MW01292423

MURDER *at* SOMERSET HOUSE

Books by Andrea Penrose

The Diamond of London

The Wrexford & Sloane Mysteries

Murder on Black Swan Lane

Murder at Half Moon Gate

Murder at Kensington Palace

Murder at Queen's Landing

Murder at the Royal Botanic Gardens

Murder at the Serpentine Bridge

Murder at the Merton Library

Murder at King's Crossing

Murder at Somerset House

MURDER *at* SOMERSET HOUSE

ANDREA PENROSE

KENSINGTON
PUBLISHING CORP.
www.kensingtonbooks.com

KENSINGTON BOOKS are published by

Kensington Publishing Corp.
900 Third Avenue
New York, NY 10022

All Kensington titles, imprints, and distributed lines are available at special quantity discounts for bulk purchases for sales promotion, premiums, fundraising, educational, or institutional use. Special book excerpts or customized printings can also be created to fit specific needs. For details, write or phone the office of the Kensington Special Sales Manager: Attn. Special Sales Department, Kensington Publishing Corp., 900 Third Avenue, New York, NY 10022. Phone: 1-800-221-2647.

Library of Congress Card Catalogue Number: 2025936241

KENSINGTON and the K with book logo Reg. US Pat. & TM Off.

ISBN: 978-1-4967-3999-5
First Kensington Hardcover Edition: October 2025

ISBN: 978-1-4967-4001-4 (ebook)

10 9 8 7 6 5 4 3 2 1

Printed in the United States of America

The authorized representative in the EU for product safety and compliance is eucomply OU, Parnu mnt 139b-14, Apt 123
Tallinn, Berlin 11317, hello@eucompliancepartner.com

For all librarians,
thank you for all you do to inspire a love of books
and reading in your communities.
You are true heroes.

PROLOGUE

"You, sirrah, are a disgrace to the Royal Society!" A rail-thin gentleman with bushy black brows and a balding pate leapt up from his chair and blocked the aisle as the evening's featured speaker gathered up his notes and stepped down from the stage. "The members of our august institution are the most respected scientific scholars in the world. For you to spout such addlepated ideas in this lecture hall is an embarrassment to rational thought and empirical observation."

"Here, here," muttered one of the onlookers.

"Stop shaking your fist under my nose, Milford," retorted the speaker. "Unless you wish to have it crammed down your gullet."

"Gentlemen, gentlemen!" Punctuating his admonition with a chiding clap of his hands, the secretary of the Society hurried over to quash the confrontation. "Come, come, let us maintain the dignity and decorum expected of our learned members."

"It is Milford who is the bloody fool, not me," retorted the speaker. "He has no imagination."

"Science is about facts, not imagination, Boyleston!" sputtered Milford.

Boyleston made a very rude sound, which earned him another rebuke from the secretary.

Milford turned to confront the Society's officer. "In all seriousness, how can you consider publishing Boyleston's drivel in the *Philosophical Transactions*? Our journal is the world's leading periodical for scientific progress. It's utterly ridiculous for him to suggest that electricity and magnetism are the same thing, rather than different forces. We'll be the laughingstock of all rational men if we put his words into print."

"Indeed!" chimed in one of the scholars who had gathered around the verbal combatants. "Think of our motto—*Nullius in verba*! Which as we all know means *Take nobody's word for it*. I agree with Milford that we've not seen a shred of evidence that Boyleston's theory has any merit."

"What fustian! The French men of science have been working with that idea for years!" countered Boyleston.

"Yes, we know how *very* fond you are of the French," piped up another member.

The speaker's cheeks flushed with anger. "H-How dare you question my loyalty as an Englishman, Fogg!"

"Because you were damnably slow to leave Paris when Napoleon crowned himself emperor and reignited war throughout Europe," shot back the gentleman standing next to Fogg.

A rumble of agreement rose from the crowd.

"Science shouldn't be colored by politics, Redding," replied Boyleston in a querulous tone. "The French men of science were performing far more sophisticated experiments with electricity than we were doing here in Britain. I stayed because I wished to *learn*!" He looked around in mute appeal. "Surely we all agree that Knowledge knows no political boundaries."

"Save for when a murderous emperor uses it to spread death and destruction across an entire continent," retorted Redding, his voice shaky with suppressed rage.

"Redding is right. Your high-minded sentiment may sound

reasonable in the abstract," responded Fogg. "But when science aids the enemy in battle, it's an entirely different matter."

Boyleston turned white as a ghost. "I gave no aid to the enemy! I returned to England as soon as it became clear that Napoleon was going to put an end to the Peace of Amiens."

"Don't prevaricate," said Redding. "The truth is, you went back to France several years ago to study with your Parisian friends."

More mutters of agreement.

"They were all men of exemplary scientific reputation," exclaimed Boyleston. "And Napoleon was half a world away, attempting to conquer Russia! As soon as he fled back to France, I returned to London. In any case, our experiments had *nothing* to do with war. We were working on important theoretical concepts that will help change the world for the better."

He gave an impatient wave. "Why are we brangling about Napoleon and the past? He is exiled to Elba and no threat to anyone now. Europe is enjoying peace and the prospect of great prosperity due in no small part to science. So let us look to the future!"

"How dare you suggest we forget about your past actions," countered Redding, the softness of his voice belying the emotion on his face. "My son is dead because men like you admired a tyrant."

Murmuring in sympathetic support, several of Redding's companions drew him back from the fray.

A crowd had formed around the combatants, and the muttering was growing more hostile.

"I tell you, I had no love for Napoleon." Eyes narrowing, Boyleston clenched his jaw for a moment. "As for disparaging the paper on electricity and magnetism that I plan to submit to our journal, you'll all soon have to eat your words—just you wait and see! I intend to prove my theory with a grand public demonstration in the very near future—"

"I trust we're all invited to see you make a fool of yourself," snapped Milford.

"Enough, everyone! Let us cease this argument before it turns truly ugly," commanded the Society's secretary, anxious to put an end to the confrontation. "As is our tradition, the committee responsible for choosing the scientific papers to be published in our periodical will make the final decision on what merits appearing in its pages."

A pause. "If you insist on continuing this unseemly bickering, do it elsewhere." The secretary smoothed the folds of his cravat. "For those who prefer to behave in a more civilized manner, the usual after-lecture champagne and lobster patties are being served in the reception hall."

Looking somewhat abashed, the crowd quickly shuffled away, leaving Boyleston standing on his own.

After a sharp exhale, he turned and exited the lecture hall through one of the side doors, where a corridor led to the back of the building and an ornate oak portal gave access to the back terraces overlooking the River Thames.

Moonlight played over the rippling water. The low *whoosh* of the eddying currents caught in the breeze, bringing with it the mingled stink of coal smoke and decay as the tide ebbed toward the Isle of Dogs. Boyleston hesitated, then crossed to the marble balustrade and braced his hands on the cold stone.

"To the devil with all their petty minds." Looking up at the night sky, he picked out the diamond-bright stars of the constellation Orion through the scudding clouds.

"Just where it should be," he muttered. "The heavens run on clockwork precision, not unstable emotion." The thought helped cool his temper. As did the fact that anger had impelled him to leave the stuffy confines of Somerset House without fetching his overcoat.

"The world is in constant motion," he continued, ignoring the night's chill. "Change is an elemental force of Nature. Why are my fellow members so incurious about understanding all the myriad natural phenomena that are still a mystery to us?"

A wherry, no more than a hazy silhouette against the iron-grey water, made its way across the river to the Old Barge-house Stairs. Silvery tendrils of fog drifted low over the landing area. Boyleston drew a cheroot from his coat pocket and lit it with a quick strike of flint against steel. Drawing in a mouthful of the sweetly scented smoke, he contemplated the quicksilver play of light and dark, welcoming the solitude after the crowded commotion of the monthly Society meeting. He much preferred the company of ideas to the company of people. The discourse was far more rational and methodical.

Once the cheroot had burned down to precisely a quarter of its original size, he dropped it onto the stone tiles and ground out the glowing tip with the heel of his boot.

Order and precision. A methodical approach to scientific re-search—as well as to most every other aspect of life—yielded the best results.

His anger flared again as he recalled the earlier attacks on his research as well as his character. Rather than return to the grand entrance cloakroom for his overcoat—he had no stom-ach for another confrontation—Boyleston turned for the ter-race stairs that would take him down to the embankment walkway skirting the river and the footpath to Surrey Street.

"New ideas make people fearful." A voice floated out of the shadows of the stately rear portico of Somerset House, fol-lowed by a figure in formal evening attire. "And thus angry."

Boyleston didn't recognize the gentleman as a fellow Society member, but then, he rarely attended meetings. "Only narrow-minded halfwits are frightened by things they cannot under-stand," he responded. "A true man of science should embrace the unknown and celebrate new discoveries that help us better understand the workings of the universe—regardless of where they originate."

"I don't disagree with you, sir," replied the Stranger. "In the past, brilliant thinkers like Galileo and Copernicus were persecuted—"

"For speaking the truth!" interrupted Boyleston.

"Yes, of course. We know that now. But often it takes time for a radical new idea to win acceptance. Not everyone is a genius and recognizes the truth on seeing its first spark."

"Be damned with the idiots. They should step aside and not block the path to Progress." Nostrils flaring in irritation, Boyleston turned his back on the fellow and started down the stairs.

"No need to get in a huff, sir," soothed the Stranger as he hurried to catch up. "I'm simply counseling you to use discretion—which as any military man will tell you, is often the better part of valor. Perhaps if you would simply temper your tongue—"

An irascible snort. "Why should I?"

"Because honey wins more friends than vinegar."

"Friends are fickle," snapped Boyleston. "Ideas don't trip over their own toes trying to follow the latest fashionable theories."

"I'm trying to help you, sir," said the Stranger. "It seems to me that a demonstration of your theory is premature. If you wish to earn the accolades that your discovery merits, why not allow people some time to discuss your paper and its—"

"My duty is to the spirit of Discovery and the dissemination of new knowledge!" retorted Boyleston. "Truth is Truth. So stop badgering me, sir, and be on your way. I shall not under any circumstances delay my demonstration."

The Stranger heaved a mournful sigh. "That's a pity."

"I don't give a fig what you think."

"That's a pity, too." The Stranger appeared to stumble and lurched against his companion.

"Go to the devil—" began Boyleston, feeling a sudden chill against his chest as the Stranger reached out a hand to steady himself. But then his words gave way to a muffled bang and the smell of singed wool and linen—and in the next instant a bullet punctured his heart.

"Alas, you'll be seeing him first. Do give him my regards," said the Stranger as he quickly withdrew the pocket pistol gripped in his right hand and danced back, letting the lifeless corpse crumple like a rag doll and roll with a muffled *thud, thud, thud* down to the lower landing.

In contrast, the lecture notes that spilled from the scholar's coat pocket fluttered away in ghostly silence, rising and falling with the vagaries of the breeze, until a final swirl scattered them over the footpath skirting the river's edge.

Glancing around at the stately façade of Somerset House and the mellow glow emanating from its myriad windows, the Stranger cocked an ear and after a moment or two allowed a smile. The reception hall was on the other side of the building's east wing, and a surfeit of champagne and scholarly camaraderie had ensured that the sordid reality of the outside world hadn't disturbed the cozy bastion of intellectual thought.

The Stranger turned back to the river, whose dark currents and eddies moved in concert with the tide. *Life's messy little hiccups had no effect on the ebb and flow of the elemental forces that ruled the universe*, he reflected. *One must always keep one's eye on the grand scheme of things.*

After brushing out the creases from his evening coat, he descended the stairs, passing the corpse without a glance, and carefully placed the spent pistol in a gap between the balustrades. Satisfied, he hurried back inside the building and made his way to the crowded reception room.

The mood, well lubricated by the fine wine and food, was relaxed and the conversations convivial, all thoughts of the brief, unpleasant confrontation in the lecture hall lost in the gentle-manly buzz of bonhomie. Glass in hand, he moved away from the refreshment tables, giving a nod and smile to those he passed before joining a group discussing the arrival of new specimen plantings from America for the Chelsea Physic Garden.

If anyone was asked about a stranger in their midst at a later date, he would be recalled as a most excellent fellow.

CHAPTER 1

Rolling her pen between her palms, Charlotte, Countess of Wrexford, huffed a sigh as she stared at the blank sheet of watercolor paper on her desk. It wasn't often that she dithered over a subject for one of her drawings.

As London's most popular—some might say infamous—satirical artist, she felt it was her solemn duty to keep the public informed about the important social and political issues of the day that affected their lives. *Corruption, misuse of power, the personal peccadilloes of the high and mighty, laws that placed unfair burdens on the poor*—her sharp-tongued commentaries spoke out for the masses who had no real voice of their own.

Of late, however, things had been awfully quiet in Town.

"No wars, no political crises, no scandals." Her lips twitched. "Which, of course, is a good thing." The only bit of current news was the daring escape of an exotic monkey—a gift to the king from an Indian sultan—from the Tower Menagerie. Having taken Hawk, a budding artist and one of the three orphan boys for whom she and her husband served as official guardians, on a recent expedition there to sketch the famous lions, Charlotte had actually seen the creature.

Long, feathery silver-grey fur framed an ebony-black face, whose darkness was accentuated by a pair of luminous yellow eyes . . . After quickly dipping her pen into the inkwell, she began to doodle. *Elongated arms and legs, curious fingers that seemed to be constantly exploring his surroundings . . .* Apparently a keeper had left a key in the cage's lock, and the clever monkey had let himself out—

"Are you perchance going to comment on the Marauding Monkey?" asked McClellan as she nudged open the workroom door and placed a tray replete with tea and pastries on the side table. Officially, her title was lady's maid to the Countess of Wrexford, but that did not begin to encompass the full range of her duties. *Taskmaster of the three Weasels, sometimes sleuth, baker of ambrosial ginger biscuits*—she was, in a word, the cog who kept all the various gears of the admittedly eccentric household running smoothly.

"Apparently, the animal broke into the kitchens of Carlton House last night and ate all the special fruit and custard pastries that had been prepared for the Prince Regent's supper," added McClellan. "Which, of course, has captured the public's fancy. They are all cheering for the monkey to remain on the loose and can't wait to hear what havoc the rascal will wreak next."

Charlotte pursed her lips in thought and then let out a chuckle. "Ah, I have it—the Pirate Primate!" she announced, already envisioning a composition featuring a gleeful monkey eluding a crack regiment of the Coldstream Guards led by the apoplectic royal regent. "Prinny must be furious. Not simply because of the ridicule that is about to explode, but because he is a glutton for sweets."

"Among other pleasures," said the maid dryly. She poured two cups of tea and carried one over to Charlotte's worktable. "Adding to the drama of the story, the palace has just announced that a very handsome reward of five gold guineas will be paid to the person who returns the fugitive to the Tower."

"This gets better and better by the moment," said Charlotte with an evil smile, mentally picturing the monkey in a fancy embroidered waistcoat and tossing gold coins to the pursuing soldiers. "But this is a perfect solution. I've been dawdling, but now I had better get to work, so Raven can deliver the drawing by midnight."

"Be careful what you wish for," warned McClellan after taking a sip of her tea. "The Weasels had a decidedly worrisome gleam in their eyes after I told them the news of the reward."

Charlotte was suddenly not feeling so amused. "Drat."

"I heard them rummaging in the attics when I stopped to leave a plate of ginger biscuits in the schoolroom just now." A cough. "The words *fishing nets* and *coils of rope* were repeated several times."

Expelling a sigh, Charlotte closed her eyes for a moment, trying not to picture the diabolically creative plans that three exceedingly clever boys could concoct for snaring the fugitive monkey . . .

"M'lady, m'lady!"

Hawk, the younger of the two brothers whom Charlotte had taken under her wing when she was a struggling widow, raced into her workroom.

Has it only been three years? It felt like a different lifetime. Her smile quivered ever so slightly, recalling both the sorrows and the joys of that fraught time when she had been an outcast from Society, trying to eke out a living with her satirical art after assuming the persona of A. J. Quill, her late husband's *nom de plume* . . . until Fate in the form of a gruesome murder had thrown her and the notoriously short-tempered Earl of Wrexford together.

It had not been a match made in heaven. *But strangely enough, our mutual antipathy turned to grudging respect . . . and then friendship.*

And then—

Her musing was wrenched back to the present moment by a loud chortling from Hawk's older brother Raven and Peregrine, the recent addition to the band of fledglings, as they appeared in the doorway.

An orphan—although because of the death of his aristocratic father, he was now Lord Lampson—Peregrine had come to be involved with their family during the murder investigation of his uncle, a brilliant inventor who had been working on a secret project for the government. Due to a number of complexities within his own family—his aunt bitterly resented the fact that the family's title had gone to a boy whose mother was of African descent—Charlotte and Wrexford had offered him a loving home, and his kindly cousin had agreed to transfer legal guardianship to her husband.

"Ha! I'm willing to wager we'll have the monkey in our sack by dawn!" crowed Raven as he held up several coils of rope and a bag of overripe fruit from the kitchen.

Peregrine raised the two long-handle fishing nets cradled in his arms and nodded enthusiastically.

Charlotte noted that Raven was, like his fellow Weasels, also wearing a bulging rucksack strapped to his shoulders. She decided not to inquire what was inside it.

"The three of you must realize that the money—" she began.

"Oh, we are well aware that seeking the reward money would threaten our family secrets," assured Raven. "If we catch the monkey, we're going to give it to Scratch, the street sweep who took over Skinny's corner, so he and his friends can claim the reward."

"We are looking at the hunt as an educational experience, m'lady," piped up Peregrine. "We'll need to use geometry to figure out the angle of approach if the creature is hiding among the buildings, and I'm sure our tutor will applaud the reading we have been doing on monkeys." A pause. "Did you know that the word *simian*, which is used to describe the broad family of monkeylike animals, derives from the Latin word for *ape*?"

She smiled. "Actually I did. But I give you high marks for creativity in trying to convince me that this expedition has any relation to your schoolwork."

The boys all grinned.

"Don't look too smug yet, Weasels," warned McClellan. "I have a feeling that m'lady is about to lay down some rules before you hare off."

"Correct," replied Charlotte. She deliberately took her time in eyeing their urchin garb and the sooty filth streaked on their faces. Raven and Hawk had spent their early years fending for themselves in the slums of London, so their rags were like a second skin. And Peregrine had quickly learned how to blend in.

"If you spot any official authorities while you are on the hunt, you are to immediately give up your chase and melt away into the shadows."

"Oiy," agreed Raven.

"If you corner the monkey, you must be extremely careful about being bitten or scratched. No attempting to approach it unless you are wearing a pair of thick leather gloves."

"Oiy!" answered Hawk. "I put three pairs in my rucksack."

"One last thing," she added. "You will have to put off your departure for an hour. I need to finish my drawing and have you drop it off for Mr. Fores before you set out on your great hunt."

"Oiy!" The three of them looked a little disappointed at the delay, but they answered in unison without hesitation.

"There are ginger biscuits in the schoolroom, which should help sweeten the wait," said McClellan, which had them jostling with each other to lead the way to the stairs.

"Well, then, I had better get to work," replied Charlotte, though her voice betrayed a flutter of uncertainty. "Though I do wonder whether this particular night is a wise time for them to be out in the city. Given the reward, I daresay a great many people who aren't the usual denizens of the night will be on the prowl for the fugitive monkey."

"Don't fret." The maid gathered up the tea things to take back to the kitchen. "The boys are experienced in navigating all the ins and outs of the stews and know how to stay out of trouble. I don't think there's any danger of them getting into any serious mischief."

Charlotte drew in a deep breath as she dipped her pen into the inkwell. "From your lips to the Almighty's ears."

Steam rose from the liquid gurgling at a soft boil in the iron cauldron. Wrexford consulted his pocket watch and then made a notation in his log book. *Two more minutes.* He watched the second hand move through the increments, finding scientific satisfaction in the unwavering precision.

He couldn't remember the last time he had been able to devote several uninterrupted days to chemical experiments, and the orderly sequence of thinking demanded by testing his theories was calming as well as demanding.

"Reason rules in science," he murmured, extinguishing the flame at exactly the right second. "While in Life, chaos is king."

Grasping the cauldron with the two ends of a towel, he moved it to a trivet on the counter and covered it with a sheet of glass. Once it had cooled overnight, he would be ready for the next step in his experiment. But for now . . .

Wrexford straightened and took a moment to massage a kink in his neck. A glass of Scottish malt and a bit of reading by the banked fire would be a pleasant way to spend the rest of the evening. *Indeed, the pleasures of a quiet evening at home feel even sweeter in this new year*, reflected the earl, as he moved from his laboratory and poured himself a measure of spirits.

"*Sláinte*," he said to the cosmos in general before settling into the soft leather of the armchair angled by the hearth in his workroom. The previous summer and autumn had brought a number of unexpected upheavals—

"You look thoughtful," said Charlotte as she appeared from the shadows of the corridor and joined him in the mellow glow of the glass-globed oil lamps and red-gold coals.

"Grateful," he replied with a wry smile. "To think that we've had blessed peace and quiet for over—"

"Ha! Cast *that* thought to the wind." She took a seat in the facing chair. "Ensconced as you were in the cerebral solitude of scientific inquiry, you've not yet heard of the Great Escape!"

Wrexford tightened his grip on his glass. "Bloody hell, don't tell me that Napoleon has—"

"What a macabre imagination you have! But *grâce à Dieu*, no, it's not quite that dire." Charlotte allowed an amused smile. "The monkey—a grey langur—recently gifted to the king by the Sultan of Golcanda escaped from the Tower Menagerie yesterday . . ."

She proceeded to explain about the animal's pilfering of the Prince Regent's special sweets from Carlton House and the subsequent reward being offered for its recapture.

Wrexford chuckled.

"You might want to stifle your mirth until I finish," she warned.

"Ah." He took a prolonged swallow of whisky and stared down at the dregs in his glass after hearing what the Weasels had in mind. "I should have known better than to spit in the eye of Fate by raising a toast to the fact that we've eluded murder and mayhem for several months."

Charlotte rose in a rush and grabbed a bottle from the sideboard. Pulling out the cork, she splashed a measure of the amber liquid into the coals.

Smoke and steam billowed up with a serpentine hiss.

"May Eris, the goddess of Chaos, accept this libation as an apology for a mere mortal's hubris," she intoned.

"Amen to that," responded Wrexford. He blew out his

breath. "A lone monkey on the loose in a very large city filled with all manner of buildings and hidey-holes . . ." He pursed his lips. "The odds of the boys finding it are not good."

"Indeed not," announced their close friend Kit Sheffield as he entered the room. An unofficial member of the family, he—along with his now-wife Cordelia—came and went as he pleased at the Berkeley Square townhouse.

"If you wish, I could do the mathematical calculations." Sheffield pinched at the bridge of his nose. "But I'd rather not. I've spent the last five hours wrestling with mind-boggling numbers and equations."

"A budget meeting for the Bristol Road Commission?" asked Wrexford.

Sheffield and Cordelia were the owners of a highly profitable shipping business, though as members of the beau monde they had to keep their involvement in trade a secret. He had become a vocal critic of Britain's antiquated system of roads and transportation infrastructure for moving goods and people around the country, and when the opportunity had arisen to have a voice in shaping the future, he had seized it with great enthusiasm.

However, observed the earl, their friend was presently looking a little deflated.

"Yes," replied Sheffield, frustration sharpening his voice. "And I decided to stop here and whinge before heading home. Cordelia has listened to my recent rants about our lack of progress with grace and good humor." He made a face. "However, patience has its limits."

"But Love does not," observed Charlotte. "Cordelia admires and applauds your dedication to making the country a better place for all who live here. Nonetheless, you are always welcome to unburden yourself here. Heaven knows, we've drawn you into enough of our troubles."

"So what's the current issue?" queried Wrexford.

"We've a number of important projects planned and have spent months hammering out the final costs. But the funds promised by Parliament have slowed," replied Sheffield. "I've been told that there has been some unexpected fluctuation with the sovereign debt, and thus government spending has been cut back for the moment."

The earl frowned. "My understanding is that financial markets are always fluctuating."

"Don't ask me to explain how they work." Sheffield blew out a mournful sigh. "I liked it better when I was a feckless fribble and everyone assumed that I wasn't capable of intelligent thought."

Their friend had a reputation in Society of being a charming but ne'er-do-well rascal. However, over the past few years he had proved himself to be an astute entrepreneur and had recently taken an interest in the world of finance.

Charlotte smiled. "No, you didn't."

That drew a wry chuckle. "I suppose not. Cordelia wouldn't have given me a second look if I was a complete lackwit." He fluttered his lashes. "Despite my *beaux yeux*."

"You're an idiot," commented Wrexford as he rose to refill his glass. "Would you like a drink?"

"True. However, I do appear to have some people fooled," drawled their friend after giving a grateful nod. "A fellow member of the Bristol Road Commission just asked me to be chairman of the Finance Committee and take charge of trying to convince the government that funds for the project are an important investment in the future of our country."

Sheffield paused to accepted a glass of spirits from Wrexford. "But getting back to Cordelia, I've received an even more important invitation because of her. Several weeks ago, she met a very interesting fellow at a symposium held by the London Society of Mathematics, and they spent a great deal of time discussing economics and the use of mathematics for modeling risk and reward."

"A subject that Cordelia no doubt found fascinating, both for its abstract intellectual challenges and its practical applications for your shipping business," mused Charlotte.

"Yes. They've met several more times at the society's frequent lectures, and when she mentioned that I was a member of the Bristol Road Commission and unhappy with the cutbacks in government funding for the project, the fellow—by the by, his name is David Ricardo—invited me to become a member of the Society for International Banking and Commerce, whose members include prominent leaders in the finance community."

"David Ricardo," mused the earl. "I've heard that he's a brilliant financier and is involved in helping to finance the government's debts."

"Yes, he's apparently *quite* brilliant. Word is he started out in 1793 with only £800 in capital, and he's now one of England's richest men," replied Sheffield. "He's also published articles on economic theory, which are highly regarded by leading thinkers in the field."

"I've also heard that he has a reputation for integrity," added Wrexford.

"Now that you mention it, I included David Ricardo in a series of drawings I did several years ago on how our government financed the astronomical amount of money needed to wage war against Napoleon," said Charlotte.

"As I recall, he also has an unusual personal background," interjected the earl.

Sheffield nodded. "His family are Sephardic Jews of Portuguese descent, who relocated to Britain during the last century from the Dutch Republic. His father was a successful financier who traded on the stock market. However, Ricardo fell in love with a Quaker Englishwoman, and after eloping with her, he renounced his faith, which caused an irreparable break with his family."

Charlotte's expression turned pensive, mingling sadness and regret. "How unfortunate. Families are precious."

Wrexford knew she was thinking of her own estrangement from her straitlaced father and mother, and how she had never had the chance to reconcile with them before they passed away.

"Families are complicated," he replied.

That made her smile.

"Amen to that," said Sheffield. "But sometimes they can surprise you in ways that you never, ever imagined."

He spun his glass of whisky between his palm and took a meditative sip before abruptly turning the talk back to a less fraught subject. "Ricardo has become very wealthy through his profession as a stockjobber—"

"I confess, I'm confused by that term," interrupted Charlotte. "Is it simply another name for stock trader?"

"No, Ricardo has explained to me that there is an important distinction. A stock trader picks and chooses whatever securities he wishes to buy or sell and only trades at times of his own choosing. A stockjobber plays a far more complex role in keeping the Stock Exchange functioning smoothly. He acts as a middleman of sorts, or a market maker—"

"What does *market maker* mean?" interrupted Charlotte.

Sheffield hesitated. "I'm still learning, so I can't yet explain all the nuances. But a stockjobber is, in a sense, the oil that keeps the gears of the London Stock Exchange turning smoothly. He stands ready at all times to buy and sell whatever securities someone wants to trade, setting a stated price for each specific security at which he will buy it and a slightly higher price for which he will sell it."

A pause. "As I understand it from Ricardo, a stock trader usually buys from or sells to a stockjobber," he continued. "As does a broker, a bank, or an individual. It's much easier for them to trade with a stockjobber, who is always there quoting a price, than to find an individual party and have to negotiate the terms. By serving as an intermediary, the stockjobbers allow the market to function efficiently."

Charlotte thought for a moment. "But as Wrex pointed out earlier, aren't the markets always fluctuating? How can a stockjobber possibly know how to price a security?"

"A stockjobber is constantly adjusting his prices for buying and selling," answered Sheffield. "Yes, he takes a significant risk that he may misjudge the direction of the market and incur losses. On the other hand, he can make considerable profits if he correctly anticipates where market prices are likely to go in the future. A major stockjobber like Ricardo will also use his central position on the floor of the London Stock Exchange to buy and sell securities for his own investment when he believes their prices warrant."

Sheffield made a face. "And before you ask, I can't explain all the various forces that affect the rise and fall of stock prices, but I hope to learn more about it from Ricardo. He is said to have an uncanny ability to read the trends of the market through mathematics—so much so that many other investors tend to be guided by whatever Ricardo is doing if they can learn of his trades, which in itself makes it all the more likely that his investing will lead to favorable market developments."

"That certainly sounds like a demanding business, even if it can be highly profitable for those with the necessary talent and temerity," mused Charlotte. "But as I said before, I seem to remember from those previous drawings I did that Ricardo played a key role managing the large borrowings the government has had to make each year to pay for all the wars against Napoleon and his allies."

"Yes," Sheffield said, "that's a somewhat separate but intriguing part of Ricardo's business. Those annual loans raised by the government are enormous. For example, two years ago, the government borrowed £49 million."

The earl raised his brows at the mention of such a staggering amount.

"To facilitate the government's borrowing of such immense sums," Sheffield continued, "rival consortiums of a dozen or so bankers, stockjobbers, brokers, and other professional investors form each year to bid on making the loan to the government—but that process and how the public participates is a complicated story that I will leave for another day."

A pause. "And besides, with Napoleon now locked safely away on the isle of Elba, such large-scale loans are happily a thing of the past."

"That's all very fascinating." Charlotte massaged at her temples. "Though the thought of parsing all those numbers makes my head hurt."

"Mine, too," agreed Sheffield with a self-deprecating grin. "But enough jabbering on my various concerns. Let us return to the boys and their current escapade."

A laugh rumbled in his throat. "Weasel versus simian? Hmmm, this could prove exceedingly interesting."

CHAPTER 2

Raven darted a look over the stone parapet of the outer walkway ringing the warehouse roof and then ducked back down into the shadows. "We'll need to rig Peregrine's new ratcheting winch and a length of rope," he whispered. "But we need to be quiet about it so we don't wake the rascal."

Their strategy had paid off. Though finding a runaway monkey in a city the size of London was perhaps even more daunting than searching for a needle in a haystack, Raven had come up with a plan. Based on the location of the Tower Menagerie and the Prince Regent's residence, and the fact that the monkey had arrived at the East India docks, he had come up with an educated guess that the animal would stay near the river and then made clever use of their network of urchin friends. While Peregrine had waited for Charlotte to finish her drawing, he and Hawk had set up a surveillance system to funnel any information on sightings of the monkey to several key checkpoints.

One tip-off had led them east, another tip-off had turned them south . . . and lo and behold, a third had sent them climbing to the top of a riverside trading company, where they had spotted the monkey sleeping atop the entrance portico of the loading bay in a secluded courtyard space.

"Who has the fruit?" added Raven, as he began unfolding the large square of fish net that he had found in the attic.

"Oiy." Hawk held up a burlap bag with several overripe apples that McClellan had unearthed in the back of the pantry.

Peregrine sniffed the air and grinned. "Sweet!"

"I daresay the monkey will be hungry when it awakes." Raven threaded a rope through the center of the netting and tied a fist-sized knot at the end of it.

"Explain to me again what you have in mind," said Peregrine.

Raven gestured for his brother to hand him the bag. He withdrew one of the squishy fruits and cut it into quarters with the knife he carried in his boot, then tucked the pieces in his coat pocket before carefully tying the bag's drawstrings to the rope just above the knot. "Once you two lower me close to the monkey, I'm going to toss some pieces of the apple to wake it. Then I'll let down the rope holding the bag—"

"What about the netting?" demanded Hawk.

His brother responded with an evil grin. "I'll be holding the netting, which as you see has the rope threaded through its center, and once the monkey begins fiddling with the bag, I'll let it drop." He gave it a jiggle. "Mac sewed lead fishing weights around the perimeter for me, so it will drop like a stone and entangle the monkey before it can flee."

"Ingenious," said Peregrine with an admiring nod.

"Assuming it all works as planned," replied Raven dryly. He buckled a heavy belt around his middle and centered the large iron ring that the thick length of leather was holding in place. "Is the winch ready?"

"Oiy." Peregrine, who had learned a great deal about engineering from his late uncle, double-checked the apparatus that he had built to lower Raven down from the roof and then fastened the brass clip that was tied to one end of the pulley rope to the ring. "Ready?"

With catlike stealth, Raven climbed over a parapet and noiselessly dropped down several feet until the gears of the rachet clicked softly into place. After a downward glance, he signaled for Peregrine and Hawk to begin slowly lowering him toward the sleeping monkey. The breeze gusted as it squeezed through the gaps between the buildings, but Raven adjusted his weight to keep his descent steady. He passed by a darkened window of the top story, and then one on the story below it.

On catching a glimmer of light reflecting off his boots, Raven realized that the room he was about to pass was illuminated from within.

Mouthing a word he was strictly forbidden to say aloud in front of Wrexford and Charlotte, he looked up and gave a quick wave for them to hurry in lowering him through the glow.

His descent quickened—

And then snapped to a halt.

Giving thanks for his dark clothing and soot-streaked face, Raven held himself very still. He was hanging uncomfortably close to the glass, but clouds had scudded over the moonlight, deepening the midnight gloom. With luck, he would go unnoticed.

He silently counted to ten . . . And then did it again.

The wick of the oil lamp on the table facing the window suddenly sparked, and its flame flared up for moment, illuminating a number of papers spread over the dark-grained mahogany.

Piles of banknotes, letters of credit issued by several of London's leading banks, stacks of stock certificates, along with what looked to be pages of mathematical calculations . . .

Raven recognized the bank documents, as Sheffield had once explained to him how they were used extensively by international merchants because they were as good as money in many places around the world. One simply presented them to the local agent representing the London bank in order to convert them into the local currency. Sheffield had also explained stock certificates—

A movement deep in the shadows caught his eye. A gentleman—no, two gentlemen—entered the room. They were both well-dressed, though oddly enough, there seemed to be a length of crumpled silk tangled with some sort of silvery fur lying on the edge of the table.

They appeared to be engaged in serious conversation. One of them consulted a pocket notebook while the other one began to shuffle through the papers, putting them into several stacks. A moment later, they were joined by a third gentleman—a thick-set, florid-faced fellow with beady eyes, whose lace-trimmed cravat and cuffed coat with oversized brass buttons looked out of place in London.

The breeze had died away, and in the stillness of the space created by the buildings that surrounded the courtyard below, Raven was able to make out a few passing words.

Exchange . . . stock issues . . . coordinated positions . . . selling . . .

Business matters, decided Raven, who quickly returned his attention to his own predicament.

"*Goddamn.*"

Raven froze. Had he been spotted?

But no, Florid Face was speaking to the others. A moment later, another "goddamn" floated out into the night

What was delaying Peregrine and Hawk? He didn't dare look up, for he feared that the slightest movement would alert the three men to his presence.

The rope gave a lurch, dropping him down several inches, and then jerked him upward.

"Bloody hell," he whispered as the man with the notebook looked up with a frown.

Their gazes locked . . .

And Raven saw something far more ominous than mere surprise flash in the fellow's obsidian eyes.

"Oiy, pull me up!" he shouted, abandoning thought of stealth. "And hurry!"

But Obsidian Eyes had already turned away and moved with pantherlike quickness back into the shadows.

"Sorry! The rachet gears have jammed!" called Peregrine.

"Haul me up by hand!" answered Raven, shifting the coiled rope and netting clutched in his arms. Obsidian Eyes was back and calmly checking the priming of a lethal-looking pistol.

"*Now*," he added. "I may not have a chance to ask again!"

Obsidian Eyes thumbed back the weapon's hammer to full cock and started to round the table . . .

The rope gave a mighty jerk, and Raven began to rise.

"Faster, faster!" urged Raven as the iron-framed window swung open with a rusty groan.

Looking up, Raven saw the top of the parapet was almost within reach. Shifting the bundle of netting and coiled rope, he twisted around and heaved it down at the snout of the pistol aimed at his chest, then turned and grabbed for the coping.

BANG!

The pistol shot was loud as thunder.

In the same instant, Raven felt a mighty wallop strike between his shoulder blades that rocketed him upward. His chin hit against stone . . .

And then everything went black.

The loud *rap, rap* of the brass knocker broke the midnight stillness that had settled over the townhouse.

Jarred back to the present moment—she had stayed up late in order to clean all her paint brushes, and her thoughts had drifted off to a recent art exhibit she had seen of J. M. W. Turner's watercolors—Charlotte felt her heart clench.

The Weasels.

Tossing aside her rag, she fisted her hands in her skirts and hurried for the stairs. That a premonition of danger had been lurking in the shadows of her conscious thought added a sense of urgency.

Wrexford, who had also not yet retired for the night, was already in the foyer and unbolting the door. It swung open, revealing a gentleman impeccably dressed in a fancy overcoat and curly-brimmed beaver hat.

A rush of relief flooded through her as she saw it was not a watchman or Bow Street Runner. But who—

"Forgive me for intruding on you at this ungodly hour, milord."

The voice sounded vaguely familiar, but Charlotte couldn't place the gentleman.

"But I . . . I . . ." The rest of the fellow's words seemed to stick in his throat.

"Do come in, Bethany, and allow me to pour you a brandy," said Wrexford as he stepped aside and gestured for the gentleman to enter.

"Dear heavens, I am so sorry for disturbing you as well, Lady Wrexford," added their visitor, on spotting Charlotte in the shadows.

"No need to apologize, Lord Bethany," she replied. On hearing his name, she quickly remembered that he was secretary of the Royal Society. "As it happens, I was in a creative state of mind and ended up working late on one of my watercolors."

"Ah, yes, as I recall, one of your wards is a budding botanical artist," replied the secretary with an effort at politeness, though clearly his concerns were elsewhere.

"He is, sir. But please, I am aware this isn't a social call. Allow me to escort you to the parlor."

Bethany swallowed hard and gave a grateful nod. "Thank you, milady."

The click of their shoes crossing the marble tiles sounded unnaturally loud in the silence. The sounds stirred a frisson of alarm as Charlotte recalled the details of Wrexford's last encounter with the secretary. The earl had been drawn into investigating the suspicious death of a Royal Society member during a gala celebration at the Royal Botanic Gardens.

Granted, there was an old adage about lightning not striking in the same place twice . . .

But that hope quickly went up in smoke. Bethany entered the parlor and turned, his ashen face taking on a sickly yellow glow in the lamplight as the earl followed him into the room.

"The unthinkable has happened, Wrexford," he intoned without preamble. "Violent death—a ghastly murder—has struck down another member of our august Society this evening."

"Sit, milord," counseled Charlotte, taking his arm and guiding him to a chair facing the sofa.

"I'm sorry to hear such terrible news," replied Wrexford as he poured a glass of brandy from the decanters on the sideboard. "How and where did this happen?"

Bethany accepted the spirits but merely held the glass between his trembling palms and stared down into the amber spirits. "He was shot on the back terrace stairs of Somerset House after our monthly meeting."

"A robbery?" asked Charlotte.

"It does not appear so. His purse was untouched." He closed his eyes for a moment, as if the gesture might erase the awful incident. "The victim was Atticus Boyleston, the main speaker of the evening. He was an odd, abrasive fellow and not well-liked by his fellow members because of his fraternization with French scientists during the Peace of Amiens as well as a shorter sojourn to Paris during the autumn of 1812."

"But surely those past interludes weren't a reason for murder," said Wrexford.

"There was a confrontation between Boyleston and several

other members right after he finished presenting his paper. The initial argument was over Boyleston's research conclusions, which sparked much derision," responded the secretary. "However, things turned very personal—and very ugly—when someone in the crowd who had lost a son in battle during the Peninsular campaign accused him of aiding and abetting the enemy."

"That doesn't necessarily mean his sharp words translated into lethal action," mused the earl.

A glimmer of hope came to life in Bethany's eyes.

"However, I'm not quite sure why you are coming to me."

"I . . . I suppose I was hoping . . ." The secretary drew in a shaky breath. "I suppose I was hoping that you would consent to help with the case. Your investigation of the murder at the Royal Botanic Gardens was done not only with great skill but also with great discretion. It saved our Society's good name from being dragged through the mud of lurid gossip and wild speculation."

Charlotte sympathized with the secretary's concerns. But murder had taken a toll on her family of late. Solving a violent death, no matter how seemingly simple, was always fraught with complexities. One never came away emotionally unscathed.

She looked at Wrexford, hoping that he would not feel compelled to get involved. Recent circumstances had demanded that he put off dealing with a personal conundrum, and she was aching for him to have the peace and quiet in which to finally do so.

To her relief, he appeared to be of the same mind. "Again, I'm sorry to hear of the murder. But as I have no knowledge or connections that would give me any unique advantage in solving this crime, I don't see that I can add any meaningful assistance to the duly appointed authorities in charge of solving the city's crimes," replied Wrexford. "This is clearly a case for the Bow Street magistrate to handle. Ask him to assign Griffin to investigate. I assure you, he is the very soul of discretion and extremely good at what he does."

Bethany's face fell. "We have already sent word to Bow Street, and as I remembered Mr. Griffin as someone you held in high respect, I did request him. But—"

"Then you are in good hands, sir," interjected Charlotte before he could go on. "Given the facts you have presented, I am quite confident that Griffin will bring about a quick resolution to the case."

The secretary looked about to argue, but on meeting her steely stare, he merely put his glass on the tea table and rose. "Thank you both for your counsel. Again, my apologies for disturbing your evening."

Wrexford saw Bethany out and returned within a few minutes.

"You did the right thing," she said, before he could speak.

"I don't doubt that," replied the earl. And yet his expression belied his words.

Charlotte quickly changed the subject, intent on turning his thoughts back to family concerns. "Now that the major issues have been hammered out by the leading powers of Europe at the Congress of Vienna, I am hoping that our friend Herr von Münch will finally follow up on the cryptic note he left for you after our unexpected meeting at Eton."

"Wishful thinking," muttered the earl.

"Despite his occasional falsehoods, I don't think he was lying," she countered. "He claims to have information regarding your father and the mysterious person that we know only as 'A.'"

They had met von Münch during the investigation of a murder at Oxford's Merton College Library and had encountered him again during the course of dealing with a more recent crime. He was, to say the least, an enigma. Especially as von Münch had promised to pass the information along as soon as he had confirmed a few more details—and that had been months ago.

"And when von Münch does reveal what he knows," continued Charlotte, "we can focus all our efforts on learning what secrets your father might have been hiding from you, and—"

"I'm beginning to think that solving the mystery doesn't matter." Wrexford's gaze turned shuttered. "After all it's too late to make peace with him."

"On the contrary," said Charlotte. "You will never put your old ghosts to rest until you understand all the aspects of your father's life." A pause. "And forgive yourself for the fact that your own pain and suffering over your brother's death kept the two of you apart."

The earl looked away.

"Our friend sensed your inner struggle—" began Charlotte.

"Like Cordelia and Kit, I take issue with you calling von Münch a friend," groused the earl. "The jackanapes stole a goodly amount of money from my workroom."

She raised her brows. "It wasn't ours to begin with."

"That doesn't make it right."

"No, but as it was originally meant for a nefarious purpose, I trust that he has put it to better use."

"You have more faith in him than I do."

"I daresay that at some point in the not too distant future we will learn which of us is right."

The soft chiming of the mantel clock drew Charlotte's attention to a different subject. "I do hope the Weasels are growing bored with their nocturnal hunt and will return home soon."

Hawk screamed and grabbed at the straps of Raven's rucksack before he slipped off the top of the coping.

"Hold tight!" Peregrine kicked aside the jammed rachet apparatus and rushed to help drag Raven over the stonework and lay him face down on the shingles of the roof.

The bullet had blown open a gaping hole in the rucksack, the edges singed with gunpowder.

"Raven?" Hawk crouched down and gently shook his brother's arm. "Raven?"

On getting no response, he looked up, tears streaming down his cheeks. "I . . . I think he's dead."

"Ha—not a chance! Lucifer would spit him back in a heartbeat," said Peregrine, refusing to believe the worst. He gently eased the rucksack off Raven's back, then reached into his rope bag and fished out a small flask.

"Help me turn him over."

Gripped by shock, Hawk fumbled to do as ordered, but on seeing his brother's lifeless features limned in the moonlight, he froze and choked back a sob.

Pushing him aside, Peregrine uncorked the flask and dumped the contents over Raven's face.

"A-A-Arrgh!" Sputtering for breath, Raven winced and then his eyelids fluttered open. "That bloody *stings!*"

"Good!" Peregrine grabbed up his bags. "Can you stand?"

After pushing himself up on one elbow, Raven flexed his legs, still looking a little groggy. "O-Oiy."

"Then stop lollygagging and do so!" He took hold of Hawk's collar and hoisted him up. "We need to fly." He pointed to the wooden structure on the middle of the roof. "Because my guess is whoever fired that shot at you is going to be bursting through the stairwell door at any moment."

As Raven scrabbled to his feet, a small *thunk* sounded as a small round bit of metal fell from his rucksack onto the roof shingles.

Hawk grabbed it before it rolled away. "Lady Luck—"

"Never mind Luck! Run!" Peregrine punctuated the order with a hard shove to his fellow Weasels as the echoing of hurried steps grew louder within the stairwell.

The three of them raced to the right rear corner of the building where the decorative cornerstones and drainpipe afforded handholds for making their way back down to the street.

With monkeylike quickness, they hurried through the descent and reached a narrow ledge crowning a set of padlocked double doors

"Jump!" cried Peregrine, after a glance upward showed a black silhouette suddenly appear at the roof's edge.

They hit the dirt footpath just as a shot rang out, regained their footing, and were off in a blur before their assailant could fire again.

Wrexford brushed back a lock of unruly hair as he made his way down to the kitchen. He had awoken at the crack of dawn, and finding his thoughts too unsettled for further sleep, he had decided to brew himself a pot of coffee and face his inner demons while the rest of the house was in repose.

Solitude offered few convenient distractions. It forced the mind to focus, no matter if the picture was not a pretty one.

However, a bustling in the pantries warned that he wasn't alone.

"There is coffee on the hob, milord," called McClellan. She appeared a moment later with a basket of eggs and a bottle of milk. "Shall I fry up some gammon for you?"

"Thank you, but just coffee for now." He poured himself a cup and savored the rich spice of the dark roasted beans. "You're up even earlier than usual."

"As are you." She opened the oven door to check on the pan of baking muffins. "By the by, in case you didn't hear them, the Weasels returned safe and sound—without the monkey, I might add—several hours before dawn. The hunt must have proved more difficult than they imagined, and pragmatism won out over the thrill of adventure."

"I did hear them," answered Wrexford, "and the fact that they proceeded so quietly to their rooms led me to the conclusion that the monkey was not part of the menagerie." A wry smile. "Thank heaven. Our household is eccentric enough as it is. Any addition might . . ."

The thought made him pause. "Actually, I prefer not to contemplate the idea."

The maid chuckled. "We have managed quite well with all the changes here at Berkeley Square over the past few years. I daresay we would adapt to any further surprises that Life chooses to toss our way."

Changes. Wrexford took a meditative sip of his coffee. Never in his wildest dreams would he have imagined the twists and turns that had altered his previous existence. Several years ago, he had been a solitary bachelor, sharp-tempered, and prone to dark brooding.

He leaned back in his chair, still a bit bemused by how all that had changed. Now he was married to a lady he admired and adored, and the two of them were surrogate parents to three lively boys.

Wrexford wasn't quite sure what he had done to deserve such happiness, but he was grateful beyond words.

"Indeed," he replied. "It seems that we have ceased to be shocked by anything that comes our way."

"You might want to reconsider those words," said Charlotte as she entered the kitchen, a grim expression darkening her gaze. Without further ado, she held up a rucksack and put a hand inside it—then poked a finger through the rather large puncture in the canvas.

CHAPTER 3

The earl put his cup down and took a long moment to assess the damage. "Is that . . ."

"Yes, it's a bullet hole," confirmed Charlotte. "I went into the schoolroom just now to tidy up all the equipment from last night's adventure that the boys had dropped on the floor." She blew out a troubled sigh. "I imagine they meant to hide the incriminating evidence this morning before any of us had a chance to spot it."

After gingerly setting the sack aside, Charlotte added, "The Weasels have a great deal of explaining to do."

"For many struggling souls here in the city, the five gold guineas offered as the reward for the return of the monkey is a fortune," observed McClellan. "The boys must have been close to capturing the animal."

"Oiy, we were *oh-so* close," intoned Raven from the depths of the darkened corridor.

"Our cleverly constructed net was poised to drop—" began Hawk.

"Stubble the details," counseled Peregrine in a hurried whisper. "I don't think they are interested in hearing about *that* part of the evening."

"Correct," said Wrexford in a tone that didn't hold a hint of amusement.

"You might as well come in, Weasels," added McClellan. "The breakfast muffins are just about to come out of the oven, and no doubt you are famished."

The three boys reluctantly filed into the kitchen, still clad in their nightshirts.

"As m'lady would say, *Festina lente*," mumbled Hawk. Charlotte was in the habit of muttering Latin aphorisms in the face of trouble. "I told you we should have put everything away before seeking our beds," he added.

"*Make haste slowly* is a wise concept to keep in mind," she agreed. "However, let us not digress into discussing philosophy." Her eyes narrowed. "Tell us exactly what happened."

With a sigh, Raven dutifully recounted their hunch concerning the monkey's likely whereabouts and their spotting of the animal after following several sightings by their urchin friends . . . which led them to a brick building by the river.

"All was going exactly according to plan," he continued. "And then, as Hawk and Falcon were lowering me to the portico roof, the ratcheting gears of Falcon's ingenious winch jammed and the rope got stuck . . ."

Charlotte listened in growing horror as he explained about the two gentlemen who were then joined by a florid-faced fellow, and the trio's reaction to spotting him.

"The man with the pistol had devil-dark eyes and a pointy chin. As for what they were doing, there was a large pile of banknotes on the table, along with what looked to be a wig and perhaps false side-whiskers atop a piece of crumpled cloth," he said. "But what really caught my eye were the other financial documents. From what I saw, the papers appeared to be stock certificates. Mr. Sheffield has shown me some examples of them and explained how a single document can represent a great deal of money."

He frowned in thought. "I also caught snatches of their conversation, though it was just random words here and there—stocks, exchange, coordinated positions, a few goddamns. And then, just before the shot was fired, I heard Florid Face cry out another 'Goddamn.'"

A shrug. "Sorry. That's all I heard."

"Merchants often accept letters of credit from their buyers, which can be redeemed at a local bank," mused Wrexford.

"It's hard to blame them for thinking you were part of a gang of thieves intent on robbing their business," interjected McClellan. "My guess is, they had just made a lucrative sale of merchandise and suspected that one of the criminal consortiums who control thievery along the River Thames had gotten wind of it."

"But shooting at children?" Charlotte tucked a lock of loosened hair behind her ear. "Money doesn't grant anyone the right to serve as judge and executioner. The law of the land decrees that only the duly appointed representatives of the government have the authority to make those solemn decisions."

"You're right, of course," said Wrexford. "In principle. Unfortunately, people taking matters into their own hands to protect their assets happens more frequently than we would like to think. We all know that the law of the jungle rules along the riverside wharfs and warehouses. Even the mighty East India Company has been forced to hire its own private army of guards to keep from being robbed blind."

"Perhaps I should do a series of drawings on the subject," responded Charlotte. "That might help put pressure on the government to finally move on creating a professional police force."

A pause. "We should at least mention to Griffin that lawlessness is getting out of hand along the river."

"I agree that agitating for proper policing is a worthy endeavor. But in this particular case, I think it wise that we don't kick up a dust." Wrexford met her gaze. "For all the obvious reasons."

Charlotte looked away, unable to muster an argument. However, another thought suddenly came to mind. "But what about the wig and false whiskers? That strikes me as very strange—unless they themselves are criminals and were up to no good."

Wrexford was about to retort but then simply lifted his shoulders in a shrug. "Speculation seems pointless, my dear. Whatever their reason for firing on Raven, I think we can assume it was to protect the money, whether or not it was theirs legally."

"Or to make sure that Raven couldn't tell anybody about what he saw," she countered.

Wrexford understood why she was loath to let go of her concerns. And yet . . .

"Come, let us not spin this unfortunate incident into a complicated plot worthy of an Ann Radcliffe novel," he counseled. "Sometimes the simplest answer is actually the right one."

"Though rarely with the troubles that tend to entangle us," pointed out McClellan.

Charlotte appeared to ignore the maid's comment and merely gave a wordless nod, but he could see in her eyes that she hadn't surrendered her misgivings.

That was what made her such a good commentator on social ills and issues, he reflected. She kept poking and prodding at a conundrum, looking at it from every possible angle until she was confident that she had spotted the truth among all the flitting shapes and shadows.

He couldn't help but applaud her stubborn courage.

Even though it frightens me half to death.

The rattle of plates and cutlery broke the awkward silence as

McClellan assembled a tray of fresh-baked muffins and jam and carried it to the kitchen table. "Who would like eggs and gammon?"

The boys eagerly accepted, and though Charlotte demurred, she asked for a plate of toast. But after refilling his coffee cup from the pot on the hob, the earl excused himself and headed for his workroom.

The parlor maid had kindled a fire in the hearth, and the cheerful crackling of flames had already dispelled the chill from the air. Wrexford paused and rubbed his palms together before moving to his desk. The soothing sounds and familiar sight of his well-worn books and research papers was usually a balm for the spirits, and yet he couldn't quite shake a vague sense of malaise. It was as if an unseen specter was dogging his steps.

Watching and waiting.

Dismissing the thought with a gruff oath, the earl took a seat and began to sort through a pile of unopened letters from the early morning post.

"What the devil is von Münch up to?" he muttered, the rustle of paper reminding him of Charlotte's comment from the previous evening. "Why hasn't he been in contact as he promised?"

A pointless question, given that the rascal couldn't be trusted to tell the truth about anything. "The damn fellow is an insufferable arse," he added, a sentiment punctuated by the snap of a wax wafer as he opened an official-looking missive.

Seeing it was only an invitation to a lecture at the London Geological Society, Wrexford tossed it aside.

"Milord?" A tentative hail drew him back from his brooding. "Riche said you were already up and wouldn't mind being disturbed."

"Don't just stand there, Griffin," said the earl, gesturing for the Bow Street Runner to enter the room. "The sooner we finish with whatever business you have in mind, the sooner you can toddle off to the breakfast room and plunder my well-stocked larders."

"It shouldn't be termed *plunder* quite yet. By my reckoning you still owe me several meals to make up for your shabby treatment of our friendship during the last investigation, milord. "

The earl allowed a grudging smile. "I've apologized for that." A pause. "Several times, in fact."

"Yes, but your words will taste far more sincere if accompanied by some of Mac's excellent cooking."

A bark of laughter. "Then let us be quick. What business do you have with me?"

"The murder at Somerset House—" began Griffin.

"The answer is no," snapped Wrexford. "Bloody hell, I don't know why Bethany wished to have me involved. I've already informed him that I have no unique skills or knowledge that would help solve this particular crime."

"Nonetheless, he wants you, sir," answered the Runner.

"Well, we all must learn to live with disappointment."

Griffin coughed to cover a snort. "I'm not sure that Lord Bethany would agree."

"Don't worry about Bethany. I shall write him a note this morning and clarify my position on the matter. And unlike you, I won't go out of my way to be tactful."

"Very good, milord."

"Any clues yet as to who might have murdered Boyleston?" asked the earl as Griffin turned to leave.

"I thought you weren't interested."

"I'm not interested," he replied. "I'm merely curious."

"We found what appears to be the murder weapon at the scene of the crime. Though I shall send both it and the corpse to Henning in order to confirm the surmise."

The earl's good friend, Basil Henning, was not only a skilled surgeon but also possessed the uncanny ability to coax secrets from victims of foul play and help bring their killers to justice.

"Ah. How convenient for you," replied Wrexford.

Griffin's brows twitched, which for the taciturn Runner was an unusual show of emotion. "Yes, it is." He shuffled his feet. "Though perhaps too convenient. It's a rather distinctive weapon."

"My understanding is that Boyleston had an ugly altercation with several fellow Royal Society members. It could very well have been a crime of uncontrollable passion, sparked by the heat of the moment. And the killer—normally a law-abiding gentleman of sound moral character—then panicked on realizing what he had done."

"Aye, all signs point to that," admitted Griffin. "In fact, I am off to question the gentlemen with whom Boyleston quarreled."

"Cheer up. Sometimes crimes do prove to have simple solutions," quipped the earl. "I daresay you'll be in a better mood once your breadbox is full."

"No doubt you're right, sir." And yet the tautness at the corners of the Runner's mouth said just the opposite.

Charlotte picked up her pen. But rather than reach for a sheet of watercolor paper, she took out a piece of stationery from her work-desk drawer and centered it on her blotter.

How to begin?

"Hmmm . . . *My dear Ernst* is far too intimate," she murmured aloud, "while *Greetings, Herr von Münch* feels too breezy."

She was quite certain they weren't enemies, but whether they were truly friends was a question she couldn't honestly answer.

"To me, real friendship means there is a bond of trust," she mused. "It demands honesty, no matter that a lie might be more expedient." And despite her defense of the fellow to Wrexford, she didn't trust von Münch farther than she could spit.

Charlotte pondered the dilemma, the muted ticking of the mantel clock an unwelcome reminder of her dithering. And then with a harried sigh, she made her decision.

Where the devil are you? she wrote in a bold black script, echoing Wrexford's frustration. *And when are you going to keep your promise?*

She didn't bother signing it.

As for an address . . . Assuming he hadn't fobbed her off with a tarradiddle, von Münch had told her that any correspondence sent to the Ludwigsburg Palace in the Kingdom of Württemberg would reach him. After taking that leap of faith, Charlotte quickly folded the note and sealed it with a wafer of rose pink wax stamped with the earl's armorial crest.

Alea iacta est. There is no turning back.

The enigmatic von Münch had hinted on several occasions that he held the key to unlocking a secret about Wrexford's father. And she meant to wrest it from him.

Forcing aside all thoughts of murder and monkeys, Wrexford turned his attention to the chemistry experiment he had begun the previous day. The liquid mixture had sat for the allotted time, and before continuing, he wanted to observe a drop of the compound through the magnifying lens of his microscope.

The rhythm of experimentation—the clink of glass and metal as he prepared the scientific equipment, the tingle of heat in the air as he used a flame to alter the chemicals, the soft scratch of pencil on paper as he kept a careful record of his observations—had its own unique allure. Empirical observation was, in many ways, the opposite of emotional response. There was no good or bad. One simply sought to identify the results as accurately as possible.

Wrexford enjoyed the challenge of careful observation, unaffected by personal preferences. It required discipline and detachment, skills that didn't come easy to many people.

He had always thought that way of looking at things was best. But because of Charlotte, he had come to see that emotion added color and texture to Life in ways that no scientific explanation could. *Head and heart.* Together they were greater than the sum of their parts.

Another truth that defied rational explanation.

And that made him smile.

After putting his microscope and glassware away, he carried his notes and rough sketches back to his desk in the main workroom and began meticulously transcribing all the information into his laboratory logbook. He was so engrossed in the task that it took several moments for him to realize that the vague thumping sound teasing at corners of his consciousness was someone knocking on the door.

"Come in," he called reluctantly.

The earl's butler clicked open the latch and then discreetly retreated into the shadow of the corridor.

A short, slender man with his grey hair pulled back in an old-fashioned queue took a tentative step into the room, bringing with him the faint scent of wood shavings and gun oil.

"Lord Wrexford, please forgive my presumption in calling on you at your home—"

"No apologies are necessary, Mr. Egg." The earl rose. "It's always a pleasure to see you." He indicated the chairs by the hearth. "Come, let us make ourselves comfortable."

Egg's features pinched in embarrassment as he looked down at his baggy breeches, which had several greasy stains darkening the mud-brown wool. "I—I would rather not impose on your hospitality, sir."

Sensing the man's deep discomfort—Egg was not used to consorting with the aristocracy outside the tiny kingdom of his workshop, where he reigned supreme—Wrexford gave a solemn nod and reseated himself at his desk. "I take it this isn't a social call."

That drew a ghost of a smile. "It is not, milord."

Durs Egg, a Swiss émigré, was one of London's most eminent gunsmiths, a man greatly admired by the cognoscenti of firearms for both his artistry and his technical innovations. Many of the most prominent gentlemen in the country owned weapons made by Egg, including the Prince Regent and the Duke of Wellington.

And me, thought Wrexford.

"How can I be of help?" he asked. The question was entirely sincere. Egg was not only a modest, self-effacing fellow, but unknown to most people, he had also provided technical expertise to the government on several important top-secret military projects. Indeed, it was because of Egg's razor-sharp memory that the earl had managed to catch a cunning traitor the previous year. Now he was ready to return the favor if he could.

"I—I hardly know where to begin, sir."

"No need to dress it up in fancy words," he encouraged. "Just tell me the problem."

Egg blew out his breath. "There was a murder at Somerset House last night . . ."

On recalling Griffin's words, Wrexford gave an inward sigh. "And you are about to tell me that one of your pistols was the murder weapon."

"Alas, yes. However, that's not the worst of it." Egg shuffled his stance, his already pale face now looking leached of all color. "My brother-in-law has just been arrested for the crime."

"The pistol was his?"

"It was not. The only firearm from my workshop that my brother-in-law owns is a military-size pistol with a burled walnut stock and rifled bore that I made specially for him as a wedding present. The murder weapon is a short-barreled pocket pistol, a prototype design that my nephew Joseph Egg and I were working on. When Bow Street's Runner came to confront me about the murder, I discovered that it had been stolen from the building behind my shop that houses our indoor shooting range."

The shadows beneath Egg's eyes turned dark as bruises. "But the authorities think that despite my sworn testimony, the co-incidence is too great to believe that my brother-in-law isn't the murderer."

"What coincidence is that?" asked the earl.

"As we've just discussed, the murder weapon was made by my workshop." The gunmaker hesitated before adding, "But even more damning in the eyes of Bow Street is the fact that my brother-in law was known to have a long-time grudge against the victim."

"What sort of grudge?" encouraged Wrexford when the gunmaker's voice once again faltered.

"His son was killed in the Peninsular War, and he felt that Boyleston's time in Paris working with French scientists during the Peace of Amiens and again two years ago had been treason-in-spirit."

Egg paused to steady his voice. "And it seems that the two of them had a very ugly confrontation witnessed by a number of their fellow Society members just a short time before the crime was committed."

Wrexford felt an immediate twinge of sympathy. His beloved younger brother had perished in that same conflict, a brutal and bloody back-and-forth clash of armies and partisan guerillas until Arthur Wellesley—now the Duke of Wellington because of his battlefield victories—had finally booted the French out of the region.

"Forgive me, but I must ask you—"

"Whether I think that my relative is guilty?" interjected Egg. A moment of silence hovered between them.

"Please be assured that I would not impose on your goodwill

or your sense of honor, milord, if I didn't wholeheartedly believe him to be innocent," added the gunmaker with grave dignity.

"Well, then." Wrexford tapped his fingertips together. "It seems that I must get to work and endeavor to prove that you are right."

CHAPTER 4

"The monkey is still on the loose." Raven tossed aside the copy of the morning newspaper that he had just finished perusing. "And the reward has been raised to ten guineas."

"I don't suppose m'lady would let us—" ventured Hawk.

"Ha!" Raven added a very rude sound. "And pigs might fly."

"If it hadn't been for the bullet hole, we might have had a fighting chance to plead our case," reasoned Peregrine.

"Oiy, she and Wrex tend to get a bit squeamish when the possibility of mortal peril is involved."

"The newspaper mentioned a murder at Somerset House," mused Raven. "It's also right on the river, not far from where we were last night." A pause. "I don't think Wrex and m'lady could object if we visit some of our urchins friends who live in the area and ask whether they observed anything suspicious. That way, if we learn something, we can pass it on them, and they in turn can tell Mr. Griffin."

"I suppose not," agreed Peregrine.

"And if we just happened to to spot the monkey . . ."

Hawk grinned, and then rose in a flash, startling Harper out of his slumber by the hearth. "Well, what are we waiting for?"

The hound pricked up his ears.

"Sorry, you're far too noticeable, Harper. You have to stay here."

A gusty canine sigh sounded as the Weasels headed for the door.

Wrexford hurriedly finished transcribing his scientific notes into his logbook, then put aside all thoughts of chemistry to concentrate on . . .

Murder.

Yet again.

Charlotte wouldn't be happy about his decision. But she would understand and applaud it. For her, there was never a question of whether friendship and loyalty took precedence over personal matters. And so his search for the mysterious "A" with whom his father had an intimate correspondence would once again have to be delayed.

The day looked to be overcast and chilly. After donning his overcoat, he summoned his carriage and set off for Somerset House, the logical place to begin an investigation into the tragic turn of events. But after turning onto the Strand and passing St. Martin's Church, he decided to walk the rest of way, in order to clear his head and compose the first list of questions that would—*Deo volente*—eventually lead him to the Truth.

Gulls dipped and darted overhead, white flashes against the gunpowder-grey clouds. The air felt heavy with impending rain.

In a sense, he was killing two birds with one stone, thought Wrexford with a touch of gallows humor. According to Egg, Lord Bethany had witnessed the entire quarrel, so the secretary should be delighted that he had changed his mind about investigating.

"Until I ask the first uncomfortable question," uttered the earl.

The wind gusted, grabbing at the capes of his overcoat. After another look at the river, whose swirling currents suddenly conjured up a fanciful image of serpents writhing just below the surface, the earl turned and hurried on to his destination.

"Lord Wrexford." Bethany looked up in surprise as one of the porters escorted the earl into the secretary's office. "What an unexpected pleasure."

"Be careful what you wish for," he responded, which drew an even more quizzical expression.

"You did ask me to investigate Boyleston's murder," explained Wrexford, "and I have decided to do so."

"But . . ." Bethany blinked in confusion. "But there's no further need. I've just been informed that your Runner, Mr. Griffin, has made an arrest." A mournful sigh. "It doesn't reflect well on our learned Society that one of our members would turn so violent. But alas, I fear that grief had gnawed away at Redding's mind until he lost all sense of reason."

"From what I have heard, the evidence against Redding is merely circumstantial."

"B-But who else would have committed such a heinous act?" stammered the secretary.

"That's precisely the question that needs to be asked." Without asking for permission, Wrexford took a seat in the chair facing the stately mahogany desk. "It seems that Redding was arrested for the murder simply because the weapon found at the scene of the crime was crafted by his brother-in-law, Durs Egg. And yet Egg has assured me that the pistol was not owned by Redding."

A sniff. "Clearly the fellow is lying out of loyalty."

"On the contrary," said Wrexford. "I know Durs Egg to be a man of great integrity and bone-deep honor."

Bethany leaned back in his chair. "I—I don't know what to say, milord. Griffin—"

"I shall be chatting with Griffin later. But first, I wish to ask you some questions, as I've been told that you witnessed the altercation."

The secretary's lips puckered in distaste. "I would prefer not to recall that unpleasantness."

"Even if it means sending an innocent man—and longtime colleague—to the gallows?"

Bethany had the grace to flush. "I did not mean . . ." He cleared his throat. "I shall, of course, do my duty to ensure that justice is done."

"I expected no less," replied the earl. "So please begin by describing exactly what happened as Boyleston stepped down from the stage."

"It was Milford who first confronted Boyleston and challenged his scientific findings . . ."

Wrexford listened intently, interrupting frequently to clarify how the argument escalated into personal insults and then turned truly ugly with veiled accusations of aiding the enemy.

"So, both Milford and Redding exchanged nasty words with the victim," observed the earl, once he had guided the secretary through his grudging account of the quarrel. "Anyone else?"

"There was a small crowd gathered around them, some of whom muttered in sympathy with Redding," replied Bethany. "Most of the audience chose to avoid the unpleasantness and went directly to the reception hall for the post-lecture refreshments."

"Can you name the gentlemen who stayed behind to listen to the argument?"

Bethany blew out his breath, his brow furrowing in thought as he took some time to consider the question. "I was there, of course . . . and Elias Fogg was standing close to me. I—I believe he also had harsh words for Boyleston." A querulous frown. "I simply can't remember exactly who else. It didn't occur to me that I might be interrogated on the incident."

"As I said, I am simply trying to ensure that justice is done," responded Wrexford. "If you recall anyone else—"

"Wait, there *was* someone else," said Bethany, "though he must have been a guest of one of our members because I didn't recognize him."

"Can you describe him?"

"A tall, distinguished fellow," answered the secretary. "Silvery hair, thick side-whiskers accentuating a pointed chin, well-tailored evening coat, and blue silk sash, so perhaps he was a visiting diplomat. He spoke perfect English, but there might have been a hint of an accent." A pause. "The fellow was very affable. During the refreshment hour, he joined a conversation that a group of us were having on the Chelsea Physic Garden and its latest delivery of medicinal plant specimens from America. His questions were quite thoughtful."

Wrexford considered the information. "Have you no idea who invited him?"

Bethany shook his head.

"Perhaps the Society's staff would know," mused the earl. "In any case, I would like to talk with the porters and footmen who were on duty for the meeting." Servants were keen observers and were more apt to have noticed the coming and goings of the members throughout the evening. "And I would like a full list of all the members who were in attendance."

A pained sigh. "Is that really necessary, milord?"

"I'm afraid it is."

With ill-concealed reluctance, Bethany summoned a servant with a shrill ring of the handbell on his desk. "Hopkins will arrange it for you." After returning the bell to its place by the inkwell, he picked up his pen. "Have you any further questions for me?"

"No." Wrexford rose. "Not at the moment."

Rendered unrecognizable by their soot-smeared faces and ragged clothing, the Weasels crept out of the mews located behind the back gardens and shimmied into a narrow alley through a loose plank in the high wooden fence. From there, a network of footpaths, a world within a world, well hidden from the elegant walkways of the beau monde, took them to the southeast corner of Hyde Park and a roundabout route through Green Park and the northern edge of St. James's Park.

"Should we have a look around the warehouse, as well as the area around Somerset House, and see if we can learn anything more about the dastard who shot at you?" said Hawk to his brother as the three of them headed east and joined the flow of foot traffic along the Strand.

Raven shook his head. "Wrex and m'lady told me in no uncertain terms that we must stay away from the place."

"Well, that's that," replied Hawk. "House rules strictly forbid disobeying a direct order."

"Neither of them said anything about avoiding Somerset House and the surrounding area?" asked Peregrine.

"Not a peep," answered Raven with a note of satisfaction. "Griffin told Mac that Wrex refused to get involved in the investigation."

"So that leaves us free to see if *we* can uncover anything useful," observed Peregrine.

"Precisely." Raven gestured for them to quicken their pace. "Ollie-Oyster loiters around the Surrey Stairs by Somerset House most nights, making a few farthings by offering to fetch a hackney or summon a wherry to cross the river for the gentlemen who frequent the Royal Society. And Billy Bones and his gang prowl the area looking for any bits and bobs that they can sell to the rag-and-bone men."

Another jingle of his purse. "One of them may have seen something useful."

It took a bit of poking around to find their raggle-taggle friends, whose activities tended to be done under the cover of night. But the effort proved worthwhile. Billy Bones and his companions had been working farther east, around the temple gardens. However . . .

"Oiy, we need to head back right away and present Wrex with what we have learned," said Hawk, once they had finished questioning Ollie-Oyster and tucked the papers that the urchin had given them into their pockets.

Wrexford left Somerset House with more questions than answers. None of the staff had noticed any suspicious comings and goings during the post-lecture reception. But by their accounts, the members kept them so harried with constant demands for food and spirits that the evening had passed in a blur. Still, it bothered him that nobody could explain the stranger circulating through the reception. It would be a tedious chore to interview all the attendees in order to determine who had invited him.

But first things first, he decided. His next stop was Bow Street and the building housing the magistracy, where he hoped to find Griffin within the cupboard-sized confines of his office.

"Why the sudden change of heart?" inquired the Runner, holding up a hand to halt the earl's initial rapid-fire questions concerning Redding's arrest.

"Because it galls me to think that a miscarriage of justice is taking place," answered Wrexford. "And as I know your sense of integrity is just as finely honed, I'm surprised that you've made an arrest based solely on the evidence of the pistol found at the scene of the crime."

"The coincidence is too important to ignore—"

"Oh, be damned with the bloody coincidence. The scenario smells as rotten as five-day-old fish. You even admitted so yourself when you first came to see me about the murder."

Griffin maintained a stoic face. Only a momentary ripple in his eyes betrayed a reaction to the criticism. "Since you're so knowledgeable about my profession and its protocols, milord, did it not occur to you that a decision about an arrest is not always solely mine to make?"

Wrexford drew in a breath and let it out in a sharp exhale. "Forgive me. I should have guessed that there are other forces at play."

"I don't like it any more than you do," responded Griffin in a low voice. "But as you well know, the Royal Society has a number of powerful gentlemen as members—including yourself. And I daresay they have put pressure on my superiors to have the case closed as quickly as possible to avoid the embarrassment of having the less respectable newspapers and broadsheets sully their name with lurid headlines."

The Runner's jaw tightened in frustration. "So for the moment, my hands are tied."

"Well, then it's fortunate that I feel no such constraints." The earl perched a hip on a corner of the Runner's small desk and leaned in a little closer. "Have you any information to pass on that may be of help?"

"To be honest, milord, I never had a chance to do more than have a meeting with Durs Egg concerning the provenance of the pistol before I was, shall we say, encouraged to arrest Redding before he could abscond."

"Justice demands that we not allow power or influence to obstruct the path to the Truth," replied Wrexford. "I did learn one other detail during my visit to Somerset House that merits further investigation." He quickly explained about the unidentified stranger who was present at the Royal Society's meeting. "I shall make discreet inquiries and see if I can identify him."

"I'll have another talk with Redding, who is currently ensconced in Newgate Prison," said Griffin. "Perhaps he can help."

"Also ask him if he's made any recent enemies," replied the earl. "Though I have a feeling the answer to the crime won't prove to be as simple as personal grudges or jealousies."

CHAPTER 5

Feeling unaccountably uneasy, Charlotte abandoned all pretense of sketching out a new drawing on the ongoing hunt for the escaped monkey. It was true that the public needed to have occasional interludes of humor interspersed between her serious commentaries on the various threats and challenges facing society. *Abuse of power, frightening new technology, the loss of jobs, the rising costs of basic sustenance . . .*

But somehow, her mind simply wouldn't focus on the task at hand.

Putting aside her pen, she rose and decided to pay a visit to Hatchards bookstore, hoping a brisk walk down to Piccadilly would help clear her head. An illustrated volume on the flora and fauna of India, including the grey langur monkey, might amuse the Weasels.

The sun was shining, but there was a bite to the blustery breeze, and a bank of grey clouds creeping in from the west warned that the weather might take a turn for the worse. Quickening her steps, Charlotte soon reached her destination and slipped into the welcome warmth of the shop. Drawing in the soothing scent of paper and ink and leather, she felt herself relax. Throughout her life, books had always been welcome companions, offering wisdom, inspiration, and a wondrous sense of adventure as one journeyed to the world of imagination.

"Ah, great minds think alike." The voice of her dear friend Cordelia, who was still settling into married life as Mrs. Sheffield, drew her back from her musing. "What brings you here today?"

"No pressing reason. I thought the Weasels might enjoy reading about simians," answered Charlotte, then took Cordelia's arm and drew her into one of the many alcoves of the bookshop. Seeing that they were alone, she added, "But to be honest, I'm feeling at sixes and sevens. The last few days have been unsettling . . ."

She recounted the news of the murder, along with an account of the troubling encounter experienced by the Weasels during their hunt for the fugitive monkey.

"Good Lord," intoned Cordelia. "Someone actually fired a pistol at Raven?"

"If not for the rucksack filled with iron grappling hooks and rope . . ." A shudder caused her voice to stick in her throat for a moment. "He was awfully lucky."

"The boys are strong and resilient. They won't suffer any lasting aftereffects of the scare." Cordelia gave her a quick hug. "And as for you, it does no good to fret on what might have been. Put it out of your head."

"Wise advice," she murmured. And yet she couldn't help thinking that no amount of strength and resilience would stop a bullet.

"That's interesting about the financial papers," said Cordelia, clearly intent on changing the subject. "Talk of 'stocks' and 'coordinated positions' strikes me as very odd if the two men were simply organizing the banknotes and other documents related to the sale of merchandise." She thought for a moment longer. "Raven said the building was a shipping ware-house?"

"Yes, he mentioned that it was made of brick, with a flat roof and small cobbled courtyard abutting the river just east of White Lion Wharf," answered Charlotte.

"Very odd," repeated Cordelia, a furrow forming between her brows. "I think I know the place, and my understanding is that the previous tenant's business failed after several of his ships fully laden with spice went down in a typhoon off Madagascar. And so it's been empty for the last few months."

The news only further unsettled Charlotte's nerves.

"But I may be mistaken," added Cordelia, on seeing her expression. "Come, let us move on to the shelves devoted to mathematics. I wish to purchase an updated edition of *The Doctrine of Interest and Annuities* by Mr. Francis Baily for my next lesson with Raven."

"Francis Baily?" Charlotte's brows winged up in surprise. "But isn't he an ardent astronomer? Wrex introduced me to him recently at a scientific soiree and mentioned that Mr. Baily and several other gentlemen were trying to organize a Royal Astronomical Society."

"Yes, Baily is currently focused on the science of the heavens," answered Cordelia. "But he began his career on the London Stock Exchange. His inventive use of mathematics allowed him to earn a considerable fortune on the Exchange, allowing him to retire from stock trading and devote himself to astronomy. His book, however, is a significant contribution to the field of financial mathematics and it sets out many of the methodologies he employed while trading on the Exchange."

"Ah, how interesting. I'm sure Raven will find it fascinating." Charlotte readily followed her friend to the back of the bookstore, but her thoughts had already wandered elsewhere. *If the warehouse was supposedly unoccupied, who were the men doing business there in the dead of night? And why did one of them shoot at Raven?*

Wrexford would likely say they were simply two of the many cunning criminals who made their living along the river, where the myriad wharves and storage enclaves offered a wealth of opportunities to profit from the lack of security.

"Are you all right?' Cordelia turned from perusing the shelves and fixed her with a look of concern.

"Just fatigued," answered Charlotte. "I didn't get much sleep." *And likely I will get even less tonight.*

After quitting the card room at White's, Wrexford was about to exit the exclusive gentlemen's club on St. James's Street when he spotted Sheffield seated by the fire in the reading room, a glass of tawny port in hand as he studied what looked to be a table of numbers.

"Excellent," said the earl. Tired and frustrated, he decided to join his friend. Since leaving the Bow Street Magistracy, he had managed to track down a dozen members who had witnessed the argument at the Royal Society on the night of the murder. Several of them recalled the stranger, but nobody had any idea who had invited him. Which meant that tomorrow he would have to begin pursuing the rest of the gentlemen who had attended the monthly meeting.

"Seeing as you can finally afford to buy a decent bottle of spirits," said Wrexford, "you may pour me a glass."

"With pleasure." Sheffield chuckled. "The porter still thinks I'm a feckless wastrel and puts it on your bill."

"Arse." More tired than he cared to admit, the earl sank into the soft leather cushions of the nearby armchair and released a sigh.

"So," said Sheffield, interrupting Wrexford's brooding, "I take it the Weasels didn't succeed in their hunt for the monkey?"

"Actually they did."

"But the newspaper says—"

"Yes, yes, I know. It's still on the loose. But according to the boys, they would have netted the rascal if some unknown gentleman hadn't opened a window and fired a bullet into Raven's back."

Sheffield slowly put down his drink. "I'm more used to your sardonic humor than most people, but still, that's not remotely funny."

"It wasn't meant to be." Wrexford took a long swallow of port and then recounted all the details of the ill-fated expedition.

"Bloody bastards," muttered Sheffield. "So what are we going to do about it?"

"Nothing."

A look of surprise flitted over his friend's face, followed by consternation, which then quickly surrendered to grudging understanding. "I suppose any report of the incident could lead to . . . uncomfortable questions."

"That's putting it mildly." The last thing Wrexford wished to do was draw attention to his unconventional family. To the beau monde, the boys were merely a shadowy presence. People knew of their existence but rarely saw them in public—at least, not knowingly. That was de rigueur among most aristocratic families. And he wished to keep it that way.

The fewer questions asked about them, the better.

Sheffield remained tactfully silent as the earl quaffed a few quick swallows of port and refilled his glass, but then couldn't help but ask, "Is there something else bothering you?"

"Aside from the fact that I've been drawn into yet another murder investigation?"

"Another murder?" Sheffield raised his brows. "I thought you and Charlotte had made a pact—"

"Yes, and I intended to keep it." Wrexford made a face. "But the best-laid plans of mice and men . . ."

"Surely you could have found a way to say no," mused Sheffield.

"Alas, it's not that simple." He recounted what had happened at the Royal Society and how he had come to be involved in the crime. "I feel that I owe Durs Egg, the fellow who requested my help, a debt of gratitude for his assistance last summer," added Wexford. "And I'm also convinced that the wrong man has been arrested."

"But can't Griffin handle the situation?" asked his friend.

"Griffin was pressured to make the arrest," answered Wexford.

"Why?"

"A good question." The earl stared into the measure of tawny port in his glass, as if an answer might be hidden in the depths of the wine. "That's one of several things that bothers me about this murder. Another is the whole scenario. It seems so well planned—and yet, how could the killer know that Egg's brother-in-law would get into a very public altercation with Boyleston and thus be able to plant a weapon that would incriminate the fellow?"

Sheffield contemplated the question. "The easy answer is that Egg's relative did in fact commit the crime, and Egg is lying out of a sense of loyalty to his family."

"True," he conceded. "But I'm not yet ready to believe that."

"So what's the alternative?"

Wexford closed his eyes, listening to the crackle of the coals as he pondered the few bits and pieces that he knew about the murder and admitted that for now he couldn't see how they fit together.

There had to be a logical explanation.

So why can't I see it?

Sheffield edged back in his chair and recrossed his legs.

"If Charlotte were here, she would suggest that we look at the conundrum from a different perspective." Wexford frowned in thought. "What if . . ."

His friend stopped fidgeting.

"What if we're asking the wrong question?"

"What do you mean?" demanded his friend.

"Perhaps the key to the crime is not who killed Boyleston." Wrexford considered the matter for a bit longer before continuing. "Boyleston's scientific paper had stirred controversy and ridicule among his fellow members. And in response, he announced that he was going to give a momentous demonstration in the near future that would prove he was right."

"You think he was murdered because of his scientific ideas, rather than any personal grudge?"

"I'm simply suggesting that we need to keep an open mind and consider the possibility."

Sheffield gave a noncommittal grunt.

The two of them sat in silence, each seeming lost in their own thoughts. And then Wrexford put aside his unfinished drink and rose abruptly, an idea suddenly springing to mind. "Thank you for listening. But I shall now bid you goodnight."

"Where are you going?" inquired his friend.

"Never mind."

"I know that look in your eyes." Sheffield got to his feet with a long-suffering sigh. "Wherever it is, I had better come with you."

The faint click of glassware emanating from the laboratory was a good sign, decided Charlotte. Tyler, the earl's valet and scientific assistant—not to mention occasional sleuth—had just returned to Berkeley Square earlier in the evening from the family's country estate, where he had been dealing with a few routine matters. He was now dutifully cleaning the beakers and vials used by the earl in his earlier experiment.

Smiling, she approached the half-open door. And as Wrexford had sent word that he would be away interviewing members of the Royal Society until quite late, the conversation she planned to have with the valet was not likely to be disturbed.

"Welcome home, Tyler. I trust you had a productive visit with our estate steward?"

"Jenkins and I managed to deal with His Lordship's requests without any problems. Though we decided that work on the millpond sluice gates should wait until warmer weather."

"That makes sense." She stepped into the laboratory. "Ummm, might I ask you set aside your household chores for a moment? I have something that I wish to discuss with you."

"Indeed, you have my undying gratitude for interrupting my labors, m'lady." Tyler slapped down his polishing cloth and massaged the back of his neck. "Forgive me for saying so, but things have been awfully quiet among our family and friends for the last several weeks." A cough. "Not that I'm wishing for Evil to rear its ugly head—"

"Nonetheless, it has done so," she interjected, deciding to get right to the point. "Did Mac not tell you about the Weasels and the hunt for the escaped monkey?"

A sound—something between a cough and laugh—stirred in his throat. "Mac was out when I arrived. Apparently, the dowager has just returned from her stay in Bath and sent a note asking for her advice in choosing fabric for new draperies." His brows waggled. "The Weasels versus an exotic beast? I can't even begin to imagine what chaos could have erupted."

Charlotte gestured for him to keep his voice down. "I would prefer that the boys don't overhear our conversation," she added in a whisper.

"Oh?" Tyler edged a little closer and cocked an ear. "Go on."

"There was an unsettling incident during the hunt . . ." Charlotte quickly explained about the warehouse by the river, the jammed winch, and the shot fired at Raven.

"Ye gods." Tyler's eyes widened in shock. He was very fond of the boys. "I—I trust the injury isn't serious."

"Lady Luck was kind. He escaped unscathed thanks to the rucksack he was wearing," answered Charlotte. "Wrex is of the opinion that we should count our blessings and forget about the incident. He says that skullduggery is rife along the river and that violence is an everyday occurrence as criminals can make a fortune through the heist of valuable goods from ships and warehouses."

"Definitely true." Tyler pursed his mouth . "But then, I'm sure you're aware of that."

"I am." Charlotte hesitated. "However, I am concerned about what Raven saw in the moments before the gentlemen noticed his presence just outside the window . . ." She went on to recount what the boy had observed.

"Money and financial documents," mused the valet. "That's not surprising if they had just sold a lucrative shipment of goods. In truth, it would explain why one of them had a hair-trigger temper—"

"Yes, but I just learned from Mrs. Sheffield that the warehouse in question has been empty for several months, as the previous occupant went bankrupt after suffering the loss of several merchant ships in a storm," replied Charlotte. "So it stands to reason that the gentlemen Raven saw were criminals." A pause. "And not petty ones."

"Perhaps that's even more reason to follow His Lordship's suggestion of not poking a stick into a nest of vipers."

Charlotte conceded that there was some sense to Tyler's statement. Indeed, a part of her desperately wanted to agree and walk away.

"I wish I could do so in good conscience, Tyler. However, I worry that the Weasels may have stumbled onto something that wasn't simply a single robbery or swindle which created a spur-of-the-moment threat to our family. The false hair and side-whiskers, along with the presence of someone who looked to be a foreigner, hint at something more sophisticated. It's possible that whatever plot these unscrupulous men are involved in has far-reaching implications."

A wariness flickered in his gaze. "So what are you suggesting?"

"That we have a look inside the building and see if there are any other clues as to what they might have been up to."

The valet pinched at the bridge of his nose. "You do know that Wrex will have my guts for garters if I go along with your request."

"Yes, he will ring a peal over your head—"

"A more accurate description is that he will spit fire and brimstone," grumbled Tyler.

She smiled. "But only for a short interlude, after which he will express his gratitude for not letting me go on my own."

The response drew an unintelligible mutter.

"Oh, come—you know that you're curious."

"There is an old adage about curiosity killing the cat," he shot back.

"Felines are said to have nine lives," she observed.

"I would imagine that both you and I have already used up twelve lives." The valet paused. "Or possibly thirteen."

"Very well. Your reluctance is entirely understandable." Charlotte turned. "I'll let you get back to your polishing."

"Oh, bloody hell. Meet me in the scullery in a quarter hour." Tyler narrowed his eyes. "And bring the pocket pistol that Wrex purchased for you last summer. Given what happened with Raven, I think it best that we don't venture into the building unarmed."

CHAPTER 6

The *whoosh* and gurgle of the ebbing tide rose up through the night mist hanging low over the river. Save for the light scuff of their boots on the cobblestones, all was quiet as Wrexford and Sheffield made their way into the courtyard.

"No sign of life in the building," observed Sheffield after a glance at the unlit windows.

The earl made a survey of their surroundings before indicating that they should proceed to the doorway half hidden in the shadows of the loading area. The latch clicked open at his touch, causing him to step back and draw the pistol from his coat pocket.

"We may not be alone," he whispered, "so it's best to be prepared for any surprises."

Sheffield wordlessly readied his own weapon and followed Wrexford into the cavernous storage space. A weak dribble of moonlight coming in through the windows revealed that it was empty, save for a few broken crates, and they moved on to the stairs located by the far wall.

"Raven said his assailants were on the third floor," remarked

Wrexford. "But I suggest we check around carefully as we head up, so as not to miss any clues."

He had brought along a small folding tin lantern and a single candle for illumination. The shuttered opening would allow him to focus the beam of light and minimize the chances of anyone outside the building noticing any activity inside.

"It sounds quiet as a crypt," replied Sheffield, after cocking an ear.

They moved stealthily up to the first story, which held a large reception room and several smaller spaces filled with desks for the clerks and scriveners. A quick search revealed nary a paper within the cabinets, and Wrexford signaled for them to continue their ascent.

The second story proved equally uninteresting. But as the earl turned, something caught his eye in the faint flicker of candlelight, and he dropped down to a crouch.

"What is it?" whispered Sheffield.

He pointed to the planked floor, where a small area was just a shade darker than the surrounding wood, and touched his finger to the faint remains of a footprint. "Moisture," he explained. "Someone walked through here very recently."

Sheffield silently eased the hammer of his pistol to half-cock as both of them gazed up at the shadowed ceiling and listened intently.

It might have only been the creaking of the beams, but Wrexford thought that he heard a hint of movement.

"Let us proceed carefully," he cautioned, mindful of the attack on Raven. The villains had shown themselves to have no compunction about taking lethal action at the first sign of trouble.

Rising, he took the lead and made his way back to the stairs.

The little squeaks and groans of the old treads beneath his boots sounded as loud as gunfire to his ears.

Halfway up, he froze. *Was that a glimmer of light to the left of the landing?* It disappeared too quickly for him to judge whether it was merely a figment of his imagination.

He drew in a steadying breath and blew out his candle, then signaled to Sheffield that there might be trouble up ahead. His friend gave a grim nod and eased his pistol's hammer to full cock.

The two of them resumed their climb.

On reaching the foyer, he darted into the room straight ahead, with Sheffield close on his heels. Given the layout of the floor below, Wrexford guessed that he could angle into either the right or the left adjoining room through a side door.

He froze on hearing a sound—definitely a low whisper—and spotting a flicker of light from under the closed door to his left. He edged closer to it, and after putting his unlit lantern on the side table, he took hold of the latch.

Sheffield raised his pistol . . .

"Damnation, lower your weapon, Kit!" called an all-too-familiar voice from behind them, "before one of us gets hurt!"

"What the devil are you doing here?" demanded Wrexford.

"I might ask the same question of you," responded Charlotte, her heart still pounding hard as a hammer against her rib cage at the realization of how close they had come to . . .

She shoved the thought from her head as too awful to contemplate. "I thought you were interviewing the witnesses to the quarrel at Somerset House."

"I thought you were at home, working on your next drawing," he countered.

"Clearly, you were both wrong," said the valet, as he came out of the room on the left, his own weapon now pointing harmlessly at the floor. "We thought we detected movement on the floor below, so we set up an ambush." To Sheffield he added, "It's a good thing you have that flaming gold hair, else things could have turned rather unpleasant."

"Bloody hell, Tyler, you have a good deal of explaining to do—" began the earl.

"But not now," interjected Charlotte. "Let us save our brangling for later and finish searching this place. Tyler and I had just spotted a few things of interest when your presence distracted us."

"Lead the way," replied Wrexford, though his voice warned that the discussion of the night's unexpected confrontation wasn't over.

After everyone filed into the adjoining room, Tyler relit his lantern and set it on the floor, where it cast just enough of a glow for them to examine the contents.

"That must be the table that Raven saw through the window," said the valet. "It's the only one in the building that fits his description."

"Any sign of papers?" asked Wrexford. "Though I don't imagine that the two men would have been that careless."

"Not as of yet," answered Tyler. "But m'lady and I didn't have a chance to look through the cabinets in the room to the right of the foyer."

"Come, you and I will search there while Kit and Charlotte make a thorough check of the areas on this side of the staircase," decided the earl. "I would prefer not to linger here any longer than necessary."

Charlotte was already down on her hands and knees beside the table. A tattered oriental carpet, its swirling pattern much stained by spills of wine and brandy, had been left behind, and she began running her fingers over the woven wool, examining it closely for any small objects that might have been dropped and gone unnoticed.

Sheffield had moved into a back room that faced onto the street. A muffled series of thumps seemed to indicate that he was going through a set of drawers.

Charlotte refocused her attention on the job at hand. The

rug—it clearly hadn't been swept in ages—was turning out to be a repository of broken pencil lead, cuttings from quill pens, copious bread crumbs . . .

Her fingers brushed against something more interesting. On closer inspection, she saw it was a cluster of silvery hair that looked as though it might have been tugged free from a wig.

She put it into her pocket. But before she could alert the others to her discovery, a hail from Sheffield announced that he, too, had found something.

"Bring the lantern here!"

She found him crouched down in front of a stone hearth.

"There appears to be a pile of ashes," he explained, "and perhaps a few fragments of paper."

"Let's have a look," said Wrexford, joining him on the floor and angling the beam into the fireplace. The flickering light picked out a mound of powdery grey ash . . . and the remains of a few singed scraps.

"Well spotted, Kit. It looks as though there might be some writing on the bits that didn't burn to a crisp."

The earl tilted his head and thought for a moment. "Damnation, it won't be easy to preserve the fragile scraps," he muttered.

"If we can find some sheets of paper—or even better, a book—we should be able to transport them back to Berkeley Square and examine them under our microscope," said Tyler. "I'll go back and check in the workrooms."

"Wait—no need," exclaimed Charlotte, suddenly recalling the small notebook she had, on impulse, slipped into her coat pocket before leaving home.

She pulled it out and handed it over.

"Allow me to help, sir," offered Tyler. "I brought along pincers." He held up a small metal tool. "If you hold the notebook open, I can pluck up the fragments and layer them in between the unused pages."

The two of them worked in silence, their attention riveted on the delicate task at hand. Once they had finished retrieving the evidence, Wrexford tied his handkerchief around the book to keep the pages firmly shut and got to his feet.

"I've no idea whether this has any relevance to our concerns—"

"I also found a hank of silvery hair in the pile of the carpet," interrupted Charlotte. "It may have come from a wig or false side-whiskers, given that Raven said he saw something that looked like fur on the table."

"Hard to say whether the hair has any meaning," replied Wrexford. "In any case, let us return home without delay and see what secrets we can coax out of the paper clues we've found."

The fire's heat had faded the ink on the singed scraps of paper, and even when magnified by the earl's powerful microscope, the writing couldn't be deciphered. But luckily, Wrexford's expertise in chemistry offered a possible solution.

"I have an idea," he said, and then ordered Charlotte and Tyler to get some sleep while he prepared a special potion.

After consulting his research files, he copied out several recipes and began the process of brewing up a mixture of various ingredients over his spirit lamp.

Just as he added a last measure of ox gall, the Weasels rushed into the laboratory, all afire to show him the muddy batch of papers they had collected from their urchin friend.

"There appears to be a lapse in my memory," he said as he thumbed through the evidence, "for I don't recall asking you to see what you could learn about the murder at Somerset House."

"You didn't tell us *not* to ask any questions of our friends," pointed out Raven.

"So we didn't disobey orders," added Hawk.

The earl's grunt was deliberately vague.

"Are the papers any help?" ventured Peregrine after Wrexford looked up.

"Not particularly, lad." He took a moment to stir the bubbling brew. "Though I concede that it was clever of you three to think of asking your friends whether they had witnessed anything suspicious."

The earl folded the papers and put them on the work counter. "These are simply the notes for Boyleston's lecture to the Royal Society. Apparently his talk was mostly about the history of research into electricity over the past few centuries and gave no details regarding the scientific paper he planned to submit for publication in the Society's journal."

Raven's face fell. "What else can we do?"

"At the moment, nothing," said Wrexford. "Given how much time you've spent on your outside activities over the last few days, I would imagine that your primary concern should be preparing for your upcoming lessons with your tutor."

At the mention of schoolwork, the boys slunk away without further comment.

Wrexford finished the final steps of brewing his concoction and then left a note for Tyler, delegating him to oversee the tedious task of soaking the papers in the chemical bath he had just designed to bring the ink back to life. After grabbing a few hours of sleep—Charlotte was still in the Land of Nod—he headed off to track down Edward Milton, the Royal Society member who had initiated the confrontation with Atticus Boyleston on the night of the irascible engineer's murder.

Knowing that Milton was a member of Boodle's, the gentlemen's club that catered to the gentry rather than the aristocracy, the earl cut through the center garden of Berkeley Square and headed for St. James's Street.

"Really, sirrah, there is nothing more I can add to my account of the confrontation with Boyleston," said Milton, lowering his newspaper with ill-disguised impatience as Wrexford approached him in the reading room of Boodle's and requested a moment of his time to discuss the altercation with the murdered gentleman. "I told that lummox of a Bow Street Runner everything that occurred—which had nothing to do with the ghastly crime that followed."

"Nonetheless, I ask that you humor me," replied Wrexford. "I have just a few additional questions."

A wordless grumble, followed by an aggrieved sniff. "Very well. But only because you are known to be a gentleman of razor-sharp reason and logic."

Wrexford made himself comfortable in the leather armchair next to Milton, which only deepened the man's scowl. "As I understand it, the unpleasantness was instigated by you challenging Boyleston's scientific conclusions."

"His conclusions were *not* science, they were quackery!" exclaimed Milton. "Surely that's evident to you."

"My expertise is in the field of chemistry, and my understanding is the argument had to do with electricity and magnetism," replied the earl. "As I have little knowledge in either discipline, might you explain to me why you think Boyleston's ideas are all wrong?"

Newsprint crackled as Milton crumpled *The Morning Gazette* and let it fall to the carpet. "*Because . . .*" Milton paused to modulate the sharpness of his tone. "Because it's obvious that electricity and magnetism are two completely different forces."

"Could you explain that to me in a little more detail?"

A sigh. "Surely you are familiar with the esteemed man of science Alessandro Volta, who invented the voltaic pile in 1800."

Wrexford confirmed the assumption with a nod.

"Then as you know, the voltaic pile uses copper or zinc plates interleaved with cloth or paper soaked in liquid brine to create a chemical reaction, which in turn creates an electrical current."

Milton stabbed a finger into the air, his sallow cheeks suddenly turning an angry shade of crimson. "Magnetism is a completely different force! Bloody hell, you've seen a lodestone or a compass, milord—it's a force that *attracts* certain metals."

"I understand your examples, which offer empirical evidence that the two forces can effect different reactions," replied the earl. "But according to most people—even his detractors—Boyleston possessed a brilliant scientific mind, so I'm finding it hard to dismiss him as a quack or idiot."

Milton looked away and muttered something under his breath.

"Boyleston thought his discovery was revolutionary—and he promised a momentous demonstration. Did he really give no hint as to what it was?"

'He blathered on about some papers written by the French men of science with whom he worked in Paris, and several experiments conducted by the French Academy," came the grudging reply.

"Can you be more specific?" prodded the earl.

"No, I cannot, sirrah!" blustered Milton. "I give little credence to 'Continental science'! Why, since the days of our great Sir Isaac Newton, it has proved far inferior to our own understanding of natural phenomena."

"I didn't realize that science had a nationality," murmured the earl. He couldn't help but add, "By the by, isn't the esteemed man of science Alessandro Volta an Italian?"

Milton's only answer was an ill-tempered sniff.

Sensing that he would get no further useful information out of the pompous arse, Wrexford rose and with a brusque word of thanks took his leave.

Annoying though the encounter had been, he at least had a clue to follow. His next step was to identify someone in London who was familiar with the experimental work in electricity being done in France since the turn of the century.

CHAPTER 7

Charlotte slept until nearly noon—an ungodly show of sloth for her—and yet still felt oddly muzzy as she went through the motions of dressing and making her way down to the kitchen.

In no mood for conversation, she was relieved to find that McClellan was busy with the housekeeper in another part of the house. After fortifying herself with a cup of black coffee and a slice of fresh-baked bread slathered with butter, Charlotte sat for an interlude in the welcome warmth and solitude, simply letting the sweetly familiar yeast-scented air clear her head before heading off to her workroom.

However, drawn by the murmur of voices from the schoolroom, she turned left instead of right at the top of the landing. The door was slightly ajar and on impulse, she crept closer and took up a position where she could safely eavesdrop without being seen. Hearing the boys engaged in their studies—the lesson this morning was geography, and punctuated by the whispery turn of a large globe, their tutor was explaining the location and history of the Spice Islands—reminded her that for the most part, their lives were filled with light and laughter, not darkness and danger.

The thought helped loosen the knot in her chest.

A flurry of questions and answers followed. She appreciated how Mr. Lynsley challenged them, forcing them to think about their answers and whether there might be alternative perspectives. Most of all, the tutor did what a good teacher should do—he sought to spark their curiosity . . .

Not that the Weasels needed any encouragement!

After another few moments, she retreated to the quiet of her workroom, satisfied that at least for now they were in no danger of getting into mischief.

Speaking of mischief, news had reached their residence at first light that the monkey was now back in place at the Tower Menagerie—but not because it had been recaptured. The animal had been discovered by its keeper, wrapped in its woolly blanket and fast asleep in the snug little wooden hut within the unlocked cage.

Charlotte's lips quirked. No doubt the monkey had been smart enough to realize that being provided with food and shelter was far more comfortable than foraging through London in the dead of winter.

The public would, of course, wish to see a final drawing on how the Great Escape had come to an end. Humor helped relieve the fears and stresses of their own everyday life.

"We all need a good laugh," she observed as she picked up her pen knife and sharpened her quill.

And yet her mind refused to focus on the task at hand. Charlotte sat for a long moment, trying to force her fingers to begin the familiar process of creating a drawing. But instead, she put down her pen and slid open the bottom drawer of her work desk. The sight of the grimy canvas sent a shiver down her spine.

"Don't," she whispered, knowing that no good could come of keeping the macabre reminder. "Don't look at it, don't touch it . . ."

If he knew of the hidden talisman, Wrexford would use reason—along with an edge of sarcasm—to chide her for letting the incident spook such elemental fears.

Still, Charlotte couldn't help but pick up the damaged rucksack and run her hand over the singed—

"Good heavens, what is that revolting object in your lap?"

Lost in her brooding, Charlotte hadn't heard the *tap-tap* of her great-aunt's cane as Alison, the dowager Countess of Peake, marched into the room.

"I would rather not speculate," added Alison. "The possibilities that come to mind aren't very pleasant."

"Neither is the reality." She sighed, deciding not to try to pull the wool over Alison's eyes. Such tactics were usually a waste of effort. Age had not dimmed the dowager's sapphirine gaze. "Come, let us sit by the hearth. Much has happened during the fortnight that you were visiting your friend in Bath and taking the waters."

"Yes, McClellan and I had a long talk as we sorted through samples of drapery fabric last night." Alison raised her quizzing glass after settling on the sofa and subjected the rucksack to a thorough scrutiny. "I see that she wasn't exaggerating about a bullet hole."

"Alas, no." Charlotte set the rucksack on the carpet, suddenly feeling as if the worn canvas was about to scorch her flesh, and went on to explain about the murder at Somerset House, and how Wrexford had felt compelled to help Durs Egg prove that his relative was not guilty of the crime.

After drawing a deep breath, she continued with the account of Raven's brush with death and the suspicious evidence that had been recovered from the warehouse.

"I confess, I find myself . . ." she added after pausing to steady her voice. "I find myself quite unsettled."

Alison edged closer and gave her a reassuring pat. "That's very understandable."

Charlotte responded with a wry smile. "Your presence is already helping to sooth my spirits. Just like when I was a child, your stalwart support always seems to frighten away the worst of my inner demons."

"Ha! That's because they know a fire-breathing dragon will burn them to a crisp if they don't take to their heels." The dowager had been dubbed "The Dragon" by the beau monde for her sharp tongue—and equally sharp cane, which she wielded with wicked accuracy.

"Now, enough Sturm und Drang. Tell me what worries are preying on your mind."

Choices, choices. Wrexford paused as he approached the corner of Haymarket Street, uncertain of whether to go straight to the Royal Institution—he had suddenly realized who might be able to give him some advice—or to head back to Berkeley Square to check on the progress of deciphering the flame-damaged scraps of paper found in the warehouse.

"Or perhaps I should simply choose to be an indolent aristocrat, who doesn't give a rat's arse about Truth and Justice," he muttered. The idea had its appeal . . .

"But alas, I appear to be cursed with a conscience."

After another few steps, the thought of returning home was too appealing to resist. Wrexford quickened his steps and turned onto Haymarket Street.

A carriage passed, its iron-shod wheels thumping over the uneven cobblestones, followed by a brewery wagon filled with sloshing barrels. The earl turned up his coat collar to ward off the freshening breeze as another carriage clattered past him . . .

And then came to a sudden halt.

The door flung open as Wrexford came abreast of the vehicle.

"Get in, milord," called a voice from within the shadows.

"I'd rather not," he replied, without breaking stride.

An oath sounded, followed by a barked order to the coachman. The carriage moved up another five yards and stopped again.

"*Please.*"

"Well, since you ask so politely . . ." The earl exhaled a sigh. "In any case, I expect that you would continue to plague me all day if I don't, so I might as well get it over with."

He climbed into the carriage and shot a sour look at George Pierson, a top operative and second-in-command to Lord Grentham, Britain's shadowy minister of state security. "Kindly make it short. I'm busy."

"I'm worried about Wrex," admitted Charlotte. "We all think of him as a pillar of strength, impervious to the doubts and emotional uncertainties that plague the rest of us. But I fear this mystery regarding his father and a possible intimate liaison is weighing heavily on his mind. And yet, he feels compelled to put aside his own troubles and take on the conundrums of others."

She looked away, and as if mocking her concerns, the shadows within the unlit corners of the room seemed to darken and swirl. "Perhaps I'm seeing specters where in fact there are none, but I have an unsettling feeling that this current murder is a crime that will have no easy answers."

"We are very good at untangling conundrums," pointed out Alison, who had proved herself frightfully good at sleuthing.

Charlotte smiled in spite of her worries. "Ha! I'm not sure whether that is a blessing or a curse."

"Yes, you are."

Her lips quirked again, then quickly thinned to a grim line. "I'm also concerned about the Weasels. The frightening incident with Raven the other night marks a momentous turning point."

"In what way?" asked Alison.

"They are . . ."

Charlotte hesitated for a heartbeat, searching for the right words to express her concerns. "They are growing up—way too fast for my liking." Another pause. "I can't help but notice that they are becoming more independent-minded and taking more risks. I fear . . ."

A sigh. "Ye gods, I can't even begin to articulate all the fears and worries that keep me awake at night."

"Change is inevitable," said the dowager softly. "Growing up is part of life." A smile. "Alas, so is aging."

The dowager's pithy sense of humor served to soften the seriousness of the moment.

"If it's any consolation, know that all parents worry incessantly about their children, especially during the fraught transition from child to adult," continued Alison. "But the Grim Reaper can strike at any moment—a wayward carriage as one crosses the street, a bout of influenza, tainted food. Obsessing about all the dangers that lurk in Life will only drive you mad."

A harried nod acknowledged the statement. "So I am learning."

"You and Wrex believe in your hearts that it's elementally important that Good triumph over Evil, and there's no denying that such dedication calls for taking some risks. It's who you are," said the dowager.

She touched a caress to Charlotte's cheek. "Inspired by your example, it's who we all are in this family."

Charlotte reached for the dowager's bejeweled hand. Their fingers twined together, setting off a flash of sapphire blue.

"We all have black moments of doubt and fear, my dear," said Alison. "But such sentiments are corrosive—they rob you of strength and the will to fight back, which is what you need most in dark times."

The dowager cleared her throat. "Whatever challenges we must face in the future, we will find a way to overcome them."

"Indeed," Charlotte agreed. In fact, her earlier fears were

giving way to a far more bellicose mood. "In fact, the more I think about it, the more I am determined to see that the varlets from the warehouse don't get away with whatever crimes they've committed." A scowl tightened on her features. "Anyone who dares to attack the Weasels will have to answer to *me*."

"And *me*," added the dowager.

"Thank you for coaxing me out of my sullens," said Charlotte. Indeed, her spirits felt infinitely lighter.

"You're very welcome," replied Alison. "And now, I think we both could use a spot of tea and a plate of Mac's ginger biscuits."

"You know, at some point, your sarcastic sense of humor is going to get you into trouble," observed Pierson.

"Quite likely. But your appearance always seems to follow with *you* asking *me* to get the government out of trouble."

Grentham's second-in-command didn't crack a smile.

"What is it this time?" demanded Wrexford.

"Word is, Durs Egg has appealed to you to help prove that his brother-in-law didn't kill Atticus Boyleston."

"He did," confirmed the earl.

"Well, *don't!*" snapped Pierson.

Wrexford narrowed his eyes, his mind beginning to whir as he took a moment to parse through the ramifications of the admonition. Power and influence could be wielded to pull in personal favors, even at the highest echelons of government.

"Who the devil are you protecting?"

Pierson heaved a long-suffering sigh. "Oh, bloody hell, the situation isn't that simple."

"It never is with you and Grentham," he retorted.

"This isn't a bloody game, Wrexford. It's a matter of the utmost importance to our nation's security."

The earl chuffed a laugh. "You know me better than that. You'll have to be a tad more specific."

"That would require me to confide highly secret information."

"Suit yourself." Wrexford reached for the door latch.

Another sigh. "Look, the government is well aware that Redding is innocent."

A growl rumbled deep in Wrexford's throat. But before it could reach his lips, Pierson made a pained face.

"And before you start frothing at the mouth about justice and fair play, I assure you that we have no intention of stringing him up on the gallows. We simply . . ."

A hesitation. "We simply want to keep him locked up for a while so that the public assumes the murder has been solved and people forget about the crime."

The unexpected admission puzzled Wrexford. "But why?"

Pierson leaned back against the leather squabs, allowing a moment of silence . . . and then another.

The earl swore under his breath and once again reached for the door latch.

"Because you are barking up the wrong tree, milord! Forget about the murder and who did it—that isn't important!"

Before Wrexford could react, Pierson added, "We need you to use your sleuthing skills on a conundrum that has far more momentous consequences for our country."

He flicked a mote of dust from his sleeve. "And the clock is ticking."

CHAPTER 8

"Explain yourself," said Wrexford. "Not that I'm entirely sure I can trust your answer."

"Then I shall try to be *very* convincing, because I wasn't jesting about the possible threat to our nation," retorted Pierson. "And though it pains me to admit it, you are the one person we trust with this secret."

"I'm listening."

"One of our operatives in Paris discovered a certain letter that raises some profoundly disturbing questions."

The mention of France prompted Wrexford to sit up a little straighter. "But the newly restored Bourbon king is our ally—and a grateful one at that." A pause. "Isn't he?"

"Don't be so naïve, milord. We don't just spy on the official government. Our network keeps a close eye on foreign operatives, as well as any other groups that may pose a threat to our interests." Pierson tapped his fingertips together. "As you can well imagine, there are a great many people in Paris whose sympathies lie with someone other than the king."

Wrexford remained silent.

"Getting back to the letter, it was written by Pierre-Simon Laplace, who as you know is considered the French Sir Isaac Newton—in other words, a genius in scientific thinking. It was written to André-Marie Ampère, another leading man of science in France who has been experimenting with something he calls electromagnetism."

Electricity and magnetism—the exact subject of Boyleston's presentation to the Royal Society, thought the earl. And suddenly a current of sparks was prickling down the length of his spine.

"The letter implies that Ampère's work in developing a theory of electromagnetism—if such a force actually exists—may be leading him to experiment with a revolutionary means of communication—an electric telegraph, if you will," explained Grentham's operative. "One that could send a message almost instantaneously from one point to another."

"Revolutionary, indeed," murmured the earl.

"As you can imagine, this discovery would have momentous implications for the world of economics, politics . . ." Pierson allowed a deliberate pause. "And, of course, for military applications."

"But the world is at peace," pointed out Wrexford.

"So it is," responded Pierson.

Which was, decided the earl, an oddly evasive response.

"Nonetheless," continued Grentham's operative, "we have our operatives doing all they can to discover whether or not the French have created such a technology."

"So what does that have to do with me?"

"Don't play the fool, milord."

"You think that Boyleston was experimenting with the same concept?" said Wrexford.

"It seems highly likely, given his fraternization with the French luminaries of science over the course of the last decade," replied Pierson. "As I said, finding Boyleston's killer isn't our main concern. We need you to find out whether Boyle-ston's research papers reveal whether the French have a working telegraph—and at the same time discover whether Boyleston has succeeded in creating one, too."

The earl turned to stare out the small paned windows of the carriage, watching the familiar buildings of Mayfair pass by as he considered what he had just heard.

"So, will you agree to take on the mission?" asked Pierson, after the carriage turned onto Berkeley Street.

"First of all, I need to ask the key question—what's the threat to our government?"

A humorless laugh. "Oh, come, you're a clever fellow, Wrex-ford. Use your imagination."

The earl took his time to mull over what he had just heard. It required damnably little imagination to comprehend what Pierson meant. *A former ruler and indisputable military genius sitting just a stone's throw from his former throne?* Much as he wished to dismiss the threat of Napoleon seeking to recapture his former glory as absurd, he couldn't in good conscience do so.

"So, you think Boyleston was murdered to keep him from sharing his momentous invention of an electrical telegraph with our government?"

"Possibly. But we can't afford to merely guess."

"Is there any other information that you're holding back from me?" he demanded.

"No."

"And do you give me your word that I have free rein to in-vestigate without your minions attempting to shadow my every move?" said Wrexford. "I refuse to be constantly tripping over their clumsy feet. You either trust me, or you don't."

"I don't quite know how you manage it, but your operatives do seem to be cleverer than ours," said Pierson. "So it would be foolish of me to stand on protocol."

"Lastly, you must inform Durs Egg that his relative's incarceration is needed for a time to help the government in an important investigation. He's proved his trustworthiness regarding sensitive government secrets, so you owe him that."

"Fine," muttered Pierson.

"Then, yes. I'll accept the assignment—on the understanding that I'll withdraw in a heartbeat if I sense that you've reneged on any of your promises."

"Excellent, we have a deal." Pierson's face was in shadow, so it was impossible to make out his expression. But Wrexford thought he detected an uncharacteristic note of relief in the operative's voice.

"There is just one administrative matter to add. I will be leaving the country this evening, so any further communication about this matter must be with Lord Grentham—and only Lord Grentham."

The two bits of news only amplified the crackling of tension in the air. "Where are you going?"

"I have some business to attend to in the Mediterranean," answered Pierson. "I can't stress enough that the reason for this investigation must remain a secret."

Wrexford didn't bother to reply. "Anything else?"

"Don't let us down."

Wrexford clicked open the door and stepped out of the carriage.

"Good luck, milord. And good hunting."

"Well, did you manage to winkle any information out of Tyler?" demanded Hawk, looking up from the watercolor sketch he was making of an orchid as Raven hurried into the schoolroom.

"Yes and no." He made a face and punctuated the answer with a frustrated sigh.

Aware of the activity in the earl's laboratory since early morning, the boys had been all afire with curiosity to know what was going on. But with their lessons looming, they had wisely decided to defer any investigation until after their tutor had left.

"It seems that the varlet who shot at us and his cohorts were indeed up to something havey-cavey," continued Raven. "Wrex and Mr. Sheffield went to the warehouse late last night to have a look around—as did m'lady and Tyler . . ." He quickly explained about the encounter, as well as the burned papers that had been fished out of the fireplace.

"What do the papers say?" pressed Peregrine.

"Dunno yet. Tyler has them soaking in a chemical solution that Wrex concocted to see if the ink can be brought back to life. He said it will be another few hours before he can begin the process of drying them."

"Then it seems we must be patient," mused Peregrine. He was lying on his belly, tinkering with the balky winch mechanism that had nearly cost Raven his life. A metallic rattling sounded as he sorted through a can of screws and chose one. "There's nothing we can do at the moment to help."

"Oiy, Falcon is right," agreed Hawk. "We ought not go flapping around on our own. Wrex and m'lady appear awfully unsettled by recent events. It's best for us to wait for specific orders."

"I don't like it." Raven's expression turned mulish. "If they think that they can start coddling us as if we are normal little aristocratic schoolboys with no clue as to what goes on in the wolf-eat-wolf real world, they had better think again."

"They wouldn't," assured Hawk. His brow puckered. "*Would* they?"

The question hung in the air, the silence growing heavier with every passing moment.

Harper stirred from his sleep and pricked up his ears.

"As m'lady is wont to say, let's not start seeing specters lurking in every corner when there's naught but harmless shadows flitting in circles," counseled Peregrine.

Raven muttered something under his breath, but aware that his fellow Weasels were watching him intently, he gave a gruff nod. "I s'ppose that makes sense." A pause. "For now."

Hawk and Peregrine returned to their projects, but after picking up a book on mathematics and finding it impossible to concentrate on the contents, Raven quietly closed the covers and left the room.

It was a short walk from Berkeley Square to the Sheffield residence on Half Moon Street. The butler, who was used to Raven's frequent visits for his mathematical lessons with Cordelia, welcomed him with a smile.

"She is in her workroom, Master Thomas." Like all proper butlers, he was a stickler for the rules of Polite Society and insisted on calling Raven by his official name. "Mister Sheffield is with her."

A pause. "Brush the crumbs from your jacket before you enter. A gentleman must mind his manners."

After obeying the admonition—though not without rolling his eyes—Raven hurried down the corridor to the rear of the house.

Cordelia had chosen a light-filled room overlooking the back garden as her study. The door was half-open, and loath to interrupt the conversation in progress, he paused for a moment to comb his fingers through his unruly hair and straighten his lapels.

". . . As I've mentioned, over the last few years, David Ricardo has participated in several syndicates which have brought to market large flotations of British government debt, which our country has issued for the last sixty years to pay for our military activities abroad—in particular, the last two decades of our wars with France."

It was Sheffield speaking.

"However," he continued, "with Napoleon now safely locked away on the isle of Elba, the government will likely only need to float a small loan this year. Thus Ricardo may not need to form a syndicate of fellow stockjobbers, bankers, and other investors to finance the needed funds. So he'll be working on other financial projects."

"And you wish to work with him on those new projects?" asked Cordelia.

"Given the volume of trading he handles, he's open to accepting extra capital from personal acquaintances. If you agree, I would like to invest some of our savings in his ventures," replied Sheffield. "I think it will not only give us a good return on our money but also allow me to learn more about the world of finance and how the London Stock Exchange works."

He allowed a fraction of a pause before adding, "Ricardo is highly mathematical in his approach—"

Cordelia cut him off with a chuckle. "You need not coat your tongue with honey in order to win my approval, Kit. I'm well aware of Ricardo's genius with numbers. In fact, I've already agreed to work with him in refining the mathematics he uses in his business of buying and selling on the Exchange."

Another chuckle. "In fact, I was just about to broach the same question to you about investing in his firm."

Sheffield added his own bark of humor. "And here I thought I was being exceedingly clever."

Seizing the opportunity offered by the lull in the conversation, Raven cleared his throat and rapped his knuckles on the door.

"Come in, come in!" called Cordelia, on spotting him peering in from the corridor. "Forgive me. Did I forget that we had scheduled a lesson?"

"No, I—I just had some questions . . ." Raven hesitated.

"You are always welcome to ask me anything," assured Cordelia.

"You and Mr. Sheffield have mentioned buying and selling securities on several occasions. I'm curious to know more about the London Stock Exchange and how it works."

"Excellent," said Sheffield. "Why don't I start with a brief history of how it came into being?" He gestured for Raven to join them at the small worktable. "And then we shall get into some of the details of stock and securities trading."

Raven leaned forward, an expectant look on his face.

"To begin with, the first stock exchange in England was the Royal Exchange, founded in 1571 by Thomas Gresham with the approval of Queen Elizabeth I. As for the London Stock Exchange, it had its roots in Jonathan's Coffee House near the Royal Exchange," explained Sheffield. "A number of stockbrokers were banned from the official exchange because of their rude and rowdy behavior and began meeting there informally to trade among themselves. One of them, a fellow named John Casting, began creating broadsheets several times a week listing the prices of commodities, offerings, and exchange rates. And these informal sales continued well into the 1700s."

"It sounds like it wasn't for the faint of heart," observed Cordelia.

"Indeed not," agreed Sheffield. "It wasn't until 1801, after a series of frauds had occurred, that the informal group required an annual membership, which turned it into a subscription room, open only to members. They then moved to their current building on Capel Court—and that led to them being formally recognized as the London Stock Exchange."

Sheffield leaned back in his chair. "But despite its long history, the London Stock Exchange as we know it is in many ways quite new. It didn't have a formal set of rules governing trading until three years ago. Before then, its activities were mostly governed by informal practices and customs."

"Mr. Ricardo helped draft those rules," interjected Cordelia. "Which he told me were much needed to create a more orderly and much larger market and to reduce fraud."

"It's also important to note that the name *Stock Exchange* is a bit misleading," said Sheffield. "Most of the securities traded there are in fact bonds issued by the British government. Because of the wars with Napoleon and all our earlier military activities, nearly £1 billion of British public debt is outstanding."

"Oiy!" Raven's eyes widened on hearing the sum.

"Other securities, such as shares of companies, constitute only a small portion of the financial market. Mr. Ricardo and most other professional investors focus mostly on government bonds," continued Sheffield. "It's interesting to note that many of the securities issued in Britain are held by foreigners. Almost half the British public debt is held by Dutch bankers."

"I didn't know that," said Cordelia.

Raven, who had been following the explanation intently, cleared his throat. "After hearing all this, I have a big question. Can mathematics really be used to make sure one always makes money trading stocks and securities?"

"It's not quite that simple," answered Cordelia. "There are a myriad of factors which affect the value of a security or how a given transaction will fare. However, Mr. Ricardo believes that by using mathematics in a variety of ways to model these factors, he can substantially increase his likelihood of making winning investments. And even if mathematics only gives him a slight edge in choosing what to sell and what to buy, that can amount to a great deal of profit if it is done consistently in large volumes over a long period of time."

Raven's face scrunched in thought.

"Here's just one example," offered Sheffield. "Almost every year he forms a syndicate with other investors to buy bonds from the government when it makes its annual effort to raise funds needed for the military or other major endeavors. The syndicate, or syndicates, which win the bid take the securities and resell them to a large group of other investors—"

"That is how individual investors have access to buying them," explained Cordelia.

Sheffield nodded. "The syndicates aim to resell these securities at a higher price than they paid for them. But the securities bought from the government are a complicated package of different types of bonds. Estimating what the public will be willing to pay for them requires a great deal of market savvy and analysis. And the fact that the syndicates can pay for the securities in a variety of installments creates even more variables— but I'll leave all that for another time."

"Adding to the complexities of the calculations," added Cordelia, "is the fact that if full payment is made for the securities before a specified date, the government offers an astronomical discount on what the syndicate has to pay for the bonds."

Sheffield nodded. "As we said, it's complicated."

"Mr. Ricardo has been seen as especially talented in his ability to quickly formulate sound and ultimately successful bids for government bonds," continued Cordelia. "He has also been praised for not playing some of the unscrupulous games that other syndicates play to increase their profits at the expense of the public."

She thought for a moment. "If you are interested in all this, I think your mathematical skills would be a great help to me in working with Mr. Ricardo. Would you like to serve as my assistant on the project?"

Raven's eyes widened. "Really?"

"Absolutely." Cordelia saw Sheffield waggle his brows and quickly added, "Though, of course, we must confirm that Wrex and Charlotte have no objection."

Raven's face fell. "They're in a pucker because of the dratted gunshot. I fear they're planning to clip our wings and try to lock us away in a gilded cage." His chin came up. "I won't have it."

"Of course they're concerned with your safety, lad," said Sheffield. "We all are. But that said, I doubt they have any intention of—"

"Demanding that we behave like dull-witted little aristocratic prigs?"

"Good Lord." Cordelia appeared utterly shocked at the idea but then began to laugh. "Oh, come, not even in your wildest nightmares can you believe that's a possibility."

Raven allowed a grudging grin. "I suppose not. But they have been *very* strict about not allowing us to be part of the current investigation."

"I think that's because none of us are at all certain of what we should be investigating," said Sheffield. "The murder at Somerset House and the attack on you Weasels are both incidents fraught with questions and possible complications. But whether they are related is impossible to say right now."

"Even more reason to let us Weasels help." Raven looked at Sheffield. "I am quite certain that the villains in the warehouse were handling stocks and letters of credit and talking of bond issues—"

"As does every legitimate businessman," countered Sheffield. "Let us see whether Wrex's chemical bath coaxes any clues from the burned scraps before we seek to make any connection between the two incidents."

"Very well," conceded Raven. "But . . . but it seems to me that if the Stock Exchange is such an important and powerful force in the financial world, it can be used for Evil as well as for Good."

Sheffield gave a sardonic grunt. "As can most things that we mortals create. Nonetheless, you're right."

"So, that's what got me thinking that perhaps the men I saw in the warehouse were involved in some havey-cavey scheme," pressed Raven.

"As I said, let's not jump to conclusions," responded Sheffield. "For now it's best to wait and see."

CHAPTER 9

After taking his leave from Pierson, Wrexford changed his mind about returning to Berkeley Square and headed straight to the Royal Institution. But instead of heading up the grand staircase to where the members worked and socialized, he descended into the bowels of the building, which held the laboratories and work areas for the various assistants hired by Humphry Davy, the prominent scientific luminary who served as the director of the Institution.

Windowless workrooms lined each side of the main corridor, their gloom softened by only an occasional lit lantern flickering behind the glass inset in their doors. The air was heavy with a damp chill and a slightly noxious odor of mixed chemicals.

But beggars can't be choosy, reflected the earl. The positions were coveted by young men of modest means who hoped to forge a place for themselves within the world of science.

He stopped at one of the larger spaces and rapped softly on the glass to get the attention of the occupant hunched over his desk.

The fellow looked up with a startled expression, which quickly softened into a half smile. "Lord Wrexford! Please come in."

As the earl opened the door, his gaze immediately fell on a large voltaic pile that ran the length of the desktop. Wires curled up from each end and were connected to various devices.

"Forgive me for interrupting you, Faraday." He looked again at the voltaic pile. "How are your experiments with electricity coming along?"

"I'm compiling a host of fascinating data, sir," answered Michael Faraday, whose brilliant mind had been quickly recognized by the director. Despite his humble background, he now served in the prestigious position of Davy's personal assistant.

The young man's mouth pursed. "It's sparking a number of theories, milord, but as of yet, I'm merely speculating on what wonders I might be able to prove."

"Speaking of theories," said Wrexford, "I have heard something recently that sparked my curiosity. Do you perchance know anything about the French work in electricity since Volta's discovery of the voltaic battery?"

"I'm generally aware of the direction of their research, and I'm quite certain that they are way ahead of us in their thinking."

"How so?" asked the earl.

"Our men of science here in Britain made the mistake of seeing electricity as some magical, mystical force, rather than a scientific phenomenon that can be explained by the laws of physics and chemistry. And so they spent their efforts on fanciful ideas, like using it to reanimate the dead."

Faraday shook his head in exasperation. "While the French have concentrated their research on developing rigorous theories about the phenomena of electricity and magnetism, putting them years ahead of us. Though, mind you, I don't agree entirely with the approach their theories are taking."

"Why?" pressed the earl.

"Because their leading men of science are said to be formulating their explanations of electricity and magnetism—which the Danish scientific thinker Christian Oersted has shown are somehow linked, though in ways we don't understand—in mathematical terms," answered Faraday. "Their mathematics may work—I don't know—but it doesn't explain *how* these two forces operate."

A sigh. "Now perhaps it's because I lack formal mathematical training, but I wish to have a more physical explanation. For example, sprinkle iron filings around a magnet and they quickly move in precise spirals around the magnet. To my mind, understanding these spirals—I call them *lines of force*—and the field they describe is key to explaining how magnetism works and how it can be harnessed."

Wrexford allow a moment of silence as he watched the flame of Faraday's lamp dance within its glass globe. "This is all very fascinating. But right now, what I very much would like to have from you is an answer to a specific question."

He drew in a measured breath. "Might the French research into electromagnetism perchance involve using an electrical current traveling along a wire to send messages over a distance at nearly instantaneous speed?"

Faraday's expression turned very grave, and he gave the query a long moment of thought before answering. "From what I have heard, I would say the answer is yes, milord."

"Do you know if they have succeeded?"

"I don't, sir."

"In your learned opinion, is such an invention possible?" pressed the earl.

"Yes, milord," answered Faraday without hesitation. "But not until we know a great deal more about how the two phenomena work together. However, our scientific thinking and technology is getting more and more sophisticated, which allows us to do more complex experimentations. So I firmly believe that it will happen within my lifetime."

His eyes seemed to come alight with an inner fire. "And when that moment comes, I believe it will be the most revolutionary invention ever created by mankind."

Wrexford was reminded of a famous Greek myth in which Prometheus was punished for gifting fire to mere mortals. Zeus had created a particularly gruesome fate because he felt that the power to wield such a potent elemental force gave humans a godlike ability that threatened to upset the balance of the universe.

"Assuming you're right, let us hope that it doesn't unleash unintended consequences," he replied.

"Progress always comes with dangers," said Faraday. "We must count on the better angels of our nature to do the right thing with it."

Angels were all very well, thought Wrexford. But the Devil was too clever in luring mankind into temptation for him to feel as confident as Davy's assistant about Right triumphing over Wrong.

However, the earl pushed aside philosophical questions for the moment and made himself focus on the mission at hand.

"Do you happen to know whether Atticus Boyleston was working on an electrical telegraph?"

"The fellow murdered at the Royal Society meeting—the one who planned to submit a paper on electromagnetism for their famous scientific journal?"

On getting a confirming nod, Faraday furrowed his brow in thought. "We weren't acquainted, and what little I know about him comes through mere hearsay. That said, I'm told he was a curmudgeonly, secretive fellow but also a brilliant man of science."

The young man leaned back in his chair. "And I also know that he worked in Paris on two different occasions with some of the best minds in France. So yes, I would think it's quite possible that he was working on that technology."

"But you don't know for sure?"

"I'm sorry, but I have no idea."

Wrexford dismissed the apology with a brusque wave. "Your insights have been quite useful—"

"Wait! A thought just occurred to me." Faraday's expression suddenly brightened. "You might want to contact Jane Marcet. She is likely the only person in all of London who considered Boyleston a friend, so she may be able to answer the questions you have about him."

Alison polished off the last of the ginger biscuits. "I dearly missed Mac's sweets over the last fortnight. All that foul-tasting healthful water and bland food designed to purge one's system of overindulgences is very unpleasant—not to speak of boring."

Crunch, crunch. "I would prefer to enjoy life's little pleasures, rather than adhere to such a virtuous regime *ad nauseam.*"

Charlotte chuckled. "Virtue is vastly overrated in many respects."

The dowager dusted the crumbs from her fingers. "Speaking of virtue, where are the Weasels?"

"Up in the schoolroom, behaving like normal boys for a change," she said dryly. "Hawk is engrossed in painting a picture of an orchid that Mac brought back from a shopping trip to Covent Garden, Peregrine is tinkering with a mechanical ratcheting device that he recently designed, and Raven is reading a very weighty-looking book on some sort of complicated financial equations by Francis Baily."

Charlotte put down her cup. "They are a bit miffed that they haven't been more involved in the investigation of the recent murder."

"Given what happened, your reluctance to have them involved in this particular crime is understandable," observed Alison.

"It's not just that," she replied. "There aren't really any clues for them to follow. They've interrogated their urchin friends in the area of the crime, and none of them saw anything helpful. So for now, there is nothing further for them to pursue. Though that may change soon . . ."

She explained about Tyler's attempt to coax the burned papers into giving up their secrets. "In the meantime, Wrex is trying to learn more about the murder victim's scientific work. The fellow had apparently announced that he was soon to give a grand demonstration of his momentous new theory."

"What theory?"

Charlotte made a face. "Nobody seems to know."

"Hmmph." The dowager shrugged. "Then it seems we must wait and see what Wrex discovers before we can plan our next moves."

Charlotte chose to overlook the use of *we* and *our*. Alison was moving a little slower than usual, despite the sojourn to soak her ailing joints in the spa's famous healing waters. But tactfully suggesting that the dowager back off from an active role in the current investigation was a battle that she would wage on another day.

"Seeing as we can't go confront any villains and pummel the truth out of them . . ." The dowager reached for her reticule and pulled out a packet of fabric swatches. "Might I get your opinion on what color you like best for draperies in my breakfast room?"

"Jane Marcet?" Wrexford frowned in puzzlement. The name meant nothing to him.

"I assure you, she is a remarkable woman. Indeed, it is because of her that I am who I am today," said Faraday.

"I confess, that's a very surprising statement."

"Nonetheless, it's true," assured Faraday. "I had little formal education and at a young age was forced to find work to help support my family. I procured a position as a lowly clerk in a bookshop, which is where I happened to discover *Conversa-*

tions in Chemistry—Intended More Especially for the Female Sex, a book Mrs. Marcet wrote explaining the work of Humphry Davy in simplified terms for those with no knowledge of chemistry."

A smile. "For me, it was transformational."

"Is she a chemist?" asked Wrexford. "And if so, why have I never heard of her?"

"Mrs. Marcet is well educated in a variety of subjects. Her father, a wealthy Swiss banker, was an enlightened fellow and allowed his daughter to be educated along with her brothers in a broad curriculum of subjects," answered Davy's assistant. "But in answer to your question, no, she is not a scholar, though she does have an interest in chemistry, and she and her husband conduct experiments in their home laboratory."

Faraday gazed at the elaborate voltaic battery, with its maze of metal plates and curling wires. "Her true skills lie in having the ability to simplify complex ideas and explain them clearly to others who have little or no background in the subject."

"No easy feat," murmured Wrexford.

"No, indeed," agreed Faraday. "Mrs. Marcet and her husband are part of a literary and scientific salon, whose members also include the Scottish polymath Mary Somerville and the historian Henry Hallam. I believe that is where she came to befriend Boyleston."

"Do you know where I might find her?" asked Wrexford.

"I don't move in the same social circles as she does, so I'm not aware of where she resides. But I shall ask around and send word to you when I learn her address, sir."

"Many thanks."

The earl then took his leave of Faraday and headed back up the stairs, lost in thought as he pondered all the unexpected revelations of the afternoon. The murder investigation had, in the space of an hour, been knocked arse over teakettle, and he hadn't quite regained his equilibrium.

Pierson had told him to forget about the murder itself because it wasn't important who had actually killed Boyleston. But something about it stuck in his craw, though he couldn't quite put a finger on what it was.

In retrospect, it seemed likely that the murderer had always intended to leave a pistol made by Durs Egg at the scene of the crime. It was, he conceded, a clever red herring, given the fact that Egg's relative was a member of the Royal Society. Even without the quarrel, the evidence would have distracted the authorities. Allowing the killer to . . .

To do what?

Why go through all the trouble—the theft of a pistol from Egg's workshop, the staging of the murder scene—if the purpose of the crime was simply to prevent Boyleston from passing his invention of an electrical telegraph to the British government? The killer could easily have fled with little chance of being apprehended.

It made no logical sense. And that bothered Wrexford.

A great deal, in fact . . .

"*Alors, c'est magnifique!*"

An unexpected exclamation in French startled the earl out of his brooding. He looked around as he stepped from the top stair into the grand, marble-tiled entrance hall, wondering if his mind was playing tricks and he had merely imagined the voice.

But no—a quartet of gentlemen led by William Brande, one of the directors of the Royal Institution, was gathered by a display of gilt-framed oil paintings portraying the illustrious men of science from Britain's past, and another burst of French sounded before the speaker switched to English.

"I am a great admirer of Sir Godfrey Kneller's paintings, and this one of Sir Isaac Newton is a particularly fine example of his work."

Brande spotted the earl and beckoned him to join the group.

"Ah, Wrexford, do come and meet Monsieur Pierre Ducasse, who is visiting us from Paris. He has been hired by the French Académie des Sciences to paint a series of portraits of Britain's scientific luminaries to be displayed in their headquarters."

"As a symbol of *amitié*, now that our two great countries are at peace," added Ducasse with a genial smile. He was, noted the earl, a handsome man, with a mane of wavy dark hair, a straight nose and a sensuous mouth that likely earned him fluttery sighs from the ladies.

"You ought to consider adding Wrexford to your list of subjects, monsieur," said Brande, after he had performed the formal introduction. "He is one of the pre-eminent chemists in Britain."

"Absolutely not," replied the earl. "I lack the patience to sit for a portrait."

"What a pity," said the Frenchman. His amber-hued gaze subjected Wrexford to a prolonged scrutiny before he added, "You have a *very* interesting visage, milord."

"Choose someone who enjoys such flummery, sir," replied Wrexford. "I have no desire to have my phiz hung on a wall for strangers to ogle."

Ducasse laughed. "We shall see. I can be very persuasive."

"Lady Wrexford is a connoisseur of art," offered Sir George Woburn, a fellow chemist who was part of the group, "and a very fine watercolorist, so perhaps you can enlist her to help change the earl's mind."

The suggestion was seconded by the gentleman next to Woburn, another of the earl's scientific colleagues.

Wrexford raised a brow in warning at the two of them. "I assure you, my wife has better things to do with her time. As do I."

"We are having a reception tomorrow evening for Monsieur Ducasse, which will include some of the leaders of the French émigré community here in London," said Brande. "As an esteemed member of our board of governors, I hope you will be able to join us, Wrexford."

Wrexford was about to demur but then decided that the opportunity to mingle with Ducasse and his fellow countrymen might be of use to his new mission. "Very well," he responded.

"*Bon!*" exclaimed the Frenchman. "I look forward to furthering our acquaintance, milord."

Another thought came to mind. "Faraday was just telling me about a scholarly woman named Jane Marcet, who made Humphry Davy's chemistry more accessible to laymen. Perhaps we should show Monsieur Ducasse how broad-minded the scientific world is here in Britain and invite her to attend as well."

Brande made a face. "The event is not a social event, milord. It is a serious gathering for gentlemen only, as we shall be discussing scientific issues as well as the business of forging closer ties with our French counterparts." He forced a prim smile. "We would only bore the ladies."

"Because those of the opposite sex have naught but feathers for brains?" retorted Wrexford.

Nostrils flaring in irritation, Brande chose to ignore the comment. He looked to Ducasse, whose eyes held a glint of amusement over the exchange. "Shall we move on to the library, where we have some champagne set out for a welcoming toast?"

"Would you care to join us, Wrexford?" asked Sir George.

"Thank you, but I must be going." The earl took his leave from the group with a gruff nod, happy to have at least poked a pin into Brande's puffed-up pretentions of male superiority, and made his way out to the street. He was anxious to return to the quiet of his workroom and reflect on the sudden new twists in the investigation.

CHAPTER 10

A short walk brought him home, and as he headed down the corridor toward the back of the townhouse, a peal of laughter from the Blue Parlor informed him that Charlotte's great-aunt had returned from her stay in Bath.

"I trust you had a pleasant visit with your friends," said Wrexford as he joined them.

"I did," replied Alison, "aside from the dreadful hours spent soaking in the sulfurous-smelling pools of the spa."

"You did admit that your knees feel better," said Charlotte.

"Which is quite fortuitous, as it appears we have yet another diabolical intrigue to unravel," responded the dowager.

Charlotte locked eyes with the earl. "Alison is now aware of all that has happened while she was away."

"Be that as it may, things have changed considerably in the last few hours," he replied. "I had a brief encounter with George Pierson, who as you both know is Grentham's most trusted operative."

The dowager darted a quick look at Charlotte before releasing a troubled sigh. "It's always worrisome when our investigations cross paths with those of Lord Grentham."

Wrexford didn't disagree. There had been several times in the past when they all had feared that the minister of state security had discovered that Charlotte was, in fact, the infamous satirical artist A. J. Quill. But so far, there had been no indication that there was any truth to their worries.

However, the less they dealt with the minister, the better.

"Indeed," he said. "I have agreed to undertake a mission for the government, but with the firm understanding that Grentham and his operatives stay well away from us and don't interfere."

"What sort of—" began Charlotte.

"I need to think things through a bit more before gathering our inner circle and having one of our councils of war," interjected Wrexford.

Alison nodded in understanding. "Of course. Though it goes without saying that I'm to be included when the time comes."

Wrexford eyed her cane and smiled. "I prefer my shins to remain unbruised, so you may count on it."

He turned to go, then paused. "By the by, do either of you know a Jane Marcet?"

"Why yes," answered the dowager. "She frequently attends Lady Thirkell's salon for intellectually minded women, and I find her to be very engaging and quite knowledgeable on a wide range of subjects."

To Charlotte, she added, "As I recall, you met her once and had an interesting conversation on the art of Thomas Lawrence, with whom she studied painting for a time."

"Ah, I do remember her," mused Charlotte. "A fascinating woman. She writes books on science that aim to explain complex ideas to those with little knowledge in the field."

"I recently heard she's in the process of penning a new work called *Conversations on Political Economy*," added Alison, "in which she aims to explain the ideas of Adam Smith, Thomas Malthus, and David Ricardo."

"You've already proved to be an invaluable sleuth," observed Wrexford, his interest in the lady further piqued by the mention of Ricardo. "Do you perchance know where she lives?"

"No, but it so happens that Lady Thirkell is having a soiree tomorrow evening." She raised an inquiring brow at Charlotte. "Perhaps you should come. Mrs. Marcet occasionally attends the meetings."

"A good suggestion," agreed Charlotte. "I shall do so."

The dowager raised her quizzing glass and regarded the clock on the mantel. "Good heavens, it's later than I realized." A sigh. "I ought to toddle home. I confess that I'm still feeling a trifle fatigued from the traveling."

Charlotte quickly rose and offered her a hand up.

"Don't forget, Wrex . . ." Alison grasped her cane and gave it a waggle. "I expect to be kept informed."

After escorting the dowager to her waiting carriage, Charlotte re-entered the townhouse and made a beeline for the earl's workroom. Wrexford was at his desk, papers filled with scribbled notes spread out across his blotter.

"What did Pierson want?" she demanded without preamble. "Nothing good, I imagine."

The earl sat back in his chair, the flicking lamplight accentuating the lines of fatigue etched at the corners of his eyes. "The government has reason to believe that the French may have invented a new technology that would give them a critical edge over all other competitors—including us—in economics, politics . . ." His pause seemed quite deliberate. "And warfare."

"B-But . . ." Charlotte felt her innards clench. "We're not at war."

"Not at present."

"Good God." For a moment, she couldn't seem to draw a breath. "Grentham thinks it's a possibility?"

"So it would seem," answered Wrexford softly. "Pierson, who mentioned that he is leaving tonight for the Mediterranean, asked me for urgent help in learning whether the French have a working model of an electrical telegraph—a technology capable of sending messages within mere seconds or minutes rather than hours or days."

He hesitated. "Even more important, Pierson wishes for me to discover whether Boyleston had succeeded in creating an electrical telegraph. For it's possible he was killed not only to prevent him from sharing the invention with our government, but because the French haven't succeeded and wished to steal the new technology for themselves."

She stared at him in mute shock.

"Granted, it may be some elaborate ruse to trick me into doing something that I wouldn't otherwise accept." He checked his notes. "But I don't think so."

"Even they wouldn't be that manipulative." Finding her legs a little unsteady, Charlotte took a seat on the edge of his desk. "Hell's bells, so Grentham and Pierson think that the public demonstration Boyleston promised on the night of his murder was to unveil . . ."

"Yes, he had worked with the leading French men of science during his sojourns to Paris," interjected Wrexford. "And I just had a sobering conversation with Michael Faraday, who is one of our country's leading experts on electricity. He's adamant that the technology is possible, and that it's only a matter of time before someone figures out a practical way to build it."

He picked up his pencil and rolled it between his palms. "The question is, has that time arrived?"

She thought over the revelation. "So, the strategic advantage of an electric telegraph is—"

"The invention would revolutionize many aspects of life, but the government's primary concern at the moment is communication on the battlefield," interjected the earl. "The ability to react to the action as it unfolds and send messages in a flash to the different divisions, rather than dispatch couriers on horseback, would be an incalculable edge."

The ensuing silence seemed to squeeze the light from the lamp flame. It flickered for a moment before regaining its fire.

"You mentioned practicality," said Charlotte. "My understanding is that the current from a voltaic pile flows along a wire. How would an army manage the logistics of stringing wires on a battlefield?"

"A good question," conceded Wrexford. "But even a few wires covering short distances to divisional commanders would offer a huge advantage. However, you're right. There is much we need to learn."

"And you think Jane Marcet may be of help?"

"Faraday is under the impression that she had developed a friendship with Boyleston, apparently no mean feat given his crotchety personality, so I think it imperative that I meet with her."

Wrexford ran a hand through his hair. "Right after my conversation with Faraday, I had an odd encounter, and given the government's fears that a French threat is indeed looming in the shadows, it strikes me as unsettling."

"How so?" she asked,

"I stumbled into a tour being given of the Royal Institution," he continued. "One of the directors was playing host to a Frenchman who has recently arrived in London and says that he's been commissioned to paint portraits of our leading men of science for the Académie des Sciences in Paris. It is supposedly a gesture of camaraderie for a new era of cooperation."

"And you think the man may be a wolf in sheep's clothing?" asked Charlotte.

"Put that way, it does sound far-fetched," admitted the earl. "And yet . . ."

"If we're on the hunt for possible conspirators here in London, I think a more likely possibility are the three miscreants from the warehouse," opined Charlotte. "The tufts of silvery hair suggest that one of them might have been wearing a wig and false side-whiskers that night. Which could mean he was the unidentified stranger at the Royal Society—and thus Boyleston's killer."

"Perhaps you think that because you're taking the attack on the Weasels very personally," he pointed out.

"Guilty as charged," admitted Charlotte. "That still doesn't make me wrong."

That made Wrexford give a grudging smile.

"Has Tyler finished treating the paper scraps we found?" she continued. "If we find any writing in French, then I think you must take my suggestion seriously."

"Or perhaps our suspects are all part of some nefarious plot whose ultimate purpose remains a total mystery." Wrexford shrugged. "But one step at a time. Tyler is in the final stage of drying the papers in the kitchen oven. In another half hour we should know whether anything of interest has been brought to light."

Charlotte rose, impatient to act and yet aware that flailing around in the dark would do them no good. She moved to the hearth and stirred the coals to life as the earl turned his attention back to his notes.

"I have been invited to a reception in honor of the French portrait painter," he continued, without looking up. "Alas, ladies are excluded from this particular gathering, as the discussions concerning science have been deemed too serious for their flighty intellect."

"I shall refrain from voicing any gross generalizations concerning pompous prigs whose brains are pickled in brandy."

"It's a pity, as I would very much welcome your impression of the French artist," continued Wrexford. "He tried to convince me to be one of his subjects—"

"Ha! You don't have the patience to sit for a portrait!" she interjected.

"That's what I told him. However, one of my colleagues mentioned that he might have a chance of changing my mind if he spoke with you."

"Try to find out what other social engagements are planned for him, and I shall contrive to attend one of them."

He nodded vaguely as he added a few more scribbles to one of his note papers.

"Milord, m'lady." Tyler suddenly appeared in the doorway of the adjacent library. "You need to see this."

Wrexford was out of his chair in a flash. Charlotte was right on his heels as he headed to the large worktable set by the arched windows looking out over the back gardens. The draperies had been drawn, and the only source of illumination on the objects came from a powerful Argand lamp.

The scraps of paper they had collected from the deserted warehouse lay on a piece of black pasteboard. Tyler had placed a sheet of glass over them to keep the curling edges flat.

"I've brought a magnifying glass," said the valet, offering the silver-handled instrument to Wrexford.

Charlotte held her breath as he leaned down to inspect the enhanced scribbles of ink, not entirely sure of whether she wanted her suspicions to be correct.

He took his time, shifting his stance to scrutinize them from several different angles.

A glance at Tyler proved unhelpful. His expression gave away nothing.

At last, the earl looked up and offered her the magnifying glass. "*Voilà.*"

Charlotte took it without comment and made her own examination. "So, at least one of the papers the men burned was written in French!" she exclaimed "And the message included the word *rendezvous.*"

A pause. "Before you say anything, I'm aware that it doesn't necessarily mean they have anything to do with Grentham's concern." She put the magnifying glass down on the table. "But neither can we dismiss the possibility."

"Which means that tomorrow we must begin trying to find some threads to follow," said Wrexford, "so that we may quickly unravel the truth."

CHAPTER 11

The murmur of masculine voices, its buzz mellowed as it resonated off the dark wood paneling of the reception room, was punctuated by the clink of crystal and the fizz of champagne—leaving no doubt that the gathering in honor of the French artist was already in high spirits.

"Wipe that scowl off your phiz," advised Sheffield as Wrexford paused in the shadows of the entrance archway. He had been informed that morning of the latest developments, and Charlotte had deemed it a good idea for him to accompany the earl to the reception. "One coaxes out more information with honey than with vinegar," he added.

"I've no desire to sweeten up Monsieur Ducasse," Wrexford muttered. "Though given Grentham's concern and what we discovered from the warehouse papers last night, he must be considered a possible suspect."

"That's why Charlotte insisted that I come with you," replied his friend. "I have far more experience in acting like a superficial fribble. I shall do my best to strike up a camaraderie with the fellow and see what I can learn."

"Ah, welcome, Wrexford. I wasn't sure that we would have the pleasure of your company." Brande gestured for the earl and Sheffield to join the circle of dignitaries gathered at the refreshment table. "And you, Mr. Sheffield. We rarely have the pleasure of your company here at the Royal Institution."

"Oh, you know me—I haven't got a serious bone in my body," drawled Sheffield. "However, Wrex informed me that you are known for holding very festive parties."

"A fellow bon vivant?" Ducasse raised his glass in salute. "Thank heavens I'm now not alone in having no head for science."

"Monsieur Ducasse is an artist," explained Wrexford.

"Who very much wishes to paint your friend's portrait," added the Frenchman.

"I wish you luck." Sheffield took a glass of wine from one of the waiters and returned the salute. "Though Lady Wrexford has often mentioned that she would like to add his likeness to the family portrait gallery."

"Indeed?" Ducasse made a tsking sound. "Surely you don't wish to disappoint Her Ladyship, milord?"

"My friend exaggerates," replied the earl.

Sheffield waggled his brows. "I assure you I don't. Indeed, if you care to meet me tomorrow afternoon at the Royal Academy of Arts, I should be happy to introduce you to Lady Wrexford, who is a discerning connoisseur of art. I am escorting her to view the new winter exhibit, which opened last week."

"*Merci!* I accept with great pleasure," exclaimed Ducasse. "I shall, as you English say, be able to kill two birds with one stone."

An interesting choice of metaphors, thought Wrexford.

"The Royal Academy exhibit is high on my list of things to see in London," continued the Frenchman. "And now I will not only be able to do so with a knowledgeable guide." A wink. "But I shall also have the opportunity to plead my case to Her Ladyship."

"Be careful what you wish for," said the earl. "My wife has a mind of her own."

"Ah, but I like challenges," said Ducasse.

The earl's response was a cool smile.

"Shall we meet at the exhibit entrance at three o'clock?" suggested Sheffield.

"*Bien!* I am very much looking forward to it."

Brande cleared his throat. "Lord Wrexford, might I also introduce Monsieur Hubert Odilon, one of the leading members of the French émigré community here in London and an influential force in rebuilding good relations between our countries?"

"I'm delighted to hear that our Parisian men of science are expressing their respect for Britain's scientific luminaries by creating a wall of honor for them at the Académie des Sciences," said Odilon. "It is yet another sign that our two countries have put the past conflicts behind them."

The earl forced a polite smile.

"His Lordship and I consider it a very generous gesture," replied Sheffield. He raised a toast. "To a long-lasting *fraternité* between Britain and France."

The mellow clink of crystal sounded.

"Aside from the Royal Academy exhibit, what other cultural attractions here in London would you recommend, Mr. Sheffield?" asked Ducasse.

Leaving his friend and the two Frenchmen to exchange polite pleasantries about the city and its attractions, Wrexford drifted away to greet several colleagues. He joined in their discussion regarding a recent engineering innovation before moving on and taking up a position in one of the secluded alcoves of the room, which afforded a good vantage point from which to observe the gathering.

However, he quickly realized he wasn't alone. Two other gentlemen had also retreated to the quiet spot.

"Greetings, Wrexford." One of them was a casual acquaintance—the earl and Norwood had served together as fellow officers for a short time during the Peninsular War—who now worked as a senior aide to the Home Secretary.

Norwood raised his glass in friendly salute. "I'm surprised that you're here to honor a Frog."

"I'm on the board of governors and was asked to make an appearance," he replied.

Norwood's companion smiled. "And I am here because Brande can be counted on to serve an unlimited flow of very fine French champagne."

"I assume you are acquainted with Fogg," said Norwood, indicating his companion. "He's a senior official at the Foreign Office."

Wrexford acknowledged the fellow with a nod. Their paths had crossed at various receptions, but they had never exchanged anything more than passing greetings. "Yes, of course."

"I confess that I, too, stopped by because the spirits always flow quite liberally at these events," continued Norwood. "I just finished attending the lecture on the geology of Cornwall and decided to wet my whistle before heading home."

He regarded Ducasse for a long moment. "I can't say that I'm quite ready to make peace with the idea of France as an ally. There's too much intrigue for my liking still swirling through Paris."

Mention of geology reminded Wrexford that Norwood had an interest in mineralogy and was a member of the Royal Society . . .

"Speaking of intrigue, were you perchance at the meeting where Boyleston met his demise?" Wrexford knew for a fact that the answer was *yes* because he suddenly recalled that Norwood's name was on the list that the Society's secretary had given him.

"I was," said Norwood. "A nasty business, though I have some sympathy with Redding."

"As do I," said Fogg.

"You were there as well, weren't you?" queried the earl. "I seem to recall being told that, like Redding, you were rather vocal in haranguing Boyleston for his collaboration with the French."

"Yes, I was," answered Fogg without hesitation. "I think Boyleston's actions bordered on treason."

Wrexford decided to take advantage of the opportunity to do a bit more probing. "I also heard mention about a stranger at the reception. Did either of you notice him?"

Norwood's expression sharpened. "Are you involved in the case?"

"Bow Street has already made an arrest for the murder," he replied. "I'm simply curious."

"Ah." Norwood took a sip of his wine but didn't appear to have swallowed the explanation. "The Runner took my statement, but I'm happy to repeat it to you. The fellow in question was tall and broad-shouldered—and looked younger than his silvery hair and side-whiskers indicated. He also had dark eyes and a pointy chin. As for his attire, he was wearing an expensive-looking evening jacket and some sort of blue sash, though I didn't spot any medals or diplomatic insignias on it."

That echoed what Wrexford had heard from the other gentlemen he had interviewed. But knowing that Norwood had proved himself to be a careful observer during his wartime activities, he pressed for further details, however small. "Anything else?"

His former comrade hesitated, giving the question careful consideration. "I doubt it's helpful, but I did notice a slight hitch in his gait. It was barely perceptible, but when he turned to his left, his knee seemed to buckle for an instant, as if from an old injury."

A shrug. "Old habits die hard, so I tend to spot such tiny nuances. Quite likely nobody else saw it."

"As we know, tiny nuances often mean the difference between life and death," murmured Wrexford.

"On the battlefield," said Norwood softly. "But, of course, those days are over."

"And you, sir?" he asked Fogg.

"Hmm." Fogg pursed his mouth in thought and then shook his head. "Sorry, I didn't notice anyone of that description," he replied, and then gave a friendly wave to a gentleman in the group conversing with Ducasse. "If you'll excuse me, I really must have a word with Shillingham."

Norwood took several meditative sips of his champagne, and then his lips gave a wry twitch. "Fogg must have a foggy memory, for my recollection is that he was part of a small group that conversed for quite a while with the stranger." A shrug. "But most people aren't overly observant."

The comment reminded Wrexford his former comrade had risen to serve as an aide-de-camp to Wellington during the bloody march across Spain. "How are you enjoying civilian life? You seemed suited to a military career."

"My mother is a Grenville," responded Norwood, naming one of the most powerful aristocratic families in Britain. "After I was wounded at Badajoz, she asked her uncle, the former prime minister, to find me a less dangerous position. The work with Addington and the Privy Council is interesting and challenging."

Norwood smiled as he gave a small gesture at the opulent room and elegantly attired gentlemen. "And far more comfortable."

"You've earned a modicum of comfort," said the earl.

"We both have." Norwood set his glass on the nearby decorative marble plinth. "Well, I've had my fill of the festivities. Enjoy the rest of the evening."

As the earl pondered on what he had just heard, Sheffield ambled over to join him.

"The Frenchman is a pompous arse," he muttered. "But perhaps almost too much so. I shall look forward to hearing Charlotte's assessment."

"That was quick thinking on your part to create an opportunity for her to meet Ducasse," responded Wrexford, though he was only half listening

Sensing the earl's preoccupation, Sheffield asked, "With whom were you just conversing?"

"A former comrade-in-arms and another fellow who both attended the Royal Society meeting where Boyleston was murdered."

"Did you learn anything helpful about what happened during the evening?" demanded Sheffield.

"I'm not sure," answered Wrexford, taking a quick look at Fogg. "Let's be off. There's nothing more to be gained here."

"I say we stop for a glass or two of port at White's before heading home," suggested Sheffield as they made their way out to Albemarle Street. "As Cordelia and Charlotte are attending Lady Thirkell's soiree in hope of meeting Jane Marcet, they won't be returning until late."

Wrexford suddenly found himself feeling weary to the bone. The prospect of retreating to his workroom, where his only company would be far too many unanswered questions, held little appeal.

"An excellent suggestion. A vintage '97 tawny would go down rather nicely right now." He made a face. "Especially as I plan to make sure the porter puts the bottle on *your* bill."

"I must remind myself to attend these gatherings more often," said Cordelia as she surveyed the gaggle of colorful guests by the refreshment table.

"Lady Thirkell's soirees really do attract a fascinating array of intellectually minded ladies." Charlotte smiled. "One can always spot an expert in some delightfully esoteric subject and spend the evening engaged in—"

"Good heavens." Cordelia's brows shot up. "Does Mrs. Dovecote actually have a live bird nested within the coil of her braids?"

"Highly unlikely," replied Charlotte. "You missed the meeting where she came wearing her pet garter snake as a bracelet. The creature managed to slither away and wrap itself around Lady Becton's ankle, nearly causing her to have a heart spasm. After that, Lady Thirkell banned the wearing of live animals as accessories."

Cordelia choked down a burble of laughter. "Speaking of Originals, where is Alison?"

"She left early with her friend, the dowager Countess of Ingalls, who was feeling a trifle under the weather."

The crowd was beginning to move to the back of the rambling house, where their hostess always set up a late-night repast of fancy pastries and sundry puddings.

"Lady Thirkell has given me Mrs. Marcet's address," continued Charlotte. "It seems that she and her husband have recently moved to one of the grand houses in Regent's Park. So unless you are feeling in the mood to stay for some sweets—"

"No, no, I'm quite ready to return to Mayfair." Cordelia patted back a yawn. "Kit and I must be at our office quite early tomorrow morning to discuss some shipping logistics for the transatlantic route with one of our captains before the tide turns."

The two of them took their leave of their hostess and retrieved their winter cloaks from the coatroom before venturing out into the night.

"Lud, it's turned colder than the devil's smile," muttered Cordelia through clenched teeth, her breath forming puffs of pale vapor that quickly dissolved in the breeze.

"The carriage is waiting in the cobbled square just past the neighbor's mews. It's just a short stroll," said Charlotte, indicating a graveled walkway.

"Brrr, let's not dawdle."

They set off at a brisk pace, and though the clouds were thickening, the flitting moonlight gave enough illumination for them to see their way.

"By the by," said Cordelia as the path cut through a stone archway and curled around a copse of winter-bare beech trees, "I meant to ask you earlier, but do you have any objection to Raven assisting me on a mathematical project for Mr. Ricardo that involves the stock market and the trading of securities?"

The question took Charlotte by surprise. "Is there any reason I should object?"

"None that I can think of. He seems very interested in learning more about the financial world and how it works. But as you and Wrex are his guardians, I wish to make sure we have your blessing before we tell him yes."

"Actually I'm delighted," responded Charlotte. "He's been a bit blue-deviled because there has been nothing for the Weasels to do regarding the murder investigation. That may soon change, of course, given Wrex's new mission. But regardless, the chance to work with you and Mr. Ricardo and learn advanced mathematics is a wonderful opportunity to—*ouch!*"

She stopped abruptly. "Damn, I have a pebble in my shoe."

Cordelia, who was now a few steps ahead, paused to wait.

Muttering another oath, Charlotte crouched down—

Bang!

A flash of sparks suddenly exploded from within the dark trees as a pistol shot rent the night air.

"Duck!" cried Charlotte. On instinct, she threw herself sideways and rolled onto the frozen verge. Scrabbling up to her knees, she saw her friend hit the ground.

"Cordelia!" she gasped, crawling forward as she tore open

her reticule and grabbed the double-barreled pocket pistol that she had taken to carrying since the attack on Raven.

"*Merde*," rasped Cordelia. "The bloody earth is hard as stone."

"Stay down," ordered Charlotte, quickly cocking her weapon on hearing the crackling of fallen twigs underfoot from within the trees. She shot up and took a step forward, searching through the shadows for their assailant.

A flutter of movement caught her eye. As the silhouette of a figure darted from one gnarled tree trunk to another, she fired a warning shot to scare off any further attack.

"Hell's teeth!" Cordelia grabbed the hem of Charlotte's cloak. "Let the varlet go!"

The figure appeared again, stumbling slightly as a flutter of moonlight shivered through the branches, and then raced off into the gloom.

Charlotte quickly lowered her pistol. "Are you—"

"Unharmed, save for a few bruises to my elbows," announced her friend. "What the devil just happened? If a footpad was seeking to rob us, he wouldn't have gone about it like that."

"No," agreed Charlotte. "And the bullet whistled high enough overhead that I don't think it was intended to be lethal." She uncocked the second hammer of her weapon and slid it into the pocket of her cloak. "Which means it was meant to frighten us."

"Why?"

"A good question." She stared into the dark-on-dark tangle of trees. "Though I have a sneaking suspicion that I can guess the answer."

As the sweetly mellow port suffused a pleasant warmth though his limbs, Wrexford felt his tense muscles slowly relax. Closing his eyes, he took another sip, savoring the whispery rhythm of the dancing flames in the hearth which had him drifting off . . .

"Has Cordelia talked to you about Raven?" Sheffield's question yanked him back to the moment.

"Why? Has the lad caused some mischief?" He straightened from his slouch. "I fear he is reaching an age when it becomes second nature to question authority."

"It's an elemental rite of passage, I suppose." Sheffield made a wry face. "And unpleasant for everyone involved. I shudder to think what grief I caused my father."

However, after another grimace, he quickly returned to the earl's question. "Be that as it may, Raven has done nothing wrong. Quite the opposite, in fact. He overheard Cordelia and me discussing plans to become involved with David Ricardo and his investing business. I wish to learn more about the inner workings of the London Stock Exchange and Cordelia has agreed to work with Ricardo on using mathematics to spot opportunities for turning a profit."

"Is that really possible?"

"Ricardo and Cordelia think so," said Sheffield. "And when Raven expressed interest in the concepts, Cordelia asked if he would like to assist her."

"I imagine he was delighted with the offer," mused the earl. "So what is the problem?"

Sheffield smiled. "He's beginning to spread his wings. And Cordelia and I just want to make sure that you and Charlotte feel that he is flying in the right direction. After all, you are his guardians—in truth, you are his parents in every way but biological." A pause. "And as Cordelia and I consider ourselves honorary aunt and uncle, it should be a family decision."

Family. Wrexford felt another wave of warmth wash over him. "It goes without saying that I trust your judgment."

His friend looked down, his expression suddenly shadowed in uncertainty. "I'm not sure that *I* do. I have been thinking . . . it's a momentous responsibility to be a guiding force for a young person's life. I—I am not sure that I will be any good at it."

"Bollocks! You'll be splendid at it," replied Wrexford. "Your past excesses and your head-butting with your own father have taught you that there is always more than one perspective to a conflict. That's made you wiser and more tolerant."

He swirled the tawny spirits in his glass. "Look at how you've come to be reconciled with your father, something you never thought would be possible."

As he spoke the words, Wrexford felt a sharp a stab of regret. He had never had the chance to put things rights with his own fraught father-son relationship.

Sheffield sat for an interlude in silent sympathy before clearing his throat. "I take it you've heard nothing from von Münch on your father's mysterious correspondence?"

"Charlotte has more faith in him than I do," he answered. "The rascal may have helped us on a number of occasions, but I can't help suspecting that his altruism is shaped by self-interest. If faced with a difficult choice, I doubt that the concept of loyalty would play any part in it."

"She knows him better than either of us," pointed out Sheffield. He lifted the bottle of port—it was the second one of the evening—and held it up to the light of the fire.

"Empty," he intoned, sounding a little wistful.

"It's probably for the best. We ought to return to our wives before we get truly foxed," said the earl, though at the moment he was feeling awfully comfortable just where he was.

"Indeed. Our carousing days are far behind us. As for the ladies, they are far too steady and sensible to get themselves into any mischief." Sheffield rose, looking a trifle unsteady. "I'll accompany you to Berkeley Square in case Cordelia has lingered there for a late-night cup of tea with Charlotte."

The porter fetched their overcoats, and the chill served to clear their heads.

"Bloody hell, I am looking forward to spring," muttered Sheffield, turning up his collar and hunching low against the stiffening breeze. "Despite its shortness, February is always a dreadful month."

Charlotte was waiting in the doorway of the earl's workroom, and though the shadows of the corridor hazed her face, Wrexford came to a dead stop.

"What has happened?" he demanded. "The Weasels—"

"The Weasels are safely tucked away in their eyrie," she assured him. "Let me pour you both a glass of whisky before I continue."

Seeing that neither she nor Cordelia showed any overt signs of injury, he felt himself relax. "Kit and I have already imbibed a surfeit of spirits, so you might as well just spit out what you have to tell us."

Cordelia raised her brows as they came into the workroom but made no comment.

"Sit," said Charlotte.

In the glow of the lamplight, her expression was even more alarming. He perched a hip on the edge of his desk, while Sheffield joined Cordelia on the sofa.

"Go on."

"Mrs. Marcet didn't attend the soiree, but I learned where she resides," began Charlotte. Then, without further preamble, she explained about the attack.

"You saw nothing that might help identify your assailant?" asked Wrexford once she was done.

"It all happened so quickly," answered Charlotte. "The figure was naught but a shadowy blur."

"I caught a glimpse of him as I hit the ground," offered Cordelia.

A small sound rumbled in Sheffield's throat

"My guess is it was a man because of the figure's height," continued their friend.

"I concur," said Charlotte.

A fraught silence descended over the room. Wrexford rose and moved to the hearth. He stared into the banked coals for a long moment, then wordlessly took another few paces to his right . . .

And suddenly flung open the door to the adjoining library, revealing the three Weasels and Harper huddled by the threshold.

"It's *not* an infraction of the house rules," piped up Raven, fixing the earl with an accusing squint, "as you've been keeping secrets from us."

The hound added a low *whoof*.

"Not deliberately—we've simply been trying to make sense of what's going on," said Charlotte. "However, things have now turned very personal." She looked to Wrexford. "Our family and friends are under attack from all angles."

Another *woof*.

"We need to convene a council of war first thing in the morning—I shall send word to Alison and Henning." Her hands fisted in her skirts. "Given Boyleston's murder and the reasons why Pierson requested Wrex's help, it stands to reason that there are dangerous French operatives here in London."

She drew in a sharp breath. "And it seems that Wrex's questions concerning the mysterious stranger have drawn their attention to us. So we need to draw up plans to find them and put an end to their perfidy."

CHAPTER 12

Henning was the first to arrive the following morning. "Ah, excellent! I was hoping that breakfast was still being served." He quickly heaped a plate with offerings from the chafing dishes on the sideboard, then took a seat at the table.

"I've been wondering why you hadn't yet come around to pester me about Boyleston's body and have a look at the fancy pistol that was found at the scene of the crime." After pouring a cup of coffee from the fresh pot that McClellan brought over, he added, "Well?"

"It appears that the pistol was meant as a red herring," answered Wrexford. "To make it look like the murder was because of a personal grudge."

Henning chewed thoughtfully on a kipper before asking, "Why?"

"To distract the authorities from the real reason that Atticus Boyleston was murdered," said Charlotte.

"Now you have me intrigued," mumbled the surgeon through a mouthful of sausage. "But then, we never seem to stumble over simple crimes."

The Weasels began to chortle but quickly fell silent as Charlotte speared them with a warning look. "Death and mayhem should never serve as a source of amusement," she chided.

The boys bowed their heads and quietly resumed eating their porridge.

Sheffield and Cordelia appeared a few minutes later, and a *thump-thump* in the corridor indicated that the dowager was not far behind them.

"Now that we are all here," said Charlotte, once Alison was helped to her seat by Tyler and served a plate of eggs and toast. "Wrex and I will endeavor to explain what we know—though there is still much we need to learn. Suffice it to say we are facing a . . ."

She hesitated, uncertain of how to phrase her fears without sounding melodramatic.

"We are up against a very cunning and dangerous enemy," said Wrexford, "unlike any that we have faced before."

The clatter of plates and cutlery ceased, and the room went unnaturally silent. It was as if nobody dared to draw a breath . . .

"To the devil with them," announced the dowager in a loud voice, breaking the tension. "They have never faced *us* before."

"Oiy!" Raven picked up his butter knife and cut a flourish though the air. "*En garde.*"

"Oiy!" Hawk and Peregrine brandished their own weapons. Alison flashed them a martial smile.

"Enthusiasm—and courage—are all very well," counseled Charlotte. "But we must proceed very carefully, for it's not only our fate that hangs in the balance."

Looking around at the expectant faces of her loved ones, she felt even more determined to guard them from harm. "I shall let Wrex begin."

"First of all, I shall be entrusting you with a momentous secret," he said. "And I must have your solemn promise that you will not speak of it to anyone outside of our inner circle."

All heads bobbed in understanding.

Satisfied that everyone grasped the gravity of the situation, he continued, "The government suspects that Atticus Boyleston was murdered because of a new scientific innovation on which he was working. The question of whether or not he succeeded in creating it has grave implications for our national security."

He paused. "Here's where it gets rather complicated."

"We're very good at untangling the truth," observed Alison.

"I fear that this will be a daunting challenge, even for us," responded Wrexford. "There's no hint of his research in his workspace at the Royal Institution. So I have no idea as to whether it exists."

"What is the innovation?" asked Tyler. "Or are you not allowed to reveal it to us?"

Wrexford blew out his breath. "It's a messaging system. But rather than being some sort of optical telegraph, like our established semaphore routes or the naval system of signal flags, it's an *electrical* telegraph."

Tyler's eyes widened. "You mean using some sort of voltaic pile to transmit messages through *wires*?"

"Yes, precisely. And that would allow the transmittal of messages to take mere seconds or minutes, rather than hours or days by traditional means."

"But . . ." The valet shook his head in disbelief. "But surely that's not possible."

"That's what we need to learn—and as quickly as possible," interjected Charlotte.

"If it works, the technology provides an incalculable advantage in communication, which affects so many critical aspects of daily life," added Wrexford.

"Egad," intoned Alison after giving it some thought. "the possibilities are quite earthshaking, aren't they?"

"Indeed they are," agreed Charlotte.

"Are you perchance implying our country fears that some other power is also working on developing this wondrous invention?" ventured Cordelia. "And that they may be close to success?"

Charlotte slanted a look at Wrexford, who cleared his throat. "Yes," he answered.

The room once again went very still for several long moments.

"Unless I am much mistaken," said Cordelia, "the only country with a community of advanced scientific thinkers in electricity that matches ours is France."

The earl confirmed her surmise with a curt nod.

Cordelia looked about to say something else, but on catching a look from Sheffield she dropped her gaze and remained silent.

"To be perfectly clear, the government is greatly alarmed by the possibility that France is up to no good," said Wrexford. "And it is depending on us to discover whether that is true."

He looked around. "Which means that we need to learn the answers to three questions. The first one is, do the French possess a working model of an electrical telegraph? The second and third questions are linked—did Boyleston create the plans for a working electrical telegraph, and was he murdered by the French to prevent him from sharing them with our government? Or was he murdered because the French *don't* have a working electrical telegraph, but they knew he did and so they stole his plans?"

For a long moment, nobody ventured to speak. And then . . .

"Perhaps my mind is moving as slowly my feet, but I confess that I'm confused as to why France would be a threat to us," said the dowager. "Aren't we now allies? After all, King Louis XVIII lived here in London during his exile and owes his return to the French throne to the British government."

"Let us just say that the crown rests uneasy on his head right now," responded Wrexford. "There are disturbing rumors about the former emperor . . ."

He let his words trail off.

"Dear God," intoned Alison, comprehension slowly dawning on her face.

Charlotte pushed back her plate and moved the notebook and pencil in her lap to the table. "Which means we need to draw up a plan." Paper rustled as she opened to a blank page. "Or maybe several."

Wrexford nodded. "I have been thinking about it all night," he began. "Time is of the essence, and so it seems the most logical approach is to divide our forces, with each of us assigned a task that suits our skills."

Alison's eyes narrowed and took on a suspicious glitter, but she waited for him to go on.

"As there are no research papers or prototype concerning an electrical telegraph in Boyleston's laboratory at the Royal Institution, we have to assume he was working on it somewhere else. Given that the Weasels have a network of urchin friends throughout the city, I'm tasking them with making inquiries about a single gentleman who might have been noticed as being out of place in a neighborhood. Boyleston was known to be secretive, so it's likely he chose an out-of-the-way area where he wouldn't be spotted by anyone who knew him."

The boys nodded in understanding.

"Tyler will also ask around among his sources."

Charlotte was busy scribbling notes.

"Don't forget my elderly friends and our drawing teas," piped the dowager. "You might be surprised by how much information can be learned through their gossip." A smile. "Many of the old biddies have nothing better to do than poke their noses into other people's secrets."

"That is what I'm counting on," drawled the earl. "As for you, Baz, I know a number of your physician friends are interested in the medical possibilities of electricity—"

"Thank heavens the mad idea that electricity could reanimate the dead has been debunked," interjected Henning. "But I understand your point. I can certainly ask around and see if any of them know where Boyleston might have conducted his experiments."

"As for Kit and Cordelia , they will join Charlotte and me in circulating through the beau monde social gatherings to see what we can learn about any French visitors here in London," continued Wrexford. "In fact, we already have one suspect."

McClellan, who had been unnaturally silent since the start of breakfast finally spoke up. "What about me?"

"You are in charge of keeping our strength up with your marvelous cooking and baking!" shot back Henning, after taking the last of the muffins from the basket on the table. "Like an army, we travel on our stomachs."

"Speak for yourself," said the dowager. "Her ambrosial ginger biscuits have added several unwanted pounds to my middle."

"Baz has a point, but your role is bigger than just cooking. Every army needs a quartermaster to handle all the logistics and organization," said Wrexford.

Charlotte smiled. "Without you, we would all end up going to hell in a handbasket within a week."

"No need for such effusive flattery." McClellan began gathering the empty plates. "I'm happy to be of service."

"Speaking of French operatives . . ." Sheffield gave a glance at the mantel clock and then locked eyes with Charlotte. "Don't forget that we have a rendezvous with Monsieur Ducasse at the Royal Academy's art exhibit this afternoon."

"And I shall send a note around to Boyleston's friend Mrs. Marcet and ask for a meeting with her," said Wrexford.

Henning quickly plucked up the last bit of his muffin before

McClellan could whisk his plate away from the table. "Well, then, let the hunt begin."

"Remember, Kit, you are to appear impatient shortly after we encounter Ducasse and ask if I have seen enough of the paintings," said Charlotte as she and Sheffield climbed the outdoor stairs leading up to the back terrace of Somerset House. Like the Royal Society, the Royal Academy was housed in the grand building. "From what you and Wrex have described, I'm quite sure he will offer to serve as my escort, allowing you to hare off."

"I have the distinct impression that the pompous Frog thinks his Gallic charm is irresistible to the ladies."

"And I shall not disappoint him." She took a moment to study the scene of the murder and then looked out over the pewter-dark water of the river. A sharp breeze stirred a rippling of whitecaps near the far shore, while the swirling patterns closer to their vantage point gave a hint of the treacherous crosscurrents just beneath the surface.

Turning back to the ornate façade of the building, Charlotte took Sheffield's arm. "The question is whether his show of bonhomie hides a more sinister intent."

The display rooms of the Royal Academy were crowded, as attendance at the annual exhibit was de rigueur for the beau monde so that they might show off their refined sense of taste by discussing the art at their social gatherings. Sheffield immediately spotted Ducasse standing with officials of both the Academy and the Royal Society.

"This way," he murmured, drawing them through the crush of spectators to take up a position close to the group.

"Ah, Monsieur Sheffield!" It didn't take the Frenchman long to spot them and saunter over. "Dare I hope that I'm about to have the honor of being introduced to the Countess of Wrexford?"

Charlotte had deliberately dressed in a gown of steel-blue watered silk that shimmered with subtle variations of color as the light reflected off the textured fabric. The effect, she knew, was eye-catching, and as Sheffield performed the introductions, she saw a speculative gleam sharpen in Ducasse's gaze.

"*Enchanté.*" He bowed and with a graceful flourish bestowed a kiss to her gloved hand.

Maintaining a certain sangfroid—in her experience, men like Ducasse enjoyed the thrill of the chase—Charlotte gave a cool smile. "You Frenchmen have mastered the art of shamelessly flattering a lady."

"It is not shameless flattery, milady. I am simply giving ethereal beauty and grace its due," he replied.

The fellow possessed a smooth tongue and facile manners to go along with his undeniably handsome looks, she reflected. It was up to her to determine whether or not the polished veneer hid a core of rot.

"Lord Wrexford mentioned that you have a great interest in art," continued Ducasse.

"I do," answered Charlotte. "Alas, my husband is bored to perdition by looking at paintings and says he is too busy doing important work in his laboratory to accompany me to exhibits such as these."

A glance at the myriad gilt-framed paintings crowded cheek by jowl on the main salon's walls. "Our dear friend Mr. Sheffield is more accommodating, but I fear he doesn't really enjoy the experience either."

Taking his cue, Sheffield shuffled his feet. 'No, no, I'm delighted to be here," he said in a tone that fooled nobody. "I say, er, are there any pictures of hounds or horses anywhere?"

"I'm afraid not," replied Ducasse.

"A pity." Sheffield took a quick peek at his pocket watch and cleared his throat." "Er, any idea how long we shall be here? I was hoping that I might pay a visit to my tailor . . ."

"Please, I shall be happy to escort Lady Wrexford through the exhibit at her leisure," interjected the Frenchman, "and then accompany her back to Berkeley Square."

How interesting that he knows where we reside, thought Charlotte, though her only outward reaction was a nod of thanks. "Now that I am here," she added, "I would very much like to take my time in studying the paintings."

"Then it's settled," said Ducasse.

"You truly don't mind?" Sheffield cast a longing look at the exit.

"Not at all."

"Well then . . ." A jaunty wave. "*Au revoir.*"

"A pleasant fellow," remarked Ducasse as Sheffield hurried away.

"Yes, very," agreed Charlotte.

"I've been told that he's a gentleman who enjoys the pleasures of life." A pause. "But apparently art is not one of them?"

"Not everyone sees the world in the same way," she replied.

"A very sage observation, milady." The Frenchman offered her his arm and began maneuvering through the crowd to gain a better position for viewing the art. He found a spot in front of several large portraits and drew to a halt.

"To appreciate art, I think that one must have imagination," he continued. "The ability to see beneath the physical pigment and brushstrokes and sense the elemental emotions and passions that inspire the artist's creativity."

"The ability to faithfully copy an object or scene is a decorative skill," observed Charlotte. "It is passion that transcends the ordinary and makes a painting or a drawing or a sculpture into true art."

"It seems we are kindred souls," murmured Ducasse. "Take, for example, this portrait by Sir William Beechey of your Prince Regent. It's common knowledge that His Royal Highness has a number of, shall we say, character flaws. And yet, the artist brilliantly captures the spirit of the monarchy, not the man, creating a heroic figure for the ages that will inspire his subjects."

"In other words, Beechey has transformed base metal into gold, so perhaps he's an alchemist, not an artist," said Charlotte dryly.

Ducasse gave an appreciate chuckle. "Art does involve illusion and sleight of hand . . ." They moved on and spent the next two hours discussing the merits of the many paintings on display.

Charlotte hadn't expected to have such mixed feelings about the Frenchman. Wrexford's brief description had portrayed him as an arrogant fellow—perhaps deliberately so, in order to hide the more nuanced aspects of his character. He was indeed clever and used exaggerated bluster and humor to probe for information. But he was also thoughtful and articulate, showing a keen intelligence when opining about art and human nature.

Possible friend? Or devious foe?

She wasn't yet ready to make a decision.

"*Alors*, Ducasse!" A gentleman squeezed past a trio of elderly ladies. Lowering his voice, he added, "*J'ai des nouvelles urgentes. Nous devons discuter—*"

"*En anglais, mon ami!*" interjected the artist. He turned and fixed Charlotte with an apologetic smile. "It would be rude of us to continue speaking in French." A pause. "That is, unless you would like the opportunity to practice."

"Alas, I don't have an ear for languages," replied Charlotte with a rueful grimace. "I'm ashamed to admit that the only French I understand is *bonbon* and *baguette*."

Both gentlemen laughed politely.

"Lady Wrexford, may I present Monsieur Hubert Odilon, a leader of the French émigré community here in London, to whom I was introduced just the other day at the Royal Institution's reception," said Ducasse.

Which begged the question of what sort of urgent news Odilon had that demanded an immediate tête-à-tête with the artist, reflected Charlotte, who had not been truthful about her fluency in French.

Tit for tat. She was quite sure that Ducasse had been lying through his teeth about the length of his acquaintance with Odilon.

"I had the honor of meeting your distinguished husband, milady," said Odilon after inclining a formal bow. "I understand that his scientific work in metallurgy helped the British military defeat the self-proclaimed Emperor Napoleon and restore the rightful king to the throne of France. Please pass on my gratitude to him for his part in freeing my country from that Corsican tyrant."

"Be assured I will do so, sir," said Charlotte.

"Might I steal Monsieur Ducasse away for a few moments?" added Odilon after a sidelong glance at his fellow Frenchman. "He has agreed to attend a dinner given in his honor by the leaders of our local community, and we wouldn't want to bore you with mundane talk of the logistics."

"But of course," answered Charlotte. To Ducasse, she added, "I shall be at Beechey's portrait of Prinny. I would like a second look at the nuances of his brushstrokes and how he blends light and shadow."

As they moved away, Charlotte took a moment to study the crowd. She wasn't quite sure what she was seeking. Perhaps a stranger who seemed out of place? Raven's description of a man with obsidian eyes and a pointy chin had stuck in her mind and refused to be dislodged. However, her gaze met only the familiar faces of the beau monde.

Most of whom hadn't an artistic bone in their bodies. They had simply come to see and be seen by their peers.

"Shall we sit for a bit?" suggested Ducasse after rejoining her. He gestured to the line of upholstered benches that ran down the center of the hall. "Art demands both mental and physical stamina. Shall I fetch us some champagne?"

"Refreshments would be very welcome."

Ducasse returned with the sparkling wine and took a seat next to her. 'Now that we've had a lovely interlude of pleasantries, might I broach a business matter?"

"Ladies of London's beau monde don't engage in business, sir." Her mouth quirked. "Not officially."

He smiled, as she had intended. "Actually, it's your husband with whom I would like to do a deal. Might you agree to help me convince him to sit for a portrait? I would, of course, be happy to show you examples of my work so that you may judge whether or not you like my style."

"I don't doubt your talent, sir. Alas, it doesn't matter. My husband has no interest in having his face hung on the wall of the French Academy."

"But—"

"There are no 'buts' about it. He won't change his mind." Charlotte took a sip of her champagne. "So save your breath."

He heaved a mournful sigh. "It would be ungentlemanly of me to press you, so I won't."

His gaze moved from the tiny bubbles exploding in his glass to the far wall and the large arched window just below the ceiling, which allowed in natural light to illuminate the paintings. "Might I ask what draws your husband to science? From what I have heard of the British aristocracy, gentlemen of wealth and title are usually . . ."

"Indolent?" suggested Charlotte when he seemed to be searching for the right word.

"My English leaves much to be desired," he said with an apologetic shrug.

Somehow, she doubted that.

"Wrexford likes an intellectual challenge," she answered after a moment of silence. "He enjoys solving practical problems in chemistry. He's also curious and often simply interested in understanding how the basic laws of the universe work."

Ducasse looked thoughtful "Your husband and I are more alike than you might think. I chose to specialize in painting portraits because I'm fascinated by people and their uniquely individual motivations."

Charlotte smiled. "As I said before, your charm is wasted on me."

He leaned a little closer. "That depends on what I wish to gain, milady."

She decided to challenge him. "Which is?"

"Your company on a visit to view Lord Elgin's Marbles at the British Museum," answered the Frenchman, "so that I might have a chance to forge a friendship with you."

An intriguing answer. Assuming there was a grain of truth to it.

"The Marbles possess a mesmerizing beauty that never ages and are well worth a visit," said Charlotte. "I would be happy to come along."

"*Merci!*"

She had already pulled her elegant little pocket watch from her reticule and clicked open the gold case. "And now, sir, I really ought to be returning home."

What with Wrexford and the Weasels on the move shortly, and her own efforts this afternoon, they were beginning their dangerous dance across the checkered tiles of the chessboard.

Attack. Feint. Maneuver.

It remained to be seen as to how the unknown enemies would play the game.

CHAPTER 13

A wintry darkness blanketed the streets, though the afternoon had barely given way to early evening. The earl's carriage clattered over the cobblestones, turning from High Street to make its way to the York Gate and the entrance to Regent's Park. The sounds of the city had died away, and Wrexford saw no sign of movement anywhere, adding to the aura of quietude.

He leaned back and closed his eyes, taking a moment to reflect on the morning council of war and all the events it had set in motion.

And all the worries.

Had he sent Charlotte to confront a ruthless operative of Napoleon? And were the Weasels scampering into danger by seeking to find the secret workspace of the murdered inventor? Every creak and rattle of the carriage seemed to carry with it the taunting question of whether he had put his family at undue risk.

His edginess had been exacerbated by a mid-afternoon meeting with Durs Egg, who had appeared at Berkeley Square to report that his brother-in law had absolutely no idea of who might have wished to frame him for the murder of Boyleston.

Information.

They needed to find some actual clues to follow. And quickly.

The wheels slowed and then came to a halt, signaling that they had arrived at their destination.

Shifting his thoughts to Mrs. Marcet and the questions he had for her, Wrexford climbed down from the carriage and headed to the imposing front entrance of the mansion.

The butler ushered him into a drawing room, whose understated elegance reflected both wealth and taste. "I will inform Mrs. Marcet that you have arrived, milord,"

Charlotte would have approved of the intriguing art, decided the earl, on spying several exquisite watercolors hung above a Chippendale console table. They looked to be Turner seascapes—

"Have you an interest in art, Lord Wrexford?"

He turned as a short, slender woman rounded the sofa and came to join him. She was dressed in a dove grey silk gown whose simplicity accentuated its exquisite cut and quality. Her only jewelry was a double strand of pearls and matching earbobs. But what he noticed most was the spark of intelligence that lit her otherwise unremarkable brown eyes.

"I enjoy viewing it and trying to discern what separates the sublime from the ordinary," he replied.

"That often depends on the eye of the beholder," she observed.

"True. But as in any discipline, having an understanding of the subject helps one to make an informed opinion," said Wrexford. "My wife is quite knowledgeable about art and would enjoy discussing such interesting observations with you." A pause. "She met you briefly at one of Lady Thirkell's soirees and found the conversation about your experience studying painting with Thomas Lawrence quite fascinating. He is a great favorite of hers."

"I very much look forward to further talks with your wife, milord."

The earl responded with a belated bow. "Forgive my egregious lack of manners in neglecting to introduce myself formally, Mrs. Marcet."

"Ritual is all very well, but I tend not to stand on ceremony, Lord Wrexford," she replied. "Please, let us sit." A gesture indicated one of the two armchairs facing the sofa. "Might I offer you a glass of brandy?"

"Only if you will join me in a libation."

A flash of amusement. "I quite enjoy sherry." Rather than summon a servant, Mrs. Marcet moved to the sideboard and poured the drinks from a selection of handsome crystal decanters.

"I am sorry that my husband had a previous engagement at the hospital this evening," she added as she passed the earl his brandy. "He is an enthusiastic amateur chemist and would have very much enjoyed speaking with you on metallurgy—assuming a discussion of basic principles wouldn't bore you to perdition. Word is you don't suffer fools gladly."

Wrexford allowed a small smile. "It seems we both have done a bit of research into our subjects."

"Preparation is always a sensible strategy for any endeavor." She took a sip of her sherry. "I confess, I can't contain my curiosity any longer as to why you have sought a meeting with me, milord. Somehow I doubt that you have any questions regarding my book that simplifies the basics of chemistry for those who are unfamiliar with science in general."

"On Michael Faraday's recommendation—by the by, he credits you with sparking his passion for science—I have purchased it for my wards, and on a quick perusal I can see why Faraday admires it. It's very well done," replied Wrexford. "But you're right. I wish to inquire about an entirely different subject."

Mrs. Marcet nodded for him to continue.

"Faraday mentioned that you were a good friend of Atticus Boyleston."

"Ah, Atticus." Mrs. Marcet ran a finger around the rim of her glass. "A brilliant but complicated man. I'm not sure that *friend* is the right word. I'm not sure he had any. However, I can't think of an alternative." She looked up. "It's my understanding that a man has already been arrested for the murder, so I can't imagine that you're investigating the crime."

"No," said the earl. "I'm hoping you can tell me something about his experiments with electricity."

A sigh. "Atticus was comfortable talking with me, but only about gardening. He was very secretive about his work. And suspicious of anyone who asked about it. All I can tell you is that he recently seemed excited about something and told me he would soon silence all the naysayers who thought he was a loose screw."

"But he didn't say how?" pressed Wrexford.

"He implied that it would be some sort of public demonstration." Mrs. Marcet made a face. "I'm sorry, that's all I can tell you."

His mouth thinned in frustration. "Have you any idea where he might have been working on this exciting discovery? His official space at the Royal Institution contains nothing out of the ordinary, so he must have had a private, personal space hidden somewhere in the city."

She gave an apologetic grimace. "I'm afraid not."

Damnation.

Mrs. Marcet regarded him thoughtfully. "I don't suppose you can be more specific about why you are so interested in Atticus's experiments with electricity? He was a very interesting and original thinker, but my sense is he wasn't terribly good at turning his ideas into practical innovations. If I know what you are looking for, I may be able to be of more help."

Wrexford considered the request. From what Charlotte had told him, the lady's intellectual circle of friends were made of up of highly regarded luminaries in the world of arts and science. And Michael Faraday's endorsement of her intelligence and character was another mark as to her trustworthiness.

Still . . .

"Forgive me for asking," she said. "I am aware that you are sometimes involved in matters that are highly confidential."

"Correct," he replied. "However, I do have one additional question, and your answer may help resolve a matter of great importance. More than that, I cannot say."

Mrs. Marcet nodded.

"Do you know of anyone else who, like Boyleston, believes that electricity and magnetism are the same basic force and that this "electromagnetism" is capable of creating some new and wondrous innovations?"

"Why, yes," she responded without hesitation. "It happens that I do, milord." A smile. "Not personally, mind you, but my good friend, the astronomer Mary Somerville, knows of him because she is well acquainted with his mother. Both of them are avid gardeners, and Mary often visits Kelmscott House, the lady's family residence in Hammersmith, which is set on a scenic piece of property overlooking the River Thames."

The earl sat back in surprise at the unexpected reply, hope warring with the knowledge that this was likely just another wild goose chase. "Please tell me more."

"The young man's name is Francis Ronalds, and Mary thinks he's an extraordinary young scientific talent, though he's quite unassuming and happy to simply putter about with his research at home. He's been working with electricity for the last four years and recently published a paper on dry piles, which apparently are a type of voltaic battery."

"And I may find this Francis Ronalds at Kelmscott House?" asked Wrexford.

"Yes," answered Mrs. Marcet. "If you pay him a visit, you must be sure to have a look at his mother's gardens, despite the season. Mary says that Francis has spent several years creating some sort of bizarre device out there, though she hasn't a clue as to what it is."

"Thank you." For an instant, a tiny spark of excitement lit, then quickly fizzled as he reminded himself of how unlikely it was that a young man mucking about in a garden was going to prove helpful.

Having no further questions, Wrexford set aside his untouched brandy. "Again, I appreciate your willingness to meet with me, but I ought not take up any more of your time."

Mrs. Marcet rose with a gentle rustle of silk. "I do hope you and your wife will attend one of our soirees so that we might continue to converse about our mutual interests."

"I look forward to it," he replied, and followed her lead back to the entrance hall, where the butler was waiting with his hat and overcoat.

"If I think of anything else concerning electricity that may be helpful, I will send word to you, sir," she added.

After acknowledging the offer with a bow, Wrexford stepped out into the chill of the night.

There was a brittleness to the surrounding silence—as if every sound was frozen in place. Unsure of what to make of the new information, he paused on the bottom stair of the landing to compose his thoughts, aware of how different the quiet felt here on the fringes of the city, where the meadows and groves of trees created a strange sense of solitude.

He was just about to step down to the graveled courtyard when a series of quick scuffs caught his ear,

Boots moving lightly over stone.

But not lightly enough.

The earl pivoted and hurried over a swath of frozen lawn.

On reaching the decorative fluting that edged the mansion's façade, he peered around the corner.

Nothing.

He felt rather than saw a presence in the muddled darkness. And so he waited, carefully muffling his breathing with the lapel of his coat as he watched for a telltale puff of vapor.

A moment passed, and then another.

After standing still as a statue for a number of minutes, Wrexford retreated, wondering whether all the uncertainties of the investigation had his nerves on edge. Perhaps the bootsteps had been naught but a figment of his imagination.

Unsettled by the incident, he quickly returned to his carriage and gave orders for home.

CHAPTER 14

Charlotte rose from her dressing table and froze for a moment to watch the early morning light dance through the pattern of ice crystals that had formed on the windowpanes during the night. Dipping and darting, the tiny sparks were quicker than the eye, leaving only a teasing impression of their presence.

Hide and seek. She heaved a sigh. Had Wrexford's meeting with Mrs. Marcet finally uncovered a useful clue? He seemed doubtful but resolved to leave no stone unturned and so was planning to visit Kelmscott House later in the day. Given his unsettled mood, Charlotte had insisted on accompanying him despite her lack of scientific knowledge, pointing out that her presence would make the visit appear to be one of simple curiosity.

In truth, everyone in the household was on edge. Frustration was building. It seemed to crackle and hiss like unseen electricity through every nook and cranny of their Berkeley Square residence.

Turning back to the looking glass, Charlotte added a last hairpin to secure her topknot and then headed for the stairs, trying to muster some reason for optimism.

The mood around the breakfast table offered little encouragement. A quick look around showed that everyone's expression was black as the devil's heart.

"Good morning!" Even to her own ears, her forced cheeriness had a brittle ring.

Without looking up, Wrexford made an inarticulate noise in his throat and turned the page of his newspaper with a brusque snap.

As for the boys, they continued grumbling among themselves over the fact that none of their urchin friends could offer a clue as to Boyleston and his activities.

"Hell's bells, how is it that nobody has seen a fellow matching Mr. Boyleston's description?" groused Raven, crumbling a muffin between his fingers.

"There are still one or two neighborhoods left to check," said Hawk, doing his best to put on a brave face.

"I just don't understand it. Boyleston had to be working somewhere, and our eyes and ears on the streets are aware of *everything* that goes on in their turf," continued Raven. "A bloody flea can't fart without one of them noticing it."

Hawk made a gagging noise as he laughed and swallowed a bite of his eggs at the same time.

"Language," chided Charlotte, wagging a finger in warning. "We are all on edge. But that does *not* excuse breaking the house rules on gentlemanly deportment."

"Sorry." Raven pushed back his plate and slouched down in his chair. "It's just that we don't have any idea as to where to look next."

Tyler made a face, appearing equally disgusted over his lack of progress in identifying the mysterious trio from the warehouse. "None of my contacts are aware of any illicit activities going on around the river. It's as if the man who attacked Raven and his two compatriots are supernatural afreets or djinns."

He waved his hands. "*Poof!* Gone without a trace!"

"Let us not descend into melodrama," counseled Charlotte. And yet she, too, wondered whether some unseen malignant force was making sport of them.

Wrexford finally looked up from his reading. "I've changed my mind about our original plan. Forget about Boyleston and finding his workspace for now. I have another assignment for you Weasels."

The three boys immediately perked up.

"Starting tonight, I want you and your urchin friends to organize a round-the-clock surveillance of the artist from Paris, Pierre Ducasse." He put aside the newspaper. "We need to shift the focus of our investigation. Given what Mrs. Marcet told me, searching for Boyleston's secret workspace—assuming he had one—may be a futile effort. Let us concentrate our efforts on discovering whether there is a cadre of French operatives here in London, and if they have gotten their hands on Boyleston's research."

Charlotte felt a twinge of remorse at not having made any headway in determining whether the French painter was a clandestine operative for Napoleon. "I'm still uncertain about Ducasse's motivations. His flirtations have no real edge. And while his probing for information about you and the rumors he has heard about your investigative talents are sharper, I can't decide whether he is any threat to us."

"A clever and ruthless agent's arsenal of skills would naturally include the ability to appear harmless," pointed out the earl. "The proverbial wolf cloaked in a sheep's fluffy wool."

"True." She sighed. "Be that as it may, in several days we are attending the soiree given by the Prince Regent for Ducasse and the leaders of the French émigré community. So we will have a good opportunity to watch him and his interactions. Given the copious amount of wine that flows at any Carlton House party, we might catch him making a mistake."

Wrexford let out a skeptical grunt.

"Do you really think he may be—"

"I don't know what to think," he barked. "Which is why I'm willing to put aside my usual preference for logic and simply cast out random nets and see what we haul in."

"It appears we have chosen an inauspicious moment for a visit," announced Sheffield, as he and Cordelia paused in the doorway.

"Not at all, there's plenty of food left in the chafing dishes," said McClellan.

"We didn't come here to raid the larder," said Cordelia. "We were going to suggest having a meeting on finances and the Stock Exchange with Raven, since he is eager to work with us on our joint project with David Ricardo." She gave a discreet tug to Sheffield's sleeve. "But we'll come back at another time."

"No, wait!" exclaimed Raven. "We can't set up the surveillance of the Frenchman until after dusk, and I would like to be engaged in something useful until then."

"Yes, please stay," added Charlotte. "I have a drawing due by tomorrow, and as there's no pressing issue swirling through the city—that is, not any that we are allowed to mention—I, too, ought to learn more about the London Stock Exchange."

She pushed back her chair. "From listening to you, I am beginning to realize what a powerful force it is on the country's economy. So it's important for the public to understand how it works and the effects it has on their lives."

She looked to Wrexford. "You don't plan to leave for Kelmscott House until noon, correct?"

A curt nod. "Again, you need not come along." After a moment, he added, "Though I confess, I would welcome your company, even though it likely will be a waste of time for both of us."

Charlotte smiled. "A drive through the countryside will be a pleasant interlude, regardless of what we find."

*   *   *

Wrexford apologized to Sheffield and Cordelia for his snappish show of temper and then excused himself to pay a visit to the library of the Royal Institution to see if he could dig up the scientific paper by Francis Ronalds that Mrs. Marcet had mentioned.

"We are all feeling under the gun," observed Charlotte after he had left the room. "What few clues we have—Egg's pistol, the scraps of burnt paper from the warehouse, the mysterious gentleman with side-whiskers who was likely Raven's assailant in disguise—have led us nowhere in figuring out what shadowy forces are in play, and more importantly, what they are seeking to accomplish. So at the moment, it feels as if we are—"

"It feels as if we are simply spinning in circles," finished Raven. Hawk and Peregrine, who had little interest in advanced mathematics, had returned to their eyrie to prepare for the evening's activities.

Sheffield grimaced in sympathy. "Our unknown adversaries must be diabolically clever to have flummoxed all of our efforts. However, let us have faith."

Charlotte made a face. "I would rather have a bit of luck." Of late, the cosmos appeared to have turned a blind eye on their efforts. "But be that as it may, let us head to Wrex's workroom and discuss the Stock Exchange."

Once she had settled herself at the earl's desk, she added, "I am trying to get a visual image in my mind of how the market works. The constant buying and selling—"

"Perhaps it would help if you picture it as stocks rising and falling," interrupted Cordelia. "Prices are always in a state of flux, influenced by all manner of things. Supply and demand, rumor and innuendo, political events—there are a myriad of things that affect buying and selling."

"For example, there is a form of something called arbitrage. It involves identifying two securities whose market prices bear a certain relationship to one another. Under various circumstances, you can somehow buy one and effectively sell the other security and make a guaranteed profit for a brief time as the prices of securities move relative to one another."

She paused to consider how to proceed. "It would sound dauntingly complicated if I tried to explain all the various permutations of trading in one sitting. Suffice it to say that while Mr. Ricardo does his trading mostly based on his vast knowledge of the market and intuition, the mathematics that Raven and I do can help him identify situations with a potential for profit and provide guidance on how long he should hold on to his positions before taking a profit."

"Hmmm." Charlotte thought for a moment. "Given that I have no aptitude or interest in mathematics, I can see that I'm overmatched in trying to do a technical explanation of the Stock Exchange. Still . . ."

She plucked up a pencil and put a fresh sheet of paper on the blotter. "I'm beginning to envision a composition that simply conveys to the public that it is a powerful force on their lives, whether they know it or not."

By noontime, the sky had cleared and the day had turned rather balmy for early March. Wrexford returned from the Royal Institution, and he and Charlotte climbed into their carriage to begin the journey west to Hammersmith.

"I apologize for acting like a bear with a thorn in its arse of late," he said, after settling back against the squabs. "It cannot be pleasant for you to live with my brooding."

"Human nature doesn't run in a straight, smooth line, Wrex." Charlotte found his hand and twined her fingers with his. "We all experience light and dark, peaks and valleys—and all the infinite nuances in between."

He chuffed a laugh. "I am the one who is supposed to be ruled by rational thought, not raw emotion."

"Perhaps we have learned from each other," she responded. "Though don't expect me to comprehend a word about dry piles, electrical pulses, or magnetic fields."

Wrexford felt his spirits lift as they continued their light banter. The physics of doubt was a downward spiral. It was time to shake off his uncertainties.

They were soon out of the city and rolling past villages and meadowlands. The road curled through a stretch of woods, and after another mile, the sound of the river rose above the clatter of the wheels as they approached the enclave of Hammersmith and turned up the drive of Kelmscott House.

An elderly housekeeper answered their knock and put them in a side parlor while she went to inform the mistress of the house that she had unexpected visitors.

"Forgive us for intruding on you without advance notice, Mrs. Ronalds," said Wrexford, after introducing himself and Charlotte. "But I heard a most extraordinary story from Mrs. Jane Marcet last evening about your son's work with electricity and simply couldn't contain my scientific curiosity."

"We are hoping that he might consent to show us his invention," added Charlotte.

A rose-pink flush rose to the woman's cheeks. "Oh, please don't apologize, milord! That a gentleman of your scientific renown has an interest in Francis's work is a great honor. I know he will be absolutely delighted to show you what he has created and explain how it works."

A tentative smile. "Be forewarned, it is not for the faint of heart. I do hope you wore sturdy shoes."

Charlotte lifted her skirts to show a pair of half-boots. "We have come prepared."

"Excellent!" Mrs. Ronalds gave a fluttery wave. "Then please follow me."

They exited through a terrace door and turned down a walkway bordered by a high boxwood hedge.

"You have quite a magnificent stretch of gardens," remarked Wrexford after looking around at the rolling lawns, stone walls, and various clusters of specimen trees that sloped down to the river's edge. "I daresay you—"

He stopped short as he came to an opening in the hedge and saw what lay ahead.

"Good heavens," intoned Charlotte, who was right behind him. "That is . . ."

"Remarkable," finished the earl. He stared out at two towering wooden frames, each consisting of six thick wooden poles. The first frame was barely a stone's throw away, and the second one was hardly visible in the distance. Strung between them, high overhead, was an intricate web of coiled wires that looked to be insulated in glass tubing.

Was it just his imagination, wondered Wrexford, or did he detect a slight humming sound twining with the whispery breeze?

"I did warn you." Mrs. Ronalds made a wry face that expressed both puzzlement and pride in her son's endeavor. "I shall leave all explanations to Francis." She reached beneath her shawl and pulled out a brass chain hung with a large whistle. "I'll summon him now."

An earsplitting blast cut through the pastoral stillness.

The earl studied the crisscrossing wires as they waited, impressed—and astounded—at the sheer magnitude of physical work that had gone into the construction.

As for the theory . . .

"Ha, here comes Francis," said his mother, giving a cheery wave to her son.

Wrexford watched the young man appear from within a copse of trees and hurry to join them. Ronalds looked to be in his twenties, and in contrast to his tall, thickset towers, he was small and wiry, with a cherubic face and sunny smile. One might almost call him delicate, but as the fellow came closer, the earl saw that he was all chiseled muscle and whipcord sinew.

"Halloo, Mama," called Ronalds, and then gave a friendly wave to his visitors.

"Lord and Lady Wrexford have come to see your invention, my dear," said his mother fondly.

The young man's eyes widened, and he inclined a hurried bow. "I'm honored, milord and milady." To Wrexford, he added, "Your papers on metallurgy have been instrumental in my creative process." He made a face. "Though my work doesn't merit being mentioned in the same breath as yours. You, sir, are a true inventor. I am merely a tinkerer."

"This appears to me to be far more than casual tinkering," replied the earl with a glance upward. "Was Mrs. Marcet correct in telling me that you are working with electricity?"

"She was, sir," acknowledged Ronalds. "These—"

"I shall leave the three of you to parse through scientific wonders while I return to the kitchen and have our cook prepare a hearty tea for when you are done," interjected Mrs. Ronalds, a twinkle lighting her eyes. "In my experience, visitors are in need of ample sustenance after Francis has given them the grand tour."

"I do tend to get enthusiastic, milord," admitted Ronalds as his mother hurried toward the house. "You must promise to stop me if I am prosing on too long about Ugly Betty."

Charlotte coughed to cover a laugh as she regarded the elaborate arrangement of wires. Wrexford could tell that she was itching to take out her pocket notebook and scribble a sketch.

"That is what Mama calls it." Ronalds looked up at the wires and crinkled his nose. "She's not overly pleased with what my invention has done to the aesthetics of her gardens. But she is a firm supporter of scientific progress and understands that sacrifices must be made for the future good. So she tolerates my endeavors with a good grace."

"You are a fortunate fellow," observed Charlotte. "One needs encouragement to thrive in any endeavor."

Ronalds nodded. "Indeed, milady."

Suddenly impatient to learn whether their journey had all been for naught, Wrexford put aside polite pleasantries and asked the key question.

"What *is* Ugly Betty?"

A swirl of wind rose up to rattle the wires.

The young man watched the taut lines shiver against the blue sky. "It's an experiment I created to test just how quickly electricity can travel over long distances via a wire."

"And what was the result?" asked Wrexford

"Nearly instantaneous, sir."

"H-How long is the full length of your wires?" asked Charlotte.

Ronalds pursed his lips. "Approximately eight miles."

"Astounding," observed the earl. "And how did you test the speed at which the electricity travels?"

"I connected a pistol loaded with a cartridge filled with hydrogen and oxygen at the two ends of the eight-mile length of wire," explained Ronalds, "and then I generated an electrical charge."

A boyish grin. "Both pistols exploded at virtually the same time," he continued, "which confirmed to me that electricity travels at nearly instantaneous speed!"

"Well done, sir." Wrexford meant the compliment sincerely. It was always an important moment in scientific progress when one confirmed a theory through carefully designed experiment and objective empirical observation.

However, he also couldn't help but feel a stab of disappointment that it wasn't the technology he had been hoping for.

The young man gave another fond look at the overhead wires and then smiled. "And that's what got me thinking about how to create something of real value from such a powerful force of Nature. Something that would help improve all our daily lives."

"Are you saying that you have another invention in addition to Ugly Betty?" demanded the earl.

"Oh, yes! And to me, it's far more interesting." A pause. "You see, it occurred to me that electricity may actually be employed for a more useful purpose than the mere gratification of the philosopher's inquisitive research or a schoolboy's idle amusement."

An inner light seemed to spark to life in the young man's eyes. "It may be compelled to travel many hundred miles beneath our feet as a subterranean ghost, reaching far-flung towns and cities and bringing with it much benefit for all mankind."

"A very laudable goal, Mr. Ronalds," responded Wrexford. "Could you be a bit more specific about what sort of benefit you are envisioning?'

"It's a messaging system," replied Ronalds.

"A messaging system?" repeated Charlotte.

"Yes! An electrical telegraph, to be precise."

CHAPTER 15

Charlotte let out a gasp.

"Though there is still much work to be done on refining the technology," Ronalds hastened to add.

Wrexford, too, felt a surge of excitement—and of dread. The world would be fundamentally changed by the fact that a tiny unseen pulse of electricity could communicate information over vast distances within the space of a heartbeat. And like any revolutionary invention, such power could be a two-edged sword.

But philosophical musings could wait. At the moment, he needed to understand exactly what the young man's electrical telegraph was capable of doing.

"I've no expertise in the fields of electricity and magnetism," said the earl. "So might you explain the principles of your invention to us in layman's terms?"

"I shall try." Ronalds blew out his breath. "For now, I don't use voltaic piles. I prefer another technology."

"So how do you generate electricity?"

"I use a method that I call *perpetual electrophorous*," answered Ronalds. "It's a type of frictional electricity, which has been known to men of science since the 1600s."

"Francis Hauksbee's electrostatic generator of 1709," mused Wrexford, "and the triboelectric charger created by the king's instrument maker in 1799."

"Precisely, sir! Though those machines were really just designed as parlor games," exclaimed Ronalds. "However, the idea of creating an electrostatic telegraph is nothing new. I found a fascinating article in a periodical called *Scots Magazine*, published in 1753. The author—who chose to be identified only as C. M. to avoid ridicule for his theory—postulated a way to communicate messages by sending each letter of the alphabet as a separate pulse of electricity. My system is based on the same concept."

"Have you any idea whether it actually works?" ventured the earl.

"As to that, I have actually built a working model—would you care to see it?"

"Oh, very much so," answered Wrexford.

The young man pointed across the lawn to what looked like a large root cellar built into the ground. A set of sunken steps and a heavy oak door afforded access to the interior. "We'll have to go inside my underground laboratory." He gave Charlotte an apologetic look. "I'm afraid it's rather primitive, milady. You may want to remain here as your lovely silk gown might suffer irreparable damage."

"Like your mother, I am a firm believer in making sacrifices for scientific progress," she replied. "Please lead the way. I wouldn't miss seeing this for all the tea in China."

'Watch your step as you approach. The cannisters on the outside landing are filled with highly flammable pine spirits," warned Ronalds, once he had unlocked the cellar door. He paused to light a lamp and then led the way down into the bowels of the earth.

Wrexford immediately noted a series of machines that were hooked up to a large mechanical apparatus constructed with belts, levers, and pulleys, as well as a massive crank powered by a small steam engine.

"Is that your frictional electricity machine?"

"Yes!" answered Ronalds, and pointed to a series of wires running down through a glass cylinder into the earthen floor. "The actual experiment takes place underground."

Out of the corner of his eye, the earl saw Charlotte take out her notebook and make a quick sketch.

"To create optimum conditions for the electricity to travel without interference, I dug a trench a hundred and twenty-five feet long and four feet deep and lined it with wooden boards coated on both sides with pitch to minimize moisture," continued Ronalds. "Then I constructed a line of interlocking glass tubes and sealed each connection with soft wax. The transmission worked perfectly, so the next challenge was how to devise a signaling system capable of transmitting messages."

Charlotte edged closer. "Don't keep us in suspense, sir! I am all agog to hear how you managed that!"

Ronalds gave a rueful grimace. "It is still, as inventors are wont to say, a work in progress." He gestured for her and the earl to follow him to a desk that held yet more mechanical devices and showed them a clock mechanism and a circular brass dial divided into twenty equal triangles. Each triangle featured a letter, a number, and a keyword, like *Finished* and *Ready*.

"I had to leave out some of the less-used letters like Q and X," continued the young man.

"How does it work?" asked Charlotte.

Ronalds blew out his breath. "It's a bit complicated to explain all the technical details. Basically, I have grounded an individual wire to each of the twenty segments of the dial, and an electrical pulse to a specific letter will cause the main dial to rotate."

He showed them another plain brass dial with a single hole cut out of it. "To receive a message, one places this dial on top of the other one so that you copy each letter in succession and end up with your full message."

"Why, that's incredibly ingenious!" she exclaimed.

"Perhaps in theory, milady." Another grimace. "The idea is intriguing, but in truth, what I'm doing is, like the inventions of the previous century, still only a parlor game rather than a practical innovation like a steam engine or nautical propeller."

Wrexford looked around at the laboratory, noting how meticulous about order and precision the young man was. "I have some further questions I would like to ask you, Mr. Ronalds. But they involve sensitive matters. I would need to have your solemn oath that you won't reveal what I ask to anyone—not even your mother."

"Don't let Mama's sweet smile and cheery demeanor deceive you. She's the most practical, pragmatic person I know, and in a pinch, I would trust my life to her above all others," said Ronalds. "But that is neither here nor there regarding your statement. Please be assured that you may rely on my absolute discretion, milord."

He glanced at Charlotte to gauge her reaction and received a confirming nod.

"Thank you." Wrexford took a moment to compose his first question. "I have been told that the French men of science are far more advanced in the study of electricity than our own innovators. Do you think they could have a practical working model of an electric telegraph—one that could be employed in normal everyday conditions?"

"No, sir." The young man's answer was instantaneous. "I'm quite sure they haven't."

"But Laplace's letter to André-Marie Ampère, which hinted at a scientific paper—" began the earl.

"I'm aware of Laplace's scientific paper and have analyzed

its contents. There is much interesting speculation, but I am quite sure the French have made no real progress on creating a working electrical telegraph."

Ronalds perched a hip on his desk. "My family's affluence—and their good-natured tolerance of my passion for science—has allowed me the luxury of reading countless papers from the past and learning from them. Naturally, the French men of science and their work have been of particular interest to me because of their advanced knowledge in electricity. I have studied most of their writings, and it's clear that the technical challenges of an electrical telegraph are perniciously complex."

He tapped his fingertips together, lost for a moment in thought. "Indeed, I suspect it will take at least a decade of scientific exploration before we begin to understand the key forces at work. Boyleston's colleagues called him a fool, but I think he may have been on the right track regarding the elemental connection of electricity and magnetism, though I can't yet figure out how they work together."

"You are confident that a working telegraph is far in the future?" Wrexford hesitated. "I ask because, as I mentioned, it's vitally important that I don't pass on wrong information."

Ronalds met his gaze with an unflinching smile. "I am absolutely confident, sir. We don't yet have the science to do this properly."

The earl released an inner sigh, feeling as if a great weight had lifted from his shoulders. He had done his duty for King and Country and could report his findings to Grentham . . .

And be done with all the damnable skullduggery.

Charlotte's expression indicated that she was thinking much the same thing.

"I'm much obliged to you, Ronalds." Given what the young man had just told him, Wrexford was anxious to return to Town without delay. "We've taken up enough of your time and ought to allow you to get back to your work."

Ronalds nodded as he picked up the lantern and turned for the stairs.

"Please give our apologies to your mother for not staying for refreshments," added Charlotte.

The young man looked back over his shoulder "Only if you promise to return again soon, milady. Mama makes a delicious Dundee cake. And I confess, I would very much like to discuss some metallurgy questions with you, milord."

"I would be happy to do so."

"Excellent!" Ronalds took another step up when suddenly a shadow skittered over his boots and the dark silhouette of a figure blocked the doorway.

"I'm afraid I must ask the three of you to halt where you are."

The lantern light angled up, illuminating a tall gentleman well dressed in every detail save for the black silk covering the lower part of his face up to his eyes—and the two double-barreled pistols he was holding in his hands.

Charlotte instinctively reached for the pistol tucked in her hidden pocket, but Wrexford caught her hand.

"Don't," he whispered, noting the flat, unemotional look in their captor's eyes. "He has the look of a hardened killer. Let us bide our time." In a louder voice, he asked, "Might I inquire as to why we are being detained?"

"But of course." Their captor expelled a mournful sigh. "It's because you have an unfortunate penchant for meddling in affairs that shouldn't concern you, Lord Wrexford. Things were perfectly planned—and then you felt compelled to poke your nose into the murder of Atticus Boyleston." A shrug. "I'm curious as to why."

"Because Durs Egg is a friend, and he asked me to do so," answered the earl.

"Friendship." Their captor chuckled. "Such a quaint notion.

What a pity it will be the death of you and your two companions."

His tone turned harder. "You have only yourself to blame. If you had simply minded your own business and left it to the proper authorities to handle murder, you and your companions would not be in danger. But alas, I can't permit any of you to repeat what you've just been discussing."

"Why?" asked Charlotte.

Keep him talking, thought Wrexford. There seemed precious few options for altering their present predicament, and yet . . .

He darted a look around, only to draw a snarled warning. "Twitch another muscle, milord, and I'll put a bullet through your wife's brain."

Both the earl and Ronalds froze.

"That's better." Their captor waggled his pistols. "As you see, Durs Egg is also a friend of mine, though an unwitting one. He does craft superb firearms."

"Since you're about to put a period to our existence, might we know the reason why?" asked the earl, echoing Charlotte's request.

"Because the forces in motion on the chessboard are far more momentous than you comprehend," came the answer. "While you putter around, intent on solving petty crimes, a much grander game is in play."

"I still don't see how Boyleston's murder fits in your scheme. Did you think he had actually created an electrical telegraph, and that it might give Britain a powerful economic and military advantage?" pressed the earl.

"Quite the opposite," answered their captor. "We know from the work of our own men of science that the possibility of creating an electrical telegraph still lies far in the future—"

"By *your* men of science, do you mean . . . *France*?" interrupted Charlotte.

"*Bien sûr*, madame."

"I—I don't understand. If you know it's not possible . . ." she stammered, and then paused, looking utterly bewildered.

Wrexford never ceased to be impressed by her acting skills, and how easily Charlotte contrived to appear a feather-brained widgeon. She had told him early on in their relationship that most men couldn't resist flaunting their superior intelligence to a lady who clearly couldn't follow rational thought. In her opinion, vanity was an elemental, fatal flaw in males that was laughably easy to use against them.

He hoped their captor would take the bait. Every huff of hot air from his lips gave him and Charlotte a moment more to think of a way to survive.

"I—I confess, I don't understand what is going on," she finished.

"Don't fret." A pitying smirk. "Our diversion fooled even your vaunted intelligence ministry, who are tripping over their own feet chasing after the clues we have carefully planted for them."

A diversion, thought the earl, which was meant to create a distraction.

But from what?

"Boyleston needed to die so that your government wouldn't learn that he had *not* created an electrical telegraph."

"Why?" pressed Wrexford.

"The truth in all its brilliance will become clear, not to you but to your country, in the near future—"

"Yes, well, before you start waxing poetic on the future," drawled Wrexford, his gaze suddenly focused on a spot just over their captor's left shoulder, "you might want to glance behind you."

Their captor let out a sardonic laugh. "You disappoint me, milord. Surely you're not so addle-witted as to think I would fall for that age-old ruse?"

A metallic click sounded.

"Lord Wrexford's wits are in perfectly good working order," announced a feminine voice. "Be assured that I have a fowling gun pointed at your gizzard. Granted, it's loaded with bird-shot, so it might not kill you."

Mrs. Ronalds allowed herself a grim laugh. "However, I daresay it will do a great deal of damage."

Boots scraped over the stone landing as their captor crabbed sideways, allowing him to keep an eye on both his prisoners and the threat to his rear.

"Four bullets and four targets," observed Wrexford. "However, logistics don't favor you. My guess is one of us will get to you before you're able to finish us all off."

"Shall I simplify matters and just pull the trigger, milord?" asked Mrs. Ronalds.

Their captor didn't wait to hear the answer. He fired two quick shots into the cannisters of pine spirits, igniting a *whomp* of an explosion and a *whoosh* of flames.

The percussive force of the blast staggered Mrs. Ronald, knocking her back on her heels. The gun barrel flew up, allowing their captor just enough time to kick the laboratory door shut and dart off into the trees.

Wrexford shoved his way free of the subterranean darkness and rushed to help Mrs. Ronalds regain her footing while her son and Charlotte quickly beat out the flames with heavy canvas tarps.

"Damnation!" she cursed, seeing the last little flutter of the fleeing gentleman's coat disappear as he lost himself in a stand of pine trees that led into the dense woodland sloping up the side of nearby hill. "Sorry, milord. I should have shot the poxy varlet when I had the chance."

"Tempting," agreed Charlotte as she brushed streak of soot from her cheek. "But we mere mortals do not have the right to appoint ourselves both judge and executioner. I am glad that you don't have his blood on your hands."

A question suddenly occurred to the earl. "Did you perchance notice whether the fellow had a slight hitch to his gait when he turned and ran?"

"Just one slight misstep, sir, then he ran like the devil." She muttered another oath under her breath. "As I said, I should have shot him—a hail of birdshot in his arse would have slowed him down enough to catch him."

Ronalds held out his hand for the fowling piece. "I'll take that, Mama."

She handed it over.

"Next time you go after a cold-blooded killer, choose the Baker rifle, not a bird gun."

"Bloody hell, Francis, I'm not a complete idiot. After all it was *me* who taught *you* all about firearms and shooting." She made a face. "In my defense, I was in a bit of a hurry."

"How did you know?" asked Charlotte.

"The fellow struck me as up to no good when I saw him from the kitchen window skulking up the footpath from the main road. And when he passed though one of the side entrances into the gardens, I decided to have a closer look—just in case."

"Thank heavens you did," said Charlotte.

"Speaking of thanks, the varlet ought to be thanking his lucky stars that his liver wasn't turned into mincemeat," observed Ronalds. "Mama is a crack shot."

"I grew up in humble circumstances in the north of England, and all of us children learned how to help put food on the table," she explained. "Self-reliance—the art of knowing how to think through problems and solve them—is a fundamentally important skill to have in life. Though my late husband and I were able to offer our children a far more comfortable upbringing, we thought it important to encourage all our children to be curious and unafraid of the unknown."

She smiled fondly at her son. "We wanted them to learn how to deal with all the unexpected challenges that Life throws at us."

"An admirable pedagogical goal," observed Wrexford. "We need more dons at Oxford and Cambridge who think like you."

"Let us hope such change will come. But I won't hold my breath waiting." Mrs. Ronalds shook the bits of dried grass and mud from her skirts. "Now, please allow me to offer you the promised refreshments. The cakes are baked, and I can easily reheat the kettle for tea—"

"Many thanks, but I'm afraid that my wife and I ought not delay our return to Town. I must inform certain people of what has taken place here," answered the earl.

Both mother and son nodded in understanding.

"I doubt the varlet will return, but as a precaution you might want to engage some men to keep watch here for the next few weeks," he added.

"Hmmph! Let him try!" replied Mrs. Ronalds. "My garden staff includes several former soldiers. I daresay they will make sure no further French skullduggery happens within our walls."

"Then I leave the details in your very capable hands, madam." Wrexford then turned to Ronalds.

"You, sir, are even more important than your remarkable prototypes, so please take extra care of yourself. I look forward to seeing what innovative thinking you will come up with in the years to come. It's imaginative minds like yours that will spark exciting new innovations."

He glanced up at the overhead wires. "And make the world a better place for all of us."

CHAPTER 16

Shades of muted pink and purple tinged the sky as afternoon deepened into early twilight. The last rays of the setting sun flickered through the dark branches of the trees edging the road, casting light and shadows over Wrexford's profile. Head bowed, his chin half-hidden in the lapels of his coat, he looked lost in thought.

Though a myriad of questions were swirling like whirling dervishes in her mind, Charlotte was loath to interrupt his process of parsing through what had just happened and all the possible permutations.

She could almost hear the whirr of mental gears spinning, spinning . . .

As if sensing her scrutiny, he turned, and for an instant his expression was one of surprise, as if he had entirely forgotten her presence.

"Forgive me," he said, pulling himself back to the present moment. "Given what you coaxed out of our captor — by the by, that was adroitly done — I am trying to think through all the evidence we have and piece together a pattern that may help us see what he and his fellow conspirators have as their ultimate goal."

"The fact that he intended to kill us made it easy to loosen his tongue." Charlotte thought for a moment. "So, assuming we believe that he's not so diabolically clever as to have done a double feint—"

"Heaven help us and our country if he is," murmured Wrexford.

"I don't think he is," she responded. "Which means that all the clues we've found so far have been deliberately left to send us—"

"*And* the authorities scampering off on a wild goose chase," interjected the earl. "Though Grentham and Pierson did discern that finding Boyleston's actual killer was a red herring."

"What does this tell us about our adversaries?" mused Charlotte.

"They are extremely canny and quick to seize a situation and turn it to their advantage," said Wrexford. "My sense is, Boyleston's killer would have struck anyway and left the Egg pistol, knowing there was bad blood between the victim and Egg's relative."

"Which means they are flexible and have done their research very carefully, putting themselves in position to pounce on a weakness when they spot one and manipulate it in their favor."

A chill slid down Charlotte's spine. "And that in turn tells us they are incredibly dangerous."

"Indeed." He leaned back, his gaze turning shuttered as he once again retreated into his own thoughts.

Charlotte watched the shadows dip and dart outside the windowpane as the carriage trundled toward Hyde Park. Like teasing, taunting phantoms, daring her and the earl to discern their true objective.

"However, despite all their cleverness, our adversaries made a mistake this afternoon. We now know that whatever grand scheme is in play has nothing to do with an electrical telegraph," she reasoned. "Our captor intended to kill us to prevent any word from reaching our government that an electrical telegraph is *not* currently possible to build. They wanted Britain to be wondering and worrying over whether France possessed a working model, which would distract them from another more potent threat."

"Yes, their plan was to convince Grentham that the threat to our country's security was coming from one angle, when in truth it's coming from a completely different direction," mused Wrexford.

Charlotte sat up straighter. "Is Wellington returning to London from Vienna to confer with the government on the state of affairs in Europe and whether the rumors of Napoleon's desire to return to France have any truth to them?"

"A good question. An assassination would rob any future Allied Coalition of its best military leader," responded the earl.

"What else would weaken Britain and give the French an immediate advantage if war once again breaks out?" she asked.

The wheels clattered over the cobbles, sharp, staccato raps of iron against stone.

"I don't know. But we need to figure it out—and quickly."

"Tomorrow evening's gala reception at Carlton House will afford us a chance to start the search for what it might be," pointed out Charlotte. "In addition, the Weasels must continue to keep Ducasse under tight surveillance. I can't believe that the Frenchman's sudden appearance in London is not connected in some way to our adversaries."

Wrexford nodded in agreement.

"Perhaps when that becomes clear," she added, "the other pieces of the puzzle will come together."

Flaming torchieres, red-gold points of fire against the chilly blackness of the following day's night, flanked the imposing columned entrance portico to Carlton House. A gust of wind tugged at Wrexford's overcoat as he hurried Charlotte up the shallow stairs and into the welcome warmth of the grand foyer.

Inside the Prince Regent's imposing mansion, all was aglitter. Crystal chandeliers, lit with a myriad of candles, blazed bright as diamonds, and the gilded wall sconces cast a golden glow over the checkered marble floor. Two footmen, their scarlet liveries festooned with silver braid, rushed over to take their outer garments, allowing them to join the long line of diplomatic dignitaries and influential members of the beau monde making their way into the West Ante Room and the formal receiving line.

"As we discussed earlier, I think it a wise strategy for us to split up," said the earl softly. "Attach yourself to Ducasse and see who gravitates to him. I will seek to join in conversation with any members of the Foreign Office I spot and see whether I can learn whether there's any concern over Napoleon and his recent activities."

Charlotte nodded, keeping her eyes looking straight ahead. "What about the prime minister and his council? I assume Prinny has invited a number of them to attend the festivities."

"I had a word earlier this afternoon with Norwood, my former military comrade who now serves as a chief aide to the Home Secretary and is privy to the confidential reports received by the prime minister," replied Wrexford. "Rumors are rife, but so far he's not convinced that the smoke indicates an actual fire."

He glanced around the room, taking in the ladies swathed in colorful silks and glittering gems, accompanied by gentlemen strutting like peacocks in their evening finery.

Was one of them intent on unleashing the former emperor to wreak fresh havoc across the Continent?

"Let us hope he is right," whispered Charlotte.

On that note, they both pasted on smiles and uttered the

requisite pleasantries to the majordomo in charge of greeting the guests before continuing on to the Crimson Drawing Room.

The sonorous tones of a string quartet playing a Haydn cello concerto provided a mellow undertone to the fizz of popping champagne corks and convivial conversations. The mood was festive, but Wrexford found himself even more on edge, wondering whether the bonhomie was merely a deceptive calm before the storm.

Spotting a high-ranking officer from Horse Guards with whom he was acquainted, he nudged Charlotte. "I need to go have a word with someone who might be in a position to tell me the military high command's assessment of any threat to the status quo."

"Be on your way," she urged. "Several of Alison's fellow dowagers are by the refreshment table. I'll join them until I see Ducasse and can attract his attention."

"Be careful," he added, though uncertain of what had prompted the impulse. The gilded splendor of Carlton House attracted any number of dangerous gentlemen, but the weapons they wielded tended to be power and privilege rather than blades and bullets.

Charlotte flashed him a quizzical smile. "Always."

He held her gaze for a heartbeat before turning away and striding off to one of the side salons.

"I'm surprised to see you here, milord," remarked Colonel Duxbury as the earl joined him. He was standing apart from the crowd around the refreshment table and appeared lost in his own thoughts. "I was under the impression that you have a distinct dislike for frivolities such as these."

"I do," agreed the earl, angling a quick look around to make sure there was nobody close enough to overhear them. "However, I'm not looking for mindless entertainment."

Duxbury stared down into his sparkling wine and slowly swirled his glass. "Then what is it you're seeking?" he asked, after taking a sip of his champagne. The two of them had met in a previous investigation, where the colonel himself had been the earl's prime suspect. So Wrexford didn't blame him for looking a little wary.

"I've heard some disquieting rumors about the state of affairs in Europe," said Wrexford.

"So have I," responded the colonel.

"Are they true?"

A hesitation, which stretched on for several moments. "I would dismiss them as absurd if they didn't involve a military genius who has outfoxed and outfought every general the various Allied Coalitions have thrown at him." Duxbury blew out his breath. "That said, Wellington is still in Vienna, with no plans to return to London in the immediate future, so he doesn't appear to be spooked."

A smile touched Wrexford's lips. "The duke is not prone to panicking over mere specters."

"Let us hope he knows more than we do."

They stood in companionable silence for an interlude before Wrexford changed the subject. "Is there any talk at Horse Guards about covert French activity here in London?"

"Why do you ask?" demanded the colonel after taking a long swallow of his drink.

"The recent murder of an inventor stirred some unsettling questions in my mind," he replied.

The colonel looked thoughtful. "I've heard nothing. But then, the military doesn't handle domestic threats. That's Grentham's department."

"Quite right." Wrexford wasn't surprised by the answer, but it had been worth a try. "And we both know he's rather good at what he does."

"Perhaps you should have a word with Elias Fogg at the Foreign Office," added Duxbury. "He occasionally confers with Grentham's office and reports to us if there is anything that affects our concerns."

Taking his leave with a nod of thanks to the colonel, Wrexford made a mental note to visit Fogg and then moved on, looking to find someone who might possess a modicum of scientific expertise, not for any other reason than to while away the time while waiting for Charlotte. But a quick survey of the salon dimmed his hope for intelligent conversation.

The Prince Regent and his circle of friends had little interest in intellectual pursuits.

After accepting a glass of champagne from a passing footman—Wrexford would have preferred strong Scottish malt—he returned to the main drawing room and resigned himself to suffering through the blathering of fribbles until Charlotte had finished eliciting what she could from Ducasse.

With that thought in mind, he quaffed the sparkling wine in two hurried gulps and looked around for another footman.

"I beg your pardon, Lord Wrexford . . ."

The earl turned and found himself face to face with a total stranger whose expression looked as if it had been chiseled out of granite.

"Yes?"

"You need to come with me."

Already in an ill humor, Wrexford found the fellow's presumptive manner abrasive. "Why should I?"

"Because it wasn't a request, milord." The man took his arm. "This way."

CHAPTER 17

*D*amnation. Repressing a huff of impatience, Charlotte kept up a frequent check of Ducasse while he and several dignitaries of the French émigré community continued to converse with a group of the prince's cronies. If the champagne kept flowing so liberally, her quarry would soon be in no state to pass on any useful information.

Returning her attention to the dowager Duchess of Hamden, she smiled and nodded, though in truth she hadn't a heard a word of the lady's long and meandering account involving a lost dog.

But thankfully, her next sidelong glance showed the group was breaking up.

"Forgive me, ma'am . . ." Charlotte lowered her voice to a hushed tone. "Please excuse me while I seek the ladies' withdrawing room."

On receiving a sympathetic nod, she began threading her way through the crowd . . .

Only to see Hubert Odilon, Ducasse's acquaintance from the Royal Academy art show, approach the artist and take his arm.

Charlotte wasn't close enough to hear their exchange, but she caught the look of agitation on Odilon's face before he ducked enough to hide it. The two gentlemen conversed for a moment or two longer and then began moving discreetly but with an air of urgency toward a side corridor that she knew led to the Prince Regent's cavernous conservatory.

She hesitated, debating whether to find Wrexford, but quickly decided there was no time and hurried after them, giving silent thanks that she had chosen to wear a dark, smoky-emerald-hued evening gown. With luck, it would help her blend into the foliage of Prinny's exotic trees and specimen collections.

Her kidskin slippers moved soundlessly over the Axminster runner, and as only half of the wall sconces were lit, the corridor was wreathed in shadows, allowing her pursuit to go unnoticed. Still, Charlotte took care to keep her distance from the two gentlemen, who had quickened their pace as soon as they were out of sight from the main reception room.

Though they were now just silhouettes in the flickering light, she could see by Odilon's gestures that he was upset.

A personal quarrel? Or was it something bigger?

Her heart began to thud against her ribs.

Closer, closer . . . Was she finally creeping closer to some answers?

Ducasse and Odilon reached the glass-paneled double doors of the conservatory, clicked open the brass latches, and disappeared into the gloom.

Hitching in a deep breath to steady her nerves, Charlotte counted to ten and then slipped in after them.

She was immediately enveloped in a tropical warmth. The humid air was heavy with the scent of wet soil, its earthiness edged with coal smoke from the banked stoves strategically placed around the sprawling display galleries to keep the winter chill of London at bay. The sound of dripping water punctuated the soft rustling of leaves, the scattering of overhead skylights allowing pearl-like flickers of moonglow to dance through the swaying foliage. Looking around to get her bearings, Charlotte saw that she was in a narrow rectangular space filled with various types of palm trees.

She moved to the archway straight ahead, which opened onto a wide central corridor. Ornate brass lanterns—they looked like something out of an Arabian wonder tale—hung from the decorative columns, and the vaulted ceiling, alive with a criss-crossing of whimsical geometric patterns, gave the place an exotic, otherworldly look. The aura of mystery was accentuated by skittering shadows, darting like impish afreets which had just escaped from being bottled up inside a magic lamp.

Shaking off such fanciful thoughts, Charlotte cocked an ear and strained to hear any sound of footsteps or voices.

The answering flutters of greenery seemed to mock her efforts.

She moved stealthily to the first column and listened again.

Is that a faint scuff drifting through the leaves from the narrow walkway to my right?

Deciding to take a chance—the junglelike maze of display rooms was confusing enough that she had little choice but to trust her instincts—Charlotte darted into the gloom. The winding path looped around through several groupings of strange-looking foliage that she couldn't identify. The light dimmed as she moved past the only lit lantern in the gallery. Serrated leaves brushed against her skirts, stirring a prickling of unease along her spine.

She paused for a moment, her pulse quickening as she caught a sudden murmur of voices. It died away in a moment, but she had heard enough to choose the left fork when the path up ahead split in two.

Slowly, stealthily, she crept forward.

A sudden rasping sound—a tree branch rubbing against one of the giant terra-cotta pots?—caused her to halt. But it, too, faded.

After another deep breath, Charlotte continued onward.

Up ahead, a glimmer of starlight filtered in through the overhead panes of glass, illuminating the center of a rectangular gallery. Though she couldn't yet see what lay ahead, she suspected it was one of the tranquil resting spots scattered throughout the conservatory, where a comfortable bench invited visitors to stop for an interlude of quiet contemplation.

Giving thanks for the myriad tall, sword-shaped stalks of the bushes clustered by her side, she crouched low and took cover within the greenery, silently shifting the leaves for a peek—

Eyes flaring wide in shock, Charlotte somehow managed to hold back a horrified cry.

Ducasse was kneeling beside the cushioned bench centered on the decorative mosaic floor beneath the skylight, a bloody knife in his hand.

Holy hell.

In the next instant, she realized that the odd rasping sound she had just heard was the death rattle in Odilon's throat as his lifeblood dripped down to the tiles from the stab wound just below his heart.

"*Mon Dieu, mon Dieu . . .*" gasped Ducasse. Swallowing hard, he mumbled something unintelligible and then leaned down, bringing his ear to within an inch of Odilon's trembling mouth.

Charlotte saw the dying man's lips move . . .

But then, the sudden clatter of steps fast approaching the far end of the gallery warned Ducasse that someone was coming. He shot to his feet, dropping the knife as he spun around and raced away, passing so close to Charlotte that she could have reached out and grabbed his coattail.

On instinct, she remained hidden. Too much was as yet unknown—it was best to wait and see what happened next. Once again, she carefully moved the leaves for a view of the area under the skylight.

A figure—a tall black-clad gentleman with the sleekly rippling muscles of a stalking panther—ran out from the shadows and skidded to a halt by Odilon's prostrate body.

He spat out an oath on seeing the knife lying on the tiles.

Charlotte felt her own blood run cold as he raised his gaze and looked around. He had a white silk neckerchief tied to obscure the lower part of his face, but his eyes were utterly reptilian—a rock-hard obsidian, devoid of emotion.

Her first impression—that the man was a viper—was immediately confirmed as he picked up the knife and casually plunged it back into Odilon's chest before withdrawing it.

The rasp of breath ceased.

"One nuisance is eliminated," he remarked with casual cruelty while cleaning the blade on the dead man's sleeve.

That voice! She recognized it all too well.

She froze, not daring to draw a breath.

"The second will quickly follow." Smiling to himself, Obsidian Eyes drew a snout-nosed pistol from his pocket and cocked the hammer. He listened for a long moment and then headed off down the same path that Ducasse had taken, passing within an arm's length of her.

The gallery quickly settled into silence, but it was several minutes before Charlotte could bring herself to move. Lifting her skirts, she carefully felt for the leather holster strapped to her calf—another Christmas gift from the earl, who had commissioned his bootmaker to craft the ingenious solution for how to carry a pocket pistol when dressed as a lady of the beau monde.

Gripping the butt of her hidden weapon helped quell the feeling of being defenseless prey at the mercy of a dangerous predator.

One who savored the thought of a kill..

She knew with absolute certainty that Obsidian Eyes was their assailant from the gardens of Francis Ronalds—a mask had hidden the lower part of his face on that occasion, too. She hadn't gotten a good glimpse of his eyes because of the sunlight and shadows, but she would never forget that undertone of amusement in his voice over the prospect of snuffing out their lives.

After taking another moment to steady the erratic racing of her heart, Charlotte eased her weapon free and checked the surroundings, then crept out to the path, intent on finding Wrexford as quickly as possible.

However, she dared not hurry.

"Not with a killer prowling close by—or two killers," she whispered, reminding herself that she wasn't out of danger.

Moving with deliberate care, Charlotte edged forward, making her way into the next display room . . . and then the next one, and the next . . . She paused within a cluster of long-needled pines, taking a moment to decide whether to choose another way back to the main hall—only to feel a dampness seep into her left evening shoe. Looking down, she bit back a gasp as she realized that she was standing in a pool of blood.

A meandering rivulet led her between the boughs of two of the trees . . .

"M-Milady." Charlotte's eyes met Ducasse's anguished gaze. He was lying spread-eagled on the floor tiles, his dress coat open, showing that his once-snowy-white shirt was now turning crimson from the bullet hole in his left breast. The dark powder burns on the fabric—the weapon had been jammed right up against his flesh—explained why she hadn't heard the shot.

"Please . . ." He crooked a finger, motioning for her to come closer.

"I'll fetch help—"

"No time, and you need to know . . ." A sad smile flitted over his lips. He signaled again.

Seeing that his life was fast ebbing away, Charlotte crouched down. "Why murder Odilon?" she asked gently, finding it hard to think of him as a killer.

"I didn't . . . didn't kill him. It was . . ." Ducasse drew in a rasping breath. "Forgive me—I've not been honest with you, but it wasn't for nefarious reasons. I . . . I'm an agent of the French crown and was dispatched to London because our security minister doesn't trust your Lord Grentham. He wished to have me keep watch to ensure that French interests were not compromised by . . ." A cough. "By Napoleon's operatives."

"But Napoleon—"

"Thinks he is a man of destiny." A weak wheeze. "Never mind that right now. W-What you need to know is that evil is afoot here—" A fit of coughing cut off his words.

A name. She needed a name for the evil.

Charlotte slid her hand under his head, lifting him slightly so he wouldn't choke on his own blood. "I promise you justice, my friend."

"Friend." Her words seemed to give him comfort. "Yes, I think we would have been friends."

"Who attacked you and Odilon?" she pressed.

"Le . . ." His eyes fluttered.

She willed him to hold on for another moment.

"Le-L . . ." But alas, in the next instant he was gone.

For a moment, Charlotte was too stunned to move. But then, the realization that a ruthless killer might still be lurking close by impelled her to her feet.

Tightening her grip on her weapon, she forced herself to plunge ahead and escape the maze of cursed greenery.

A sudden stirring of the leaves up ahead caused her to flinch. Curling her forefinger around the trigger, Charlotte shrank back into the palm fronds and waited. A silhouette appeared, blurred for a moment by the flutters, before the contours sharpened—

"Wrex!" Lowering her pistol, she hurried forward. "Th-Thank God I've found you."

He reached out to steady her as she stumbled over the tiles.

"There's been a murder just now—actually two!" she continued in a rush before he could speak. "Odilon and Ducasse are dead at the hands of—"

"Forget about all that for now." He took her arm. "Put your weapon away and come with me."

Charlotte pulled free and stared at him in mute confusion. "D-Did you hear what I just said—"

"I did."

She had never seen him look quite so grim.

"But as I said, put all that aside for now." Wrexford grasped her hand. One by one, he eased open her fingers, then took her weapon and placed it in his pocket.

"The game has changed yet again," he explained. "The chessboard has been reset, and a new confrontation has already begun."

"W-What are you saying?"

"I have just been informed that five days ago, on the night of the twenty-sixth of February, Napoleon made his escape from the isle of Elba."

CHAPTER 18

Wrexford poured Charlotte a glass of brandy as soon as they arrived back at Berkeley Square, but she set it aside untouched.

"Drink," he counseled. "You've had quite a shock."

"Be damned with my sensibilities," she answered. "What if the Weasels follow the coldblooded killer, thinking he is Ducasse's co-conspirator?"

"They won't," said the earl. "They have strict orders to shadow Ducasse and know better than to improvise in this situation."

"His Lordship is right," said McClellan. She and Tyler had been informed of the momentous news of Napoleon's escape and invited to the drawing room to discuss the ramifications. "The boys will be fine."

"But as for our nation and the Continent . . ." muttered Tyler.

A fraught silence gripped the room.

"Have we any idea where Napoleon is headed?" continued the valet.

"He landed in the south of France near Antibes three days

ago and appears to be heading toward Grenoble," answered Wrexford.

"Surely the French people have had enough of war and bloodshed," said Charlotte.

"The French value glory over peace," said Tyler. "My guess is that they will welcome their former emperor with open arms."

Wrexford wished he could disagree.

"We just returned from a supper soiree and saw your note." A pale-faced Sheffield and Cordelia appeared in the doorway. "I—I don't suppose there could be . . . a mistake?"

"Grentham isn't prone to making mistakes," said the earl. "Especially about something of this magnitude."

"What can we do?" queried Sheffield.

"As to that, I was told to wait for further instructions. Apparently Grentham left for Brussels earlier this evening after telling his temporary man-in-charge to alert me of the escape. Wellington is also headed there to cobble together an army to face Napoleon—for I think it's safe to assume the former emperor is intent on putting his arse back on the French throne," he replied.

"What about the murders?" demanded Charlotte. "We know the man who is responsible, but we have no idea of his actual identity." She drew in a shaky breath. "He has no name—save for the fact that I call him Obsidian Eyes!"

"Obsidian Eyes!" exclaimed McClellan. "The man who shot at Raven?"

"That's my surmise, " answered Charlotte. "As he's also the fellow who planned to murder us and Francis Ronalds in the gardens of Kelmscott House . . ."

As Charlotte recounted to the others the gruesome chain of events she had witnessed in the Prince Regent's conservatory, Wrexford moved to the window and stared out at the few flickers of lamplight still visible in the buildings across the square.

They seemed awfully puny, he reflected, compared to the vast expanse of darkness.

Closing his eyes for a moment, the earl pushed such thoughts aside before turning back to the room. "Grentham's men took care of removing the bodies from the conservatory, and the official story will be that the two men were the victims of a robbery gone bad while crossing through Green Park. So no rumors about murders within the Prince Regent's residence will spark panic in the city."

Wrexford considered their next move. So much was unknown . . . "What we need to concentrate on is figuring out what Napoleon's ultimate strategy is for weakening Britain. All these preliminary moves have been orchestrated with consummate skill to keep us off guard. We need to discover why."

"In poking around for information concerning Boyleston, the Weasels and I have had our ears to the ground for any skullduggery going on," pointed out Tyler. "And we've heard nothing about any illicit activities. Even the urchins, who see things that most people miss, haven't offered up any clue."

"Then we have to try harder," said Wrexford. "It seems to me that an assassination could cripple our ability to organize an army to confront Napoleon, as well as create fear and panic in the city."

Charlotte chafed her palms together, trying to dispel the chill forming in the pit of her stomach. "Much as I hate to suggest it, should we inform Grentham's office about Obsidian Eyes and the fear of an assassination plot?"

"As I said, Grentham is out of the country. As is Pierson." The earl made a face. "I know nothing about the fellow now in charge. But then, that's what Grentham prefers his operatives to be—amorphous swirls of smoke, hidden in the shadows, going about their wolf-eat-wolf business without anyone seeing a flash of teeth."

"Do you trust him?" queried Sheffield.

Wrexford chuffed a sardonic laugh. "Trust is most definitely not a word that comes to mind when speaking of the Machiavellian world of espionage. And both Grentham and Pierson stressed to me that I was not to discuss the French attempts to stir chaos here in Britain with any official other than them."

"In other words, it's imperative that we conduct our own investigation independently from the government's activities," said Charlotte.

"Correct. To do otherwise would perhaps threaten our country, not to speak of putting our family secrets in danger."

She nodded, relieved that he had given voice to her own inner fears. However, his next words took her by surprise.

"My first course of action tomorrow will be to have a word with Elias Fogg, a senior official at the Foreign Office." Wrexford recounted what Colonel Duxbury had said to him earlier in the evening. "As well as have a very confidential talk with Duxbury and arrange for a discreet increase in security for the prime minister and the senior generals at Horse Guards. He can be trusted to keep quiet about it."

A harried sigh. "And my second will be to pay a quick visit to Wrexford Manor."

Seeing her quizzical look, he explained. "If we're investigating on our own, I may be called on to move about Town quickly in case of a crisis, and we have only placid parkland mounts and carriage horses here in the mews. I need to bring Lucifer back to London."

Charlotte made a face at the mention of the earl's favorite stallion. "That beast is nothing but trouble. Hawk nearly lost a hand the first time he tried to feed the brute a lump of sugar."

"What Lucifer lacks in manners, he more than makes up for in stamina and fearlessness. I need to have a mount that I trust won't let me down in a pinch," countered the earl. "The boys know to avoid him."

"Very well," she conceded, accepting his reasoning despite her reservations. "As for me, my responsibilities as A. J. Quill demand that right now I give my full attention to keeping the public informed of current events—and to encourage a sense of calm rather than panic."

"I daresay even Grentham would have no quarrel with A. J. Quill's voicing such commentaries in the coming days," responded Tyler.

"The good of Britain's people—*all* of Britain's people—is always my first obligation," replied Charlotte. "Whether it suits the minister's needs or not."

Further planning was interrupted by the clatter of footsteps in the corridor announcing that the Weasels had returned from their mission.

"We waited until the last of the guests left Carlton House," announced Raven. "Each of us kept watch on a different entrance, but Ducasse never appeared."

"That's because Ducasse and his friend Odilon were lured to the conservatory and murdered," said Charlotte. "I—I think the killer may be the man you called Obsidian Eyes."

Raven gave an involuntary flinch.

"You saw him clearly," she continued. "Was he tall and sleekly muscled, with a pantherlike quickness to his movements?"

"Oiy," answered Raven. 'He had the look of a predator— one who enjoyed the hunt." He blinked. "And the kill."

"Let us be careful about jumping to conclusions," counseled Wrexford. "For now it's merely speculation that Raven's assailant and the French operative are one and the same. We can't afford to go haring off after specters."

Nobody voiced a disagreement.

"Have we anything else to discuss tonight?" he asked, looking to Charlotte.

She shook her head.

"Then let us get some rest. Come morning, we need to start unraveling this devil-cursed web of intrigue."

Charlotte stared at the blank sheet of watercolor paper, trying to visualize just the right image to inform the public of the momentous news that Napoleon had slipped away from his island prison and landed in the south of France.

She had carefully read all the morning newspaper accounts of the escape, only to put them aside in disgust. Given that precious few facts had reached London, the stories were filled with lurid speculations. Thankfully, Wrexford had received a terse note just after dawn from Grentham's office containing what little the government knew so far.

Picking up her pencil, Charlotte began a rough sketch. She deliberately chose to make the former emperor a small image on the page, showing him wading ashore from a rowboat onto French soil. Trailing in his wake was a small retinue of the Garde Impériale who had followed him into exile—she added a few moth holes to their coats and rips to their boots to make them look less threatening.

She leaned back, satisfied with the composition. It was based on facts, not rumors. At the moment, Napoleon and his loyal followers were no more than a raggle-taggle group on the run. It was still unclear what he was seeking.

That, she decided, would be the subject of her captions. *Is he seeking passage to America in order to start a new life in the New World? . . . Does he think that King Louis XVIII will grant him the right to live quietly in France? . . . Or are his desires more ambitious?*

Picking up her penknife, Charlotte sharpened her quill and set to work on inking in the final image.

* * *

"Your pardon, sir." The junior secretary tapped a tentative knock on the half-open door. "A gentleman wishes to have a word—"

"Are you daft, Hopkins?" barked Fogg. "Send him away. I have no time for visitors."

"This won't take long," said Wrexford, shouldering his way past the young man and closing the door.

"Bloody hell," muttered Fogg under his breath as he removed his spectacles and scowled. "We have a crisis unfolding here. I am not at liberty to reveal what it is, but I assure you, the Foreign Office has far greater concerns at the moment than . . ." A hesitation. ". . . than any of your pestering questions."

"If you're referring to Napoleon's escape from Elba, I learned of that last night," replied the earl.

"How—" began Fogg.

"Never mind that now. I simply wish to clarify a few things you said at the Royal Institution's reception for Monsieur Ducasse," replied Wrexford.

A look of surprise flared in Fogg's gaze—along with a flicker of unease. "I—I can't imagine why, milord," he said through gritted teeth.

"Because it puzzles me that you couldn't recall a stranger being present at the Royal Society on the night of Boyleston's murder when Norwood mentioned to me that you had spent most of the evening conversing with him."

The morning light angling in through the leaded windows caught the sheen of sweat now beading Fogg's forehead.

"Bloody hell, milord, you know how these scientific meetings go! We discuss serious topics, and afterward, the wine flows and we indulge in friendly conversation with our colleagues." Fogg's voice turned shrill. "I may have had a glass too many, because I don't remember the damn stranger you described. Is that a bloody crime?"

"Not to my knowledge," said Wrexford. Curious to hear how Fogg would respond, he added, "I don't suppose you recall the topic of conversation?"

"The Chelsea Physic Garden!" replied Fogg, his voice rising another notch. "Are you now going to demand to know the color of the undergarments I wore that night?"

Wrexford raised his brows. "Oh? Do they come in any shade other than white or cream?"

"Why the devil are you asking these questions? Have they something to do with Boyleston's murder?"

Ignoring the question, the earl abruptly switched to a new line of inquiry. "I also just learned from Colonel Duxbury that you serve as a liaison with Grentham's department for the Foreign Office and Horse Guards—"

"That is not true!' exclaimed Fogg. "I have no such official position. I do occasionally confer with Grentham's senior staff for general updates, and if I happen to hear a trivial bit of information that might interest Horse Guards, I pass it on."

"Grentham's department does not deal in trivial matters," said Wrexford.

Fogg drew in a shaky breath. "You seem intent on twisting my words, milord. Might I ask why?"

Wrexford kept his answer deliberately vague. "I'm merely trying to put together a clear picture of certain events."

"But the authorities have apprehended Redding and charged him with Boyleston's murder."

"So they have," agreed the earl.

Muttering to himself, Fogg picked up his pen. "Unless you have any more absurd questions to ask—and by the by, I answered you out of gentlemanly courtesy, as I can't imagine you have any official mandate to ask them—I have serious work to do."

"That's all," said the earl, allowing a moment to pass before adding, "For now."

Another spasm of emotion passed over Fogg's face, but he quickly looked down and began writing.

Without further comment, Wrexford retreated into the corridor. The fellow's answers were all reasonable, he conceded, knowing there were likely many times when he wouldn't have been able to identify who had been part of a group conversation. And the fellow's ire was understandable.

However, there was something about Fogg's demeanor—a tautness that seemed tinged with fear—that bothered him. As he made his way out to the street, Wrexford was not yet ready to deem the fellow free from suspicion.

CHAPTER 19

The journey home from Wrexford Manor the following afternoon passed without incident, save for a spot of rain near Foxton. Tired and dusty from hours in the saddle—the afternoon was fading into twilight—Wrexford guided his stallion into the walled courtyard of the mews and blew out a sigh as he dismounted.

"Make up a generous mash of corn for Lucifer," he called to the groom, who knew enough to keep his distance from the temperamental horse. "Just leave it outside the stall," he added. "I'll feed him once I've finished giving him a rubdown."

"Thank you, milord. I don't fancy losing a hunk of flesh to that demon from Hell."

The stallion laid back his ears and gave a sharp snort.

"Watch your tongue." The earl smiled. "There are times when I'm quite certain he understands English."

The groom retreated several steps. "I don't doubt it. He's possessed by some supernatural . . ." His mutter trailed off into a wordless scowl as he hurried away.

"Not everyone appreciates your feisty spirit," said Wrexford, giving the stallion's flank a fond pat. After leading Lucifer to a stall well away from the other horses, he removed the saddle and bridle, slipped on a halter, and rubbed down the stallion with a special soothing salve.

A pail rattled outside the stall's gate. "The mash is ready, milord," called the groom.

Wrexford fetched it and hung it on a hook over the manger filled with hay. "Enjoy a well-deserved repast," he murmured as his own stomach growled.

Charlotte greeted him at the back entrance to the townhouse with a fierce hug.

"You ought not get so close—I reek of sweat and horse," he protested, though her closeness was a balm for both his body and his spirit.

"You must be weary to the bone," she said after pressing her lips to his. Taking his arm, she headed for his workroom. "Sit by the fire while I fetch you some food and drink."

Wrexford sank into the soft leather of the armchair nearest the hearth and propped his boots on the brass fender. The coals crackled, releasing a blissfully welcome warmth. Closing his eyes, he put aside all thoughts of the daunting challenges that lay ahead and simply savored the quiet joy of home and family.

Having been through war before, he knew how those precious things could change in a heartbeat.

The muted rattle of porcelain announced Charlotte's return with a tray of tea and a large wedge of steak and kidney pie.

"I imagine Scottish malt would be even more welcome than tea," she said, after handing him the pie.

"Bless you," he mumbled through a mouthful of the savory meat and pastry.

She brought him a glass of the spirits and took a seat in the facing chair.

"Any further news from Grentham's minions on the situation in France?" he asked

"No, there seems to be no reliable information yet about

what's happening," answered Charlotte. "Things are calm here in London. My drawing announcing the news was published this afternoon, and I made a point of reminding the public that for now, Napoleon is merely a fugitive on the run with a small band of loyal followers, not the leader of a grand imperial army."

"Let us pray that Napoleon is quickly apprehended." Wrexford quaffed a long swallow of whisky. "But I fear that it may not prove so easy."

"Tomorrow, we will regroup and concentrate our efforts on figuring out the ultimate target of all the French machinations," replied Charlotte.

As Wrexford looked to the hearth, the lamplight accentuated the lines of worry etched at the corners of his eyes.

"But for tonight, let us not allow our pressing fears and worries about the future to darken the present moment," she added.

"I was just thinking the same thing," he mused. "Life is unpredictable, which I suppose is both a blessing and a curse. But you're right—let us not fritter away the evening in philosophical abstractions."

For several long moments the only sound in the room was the clink of cutlery as the earl polished off the meat pie.

"Would you care for some Stilton and a slice of apple—" began Charlotte, only to be interrupted by a knock on the door.

"Come in," called the earl.

"Forgive me, milord." Their butler's face was wreathed in shadows, but the rigid set of his shoulders betrayed that his normally unshakeable composure was a touch off-kilter. "There is a woman seeking to speak with you." A pause. "She says it is a matter of life and death."

The announcement stirred a sudden prickling of gooseflesh at the nape of Charlotte's neck.

She couldn't begin to articulate why.

I suppose it's because we are all on edge, she told herself, *making ordinary occurrences take on sinister overtones.*

There was no reason to be alarmed, Charlotte told herself. Word had spread through the network of urchins in the city about Wrexford's generosity to those in need, so supplicants appeared with some regularity at the Berkeley Square townhouse. Indeed, the only odd thing about this visitor was that Riche had felt compelled to inform them of her presence.

"If you would escort the woman to the kitchen," she said, "Mac will fix a hamper of food and pass on a purse to tide her through whatever emergency she is facing."

The butler bowed his head in apology. "I know the usual procedure, milady, and attempted to do exactly that. But there is something different about her."

Charlotte didn't like the sound of that. Riche wasn't one to indulge in drama. "In what way?" she demanded.

"Her dress and deportment," he answered. "The woman insists that it is . . . personal." He swallowed hard. "And refuses to budge until she has an audience with His Lordship."

"Then I had better meet with her," replied the earl.

"I put her in the Blue Parlor to wait while I ascertained how you wished to proceed," intoned Riche.

Wrexford got to his feet somewhat stiffly, which raised Charlotte's protective hackles. He looked exhausted.

"Sit," she commanded. "I'll see to her." Her eyes narrowed. "And if she claims to be the long-lost Countess of Wrexford, who has finally escaped from the band of malicious fairies who kidnapped her on her wedding night, I shall send her away with naught but a flea in her ear."

He allowed a grudging laugh. "If she comes up with a more outrageous story than that, perhaps she should be given an extra reward."

"On the contrary, Banbury tales should *not* be encouraged."

"Perhaps not, but I do consider myself obliged to hear her story," he said. "It would feel cowardly to do otherwise."

Charlotte heaved a sigh and gestured for Riche to lead the way to the parlor. "I'll come along, too. The sooner we hear her out, the sooner we can go back to enjoying some peace and quiet."

Despite their butler's warning that their visitor was no ordinary supplicant, Wrexford found himself surprised when the sound of his entrance into the parlor caused her to turn abruptly from gazing out the windows overlooking Berkeley Square. His first impressions were . . .

A quiet strength and determination, trying hard to conceal a rippling of fear.

He stopped short, trying to make sense of his reaction. Fatigue did strange things to one's mind.

Charlotte, however, didn't hesitate to take the bull by the horns. "Our butler has informed us that you claim to have a pressing personal matter to discuss with His Lordship." Her voice, though pleasant, carried an undertone of steel that made it clear that no nonsense would be tolerated.

"I do, Lady Wrexford," came the soft but equally resolute reply. "I apologize for intruding on your household. Please be assured that I would never do so unless there was no other alternative."

"Life and death?" said Charlotte. "Be forewarned that theatrical displays of drama do *not* play well with us."

That drew a wry smile from the woman. "I am relieved to hear that. I'm not very good at acting."

Wrexford had used the short exchange to study their visitor. Her dignified bearing—perfect posture, steadiness in the face of adversity—had at first disguised the fact that she was elderly. She was dressed modestly, but her clothing was clearly of good quality. As for her face, it was plain, with blunt-cut features that held not a trace of guile.

Their eyes met, and in that instant he was sure that the woman was no charlatan.

Which yet again begged the question of why she was here.

Charlotte, too, seemed to have retreated from her initial hostility. "Please be seated." She indicated one of the armchairs facing the sofa. "Allow me to offer you some tea, and then you can tell us the reason for your visit."

"Tea is not necessary, milady. I am already intruding on your hospitality."

"Nonetheless, the ritual is useful in smoothing the rough edges off a difficult topic of discussion."

That drew another ghost of a smile.

As Charlotte rang the silver bell on the side table and sent a parlor maid hurrying to the kitchen, the earl took a seat on the sofa facing the woman.

"Forgive my lack of manners, madam," he said. "I've neglected to introduce myself properly and inquire as to your name."

"Like Her Ladyship, I much prefer plain speaking to the platitudes of proper etiquette," replied their visitor. "You and your wife need no introduction, milord. But given my role in what I am about to tell you, it's only right that you know my identity."

The woman smoothed a crease from her skirts. "My name is Moreen O'Malley."

"Is your accent from County Galway, Mrs. O'Malley?" inquired Charlotte.

"It is *Miss*, not *Missus*, milady," replied their visitor. "You have an excellent ear for languages. Yes, I'm originally from Connemara, but I've lived in England for a number of years."

"My wife is very attuned to noticing little details," said Wrexford.

A tiny twinkle seemed to light for an instant in Miss O'Malley's eyes. "Then I shall take care to say nothing but the truth, so as not to draw Her Ladyship's censure."

It was McClellan, not the parlor maid, who bustled into the parlor with the tea tray. Wrexford bit back a smile, knowing

Riche must have mentioned the mysterious woman and her tit-illating claim.

"I've brought along fresh-baked biscuits that were meant for the Weasels," she announced.

"You keep weasels here?" inquired Miss O'Malley, sitting up even straighter. "Are you fond of animals?"

Wrexford chuckled. "The name *Weasel* is, shall we say, a term of endearment for the three exuberant boys who occa-sionally wreak havoc in this household."

Oddly enough, the announcement seemed to upset rather than amuse their guest. Her expression turned guarded. "I—I didn't realize that you had children."

"They are our wards," explained Charlotte. "But for us, love is no less an elemental bond than blood."

McClellan poured out three cups and passed them around.

"Do help yourself to a biscuit, Miss O'Malley," urged Char-lotte. "McClellan is renowned for her ginger-spiced sweets."

"Thank you." Their visitor accepted one—her hands trem-bled ever so slightly, noted Wrexford—and took a small bite. "It's delicious," she said, and then set it on her saucer.

"But let us not prolong the show of pleasantries any longer. I think you are just as anxious as I am to get to the heart of why I am here. So with your permission, I shall begin . . ."

"Oiy, did you see something move in the shadows of the mews?" said Hawk. As the afternoon gave way to early eve-ning, the Weasels had taken a break from their schoolwork and come down to the garden to practice their latest fencing ma-neuvers.

Raven lowered his foil and shaded his eyes as he stared over the low stone wall at the stable and carriage house across the back alleyway.

A breeze ruffled through the bare branches of the nearby trees, the dark flutterings blurring the fading light.

"Hard to say," he replied. "We better go have a closer look." The three of them quietly scaled the wall and crept across the narrow cart path.

"There! By the far stable door," whispered Hawk. "Someone is fiddling with the latch."

Raven raised his brows in surprise. "The cully must be a newcomer to Town, and our local gang hasn't yet had a chance to tell him the rules."

"We definitely need to set him straight. No pilfering allowed at this particular townhouse," said Hawk. He squinted into the gloom. "He looks skinny. Once we make sure he's had some supper, let's send him to Scratch, who'll take him under his wing and make sure he learns the ropes of how to survive on the streets."

"Right." Raven felt in his coat pocket for some coins. "We may be wards of an earl and live in a fancy mansion with every imaginable luxury. But we must never forget our roots."

"We better hurry," observed Peregrine. "He's just managed to open the latch."

Crouching low, they crossed into the courtyard just as the unknown urchin slipped inside the far section of the stable.

"Holy hell—that's where Wrex has put Lucifer!" said Hawk.

They quickened their steps to a run, abandoning any attempt at stealth, and raced through the half-open door just in time to see the newcomer climb over the wooden side of the stallion's stall and drop down into the hay covering the stone floor.

"Oiy! Get out of there before you get trampled!" cried Raven. Wrexford had warned them in no uncertain terms to stay clear of Lucifer, and the boys had witnessed enough temperamental behavior from the fiery stallion to take the earl's admonitions to heart.

The urchin ignored the warning and took a step toward the glowering horse.

Laying back his ears, Lucifer snorted and kicked at the

straw-covered floor of the stall with an agitated *thump-thump* of his iron-shod hooves.

"I tell you, he's a very dangerous—" Raven suddenly fell silent as the urchin began to sing in a soft but lilting voice. The words were unrecognizable, but the elemental beauty of the music transcended mere language.

The stallion shook his head but stopped snorting.

The urchin took a step closer.

Muscles rippled beneath the stallion's coal-black coat, and then he went still as a statue.

The Weasels stared in open-mouthed wonder. They, too, were mesmerized by the song.

"Aren't you a magnificent creature?" The urchin ventured a tickling caress to the stallion's velvety nose, eliciting a soft whuffle.

"W-What are you? Some sort of sorcerer?" demanded Raven. "One who casts a dark enchantment over unsuspecting listeners?"

The urchin made a rude sound. "It's not magic, it's merely a Gaelic folk song." Another caress. "All living creatures find music calming. One simply needs to have the knack of finding exactly the right tone."

"But how do you know which one is right?" asked Hawk.

"Dunno." A quick shrug. "I just do."

The sudden movement startled the stallion, who nipped at the urchin's floppy hat.

It fell off . . . allowing a riot of dark curls to tumble free.

"You're a . . . a . . ." sputtered Raven.

"A girl," finished Peregrine, looking equally stunned.

"Aren't you the bright lads?" she said mockingly as she gave the stallion another tickling caress, earning a slobbering lick to her fingers. After wiping them on her breeches, she cocked her head. "I'm Eddy. Who are you?"

For a moment, Raven appeared tongue-tied. "I'm R-Raven," he stammered. "Umm, that is, T-Thomas."

Eddy eyed him with a pitying stare. "You aren't sure of your own name?" She looked at Hawk and Peregrine. "What about you two? Are you simpletons as well?"

Peregrine quickly piped up with his name, while Hawk haltingly explained how he and his brother had chosen to go by a shortened version of their longwinded official names.

"Hawk instead of Alexander Hawksley and Raven instead of Thomas Ravenwood," mused Eddy. "Aye, I can understand that." She made a face. "My official name is Eddylina, but I much prefer Eddy."

"I much prefer Falcon," volunteered Peregrine.

She studied their clothing—as usual, they were looking more like guttersnipes than aristocrats—and couldn't seem to decide who they might be. "What do you three do around here?"

"We fence," offered Peregrine.

Her expression sharpened in interest. "Are you any good?"

"Falcon is an expert swordsman," answered Hawk. "Raven and I are getting better."

Ignoring the comment, her gaze remained locked on Peregrine. "I'd like you to teach me—"

"*Eddy!*" A loud call echoed from somewhere outside.

She sighed, suddenly looking apprehensive.

"Why are *you* here?" asked Raven.

Shoving her hands in her jacket pockets, she blew out a troubled breath. "You'll see soon enough."

"Eddy! Please come at once!"

Shoulders slumping, Eddy gave a last caress to the stallion and climbed out of the stall. She hesitated, but after another urgent call, she moved reluctantly to the stable door.

The Weasels exchanged puzzled looks, and then curiosity impelled them to followed right on her heels.

Raven edged forward to peer over Eddy's shoulder and saw Charlotte approach the back garden gate. Wrexford and an older woman were several steps behind her.

"Is that the Countess of Wrexford?" whispered Eddy.

"Oiy, that's m'lady," answered Raven.

Eddy kicked at a wisp of hay and whispered something in Gaelic. In a louder voice she added, "So much for Moreen's mad plan."

"W-What do you mean?" asked Peregrine.

Instead of answering, Eddy looked around, panic flaring in her eyes as she seemed to be searching for a last-minute escape route.

"Whatever is coming, it can't be *that* bad," said Raven.

"Ha!" She squeezed her eyes shut, as if trying to hold back tears. "Moreen is ill and can't care for me anymore. And so she is trying to foist me on the earl and his wife."

"Why them?" asked Hawk.

"Because," she answered, "the Earl of Wrexford is my father."

CHAPTER 20

Wrexford spotted a child dressed like a boy standing in the doorway of the stable and felt his breath catch in his lungs.

Quickening his steps, he hurried past Charlotte.

The girl—the last rays of sunlight illuminated the mass of feminine curls tumbling past her shoulder—flinched as he approached, causing him to halt.

He drew in a breath, utterly at a loss for words.

What the devil should I say?

Clearing his throat, he gave her a tentative smile. "Halloo, Eddy."

Her eyes widened. She was clearly nervous—ye heavens, the world as she knew it was turning upside down—but she stood her ground and lifted her chin. "G-Good evening, Your Lordship."

"I'm not 'Your Lordship.' I'm your brother."

Wrexford heard the Weasels give a collective gasp but ignored them. He crouched down bringing his eyes level with hers. "My name is Alexander, but everyone calls me 'Wrex.'"

Eddy continued to stare at him in solemn silence.

The earl held out his hand. "Welcome to our family. I am so very happy to finally meet you."

A look of wariness seemed to flicker beneath her lashes, and he felt his heart lurch.

If only I hadn't been so childish with my father . . .

Ifonlyifonlyifonly.

Shaking off such thoughts, Wrexford wracked his brain for another way to break the ice.

But then Eddy slowly reached out and touched her palm to his.

Wrexford wrapped his fingers around her hand and straightened. "Come, before I introduce you to the rest of your family, you need to become acquainted with Mac's ginger biscuits."

Charlotte gestured for the Weasels to join her and her companion. "Miss O'Malley, please allow our three wards to introduce themselves." To the boys she added, "Do show your new sister's governess that she's not abandoning her loved one to a pack of wild savages."

Hawk flashed a toothy grin after the three of them performed the polite ritual with perfect polish. "We're not really savages," he confided. He glanced down at his muck-streaked breeches. "We just look a little untidy at times."

Raven inclined a very gentlemanly bow before adding, "We will do our best to make Eddy feel welcome."

"Oiy," piped up Peregrine. "It's easy to fit in here. I've only been part of the family since last summer, but I couldn't feel more at home." Like Hawk, he gave a grin. "We may not be conventional, but as m'lady is wont to say, convention is vastly overrated."

"That is very reassuring, Master Peregrine," said Miss O'Malley after stifling a chuckle. "I couldn't agree more."

"You boys run along now and help Wrex show Eddy around,"

said Charlotte, sensing that her companion wished to have word in private.

"I'm very grateful to both you and Lord Wrexford for your generosity of spirit," began Miss O'Malley once the boys had scampered off. "Given what the old earl—that is, His Lordship's father—had told us about his eldest son, I had reason to hope that Eddy wouldn't be turned away."

She fisted her hands together. "That said, I feel I must explain some things about Eddy's mother and the late earl. It's important that you comprehend the . . . complexities of the bond. And to be honest, I feel it's easier to do it with you, milady, rather than Lord Wrexford."

"I understand," Charlotte assured her. "I know that the relationship between father and son was fraught with complicated emotions—as well as unfortunate misunderstandings." A sad smile. "Alas, men don't seem to find it as easy to talk about their feelings as women."

"So true," agreed Miss O'Malley. "Which is not to say that those of our sex are any less tangled in contradictions and conundrums."

"You may speak plainly to me," said Charlotte. "I was a rebellious hellion in my youth and chose a path in life that led me to stray far from the boundaries of Polite Society. Which means that I've experienced not only grand adventures but also adversities and heartaches."

A pause. "I say this to assure you that I truly understand that Life isn't black and white. I consider myself open-minded and accepting of ideas that don't mirror my own. Wrexford thinks the same way as I do." She drew in a deep breath. "So whatever challenges lie ahead, we will deal with them."

"Bless you," whispered Miss O'Malley, tears pearling on her lashes. "I've a wasting illness and my days are numbered. That I am leaving Eddy with family who will strive to understand and appreciate her individuality means the world to me."

She dabbed at her eyes with a handkerchief before continuing. "First, let me tell you about Eddy's mother. I was her nursemaid and continued to serve her until her death in a shipwreck while making a trip to Ireland."

"When was that?" asked Charlotte, hoping to start piecing together a picture of the late earl's relationship with the mother of his daughter.

"Six months after the late earl passed away," answered Miss O'Malley. "Ala—her full name was Aladeen—was strong, courageous, and independent-minded. She was also strong-willed— some might call it stubborn to a fault—and could be tempestuous on occasion, capable of shining bright as the sun or plunging into an abyss of darkness. I loved her wholeheartedly, but I was not blind to her faults."

"An elemental force of Nature," observed Charlotte, feeling that despite the challenges, she and Ala would likely have come to be friends.

"Yes," agreed her companion. "Ala was an extraordinary lady—a true lady, as her family was descended from a legendary Irish chieftain. Like her father, she was a renowned horse trainer . . ."

Charlotte listened intently to the story of Aladeen's life, making note of all the colorful details to pass along to Wrexford when the time was right.

"Eddy is different from other girls. Given Ala's travels, she thought it safer for Eddy to dress as a boy, and she's come to love the freedom it offers over feminine garb."

"I can understand that," said Charlotte dryly.

"Eddy also shares her mother's gift with animals," said Miss O'Malley, bringing the conversation back to the here and now. "She can create an inexplicable rapport with every wild creature she encounters. I . . . I hope you will tolerate her passion for having animal companions."

She made a face. "It grieved her deeply to leave her baby pigeons behind when we journeyed here."

"Please don't fret. Eddy will receive nothing but encouragement for her interests. Indeed, I am used to having a menagerie here in the house, as Hawk is a budding naturalist. Snakes, toads, baby hedgehogs, orphan fox kits—I have learned to tread carefully when I enter their quarters."

A smile. "We will send right away for Eddy's birds to be brought here. There is ample room on the roof for a dovecote."

"She would love that, but I'm afraid it won't be possible," replied Miss O'Malley with a wistful sigh. "Her birds were a special type called messenger pigeons, which are bred to return home to their place of birth from no matter where they are released. Once they learn the location of their home, it cannot be altered."

Charlotte thought for a moment. "Then we shall obtain eggs—"

"Squabs," interjected Miss O'Malley. "One obtains squabs, which are young hatchlings which haven't yet been trained to fly from a specific nesting area."

"Squabs," she repeated. "I will arrange for the purchase of squabs first thing in the morning."

"Do you mean that?"

"Be assured that Lord Wrexford and I will do everything in our power to make Eddy feel welcome and much loved." She glanced at the townhouse, its window aglow with lamplight. "And now, I had better return and formally meet my new . . .

Daughter?

The word stirred a spurt of panic.

Ye gods, how will I cope with guiding an adolescent girl to adulthood when I can't in good conscience demand that Eddy adhere to the strictures of Polite Society?

"Meet my new ward," she finished. "Just one last question.

It does not matter a whit to us, but we can't ignore that the answer has implications for Eddy's future—"

"You wish to know whether Ala and the late earl were legally married," answered Miss O'Malley.

"Yes."

That her companion didn't respond right away seemed an eloquent enough answer . . .

"I believe that they were. Ala told me that they had indeed tied the knot on a trip to Brittany to deliver an Irish racehorse to a wealthy client who lived there. And the late earl confirmed it to me. Indeed, at my entreaty, when Eddy was born nine months later, I asked to see the certificate and Ala showed it to me, assuring me that she kept it in a very safe place."

Miss O'Malley shook her head mournfully. "Their relationship was a complicated one, and it was made even more fraught by the late earl's reluctance to tell his sons of his marriage. Though she hid it well, I think Ala was deeply hurt, even though he tried to explain it was based on the complexities of his father-and-son relationship, not any reservation about her."

Charlotte nodded in understanding.

"I know he meant to tell your husband in person—especially after Thomas was killed in battle on the Peninsula—and present him with the document. But he kept putting it off. And then, when Ala was lost at sea …" She shook her head. "I fear it went down with her, for I've searched high and low and never found it."

"*Carpe diem,*" whispered Charlotte. "A lesson to us all not to put things off until it's too late."

After Charlotte's return and her first exchange with Eddy, things had become a blur for the rest of the evening, conceded Wrexford. But at last the house quieted and he was able to seek refuge in his workroom to ponder the . . .

Was there a word for what had just happened?

Eddy had seemed to weather the cheerful chaos of their household with admirable sangfroid as she was introduced to the mansion and all its quirks and routines.

But was she overwhelmed? wondered Wrexford. He couldn't tell. She seemed to hide her emotions well.

A family trait?

He hoped that she had more of her late brother Thomas's sunny disposition than his own tendency to brood.

A rustle of silk against the carpet drew him back from such thoughts, and an instant later, Charlotte leaned over the back of his chair and placed her hands on his shoulders.

The lamplight seemed to brighten, the flames releasing a sudden warmth into the room.

"I am sorry to have upended our life as we know it," he said, after grasping her hand and pressing a kiss to her knuckles.

A chuckle. "Our life as we know it was hardly a pattern card for peace and tranquility," responded Charlotte. "Besides, you have always told me that an elemental scientific truth is that the world is in a state of constant flux. Time ticks on, the tides ebb and flow, the seasons move inexorably through the cycle of birth, death, and rebirth."

"That is all very well in the abstract," said the earl, "but when it becomes personal—"

"Change is good. Challenges are what keep us from becoming complacent. They make us learn and grow." She moved around and settled herself in his lap. "Am I terrified of what lies ahead?" Her mouth quirked. "Absolutely. But somehow we will manage."

Wrexford felt the knot in his chest slowly loosen. "What did I do to deserve you?"

"As I recall, you were sarcastic and sharp-tongued enough to get yourself accused of a heinous murder."

He laughed. "And despite the fact that you loathed me, you cared enough about Truth and Justice to pull my cods out of the fire."

"Principle must always overrule personal feelings."

The earl put his arms around her and drew her close, savoring the sense of joy that her presence lit in his heart. He wished he could keep hold of the moment indefinitely.

However . . .

"Speaking of Principle, we have committed to helping the government protect the country from its enemies. But given how profoundly our new responsibilities will alter our family life, we need to discuss our future priorities."

"We have managed to handle complicated investigations in the past," she countered.

"Yes, but I fear that this particular demand will test our limits," he admitted. "I have no idea how to be a brother—and in some ways a father—to a complete stranger."

"You and the Weasels got off to a much less auspicious start," she reminded him. "Raven actually stabbed you in the leg during your first encounter, while Eddy made no attempt to draw blood. So I take that as a sign of encouragement."

"But you—"

"Hush." Charlotte pressed a finger to his lips. "No more doubts. First thing in the morning we will start making plans."

"Your famous lists," he murmured.

"I daresay I'll need a whole new notebook." The lamplight gilded the curl of her smile. "And the first entry will be the need to acquire pigeon squabs—and not just any pigeon squabs."

"What are squabs? And why on earth would we want them?"

She quickly explained about Eddy having to abandon her pigeons.

"Ah." Wrexford pursed his lips. "I believe that Thaddeus Howe, secretary of the London Avian Appreciation Club and a fellow member of the Royal Society, breeds messenger pigeons. I shall send a note to him in the morning. I'm sure I can convince him that his squabs will be coming to a good home."

His expression turned more troubled. "As for our damnable search for a ruthless French operative and whatever dastardly plot he and his cohorts have in mind — "

"Have faith, Wrex. Together, we shall find a way to make all of this work out."

"Do you hear any sounds of distress?"

Raven pulled his head from the corridor and closed the door. "Impossible to say. Her room is too far away."

"What if she's scared and lonely?" whispered Hawk. "What if she misses her old home?" His face scrunched in worry. "What if she doesn't like our family?"

The comment roused Harper from his slumber by the hearth. Shaking his shaggy head, he gave a soft *whoof.*

"Don't worry, Harper. I think she may like animals better than people," mused Hawk.

"She strikes me as more prickly than scared." Raven made a face. "Regardless, it seems that we're all stuck with each other. Remember, she told us that Miss O'Malley is seriously ill and can't care for her any longer."

"What if . . ." Hawk hesitated. "Should we check and make sure that she's not feeling frightened and abandoned?"

"Hammering on her door might wake her up," pointed out Peregrine. "She's likely exhausted by all the emotions of the day." He looked pensive. "I know from experience that it's not easy having your life turned topsy-turvy by circumstances out of your own control."

"We could check on her discreetly," said Hawk. "The ledge outside our bedroom window leads around past hers."

Raven muttered something under his breath but surrendered

on catching his brother's pleading look. "Very well. But we need to take off our shoes and move *very* quietly. It would be embarrassing to get caught."

The three of them quickly stripped off their footwear and tiptoed out of the schoolroom.

"I'll go first," said Raven, easing open the window sash. "Stay close."

They crept along the outcropping of stone and made their way toward the corner of the townhouse's south wing. A spill of light through the mullioned glass up ahead indicated that Eddy had not yet retired.

Ducking low, Raven scooted to the far side of window and positioned himself for a look inside. Hawk and Peregrine pressed together at the near side and did the same. On a silent signal from Raven, they pressed their noses to the night-chilled panes—

Only to see a scowling face peering back at them from mere inches away.

"Why are you three out there creeping around in the cold?" demanded Eddy.

"Ummm." Hawk and Peregrine looked to Raven.

"The moon is full—" he began.

"And the three of you change into hairy werewolves for a few days each month?"

"Ha, ha, ha." Hawk gave a weak laugh. "Would you sing to us if we were werewolves?"

"No, I would throw garlic at you and stab a silver stake through your evil hearts."

Raven narrowed his eyes. "Are you always so sarcastic?"

"No," she answered, "only when someone does something egregiously strange like creep along a window ledge in the bitter cold to stare into someone's bedchamber."

A flush darkened Raven's face. "We were just trying to make sure that you weren't . . ."

"Upset," offered Peregrine. "Or in tears."

"I never cry." Eddy then threw open the window sash and stared up at the sky. "So, one really can see the Moon from this cramped and smelly city. I feared it would be hidden by all the noxious smoke and tall buildings."

"It's not so bad here, once you get used to it," offered Hawk. "There are lots of different neighborhoods, all with interesting nooks and crannies to explore."

Eddy's eyes betrayed a flicker of interest. "What about riding trails?"

"There are plenty of those in Hyde Park, which is just a stone's throw from here," offered Peregrine.

"Do you think His Lordship—"

"Wrex," corrected Raven. "You're part of the family, and we all call him Wrex."

She looked away, making her expression impossible to read. "How do you three fit into the family?" she asked.

In the hustle and bustle of supper and sorting out all the initial logistics of familiarizing Eddy with the house and settling her into her quarters, there had been no time for personal chatter.

"Luck and chance," responded Raven. "We're all orphans, and not related to Wrex by blood." He hesitated, and then stuck to the story that all outsiders were told. "But Hawk and I have a distant family connection to m'lady through marriage, and she was kind enough to take us in. When she married Wrex, he accepted us as part of the package."

"I became friends with Hawk and Raven, as m'lady's brother is married to the sister of my former legal guardian," explained Peregrine. "His wife hated me because of the color of my skin—my mother was of African descent—and out of the kindness of their hearts, Wrex and m'lady arranged for me to live here. As of several months ago, I am now their legal ward."

"I'm an orphan, too," she mused.

"Well then, it seems that we're birds of a feather," remarked Raven.

The mention of birds brought a look of longing to Eddy's face, but she quickly masked it with a slight frown as a *thump-thump* against the bedroom door caused her to turn around and hop down from her bed.

Thump-thump.

The latch jiggled and then popped up, allowing the door to swing open. A big black nose and lolling pink tongue appeared, followed by the rest of Harper.

The massive iron-grey hound circled Eddy twice and then sat right in front of her and butted his head against her belly.

"Aren't you a beauty?" she murmured, reaching out both hands to scratch behind his floppy ears.

A blissful sound rumbled in the hound's throat, and his tail began a rhythmic thumping. Both sounds grew louder as Eddy began to sing softly.

Harper's rumbles turned into a series of soft howls as he sang along with her.

Hawk's eyes widened in awe. "Can you teach me how to do that?" asked Hawk.

"He, too, has a special rapport with animals," explained Raven.

"But not like yours," Hawk hastened to add.

"It's not something that can be taught," answered Eddy. "But if you have the gift, I can maybe help you discover it."

Hawk's response was a beatific grin.

"Seeing as you have no need of help in settling in, we ought to return to our quarters," said Raven, trying not to shiver.

"It might be easier if you climbed down and went out through the door," drawled Eddy.

"Yes, but it's much more fun to do it our way," countered Raven.

"Suit yourself," she replied.

Harper had already curled up on the rug by the bedside and fallen asleep.

"Sweet dreams," she added, as Raven slammed the window shut and disappeared from view.

CHAPTER 21

"I dressed as quickly as I could once my maid brought in the early morning post!" Alison hurried into the parlor, one diamond earbob not quite properly fastened in her right lobe. "Good heavens, what a surprise!"

"That is putting it mildly." Charlotte pushed back from her desk and put down her pen. "I am composing a number of lists for all that needs to be done—a complete wardrobe appropriate for an aristocratic young lady, sundries, books, pigeons—"

"Pigeons?" exclaimed the dowager. "Is that some sort of new-fangled euphemism for a feminine product like skin cream for wrinkles?"

"No, I am speaking of the actual bird, specifically messenger pigeons. Wrex is taking Eddy to select some squabs for her to raise and train here on the roof."

"What an unconventional hobby for a girl." Alison smiled. "She should fit right in here."

"I hope so." Charlotte looked pensive. "Eddy seems awfully composed for her age—she's only twelve years old, though she will turn thirteen in several months. I confess, it's hard to know what she is thinking."

"Give it time," counseled the dowager. "She's been here less than twenty-four hours."

Charlotte closed her eyes for a moment, knowing it was unreasonable to feel a spurt of panic. "You're right, of course. I will be depending on you for advice over the coming days."

"And you shall have it." Another smile. "Perhaps more often than you might wish."

Charlotte looked back to her lists and made a wry face. "I'm sure these will keep growing."

"Don't look so apprehensive, You've dealt with three independent-minded boys."

"Yes, but girls are different and create a whole different set of complications." She sighed. "I ought to know."

Alison took a seat on the sofa by the hearth and gestured for Charlotte to join her. "Bring your lists, and I'll have a look at them. And then, when Eddy returns, let us take her to Gunter's before the whirlwind of practical tasks begin. There's nothing like their iced confections to make all the troubles of the world seem to melt away."

Cordelia looked up from the sheet of equations and half-dozen open books spread out on the dining room table. "Oh, forgive me, Raven! I didn't hear you come in. You need not stand in the shadows. You are always welcome to enter and make your presence known whenever you come to visit."

She put down her pencil with an expectant look. "Besides, I am all agog to hear more about the newest member of your family. M'lady sent me a note about the unexpected arrival of Eddylina, but I wish to give them both some time to settle in to this momentous change in life before Kit and I rush over to make her acquaintance."

Raven sidestepped the request for information by simply ignoring it. He moved closer and craned his neck to see the string of numbers and symbols written on the paper. "What are you working on?"

"We'll get to mathematics in a moment." Cordelia gave him a quizzical look. "Is there a reason you don't wish to talk about Wrex's half-sister?"

"There isn't much to say. She's a hair taller than me, has dark copper-tinged curls, and sings exotic songs to animals."

Cordelia waited, but when it became evident that nothing more was forthcoming, she raised her brows. "Why is it that I sense you've not mentioned everything?"

Another sliver of silence.

"And she has a razor for a tongue," he blurted out in a rush.

She gestured for him to take the chair next to hers. "I gather your first impressions were not overly favorable."

Raven fisted his hands in his lap after slipping into his seat. "Doesn't matter what I think," he muttered. "Like it or not, we're stuck with her. She has nowhere else to go."

Repressing a sigh, Cordelia took her time in composing a response. Change did not come without growing pains for adolescents, but she wished to offer more than such a well-worn platitude.

"Have you considered that perhaps Eddylina—"

"Eddy," he interrupted. "She prefers to be called Eddy."

"Perhaps Eddy is very aware of the fact that she's alone in the world, and it makes her feel scared and vulnerable," suggested Cordelia. "And so she acts tough and aggressive to hide her fears."

"Perhaps," he conceded.

"I'm just saying that you might consider giving her a chance. A great many of us don't show to advantage in a first encounter."

"Like me, for example," announced Sheffield as he crossed into the room from the corridor. He dropped his hat on the corner of the table and shrugged out of his overcoat. "Cordelia thought I was an utter lackwit when we met."

"You exaggerate," she said.

"Not by much." Sheffield winked at Raven before adding, "Whom are we discussing?"

"Wrex's half-sister," intoned Raven.

Sheffield's face went through a series of odd little contortions. "S-Since when does Wrex have a half-sister?"

"Since yesterday evening," said Cordelia. "Charlotte's note arrived this morning just after you left for your meeting with David Ricardo." She went on to explain what she knew, embellished by a few grudging details from Raven.

Sheffield looked about to probe more into the matter, but a warning look from his wife speared him to silence. "I have some information to report as well, but as I'm famished, I'm going to have Cook fix me a cold collation in the kitchen. I'll rejoin you in a bit." A pause. "Once I've digested both my food and this momentous news."

After slanting a look at Raven's still-grim expression, Cordelia pulled several of the books closer. "I'm working on some formulas to model the effects of 'selling short.' Do you remember from our last tutoring session what that is?"

"I think so," Raven said, scanning the mathematical expressions on the page. "Short selling is when an investor wants to bet on a security declining in value—and making a profit if the price of the security drops."

"Correct," said Cordelia. "Do you remember how it works in practice?"

"I think so," said Raven, his scowl softening. "An investor borrows a security, usually from a stockjobber or broker who owns it, and sells that borrowed security to a buyer at the current price. But since the security doesn't have to be delivered to the buyer for a set number of days—that number varies a lot— the investor is betting that the security price will decline so that he can purchase it at a cost lower than that for which he sold it. He then returns the borrowed security to the jobber or the broker, paying only interest or a commission to the lender and pocketing the rest of the difference between the two prices as profit."

"Exactly right," said Cordelia. "Now there are other costs and charges involved in actual practice which have to be captured in the mathematics, and the risks to the investor are effectively unlimited if he loses his bet and the stock price rises rather than falls. I'm also trying to work that into the mathematics here."

The last vestige of Raven's brooding was quickly banished by the mathematical challenge. "Oiy, I see what you're aiming for." He plucked a sharpened pencil from the pile of extras and helped himself to some blank sheets of paper.

"Hmm, what if . . ."

The two of them worked in companionable silence, punctuated by the scratch of their scribbling and whispery flutter of turning pages.

Sheffield soon reappeared, dusting the lingering crumbs of a jam tart from his fingers.

"You're making me feel like a sloth," he intoned, observing the growing pile of equations. "Though in truth, I haven't been entirely idle today."

Cordelia didn't miss the edge in his voice. She paused and pushed back from the table. "What is it that you and Ricardo were discussing?"

"To begin with, I have been learning a great deal more about the type of securities called Consolidated Annuities and their importance to our nation. I must admit, I never understood their true significance."

"Yes, I've learned from Ricardo that they are a key to our country's economic strength," said Cordelia.

"How so?" asked Raven.

"First, a quick history lesson," she replied with a smile. "They were the brainchild of Sampson Gideon, who in 1750 convinced our prime minister that almost all of our government debt going forward should be issued in the form of 3 percent 'Consolidated Annuities'— which quickly became known as *consols* for short."

"As I understand it, consols are perpetual bonds," responded Sheffield. "That is, they have no maturity, but keep on paying £3 of yearly interest for each £100 of face value of the bond forever. The government has the right to redeem a bond from the holder at 100 percent of face value at any time, but other than that, a consol goes on paying indefinitely."

Raven frowned. "Why is that so brilliant? Don't interest rates fluctuate, especially in times of war or other turmoil?"

"You've asked a key question! And the answer is why Mr. Ricardo considers Mr. Gideon a genius," replied Cordelia. "The government discounts the price of consols when interest rates rise, as they do in times of war or economic troubles, like bad harvests. For example, if interest rates generally rise to 6 percent, the government will sell a 3 percent consol with a £100 face value for £50."

"And that makes consols a *very* attractive buy for investors," mused Sheffield. "When the country settles back into better times, interest rates return to their lower, non-crisis levels, and investors who purchased discounted consols may make large capital gains. Even after the American War for Independence, for example, which didn't work out as the king and his ministers planned, the consols issued to pay for our army rose over 30 percent after the war ended, and numerous investors made fortunes."

Raven nodded in understanding. "Because if they have purchased a consol with a £100 face value for £50, they are suddenly much wealthier when interest rates return to their normal range and their consols accordingly trade at much higher values than the discounted rate at which they were purchased."

"Precisely," said Cordelia. "So, let me summarize, without getting lost in the mathematical details. The consol's low annual interest charges for the government and the fact that the country never has to repay the principal unless it voluntarily chooses to redeem the debt have allowed Great Britain to afford large armies, navies, and colonial administrations around the world. At the same time, the capital gains from consols have created significant private wealth, which, along with the economic boost from increased government spending, have provided a huge part of the financing for our innovations in technology and industrialization."

"Other nations would love to copy this model of financing, but only our country has been able to implement it, thanks to our unique record of political stability and sound management of the national debt," Sheffield pointed out. "As one of our top stockjobbers, Mr. Ricardo functions as a middleman to ensure a smooth and constant market on which to buy and sell these vital bonds."

"Our mathematical calculations can be of enormous help to him in setting his prices and running these trades quickly and profitably," said Cordelia.

"Then let us get back to work," said Raven

"Before you do so, I have some other information to report." Sheffield altered his stance, his demeanor turning more serious. "Ricardo has close contacts with many of the prominent traders and bankers who do business internationally, and he gets constant updates on what is going on across the Channel."

His lips pressed together for a moment. "I have just learned from him that when Napoleon reached Grenoble, he walked unarmed toward the soldiers assigned to arrest him and bared his breast, telling them to shoot him if they thought he was the enemy. Instead, the soldiers threw their allegiance to him and joined his march on Paris."

Cordelia swore under her breath.

"The next day, Napoleon and his troops encountered Marshal Ney, who had been dispatched by the French king with a force of six thousand men to arrest the former emperor and bring him to Paris in an iron cage," continued Sheffield. "Ney mutinied, as did his troops."

"You must be sure to visit Charlotte later today and tell her these details. She may wish to use them in creating her next drawing," said Cordelia. After a fraught pause, she added, "Do you think Napoleon will march into Paris unopposed?"

"I think it quite likely. As does Ricardo." Sheffield blew out his breath. "My most important news is that he told me the government is already making discreet inquiries about financing a much larger loan than anticipated for this year."

"Because causing countless deaths and the devastation of a continent does not come cheaply," intoned Cordelia with bitter irony. "Heaven help us."

"I am loath to count on divine intervention," said Sheffield. "If utter disaster is to be avoided, I think the task is going to fall to us mere mortals."

CHAPTER 22

A week passed in a blur of activities as the family adjusted to their new member. One of the first priorities had been arranging for the purchase of pigeon squabs and a suitable home for the baby birds.

"Careful, careful," called Wrexford as he and Tyler, helped by two of the household's sturdy grooms, maneuvered a large octagonal-shaped wooden dovecote up the last flight of stairs with only a few muttered oaths and carried it out onto the roof.

"Is there a certain spot that would be best?" he called to Eddy, who was busy exploring the walkways and parapets.

Closing her eyes, she raised her face to the sky and slowly turned in a full circle before pausing.

Wrexford wondered what forces she could sense that eluded his own understanding. As a man of science, the question intrigued him.

"The west corner, please," she answered.

He waved the groom on and then went to join his sister. "How did you decide?"

"The squabs told me." Eddy shuffled the pasteboard box in

her arms, and he could hear the faint rustle of straw and high-pitched peeps from within it. "I think . . ." She cocked an ear. "I think they like it here."

"Excellent," he replied, feeling an odd rush of happiness that the baby pigeons had given the townhouse their blessing. Now, if only the stranger by his side would come to think of it as home.

A smile—the first spontaneous one he had seen from her—lit up her face. "It's a splendid dovecote!"

"Indeed, it is," he agreed. The oiled cedar shingles, mellowed to a rich shade of cinnamon, had a number of snug-looking nest openings, and the peaked slate roof was topped by a gilded wrought-iron finial designed to glow like a homing beacon when it caught the sunlight.

"Thank you, sir!"

"Wrex," he corrected softly.

"Sorry." Eddy swallowed hard. "Thank you . . . Wrex."

He wondered why she had such trouble with saying his name but decided that it wasn't a pressing question for now.

"Is there anything else you need?"

She shook her head. "Hawk and Peregrine kindly offered to gather the material I need for fashioning nests and bring it here." Hearing the echo of their voices in the stairwell, she added, "They seem . . . nice."

"Aye, that they are." Wrexford noted the omission of Raven but again let the matter pass without comment. Only a fool would imagine that a new gear added to the already complex construction of their family would spin along without a few bobbles and squeaks. He would deal with them in due course.

"Mac found all the materials you need," announced Hawk, racing around a turn in the parapet and skidding to a halt. "Can we help build the nests?"

Eddy hesitated. "They aren't something that can just be thrown together willy-nilly. There is a precise method, and it has to be followed very carefully."

"I would like to learn, " he replied.

"As would I," added Peregrine. "We're good at listening and following directions."

"Indeed, they are quick to comprehend instructions," assured Wrexford. "And they pay attention to details."

"Very well." Her voice held a note of reluctance, but Eddy gave a gruff nod. However, she hung back as the boys hurried to the dovecote with their boxes.

"M-May I ask you a question?"

"Of course," he answered

"Will you take me riding tomorrow in Hyde Park, before m'lady and Lady Peake take me on another round of shopping for necessities? I—I miss it."

"I would be delighted to do so! Miss O'Malley told me you're very at home on a horse." Wrexford was pleased by the request . . . until the next words came out of her mouth.

"May I ride Lucifer?"

Damnation. The boys had reported on the stallion's strange reaction to Eddy's presence, but he had taken it with a grain of salt. The surprise of discovering a girl in the mews had likely jumbled their normally sharp observation skills.

"Lucifer is high-strung and skittish with anyone other than me," he began.

Her chin rose a notch. "Don't worry, I can handle him."

"I admire your pluck, Eddy. But why don't we begin with a less temperamental—"

"Lucifer isn't temperamental!" she exclaimed. "He simply needs to know that his rider is a kindred spirit."

The retort rendered him momentarily speechless. *How to respond?*

"My mother was a renowned horse trainer," added Eddy. "She had an unworldly gift for communicating with animals, and I appear to have it, too. I've never met a horse I can't ride." Her jaw clenched and unclenched. "But clearly you don't wish to believe me."

"I . . . I am not doubting your word, Eddy. As a man of science, I am simply acting on empirical evidence," explained the earl. "I have seen with my own eyes how Lucifer can turn into a veritable devil when a stranger attempts to approach him. I can't in good conscience allow you to risk serious injury—"

"Why don't you let me prove it?" she challenged. "If he shows the least bit of agitation when I approach his stall, I won't ever ask you again to ride him."

Wrexford saw no way to refuse. "Fair enough." He made a face. "Though I confess that I'm having great difficulty imagining Lucifer submitting to a sidesaddle."

Eddy's grin pinched to a look of horror. "B-But I always ride astride!"

"You will not be doing so in in London, and I'm afraid that's not negotiable," he said gently. "I understand how distressing it must be to find your life changing in so many ways—though I hope you will quickly come to be happy with a number of them."

He heard her draw in a ragged breath and felt his heart clench.

"I have been warned that the beau monde—Moreen has told me that is what aristocratic society is called—has all sorts of cursedly stupid rules," she said.

"I don't disagree," responded Wrexford. "However, there are ways of navigating the rules, and things will not be as onerous as they might seem at this moment." He knew nothing about her past life, but he sensed it had been unconventional.

Was she old enough to understand what he was about to say next?

Wrexford decided to try. "Life always demands compromises, no matter who you are. The key is to pick and choose which battles to fight."

Eddy swallowed hard. "B-But how?"

"By letting your brother and your sister-by-marriage help

you learn to steer a course through the rocks and shoals of Society," replied Wrexford. "For example, when we go to the privacy of our country estate you may ride astride and gallop neck and leather. But here in London, it can't be done."

"I don't think I'm going to like being a member of the beau monde," she grumbled.

Wrexford smiled. "Perhaps we could both keep an open mind about the challenges ahead?"

Her tight-lipped scowl softened to a reluctant twitch. "I suppose that's fair enough."

After watching her walk away, Wrexford forced his attention away from family matters, feeling a prickling of guilt over doing nothing to pursue Obsidian Eyes. As for Elias Fogg . . .

Hurrying down the stairs and out to the street, he quickly made his way to the Sheffield residence, and heaved an inward sigh of relief at finding his friend in his study.

Sheffield looked up from the pile of ledgers on his desk. "How is family life going?

"I must have bats in my belfry, but we now have a dovecote filled with pigeons on the roof."

That drew a chuckle.

"But I'm here on more serious matters," Wrexford added. "I paid a visit to my friend Norwood at the Home Office the other day to ask him more about Elias Fogg . . ." He explained about his suspicions and the comment Duxbury had made about Fogg's occasional contact with Grentham's office.

"Norwood mentioned that he had heard through idle gossip that Fogg appears to have a penchant—some might call it an addiction—to high stakes gambling, though he takes great pains to keep it quiet."

"A subject with which I am all too familiar," murmured Sheffield, who had once had his own problems with such risky behavior.

"That's why I'm hoping you can help."

"Of course." His friend straightened in his chair. "What do you need me to do?"

"Make some inquiries and find out whether Fogg has a problem. If he does, that may make him vulnerable to blackmail," replied the earl. "You likely know the places that cater to a high-ranking gentleman who depends on absolute discretion."

"You think he may be working with the French operative you call Obsidian Eyes?"

"The fellow seems to have known too much about our government's interests and my occasional involvement in investigations not to have a contact somewhere in the highest levels of decision-making."

"Bloody hell," muttered Sheffield. "I'll report back as soon as I can."

Wrexford gritted his teeth to keep from barking out a warning as Eddy approached Lucifer's stall for their first ride in Hyde Park the following morning. The Weasels had assured him that she had indeed cast a magic spell over the temperamental stallion. But seeing was believing . . .

Assuming the big black beast didn't bite her nose off.

"These cursed skirts might upset him," she muttered. "I don't see why—"

"I am asking that you trust me regarding the rules of Society," he replied. "Just as you are asking me to trust you regarding Lucifer."

Eddy paused to think about that. "You're saying that we both have to take a leap of faith?"

"Friends trust each other. And I am very much hoping we can be friends, as well as family."

She looked up at him, her solemn blue-green eyes achingly similar to those of his father. "I . . . I would like that as well, sir."

"Wrex," he urged.

She dropped her gaze. "Yes. Sorry."

Lucifer blew out a low snort but remained unnaturally calm.

Wrexford decided to press her. "Is there a reason you have trouble calling me something other than 'sir' or 'milord'?"

She swallowed hard. "M-My mother had unconventional ideas about a great many things. Names were one of them. She insisted I call her 'Ala' and . . ."

Her voice faltered.

"And our father 'Wrex'?" he guessed.

Eddy shuffled her boots, setting off a crackling of straw.

"I've heard what some of our servants said about me when they thought I wasn't around. It's questionable whether I have any legitimate right to claim I'm his daughter."

"I have absolutely no doubts about that—you have his eyes and his smile." He crouched down and pulled her into a hug. "You are my sister in every way that matters. As for the tattle-mongers, you leave them to me."

She shyly circled her arms around his neck.

"If 'Wrex' is too fraught with memories, please call me 'Alex.' Or any other moniker you wish to choose."

"I—I don't really remember a lot about him. I was very young when he died," she admitted.

"Then perhaps 'Wrex' is a nice continuum," he suggested. "Because of our difference in age, I am somewhere between a father and a brother."

Eddy leaned back, a pensive look shading her face. "Perhaps you're right."

"Think about it," he suggested, then quickly rose. "Now, let us get down to brass tacks. Prove to me that you're capable of winning Lucifer's trust."

Eddy smiled and began to sing.

The stallion pricked up his ears and came to gaze at her over the stall gate. With a shake of his head, he let out a soft whinny. She moved to greet him, caressing his velvety nose while she continued her Gaelic song.

"I'll be damned," whispered Wrexford. After unlocking the connecting gate, he took the stallion by the halter and led him out into the mews.

Eddy walked by Lucifer's side, ruffling her fingers through his mane.

"You've proved your first point, imp," he said with a grin as he drew to a halt in front of the tack room. "But let us see what he thinks of a sidesaddle."

Her smile was no longer looking quite so confident.

But to the earl's surprise, after showing a quick flash of bared teeth, the stallion submitted to the indignity with docile good grace. He quickly replaced the halter with a bridle.

"Up you go." He gave her a leg up into the saddle, then hurried to fetch his own mount from one of the grooms, who was keeping a careful distance from Lucifer.

"Keep him at a sedate walk until we reach the park," ordered Wrexford, after assuring himself that she looked relaxed and comfortable atop the muscled stallion.

"And you, you had better be on your best behavior, you big devil," he added to the stallion, "or you'll answer to me."

Lucifer snorted in impatience to be off.

"Let's not dawdle," said Eddy, handling the reins with consummate skill. "Lead the way!"

"Raven?" Day had long since faded into night and Cordelia frowned, wondering whether it was merely a quirk of the muddled shadows in the parlor. "*Raven*?"

He shot up from his slouch in the armchair by the unlit hearth, blinking the sleep from his eyes.

"Good Heavens, I thought you went home hours ago!"

"I—I wanted to keep working on these equations," he answered, quickly shuffling the jumble of papers in his lap into some semblance of order. Over the last fortnight, he had become a bit of a fixture at the Sheffield residence. "I feel that I'm getting close to some insight, but it's proving damnably hard to pin down."

"Don't say *damn*," responded Cordelia. "We wouldn't want Wrex and Charlotte to think we are encouraging you to form bad habits."

"I know a lot worse words than *damn*," he replied.

"Say one of them in this house and I'll wash your mouth out with soap," she warned.

That made him grin. "You can try. But first you would have to catch me."

A chuckle tickled in her throat as Cordelia lit an oil lamp and placed it on the side table next to the burned-down stub of Raven's candle. "Is there a reason you don't wish to return home?" she asked gently.

He looked away, his features hardening to a brittle sharpness. "We're doing interesting work here. I don't much care for mucking about with baby birds."

"We could bake them in a pie," called Sheffield from the corridor.

"Kit!" she huffed, spearing him with an exasperated look.

"Just a little jest to lighten the moment, my love." He, too, looked as if he had been hard at work. His coat and cravat had been discarded, and the sleeves of his linen shirt were rolled up to bare his forearms. As he took a sip of brandy from the glass in his hand, winks of light from the cut crystal facets illuminated the smudges of ink on his fingers.

"Mac would have to make a very good sauce," observed Raven. "Otherwise they would taste horrible—they're naught but skin and bones."

"That's *not* funny." She waggled a finger at both of them. "That Eddy has a passion—and a special gift for it—is not a subject for mockery."

Raven ducked his head in contrition. "I'm not mocking her. We're just . . . different."

"Differences are what make life interesting," said Sheffield. "Look at me—I was a mindless fribble, and Cordelia was a brilliant problem solver. I didn't make a very good first impression, but she showed both patience and kindness in answering a rather dumb question I asked on card-playing and probability—"

"Actually, it was a rather insightful question." She smiled. "I realized then and there that you had a brain in your cockloft, you just had to be encouraged to use it."

"My point is," he said to Raven, "opinions can change if you keep an open mind."

"I'm not sure I'll ever warm up to the birds," muttered Raven.

"I wasn't referring to the birds, Weasel." A pause. "And you damn well know it."

Cordelia rolled her eyes, but before she could snap a retort, the sudden *rap-rap* of the knocker on the front door echoed in the corridor.

"Who could that be at this hour?" she wondered.

"The servants have all retired, so I shall go and see," said Sheffield. "It's probably Wrex, looking for the errant fledgling."

Raven shifted uncomfortably in his chair.

The sound of voices, too muddled to make out the words, drifted back to the parlor.

However, when Sheffield returned, it was not the earl who accompanied him but rather a tall, reedy gentleman with a long face dominated by a Roman nose and a genial smile.

CHAPTER 23

It was late, and while the rest of the house was settling into slumber, Charlotte leaned back in her chair and took a moment to savor the quiet solitude of her workroom.

The past few days of shopping had passed in a flurry. Acquiring a wardrobe befitting an earl's sister, along with all the countless little accessories and furbelows to go along with the new clothing, had proved particularly daunting. Eddy had shown remarkable poise and fortitude in submitting to the whirlwind even though it was clear that most of the purchases were not to her taste.

Charlotte grimaced on recalling Eddy's expression on being shown a feminine riding habit.

Thank heavens the shopgirl had not heard the muttered expletive.

However, Wrexford's sister—Charlotte was still getting used to that thought—had not uttered a further word when she and Alison agreed that the garment should be added to the pile of other clothing being packed up for delivery to Berkeley Square.

Thankfully, several visits to Gunter's for ices after the shopping ordeals had proved more relaxing. Eddy had unbent enough to giggle in delight at her first taste of the frozen confections.

"I hope that I shall soon see a good many more expressions of spontaneous happiness," she said to herself. Eddy was too young to be so serious.

"How are things progressing?" McClellan eased the door open and came in. "Things have been so hectic around here lately that we've not yet had a chance to have a good gossip about how Eddy is settling in." She set a tray on the side table by Charlotte's work desk. "I brought you some tea." A pause. "Or should I have brought whisky?"

"I'm not sure," confessed Charlotte. "Alison and I accomplished our task of assembling the basics for her new position as Wrexford's sister. But I can't tell what she thought of the experience. As with her brother, it's not easy to read her emotions." A sigh. "Actually there have been several positive moments. She seems thrilled with the dovecote, she clearly enjoyed Gunter's, and when I asked whether she would like to stop at Hatchards and see if they had any books on pigeons, she readily agreed and found three to her liking."

"It bodes well for fitting into this family that she likes to read," observed McClellan after passing Charlotte a cup.

"I hope so." Charlotte took a sip of her tea. "I plan to take her to see the Tower Menagerie soon, and I'll ask Hawk to come along. It seems a good idea to have her spend some time with each of the boys individually, rather than in a group. That way she can form a personal friendship with each of them."

The maid looked down, but not quite quickly enough to hide the skeptical twitch of her brows.

"What are you not telling me?"

"Nuffink," said McClellan with a wry grimace, imitating Hawk's tendency to mispronounce *nothing* when he was hiding something.

Charlotte didn't laugh.

"I may have misinterpreted his meaning," added McClellan, "but Raven stormed out of the house earlier, and I happened to overhear him muttering some very bad words in the same breath as Eddy's name."

"Good Lord." She put her cup down. "I shall refrain from using foul language myself. But only by exercising great restraint." After releasing a sigh, she added, "How on earth did they come to butt heads?"

A sympathetic chuckle resonated in McClellan's throat. "I've no idea. But for now, I would refrain from comment and see if the two of them can work out their differences."

"Sage advice," said Charlotte. "However, I can't help but worry. Raven is more complicated than Hawk or Peregrine, who both have sunny dispositions. He's carried such weighty responsibilities from a tender age. He broods over things."

"That's not necessarily bad," pointed out the maid. "Wrexford also broods over things. And then he uses his incisive logic to parse through the problem and comes to a practical way to solve it."

"I suppose you have a point," she mused. "Raven's mathematical skills show that he possesses an analytical mind and knows how to use it. But at his age, emotions are not as clearly defined as numbers. I hope . . ."

Charlotte closed her eyes for an instant. "But, as I assured Wrex, we shall somehow manage to deal with our new family's demands, along with—"

"Countering a nefarious plot that threatens our country?" McClellan gave a wry chuckle. "But of course we will."

"Mr. Ricardo!" Cordelia shot up out of her chair to greet their late-night visitor, looking a little flustered.

"I apologize for intruding at such an ungodly hour," he said, gesturing for her to be seated. "But you've both mentioned that you are often working late at night, so I took the liberty of seeing whether I might catch you up and about."

Raven had also jumped to his feet and was hurriedly combing his fingers through his unruly hair, trying to flatten the worst of the spiky tufts.

"I take it this young man is our new recruit," said Ricardo after exchanging pleasantries with Cordelia.

"Yes, sir." Raven bobbed a very creditable bow. "Thomas Ravenwood Sloane at your service."

Cordelia pressed her lips together to hold back a smile.

"I've reviewed some of your mathematics, Master Sloane. It's very impressive work."

"T-Thank you, sir. But I have so much more to learn," stammered Raven.

"I have a secret to share with you." Ricardo lowered his voice to a conspiratorial whisper. "So do I."

"And I," added Sheffield. He held up his glass. "May I pour you a brandy?"

"That would be quite welcome—if you're all sure that you don't mind the interruption," said Ricardo. "I was taking a walk just now, as I find the activity helps me focus my thinking, and a few things have come to mind. I would find it useful to discuss them with you."

"We would, of course, be honored, sir," replied Sheffield after a glance at Cordelia and Raven. "But I worry that we are not nearly conversant enough in the intricacies of finance to be of any help."

"As you will see, I'm seeking your counsel on a rather larger issue than any financial specifics."

Sheffield moved to the sideboard and quickly poured a measure of brandy for Ricardo. "Then please make yourself comfortable, sir. I assure you that we are all ears."

Cordelia gestured for Ricardo to take the armchair she had just vacated, and both she and Sheffield settled themselves on the facing sofa.

Raising his glass in salute, Ricardo smiled. "Let me begin with an update on current political and financial events. This will give us some context for what I want to propose as next steps in working together."

Ricardo paused to take a sip from his glass. "We must, of course, talk of Napoleon. As you know, I have various well-placed sources who keep me informed on the latest news, both here and across the Channel. Financial markets do not exist in a vacuum. Politics, economic forces, social unrest, military threats — in the blink of an eye, a shift in the status quo can cause major fluctuations."

Cordelia frowned. "I imagine that Napoleon's march to Paris is already causing uncertainty for the market."

"Napoleon has already been in Paris for several days," said Ricardo. "And has reseated himself on the throne without opposition."

"Good Lord," intoned Sheffield. "We all have anticipated such news, but still, it's a shock." He swallowed hard. "You are quite sure of this? There was no such report in today's newspapers."

"Yes, I am quite certain of the information."

"S-Surely that news will affect the London Stock Exchange," ventured Cordelia.

"Indeed, it will. Especially as our government will have no choice but to raise an extremely large amount of money to fund the coming military conflict—for I see no way that war can be avoided," said Ricardo. "Napoleon's only hope for staying in power is to strike quickly, before Britain can reassemble an Allied Coalition to oppose him, and force a decisive battle over the raggle-taggle army that Wellington will have under his command. Then he can negotiate from a position of strength."

His gaze turned troubled. "I imagine he will demand to be recognized as ruler of France in return for a promise to refrain from further military action."

Ricardo allowed a moment for his words to sink in. "But this is getting a bit ahead of events. Let us return to what is actually happening at this moment."

Sheffield glanced at the others and then gave a grim nod.

"First, it appears we all agree that this news will create further uncertainty in the market and hence push government consol values down," continued Ricardo. "So far prices have declined somewhat but have held up reasonably well in the face of all of these events, behaving exactly as I anticipated. The latest news, however, will put more downward pressure on prices and make it harder for the government to raise the enormous new loan it will need to defeat Napoleon's grandiose ambitions."

Ricardo took another sip from his drink. "So, our first task is to do what we can to prevent the government debt market from declining too much more. A decline can quickly turn into a total rout."

"Can we do that?" asked Raven. "Surely that must be awfully difficult."

"We can only do so much," Ricardo conceded. "But given that I am by far the leading stockjobber in government debt—the average volume is £50,000 per year, while mine is about £1,000,000—the prices at which I buy and sell consols help set the overall market prices for the securities. So I can help stabilize their price by offering a generous bid for what I will pay for them."

Cordelia grimaced. "That could become *very* expensive. And if the value of consols drops precipitously despite your efforts . . ."

"You're exactly right," he acknowledged. "But the calculations you and young Master Sloane perform will be very helpful in that regard. They will tell me a great deal about what I can offer to pay for consols, as well as how many of them I can afford to hold—and for how long. If we are careful and watch our timing, I think we can both help our country by stabilizing prices . . ."

A fleeting smile touched his lips. "And come out quite well financially in the end."

It was Raven who grasped what Ricardo was implying. "Does that mean you are considering putting together a consortium to bid on the annual loan for the government so we can thump Napoleon, sir?"

"Yes," responded Ricardo. "I am beginning to give the new loan some serious thought. It poses certain great difficulties . . ."

His lips compressed for a moment. "However, let us put that aside for now. I want to raise something else, which is the real reason why I decided to bother you at this late hour."

Ricardo's voice took on a troubled edge. "Your reactions and experience will be invaluable to me."

"But of course," said Sheffield, after a perplexed glance at Cordelia. "Please go on."

"I have been thinking about what you confided to me the other day," began Ricardo. "That you and Lord Wrexford investigated—and disproved—rumors that the French had developed an electrical telegraph was very important to the government because it was feared that if such rumors went public, it would cause panic here in London, which would quickly spread throughout the country."

"Yes," replied Sheffield tersely. He turned to Cordelia and Raven. "Wrex agreed that I could pass on that information. Given Mr. Ricardo's inside knowledge of the complex forces at play both here and abroad, it seemed wise for him to be aware of that piece of the puzzle."

"As it turns out," said Ricardo, his gaze taking on a martial glint, "I am now quite certain that your telling me about the threat of a destabilizing rumor is a critical piece of information."

He drew in a deep breath. "Because it hints that something even more dangerous is in play."

* * *

Charlotte extinguished the Argand lamp on her desk and took up a candlestick to light the way up to her bedchamber. Her drawing for Mr. Fores was finally done, but still feeling a bit too restless for sleep, she changed her mind and headed downstairs to see if the earl was still in his workroom.

"You must be tired from trudging around all the various shops on Bond Street," said Wrexford. He was sitting by the hearth, perusing a map of the Low Countries. "I know how much you dislike shopping."

"A little," she admitted. "Eddy seems no more eager than I am to spend endless hours oohing and ahhing over fashion plates and fabrics." A sigh. "I take that as a good sign."

"Perhaps I should take her to my tailor for a riding coat and breeches."

"Mention that at your own risk," warned Charlotte. "She will likely take you seriously."

He chuckled. "I think you're right."

Relaxing with some lighthearted banter felt good for the spirit after all the whirlwind activities of getting Eddy settled. She saw the map in his lap but decided to ignore it.

Reality would rear its ugly head soon enough.

Instead they talked of mundane things—summer plans for spending time in the country . . . perhaps a trip north to the Lake District so that the Weasels and Eddy could explore the natural beauty of the rugged hills . . . a visit to Charlotte's brother and his family.

"We should also discuss a trip to the estate in Yorkshire," she ventured, even though the mention of where his late father had chosen to live after his sons had left home would stir uncomfortable emotions.

"You mean that we should make a thorough search for an official document affirming that my father married Eddy's mother—assuming that it exists," responded Wrexford.

"We need to know, and the sooner, the better," said Charlotte. "So that we may plan how to deal with . . . whatever the truth turns out to be."

"I assume that Miss O'Malley has already searched every conceivable place," he pointed out.

"Miss O'Malley may have known your father well, but not in the elemental way that you did," replied Charlotte. "You may think of meaningful places to him that wouldn't occur to her."

A nod conceded that her instincts might be right. "When the current threat to our country is resolved," he said, "we will turn our full attention to the challenges that lie closer to home."

Several moments passed in silence as Ricardo appeared to be putting his thoughts in order before continuing. "I'm convinced that Napoleon and his operatives created their diabolically clever telegraph rumor with the ultimate aim of spreading fears on the London Stock Exchange that the French possessed an instrument of great military significance. Such fears were designed to panic investors . . ."

He paused. "And destroy our government's ability to raise money to fund the coming war."

"Do you really think—" began Cordelia.

"Yes, I do," said Ricardo. "Let me remind you of a little recent history concerning the Stock Exchange. Early last year, a group of speculators had built up an enormous position of government consols, purchased almost entirely on credit, expecting prices to rise. However, the French suddenly had unanticipated military successes on the Continent, causing the consol prices to fall sharply."

"Oiy, that makes sense," said Raven. "Good news for the French is bad news for us."

"Correct," said Ricardo. "The loans that the speculators had taken out to buy consols were coming due shortly, and they faced enormous potential losses. But then suddenly, an alleged aide to a British general in Europe arrived, claiming Napoleon had been killed in battle and the monarchy restored. The same news was also trumpeted by three men dressed as French royalist officers who drove around the city, claiming that they were on their way to 10 Downing Street to inform the prime minister." He allowed a pause. "The price of consols shot up twenty percent in a single day."

"I vaguely recall hearing about that," mused Cordelia. "But the news seemed to die down rather quickly."

"Well, the truth of the matter is that Lord Cochrane, a Member of Parliament and a celebrated naval hero, was one of the speculators involved in creating the false rumor, and so the whole miserable plot was hushed up as much as possible. Cochrane was jailed for a year and now is abroad, apparently commanding the Chilean and Brazilian navies in their wars of independence."

"It's frightening that consol prices would rise so quickly and so dramatically on an unsubstantiated rumor," muttered Sheffield.

"Exactly my point," Ricardo responded. "It doesn't take much to set off huge price fluctuations if rumors are permitted to take hold."

"Bloody hell." Sheffield shook his head. "We spent a great deal of time unraveling the hoax about the telegraph but were flummoxed in trying to figure out exactly why it was attempted."

He paused for a moment. "Wrexford was a bit surprised that Grentham's agents came into possession of the Laplace-Ampère letter so easily."

"The letter was a rather clever touch," said Ricardo. "As long as our government believed that an electrical telegraph might exist, they were not in a position to correct any market rumors about the French having developed such an important new military innovation."

"But then Mr. Boyleston was murdered!" Raven suddenly

interjected. "Not because his scientific paper was going to reveal that he had developed a telegraph, but rather because it was going to reveal that he had not!"

"Quite right, lad," said Ricardo.

"Clearly an elaborate plot of misinformation to upset British financial markets has been in play," reasoned Cordelia. "But Napoleon was rather busy planning his escape from Elba and then marching up from southern France during these events. So who was orchestrating all of this?"

"Does the name *Gaudin* mean anything to you?" responded Ricardo.

Cordelia and Sheffield exchanged puzzled looks.

"Ummm . . ." Raven cleared his throat. "I—I seem to recall that A. J. Quill did a drawing about a brilliant French finance minister who was invaluable in creating clever ways for Napoleon to pay for his wars." Another cough. "Wasn't his name Gaudin, sir?"

"Indeed it was. You clearly have an eye for detail and an excellent memory, Master Sloane." Ricardo looked thoughtful. "I confess, I was slightly skeptical when Mrs. Sheffield asked if you might join us working on our project. But now I understand why she said you would be a major asset."

"So again," said Cordelia, "if this electrical telegraph hoax was all a massive misinformation campaign by the French designed to upset our financial markets, isn't the threat now over?"

"Far from it, I'm afraid," replied Ricardo. "I rather doubt that anyone as clever and skilled in intrigue as Gaudin would have only one arrow in his quiver. I'm sure he has other alternatives planned for disrupting the market and making it impossible for us to finance a war against Napoleon."

"Dare I hope that you have some ideas on how to counter his nefarious plans?" inquired Sheffield.

"Yes, I do." Ricardo responded. "It may not be easy, given

the example of the sophisticated telegraph plot. I've seen how rumors can develop quite quickly, causing downward pricing spirals and engendering yet more rumors."

Seeing their alarmed expressions, he quickly added, "I have some specific suggestions as to how we can be on the alert for any market misinformation—and my efforts at price stabilizing can perhaps buy us extra time to quash them before the market spirals into chaos."

The room seemed to shiver with silence as the momentous threat to Britain's finances sunk in.

Ricardo gestured at Cordelia and Raven. "And I will need your mathematical assistance to help determine how we can form a syndicate to float the new government loan."

"Doing both those things presents a daunting challenge," observed Sheffield.

"Indeed," agreed Ricardo with a confident smile. "But I would venture to guess that we're all very good at overcoming challenges."

Wrexford added a chunk of coal to the banked coals in the hearth and poured himself another glass of Scottish malt. Though the spring equinox was not far off, a lingering chill still tinged the evening air.

"Getting back to our present conundrums, I stopped by Bow Street and spoke with Griffin about aiding us in the search for the man you call Obsidian Eyes," said Wrexford. "He thinks he can convince the magistrates to allow him to take up the case, at least for a short while, without any official request from the Home Office."

"Let us hope that Griffin can help us track him down." A shadow skittered over Charlotte's face. "I can't help but feel unsettled by the fact that such a dangerous operative is still at large. He's a threat to us and our family."

"He's a very dangerous fellow," agreed Wrexford. "But his

interest in sending us to our Maker was to keep our government from learning that the technology for an electrical telegraph doesn't exist. My sense is that we're no longer of any importance to him."

When she didn't react, he quickly moved on to his more pressing concern.

"I've been thinking more about Elias Fogg. Kit is following up on the rumors of his gambling for high stakes, which might have made him vulnerable to blackmail."

"You think he could be a traitor?" asked Charlotte.

"I think someone high up in the government is. The French seem to know too much about our activities and vulnerabilities for my liking." Wrexford glanced at his bookshelves. "Which is why I would like you to ask Alison to do a little research into his family background."

"She'll be pleased—" began Charlotte, only to shoot up out of her chair at the sudden clatter of running steps in the corridor. "The Weasels are up in their eyrie!"

Wrexford was almost at the door when Raven burst into the room—and ran straight into his arms.

"Hell's teeth, you gave us a fright," barked the earl after catching his breath. "Where the devil have you been?"

"With Lady Cordelia and Mr. Sheffield," answered Raven in a rush. "Discussing the London Stock Exchange with Mr. Ricardo!"

Wrexford frowned in puzzlement. "At this hour?"

"An idea occurred to him while he was out taking a walk, and he wished to discuss it," answered Raven. "But never mind why Ricardo was there—I mean, that was important, but not the most important thing . . ." An impatient wave as he gulped in a lungful of air—

"Slow down, sweeting," counseled Charlotte. "You're not making any sense."

"Then allow me to help Raven explain," said Sheffield, who

had refrained from sprinting to keep up with his companion. "Thanks to the astute eye of David Ricardo, I think that we have finally cut through all the confusion caused by the elaborate feints and subterfuges created by the French—"

"And discovered what the Frogs are really intending to do!" crowed Raven.

Charlotte and Wrexford listened in stunned silence as Sheffield recounted Ricardo's suspicions about a French plan to manipulate prices on the stock market, making it impossible for the government to raise a new loan.

"For what I have heard, Ricardo is both brilliant and not prone to jumping to conclusions, so I suppose we must accept his analysis." Wrexford released a troubled sigh. "Heaven help Wellington. A financial crisis will doom his undermanned army to certain defeat by Napoleon."

"Take heart," said Sheffield. "Ricardo is going to think over the situation tomorrow—and come up with a plan to beat Gaudin and the French at their own game."

CHAPTER 24

"You're up at the crack of dawn." Charlotte pushed back the coverlet and sat up in bed.

"Eddy enjoyed our ride so much yesterday that I wanted to take her out again." Wrexford finished knotting his cravat. "Not only is it best to head off at an early hour in order to have a good gallop, but the timing also works out well for my other plans for the day."

He pulled on his boots. "Given what we heard last night, I wish to speak with Colonel Duxbury at Horse Guards, as well as an acquaintance on the prime minister's privy council who may be willing to tell me of any clandestine French activity here in Town."

Charlotte rose, and after donning her wrapper, she fetched his riding gloves from his dressing room. "It's a lovely morning. I shall take that as a good omen."

He smiled. "The time together on horseback with Eddy is the perfect way for us to get to know each other. She's a neck-and-leather rider and possesses great pluck and spirit. Seeing her let down her guard and laugh as the wind tugs at her hair gives me great hope that she'll be happy here with us."

"It's interesting how often black clouds have silver linings," she observed.

Wrexford paused to press a quick kiss to her cheek. "You have a special gift of seeing the best in any situation."

She brushed an unruly curl back from his brow. "We are fortunate beyond measure to have each other and our loved ones. I don't intend to let anyone take that elemental joy away from us."

"Nor I," he murmured.

Another kiss.

"Now, I had better be off. Luckily, Eddy is an early riser and will be on the roof tending to her birds." The earl pulled on his gloves and headed for the stairs leading up to the roof.

Clad in her night-rail and a thick woolen wrapper, her copper-tinged curls shimmering in the soft sunlight, Eddy was just finishing her inspection of the dovecote's nest holes as he rounded the corner of the stone parapet.

"The squabs are almost ready to test their wings!" she announced.

"Indeed?" He crouched down beside her. The little birds no longer looked like awkward puffs of thistledown as their feathers had replaced the downy fluff. "That's exciting. You must show me how you begin their training."

"I didn't think you had any interest in pigeons."

"I have an interest in anything that's important to you, Eddy. Taking joy in each other's passions is part of the bonds that tie a family together."

She clucked softly to one of the squabs who poked its head out of its nest before answering. "I heard Raven tell Hawk and Peregrine that my birds were smelly."

"Have you ever invited him to see them?"

"I didn't think he would like them," muttered Eddy.

"In science we call that making an assumption about the final results before we test them—which isn't a very reliable method if one is seeking the truth."

"You think I should . . ." Her voice trailed away.

"I think you should think about it—but later." He tucked a lock of hair behind her ear. "I came up here to see if you wished to take a ride in Hyde Park before I head off to some meetings."

Wrexford rose. "If so, you'll need to change quickly, so that we'll have ample time to explore the trails up near the Cumberland Gate."

"That would be splendid! I'll be ready in a trice!" Eddy nearly tripped on the hem of her night-rail as she sprang up and darted off for the stairs.

Smiling to himself, the earl made his way down to the mews and saddled Lucifer. His own mount—he had sent one of the grooms to fetch his Spanish-bred hunter from Wrexford Manor— was already waiting impatiently by the courtyard gate.

"Behave yourself," chided Wrexford as the black stallion laid back its ears and snorted what was likely an equine insult at the other horse. "Sombra runs like the wind, and if you get his dander up, he just might beat you."

"Ha, don't count on it!" said Eddy from behind him. She whispered something unintelligible to Lucifer before rushing past him.

"Just a moment." He reached out to properly fasten the chin strap of her shako riding cap.

"It's far more fun to feel the wind in my air!" she protested, and then heaved a sigh. "Yes, yes, I know it's the rules." A sniff. "But I dislike it immensely."

He laughed. "I'm aware of your sentiments. That won't make the rules go away."

She bit back a grin. "Give me a leg up, Wrex, and we'll soon see who is fastest, hat or no hat."

They headed down Mount Street and entered the park through the Grosvenor Gate. The hour was still early, and the area was deserted. The beau monde favored the popular "Rotten Row," a section of the old King's Road that was considered the most fashionable place to ride.

Wrexford drew his horse to a halt. "Up ahead, the way forks. We can either go left, which leads through some wooded areas, or head to the right, where the trees soon open up to some rolling meadowland."

As Eddy studied the terrain, the earl heard a rider approach from the rear and was relieved to hear the sound of hoofbeats head north. He didn't wish to share this peaceful interlude with a stranger.

"Right," announced Eddy, "which I daresay doesn't surprise you. Of course I wish to gallop hell for leather, and that's best done over meadowland."

"Be forewarned, you're too good a rider for me to give you any quarter."

Her laugh kindled a sweet warmth in the center of his chest.

"Let's see if Lucifer and I are up to the challenge," she replied.

"We must take it slowly through this short stretch of the woods. The exposed tree roots can be dangerous for horses."

The bridle path was just wide enough to allow them to ride abreast, and the earl took the opportunity to ask her a few more questions about her pigeons and their upcoming training.

"They seem to like London despite the smoke and filth," she began. "So I don't anticipate any trouble . . ."

As they rounded a tight turn, Wrexford saw a man dressed in dark-hued riding clothes and a wide-brimmed beaver hat up ahead. He was standing in the middle of the bridle path and gave a friendly wave.

"Eddy, drop back behind me," he ordered softly. Perhaps he was overreacting, but something felt wrong, and his experience in the Peninsular War had taught him to trust his instincts. "Now, and without argument."

"Lord Wrexford, how nice to see you." The man's voice was

smooth as ice—and all too recognizable. "And your charming sister."

He reined to a halt. The tangle of trees pressed in tightly. There was no room to maneuver and attempt to flee. "Your business is with me," he said to Obsidian Eyes. "Let the girl go."

"That would be the honorable thing to do," agreed the French operative as he cocked his two pistols in mock salute. "But by now you must realize that I haven't got an honorable bone in my body. It's a concept for fools and weaklings."

Against a less experienced killer, Wrexford gauged that he might have had a chance to spur forward and knock the man down.

"What do you want?" he asked softly.

"Your life, of course. However, before I deliver the coup de grâce, I need to coax some information out of you regarding who else is helping you with your investigation. And your sister is going to help me do so."

Lucifer suddenly began an agitated dance, snorting and stomping, his iron-shod hooves kicking up clots of earth.

"Settle the horse," barked Obsidian Eyes.

"I—I can't," wailed Eddy, sounding on the verge of hysterics. "I'm t-t-too frightened."

The French operative took a step forward—only to stop short.

Wrexford heard it, too. The sound of a horse coming toward them from the opposite direction at a fast pace.

Obsidian Eyes hesitated, but for only a heartbeat. Keeping careful aim on the earl, he darted back into the trees.

The earl's first impulse was to give chase. However, reason quickly reasserted itself. His sister—

He whirled around in the saddle.

"What a damnable knave!" Eddy regripped her reins—Lucifer had ceased his antics—and squinted into the trees. "I don't suppose we can go after him?"

Reassured that she was not about to fall into a swoon, Wrexford whipped out his pistol and turned to face the oncoming threat.

"Milord!" Slipping, sliding, a lathered horse came to a halt in a cloud of dust as its rider waved a hand in greeting. "Do put away your weapon. Surely you're not still holding a grudge against me."

"I ought to be, von Münch," growled Wrexford, though he did put his pistol back in his pocket. "Why is it that when *you* appear, Trouble always seems to follow?"

"You wound me, sir. In this case, the order was reversed," replied von Münch. "The fellow who just accosted you is far more troublesome than I am." He gave an apologetic shrug. "Sorry. I misjudged where he meant to set up his ambush, else I would have warned you sooner and avoided the unpleasantness . . ." He gave a glance at Eddy. ". . . for your sister."

"As to *that*," began the earl.

"Yes, yes, we'll discuss that and a number of other things when we return to Berkeley Square," interjected von Münch. "Given that we are old friends, you *are* going to invite me to return with you so that I can pay my respects to Lady Wrexford, aren't you?"

Wrexford reluctantly gestured for his so-called friend to join him and Eddy.

"It is a pleasure to make your acquaintance, Lady Eddylina," added von Münch with a graceful bow.

How the devil does he know her name?

A foolish question, decided Wrexford, given the secrets-within-secrets that lurked inside von Münch's maddeningly oblique mind.

Eddy responded with an uncertain smile.

"Are you enjoying the city?" he inquired. "Given your interest in birds, you really must visit the Tower of London and meet its famous ravens."

Eddy's eyes lit with interest. "Why are they famous?"

"Ah, now that's a fascinating story. Allow me to regale you with it while we ride back to Berkeley Square . . ."

"Herr von Münch!" Charlotte rushed down to the drawing room on hearing the news of his arrival from McClellan. Unlike the earl, she had confidence that his show of friendship and loyalty in the past were not a sham.

But still . . .

"Where the devil have you been?" she demanded, after giving his hand a welcoming squeeze.

He winced but quickly covered it with a smile. "My abject apologies, milady. I truly meant to be here sooner but was detained by circumstances that were out of my control."

It was only then that she noticed the half-healed burn marks on his palms.

"Elba?" she guessed. In their last meeting with von Münch in the previous autumn, he had admitted that he was not the Royal Librarian to the King of Württemberg—his claimed persona when she and Wrexford had first crossed paths with him—but was actually a clandestine operative for the kingdom's crown prince, tasked with working with other like-minded allies to preserve the hard-won stability of Europe after years of war.

A nod confirmed her surmise. "The night of Napoleon's escape—" he began, but paused as Wrexford joined them.

"Eddy appears unrattled by the attack in the park," he announced. "Indeed, she's far too curious about how we're going to pursue the dastard and bring him to justice." Wrexford made a face. "However, I think I managed to put off further questions, at least for now."

Turning to von Münch, he added, "*You* have a lot of explaining to do. How did you know—"

"Let us discuss that later," counseled Charlotte. "I've asked Mac to send a note to Alison, asking her to come immediately and keep Eddy occupied with an afternoon of shopping and a visit to Gunter's for ices." She turned to their friend. "Herr von Münch was just beginning to tell me about Elba. We need to hear what happened."

The earl gave a curt nod.

"The night of Napoleon's escape, Grentham's lieutenant, George Pierson, attempted to prevent the brig *Inconstant* from leaving the island with the former emperor and a force of his Imperial Guards."

Dropping his gaze, von Münch appeared to be studying the pattern of the Axminster carpet beneath his boots for a moment or two before continuing. "In the confusion and mayhem that occurred on the docks that night, there was an explosion on one of the other ships," he recounted before turning to the earl. "I'm aware that you're acquainted with Pierson, milord. I regret to inform you that it appears he perished in the flames."

"I'm sorry to hear it," said Wrexford. "I wouldn't go so far as to say we were friends, but we had a mutual respect for each other."

"He was a good and honorable fellow. He will be missed," intoned von Münch. "*In absentia luci, tenebrae vincunt.*"

"In the absence of light darkness prevails," murmured Charlotte, translating the Latin aphorism.

"Our flames are still flickering," pointed out the earl. "Dare I hope that you've brought some good news to go along with the bad?"

Charlotte suddenly noted that beneath the stubble of unshaven whiskers on von Münch's face were more scrapes and burns.

She took his arm. "Come, sit."

He allowed himself to be led to the sofa and sank into the pillows with a grateful sigh. "In answer to your question, milord, I know you are concerned about whether the French have a working electrical telegraph, and I can assure you that they do not. After the disaster on Elba, I headed straight to Paris. Pierson had told me of your government's grave concern over whether the French possess such a messaging system—"

"I already know that they don't," interrupted Wrexford.

"How did you come to be so certain?" asked von Münch.

"One of my contacts in Paris has firsthand knowledge of the experiments that Ampère, France's leading scientific luminary in electricity, is conducting and confirmed that the development of an electrical telegraph is still in the theoretical stages. But as far as I know, nobody here in London knows that."

"Actually, we, too, found someone with firsthand knowledge of experiments in creating an electrical telegraph," said Charlotte, and proceeded to explain about Francis Ronalds.

"Extraordinary," exclaimed von Münch. "Think of how that technology will revolutionize the world when its time comes!"

"In good and bad ways," remarked the earl. "As with all momentous inventions, progress can be a two-edged sword."

"Which is why all responsible citizens must be vigilant to ensure that the wonders of science are not used for evil purposes," responded von Münch.

"Human nature is such that the battle between Good and Evil is never-ending," observed Wrexford. "Let us hope we can find a way to win this particular clash, because while we've dodged the bullet concerning an electrical telegraph, we suspect that there's an even bigger plot to throw Britain into chaos."

"So that's why Le Loup is in London," mused von Münch.

Wrexford's brows rose in question. "Le Loup?"

"The fellow who just attacked you," said von Münch. "Le Loup—which translates to The Wolf—is Napoleon's most cunning operative and is only used for the most important assignments."

"We're aware of his ruthlessness, but we didn't know his actual name," said the earl. "He tried to kill us during our visit with Francis Ronalds—"

"We also know that he murdered an agent of the French king and a leader of the French émigré community here in London," added Charlotte.

"Hmmph." The information caused von Münch to frown. "From what I have heard, he is not normally used as an assassin. Indeed, it surprised me that he tried to attack you just now in broad daylight. His skills are in orchestrating treachery and deception. But then, Napoleon's top henchmen are spread rather thin these days, what with all the chaos they are intent on creating."

He lapsed into a long moment of thought. "Have you any idea as to what his ultimate objective is here in London?"

"Money," replied Wrexford. "As an old adage says, *Money is the root of all evil.*"

"What Wrex means is that the man you call Le Loup is part of a French plan to manipulate prices on the London Stock Exchange and destroy our government's ability to raise funds to rebuild our army, leaving us at the mercy of Napoleon," explained Charlotte in a rush. "He's been creating diversions to keep our government's attention elsewhere while Napoleon's former finance minister—a man by the name of Gaudin—creates financial havoc."

"Bloody hell, that's very bad news," whispered von Münch. "Gaudin is considered brilliant."

"Yes, but the renowned financier David Ricardo is considered even more of a financial genius," replied Charlotte. "And as he's serving as the general for our side in this battle, I'm not ready to concede defeat."

CHAPTER 25

Hawk shimmied back into the schoolroom from the narrow ledge outside the window. "Aunt Alison's carriage just rolled into Berkeley Square."

"Something havey-cavey happened this morning," mused Peregrine. "Maybe we can winkle the details out of Eddy."

"Oiy." Hawk's mouth pinched in a scowl. "Wrex and m'lady have been huddled with Herr von Münch for most of the day." A sniff. "It seems to me that's in violation of the House Rules. When Raven returns—"

"Shhh!" Peregrine held up his hand for silence. "I think Eddy is coming up the stairs."

Woof. The sound of steps roused Harper from his slumber by the hearth. He raised his shaggy head and pricked up his ears.

Woof. A louder one.

The soft *swoosh* of skirts brushed over the corridor floor, followed by a tentative knock on the door.

Harper rose and nosed it open.

"Lady Peake thought you would like some Pontefract cakes," said Eddy, holding out a bulging paper sack.

"Huzzah, huzzah!" exclaimed Peregrine, for a moment forgetting about the mystery as Hawk accepted the treats. "Heh, heh—Raven had better hurry home or there won't be any left."

Eddy frowned in puzzlement at their obvious glee. "What are Pontefract cakes?"

"Licorice confections!" chorused both Weasels.

A blank stare. "What's licorice?'

"It's made from the root of the flowering plant *Glycyrrhiza glabra*, a member of the bean family Fabaceae," explained Hawk.

She crinkled her nose. "That sounds disgusting."

"Suit yourself." Hawk popped a confection onto his tongue and emitted a blissful sigh before passing the bag to Peregrine—who crammed two discs of licorice into his mouth and began chewing.

"You're welcome to try one," offered Hawk as he reached for another piece.

Eddy hesitated.

"Feel free to abstain!" said Raven, hurrying into the schoolroom. "All the more for us!"

Hawk grinned and tossed him a confection.

Reacting with lightning quickness, Raven plucked it out of the air, spun it between his fingers, and was about to take a bite when suddenly he paused.

"You really should try a taste," he said to Eddy. He held out his hand, the Pontefract cake cupped in his palm.

"It's . . . black." She made a face. "Ewww, I've never eaten anything black before."

"All the more reason to try it," replied Raven. "Wrex and m'lady have always encouraged us to test our preconceptions, because we might find ourselves pleasantly surprised."

Eddy didn't miss the hint of challenge in his voice. Drawing in a deep breath, she accepted the offering and took a tiny bite.

The other two Weasels waited expectantly.

A sputter. And then a horrible gagging sound.

"Hell's bells—fetch her some water!" cried Raven.

The gagging gave way to a giggle. "Just jesting," she said with a sticky smile.

"That's *not* funny," he retorted, but a grudging grin tugged at the corners of his mouth.

"It's actually delicious," added Eddy. "Thank you for sharing."

"Have another," said Hawk. "And then, you really need to tell us about what happened this morning in the park."

"So, what's our next move?" asked von Münch, once Charlotte and Wrexford finished the lengthy explanation of all the twists and turns the investigation had taken, ending with the revelation that David Ricardo had cleverly spotted what the French were planning.

"For the moment, nothing," answered the earl. "Starting tomorrow morning, Sheffield and Cordelia, aided by Raven—who, as you know, has a special gift for mathematics—will begin working with Ricardo to counter the French attack and effect their own manipulations of the stock market to keep our country financially stable. Until they have specific marching orders for the rest of us, I'll keep on trying to learn where Le Loup has his lair."

Wrexford explained about his suspicion that the French operative had an informant within the highest circles of the British government. "Sheffield is making some inquiries. I am doing so as well."

"I, too, can seek information from my contacts here in Town," mused von Münch.

"Might I also ask you to accompany my wife and my sister on a visit to the Tower Menagerie tomorrow? After all it was *you* who suggested to Eddy that she would enjoy seeing the legendary ravens." Wrexford shuffled his feet, the weight of the pistol in his coat pocket a grim reminder that danger shadowed their every move. "I wish to visit several of my acquaintances at Horse Guards to learn more about Wellington's situation in Brussels and would prefer that they don't go alone."

"Of course. I would be delighted to do so," replied von Münch. To Charlotte he added, "Shall I come around after the nuncheon hour?"

She nodded.

"I look forward to—how do you English say it?—having a comfortable coze with you, milady."

"With you, nothing is comfortable," muttered the earl.

Repressing a smile, von Münch rose stiffly. "I shall do my best to change your mind on that. However, now, if you don't mind, I am going to take my leave and get some sleep."

"Where are you staying?" inquired Wrexford.

"Don't worry, milord. I promise you haven't seen the last of me."

"An incident this morning in the park?" croaked Raven as a piece of licorice suddenly stuck in his throat. After swallowing his surprise, he looked at Eddy. "I—I thought you went out riding with Wrex."

"Oiy," answered his brother. "She did."

"And when she and Wrex returned, they were accompanied by Herr von Münch," added Peregrine. "Wrex and m'lady were closeted with him in the drawing room for over an hour before he left."

"Who *is* Herr von Münch?" demanded Eddy, noting that the name sparked a flash of alarm in Raven's eyes. "He seems a very pleasant fellow, and yet . . ." She hesitated, letting her words trail off.

"He's an old family friend," answered Raven.

"Then why doesn't Wrex seem to like him?"

"Oh, gentlemen are wont to engage in friendly banter," responded Peregrine. "Think nothing of it."

Eddy didn't appear convinced, but Raven quickly turned the conversation back to Hawk's original question. "Don't keep us in suspense. What happened during your ride with Wrex?"

"As we made our way through a wooded part of the bridle path, a man with two pistols stepped out to block our way—"

"What did he look like?" demanded Raven.

"Hard to say. His face was in shadow—he may have been wearing a cloth pulled up over the lower part of his face—and he was dressed in dark clothing with no distinguishing marks." She thought for a moment. "He was broad-shouldered and about Wrex's height." A fleeting frown. "And he had an aura of evil. Lucifer didn't like him at all."

"You're very observant," murmured Hawk.

Eddy shrugged. "Doesn't everyone pay attention to their surroundings?"

Seeing the Weasels surreptitiously glance at each other, she narrowed her eyes. "What are you not telling me?"

"Nuffink!" answered Hawk.

"We're just surprised that a footpad would be so bold as to attempt to rob a member of the beau monde," added Raven quickly.

"It wasn't a random robbery," said Eddy. "Wrex ordered me to drop back behind him when he spotted the man. Between the rustling of the trees and the restlessness of our horses, I could only catch occasional snatches of their exchange. But from what I did hear, the man appeared to know Wrex."

She tucked an errant lock of hair behind her ear. "Even odder, he knew my name, too."

"Weren't you scared?" asked Peregrine.

Eddy scrunched her face in thought. "No, I was more angry than frightened. He was pointing his pistols at Wrex, and now that I had finally met my brother, I . . . I didn't want to lose him."

"The encounter is very puzzling," said Raven, after shooting the other Weasels a warning look. "But I'm sure Wrex will pursue the matter. In any case, there's nothing we can do about it. Save, of course, to stay alert and do our best to keep out of trouble."

"Oiy," chorused Hawk and Peregrine.

"I thought you boys had more spunk than that," she muttered.

Before they could respond, McClellan poked her head into the room and shook a warning finger at the four of them. "No more sweets! Supper will be served shortly."

Harper raised his head and flashed his teeth.

"You'll be eating in the kitchen with me, as Wrex and m'lady are going to dine with Mr. and Mrs. Sheffield."

Raven scrambled to his feet. "Don't bother setting a place for me. I think I'll go along with them."

"Absolutely not," retorted the maid. "Since your name was not included in the invitation, you will be staying here and enjoying our scintillating company, along with my beef and mushroom stew."

Raven blew out his breath, along with a very bad word.

McClellan raised her brows. "I'll pretend I didn't hear that."

"I'm not hungry," countered Raven. "I'm going to stay here and work on some of the mathematical equations mentioned in the book that Mrs. Sheffield gave to me."

"Suit yourself. Just as long as you don't *subtract* yourself from this house," said the maid dryly.

CHAPTER 26

The next morning's gold-flecked sunlight brought a welcome warmth to Berkeley Square, the first tantalizing sign that spring would soon begin to blossom. Raven's mood was considerably brighter as well, as Charlotte roused him from his slumber to tell him that work on countering the French attack on Britain's financial stability was going to begin immediately.

"The Sheffields will call for you in their carriage shortly and head on to Mr. Ricardo's business establishment," she said as he blinked the sleep from his eyes. She pointed to the bundle of clothing that she had just placed on the side table. "Mr. Ricardo sent Kit the official uniform of a Stock Exchange messenger boy. Apparently, your presence on the trading floor will be a great asset."

He was up in a flash.

"Give your face and hands an extra scrub, and be sure you've no dirt under your fingernails. It's important to look somewhat respectable," counseled Charlotte as she unfolded the drab iron-grey jacket and matching pants. "And do run a comb through your hair." She held up a black cap that matched the color of the horn buttons on the jacket. Embroidered on its front in grey thread was the monetary symbol for a British pound. "This is also part of the uniform, which suits our objectives very well. The less the crowd at the Stock Exchange sees of your face, the better."

Raven hurried through breakfast while Eddy was up on the rooftop feeding her pigeons and threw open the front door before Sheffield could reach for the knocker.

"Let's not dawdle, sir!" he said, descending the front steps two at a time. "The sooner we get to work on spiking Napoleon's guns, the better."

Ricardo's office was on Nicholas Lane, just south of Change Alley and the Capel Court entrance to the London Stock Exchange. Located on the top floor of a nondescript brick building, it was a modest set of rooms, whose one distinguishing feature was a bank of tall casement windows in the main room that gave an expansive view of the River Thames as it wound its way past the Tower of London.

"I thought it would be bigger," intoned Raven, "and grander."

There looked to be only a single employee, who appeared so engrossed in his work that he didn't look up from the reams of papers and ledgers on his desk in the adjoining workroom.

"Welcome, welcome," said Ricardo as he stepped out from a tiny office at the end of a short corridor. "Sorry to disappoint you, Master Sloane. Establishments like the East India Company look to impress their clients with a fancy headquarters filled with opulent riches and numerous minions, but I prefer to let my work speak for myself."

The rapid-fire scratch of a pen moving over paper was audible in the fleeting moment of silence that followed.

"Plain and simple suits me and my assistant just fine," added Ricardo. "Come, allow me to introduce you."

He moved to the doorway. "Put down your pen for the moment, William, and come greet our new colleagues." To the others, he said, "Allow me to introduce William Arthur Wilkinson, who is the eldest son of my wife's brother. However, the real reason he is here is because he deserves to be."

"I hope you don't mind working with a woman, Mr. Wilkinson," said Cordelia, with just a hint of a challenge edging the question.

The young man smiled. "Not all, madam. Perhaps the most important lesson that I've learned from my uncle is to be open-minded and willing to see beyond the strictures of conventional thinking. He says you are brilliant, and I very much look forward to learning from you as well."

"It takes courage to go against convention," said Cordelia, meeting Ricardo's gaze.

A shadow seemed to pass over his face, but it was gone in the blink of an eye. "I'm not afraid to make unconventional choices, Mrs. Sheffield. They are not always easy, but when you follow your inner beliefs, they aren't frightening."

He allowed a moment to pass before continuing, "However, as you know, unconventional thinking concerning women and their abilities does not rule at the Stock Exchange, so alas, you will have to stay here and work with William while your husband and Raven accompany me there."

She nodded in understanding.

"I told Lord Wrexford that I trust William wholeheartedly," added Ricardo, "and he agreed with me that keeping him in the dark about the challenge we face might cause him to miss a tiny but important clue as we watch the fluctuations of the market."

"That makes great sense," agreed Cordelia. She shrugged off her cloak. "Please show me which desk I should use, Mr. Wilkinson, and then let's all get to work."

As they headed back down to Nicholas Lane and began the short walk to their destination, Ricardo gestured for Raven to keep pace with him and Sheffield. "Seeing as this is your first plunge into London's financial world, lad, allow me to give you some background on what you're about to experience."

"I, too, will welcome that information," said Sheffield. "I confess, based on my previous visits, it all seems a bit . . ."

"Chaotic?" suggested Ricardo, and added a chuckle. "It takes some getting used to, but there is a surprising amount of underlying order beneath all the habble-babble."

Sheffield replied with a skeptical grimace. "I will take your word for it."

"When the Stock Exchange building on Capel Court was completed in 1802, a more formal governing structure was also created. Management, regulation, and direction of all concerns was given to a committee of members chosen by ballot annually," began Ricardo. "The building itself was run by nine trustees and managers, who were separate from the management committee. The daily hours of operation were set at ten in the morning to four in the afternoon. Now, as to the physical layout of the building, I shall describe it in detail because it's important for both of you to know your way around once we begin our work in earnest. There are four entrances in addition to the main one in Capel Court, including a passageway through the Hercules Tavern."

He chuckled. "The landlady makes a tidy sum controlling who may pass through it. Mendoza's boxing rooms are also next door. I have known some stockjobbers to take out their frustrations on having a bad day by heading to the ring and engaging in fisticuffs with each other."

After crossing Lombard Street, he turned left before continuing. "When we reach Capel Court, you'll noticed a crowd of men loitering in Change Alley, jostling and shouting out offers to help with buying and selling securities. They are informal traders. Only those men who have been approved by the managing committee and paid their annual fee—there are approximately five hundred members—are permitted to do business inside the Stock Exchange. These others seek to attract unwary investors—usually inexperienced individuals from the country-side dreaming of getting rich quick."

As they turned into Change Alley, the loiterers spotted Ricardo and dropped their jabbering to a respectful tone.

"Any tip fer us today, Your Nibs?" called one wag.

"Yes," answered Ricardo. "Cut your losses and let your profits run."

A round of guffaws greeted the advice. "Would that we had your luck in doing that!" shouted another trader.

"It's not just luck," said Ricardo softly, quickening his steps before returning to his explanation of the Stock Exchange. "On entering, you'll see a large clock on the south wall. Under it is a tablet listing defaulters who have not made good on their purchases."

"Public shaming," observed Sheffield.

"Something that has worked for centuries," observed Ricardo. "To the left side of the entrance doors there is a house officer—a fellow dressed in a gold-trimmed navy robe and military-style hat—who stands on a podium and watches over the crowd to make sure that decorum is maintained. On the opposite side is a recessed area—there are many such spaces around the perimeter of the large trading floor—housing the Commissioners for the Redemption of the National Debt. Two long lines of Ionian columns run the length of the room on either side of the main trading floor. Well-known traders have their regular spots by these columns. You both will learn all that quickly."

"Do you have a spot, sir?" inquired Raven.

"Yes, indeed I do. Though I make a point of circulating through the room quite frequently while one of my associates remains there to transact simple buy-and-sell requests."

He gestured upward. "Above the trading floor is a gallery that runs around the perimeter of the building. It's crammed with desks and manned by clerks who are kept busy with the helter-pelter pace of business. When someone needs a reference book or ledger, they simply shout out from the floor and a clerk tosses it down to them."

After returning the greeting of several gentlemen passing in the opposite direction, Ricardo continued his explanation. "An official price list is published each day and can be located at a central podium. These days, the Stock Exchange lists British funds as well as Irish funds, American securities, and shares in bridges, roads, and iron railways."

He paused to give Raven a quick pat on the shoulder. "Traders use the official prices as guidelines. They are free to negotiate their own deals, which can become quite complicated if the transaction includes a bundle of different securities. All trades must be recorded on a slip of paper, and that's where your job comes in—messenger boys are constantly on the fly, collecting the slips from various traders and delivering them to the recording clerks stationed around the trading floor."

Ricardo lowered his voice. "Lord Wrexford and Mr. Sheffield have told me that you are quite skilled in surveillance—I did not ask them why—so as you join the fray and work with my other lads in doing all those vital tasks for me, it would be very useful for you to keep your ears open and keep track of who is selling large amounts of securities and at what price."

They began walking again and quickly reached the front entrance. "Now, enough of my jabbering. It's time for Master Sloane to see things for himself."

Ducking her head to the gust of wind tugging at her bonnet strings, Charlotte moved to a quiet corner of the Tower Menagerie's battlements and rested her elbows on the ancient stone as she gazed out at the River Thames.

"A penny for your thoughts," said von Münch, taking up a position beside her.

"Even if they were for sale at any price, I'm not sure quite where to begin," she replied.

His lips quirked. "That's entirely understandable. So much of our world is in flux right now, the very earth feels as if it's constantly shifting beneath our feet."

He, too, turned his eyes to the river, watching the sails of wherries and lighters dip and dart through the wind-ruffled water of the ebbing tide. "Don't worry, milady, I'm quite confident you'll keep your equilibrium."

She released a pent-up sigh. "You have more confidence in me than I do."

Rather than respond to her uncertainty, von Münch turned his attention to the far end of the battlements, where Hawk and Peregrine were watching in awe as one of the famous Tower ravens circled Eddy with a flapping of its dark wings and raucous chorus of *quorks* before taking a perch on her shoulder.

"Eddy is an extraordinary young lady," he said. "That she possesses the worldly experience of someone far older than her tender years will make her a perfect fit for your family."

Charlotte wondered if he knew the real story about Raven and Hawk. The thought sent a tiny shiver down her spine. No secret seemed safe from von Münch, and much as she liked him, Wrexford's doubts about the fellow's ultimate sense of loyalty had stirred her own niggling concerns.

"How did you know about her?"

He looked back to the river, and after several long moments slid by, Charlotte decided he wasn't going to answer.

At least not truthfully.

Secrets within secrets. Perhaps subterfuge had become such a way of life for him that the Truth was too entangled in shadow to ever be allowed to see the light of day.

"It's rather complicated," said von Münch.

"Wrexford would have expected exactly that answer—or

rather non-answer—from you," replied Charlotte. "While I hoped for something more befitting of our friendship."

Her remark caused an odd flicker of emotion to flit over his features. "Like His Lordship and you, milady, I must do my best to balance a number of complicated relationships whose needs do not always align. I regret that some of my actions may have led you to believe that our friendship is based on expediency, rather than true regard."

She studied his face, wanting very much to believe he was sincere.

"I was about to elaborate on my opening words. With your permission, might I continue?"

A nod signaled for him to go on.

"I met Aladeen O'Meara—or rather, the Countess of Wrexford—twelve years ago, just as it was becoming clear that the Peace of Amiens was not going to last much longer. As an Irishwoman, she had little love for the British government but even less for the French regime. Several members of her mother's family had married into the French gentry and were sent to the guillotine during the Reign of Terror," recounted von Münch.

"Are you saying that Eddy's mother was involved in some clandestine mission for the Crown?" whispered Charlotte.

"Actually, she liaisoned with a friend of mine, a top intelligence operative from the Kingdom of Württemberg. The two of them had met at the horse auctions that take place during the racing season at Newmarket."

"Why on earth would your country reach out to her?"

"Her father was a famous breeder of magnificent horses, as was Aladeen," he replied, "and it so happened that she and her father had a very influential longtime client with a large estate in Brittany, whose cousin was Marshal Ney, commander of Napoleon's Grande Armée. Our operative convinced her to use her charms to learn more about French intentions. Knowing if and when Napoleon planned to break the peace treaty meant that we could pass the information on to British military commanders so that their forces wouldn't be caught off guard if war began anew."

He paused. "I think she agreed to do so because she knew from your father that Wrexford and his younger brother planned on military careers."

Yet another surprising revelation. Charlotte was still trying to make sense of it all when von Münch cleared his throat with a cough.

"Just so you know, I wasn't aware of all this when we first met at the end of last summer. A chance encounter with my friend during the autumn led to reminiscences about the past, and he mentioned the Wrexford name. I recalled hearing you mention something about a mysterious letter to the late earl from someone identified only as 'A,' so I made further inquiries."

"Which means you were aware of the relationship when last we met but held back the information."

"Guilty as charged," admitted von Münch. "I wanted to be sure of all my facts. I had begun to uncover hints that a child existed, and it seemed both reckless and unkind to toss that bombshell into your life if it wasn't true."

"But you did discover the truth," mused Charlotte.

"Just before I was required to rush to Elba. And then there was a further delay . . ."

Charlotte nodded in understanding. "Yes, the whole world, not merely my family, seems to be turning upside down."

A moment of companionable silence settled between them, and then she suddenly frowned in thought. "Brittany—Aladeen visited Brittany approximately twelve years ago . . . Eddy is twelve years old . . ."

A spark of hope stirred in her chest. "Miss O'Malley mentioned that she thinks the late earl and Ala were married on a trip to Brittany. She assured me that she had been shown proof of the marriage, but it appears to have gone missing. It seems likely that it went down with Ala when her ship sank in a storm."

Charlotte shook her head in sadness. "Without it, Eddy's future is complicated. Wrexford could, of course, contrive to cover up the lack of an official document, but there are deep moral consequences to that."

She made a face. "I wonder how many churches there are in Brittany?"

"There are over one thousand chapels," said von Münch softly. "In Finistère, the northwest corner of the region where Ala's client had his estate, Celtic myth and Catholicism often intertwine, creating an unconventional blending of religion."

"That seems a likely place to start looking,"

He nodded. "Perhaps when the current troubled times are behind us, you and His Lordship can do some exploring in the area."

"Yes," she agreed. "Th-Thank you for all this information."

"No thanks are necessary," interjected von Münch. "It goes without saying that friends help friends."

"Wrexford will also be grateful," she stammered.

A chuckle. "Actually I think he'll be rather annoyed. He prefers to consider me a knave and a scoundrel."

A hoot of laughter drew their attention to Eddy and the boys. The Tower raven had snatched Peregrine's hat and had been joined by several feathered friends in playing a game of passing it back and forth.

A singsong order from Eddy brought the hat plummeting back to earth, and with a farewell *quork-quork*, the ravens flew off.

"It's turning chilly," observed von Münch as he offered his arm. "Shall we fetch Lady Eddylina and the boys and head back to Berkeley Square?"

CHAPTER 27

Wrexford sighed after hearing Charlotte's report of all that von Münch had learned regarding Eddy and her mother. "I suppose I must admit that you are a better judge of character than I am." He looked up. "But don't repeat that to von Münch."

Charlotte turned away and began straightening the books on his work counter to hide her smile.

"Speaking of whom," he added, "I trust you encountered no trouble during your trip to the Tower Menagerie?"

"Save for a trio of larcenous ravens who stole Peregrine's hat for an interlude, all went exceedingly well. Eddy was enchanted with the legendary birds," she answered.

"I daresay she had an interesting conversation with them." The rational part of his consciousness continued to rebel against any ideas that held a whiff of mysticism. But scientific curiosity countered such thoughts. Wrexford reminded himself that the finest scientific minds in Britain—Faraday, Brunel, Hedley, and the young Francis Ronalds—didn't yet understand such powerful forces of the cosmos as electricity and magnetism.

So it was best to keep an open mind.

"She did," confirmed Charlotte. "The ravens felt a malignant force is stirring. They warned her to be alert for trouble."

"I wonder if she could ask them whether they've seen a tall, broad-shouldered Frenchman with a hitch to his gait in Town," he said dryly, "and if so, where his hideaway is."

"I don't think that they converse in such straightforward language," replied Charlotte, a note of wry humor shading her words.

"A pity," he responded. "The birds have been cosseted and treated like royalty for centuries. One would think they could do something useful to earn their supper."

Their light banter was interrupted by Raven, who appeared in the doorway of the adjoining library, now dressed in his usual well-worn clothing. "I slipped in through the scullery and changed out of my uniform, so that Eddy wouldn't see me and ask any uncomfortable questions about my activities."

"Wise thinking," said Wrexford. "How did the first day go?"

Raven gave a nonchalant shrug, but the earl noted the gleam of boyish excitement in his eyes. "It's all hustle and bustle, and the babble of voices is so deafening that it's a wonder that any of the traders can hear themselves think."

A grin twitched at the corners of his mouth. "Actually, I found it very interesting. Mr. Ricardo quickly taught me the basics of my job and then had me accompany him as he made the rounds of his regular trading partners, introducing me as a new addition to the messenger boy contingent. However, we're going to be careful that I'm not seen as his shadow but merely one of the many scamps who run errands for him. That way, it will be easier for me to flit around without drawing notice."

"I suppose it's too early to ask if the French have taken any further steps to throw Britain's financial markets into chaos."

"Mr. Ricardo says we must be patient," said Raven. "For now he's analyzing stock purchases and sales to see if he can discern if any trading patterns are out of the ordinary."

"Time is of the essence," muttered Wrexford. "I've just heard from my contact at Horse Guards that Russia, Prussia, and Austria have agreed to each mobilize 150,000 men to help our present Anglo-Dutch army in Brussels fight Napoleon. But because of their petty bickering at the Peace Conference in Vienna, they are dragging their feet on getting their forces to move. It's uncertain whether any of those reinforcements will reach Wellington before Napoleon decides to move east and strike while he has the advantage."

"Oiy, Mr. Ricardo is well aware of that," replied Raven. "He seems to have a full understanding of what information, both real and false, is circulating through the Exchange and driving trading." He patted back a yawn. "Come tomorrow, Mr. Sheffield and I will be at the Stock Exchange at the opening bell and see what more we can learn."

"My sense is that there is some downward pressure on bond prices now the fact that Napoleon has entered Paris and seized power is common knowledge," confided Ricardo on meeting with Sheffield and Raven the following morning on a side street near Capel Court. "The decline is not yet alarming. People are understandably nervous over the news from France. However, I shall keep a close eye on things. There are always everyday rumors and innuendos which cause market fluctuations, but they usually correct themselves. What we're looking out for is an elaborate web of falsehoods and deceptions which will be difficult to counter and cause major volatility in the market."

"I imagine the government will be looking to quickly raise a huge amount of money in order to finance any coming conflict," said Sheffield. "The last thing it can afford is a market in chaos because of misinformation."

"Correct," said Ricardo. "Whatever Gaudin has up his sleeve will be elaborate and carefully crafted. Remember, it took Lord Wrexford weeks to track down the truth about the telegraph hoax—and he knew what he was looking for. I'm certain that the French will be exceedingly clever in spreading multiple layers of misinformation in the market to misguide traders. And once rumors or false information take hold, it can set off a panic."

"H-How do we stop him?" queried Raven.

"You'll be of help in spotting trouble, lad," answered Ricardo. "As you make the rounds to collect sales slips of the various transactions made by the traders on the floor who are working with me, I want you to loiter by the other major stock-jobbers and listen for information on their business. I'll also send you to the clerks on the upper gallery with routine documents, giving you a chance to ask questions. It's natural for a new boy to be curious about the Stock Exchange. If you hear anything out of the ordinary, come tell me immediately."

Ricardo's usual smile had given way to a far more solemn expression. "We have to stay alert at all times. The trading floor can be a volatile place. Rumors can spark a selling frenzy. So we must be prepared to improvise."

He eyed Sheffield. "However, for now, we simply want to be ready to stimulate sales if the downward trend continues, in order to to keep the market stable. As one of the major stock-jobbers, I can give favorable deals to fuel interest and spread word through the grapevine that I deem it a good time to find profitable investments."

Sheffield nodded in understanding. "Your word alone will have a great deal of influence."

Ricardo consulted his pocket watch and then clicked the case shut. "The Exchange will open in precisely two minutes. Let us head to the main entrance and get to work."

The next week, however, proved uneventful. Trading remained within its normal fluctuation patterns, and the activity was calm enough that Ricardo sent Raven home early each day so that he could continue to work with Cordelia on the mathematics for computing complicated interest rates. However, Charlotte had made it clear that she wouldn't allow his involvement with the stock market demands to interfere with his regular schoolroom studies, so for the moment, the townhouse at Berkeley Square was settling back into its usual routine.

"My pigeons are done with trying out their wings on the rooftop and have completed the short training flights from the gardens and the mews area back to their nests. They are now ready to make their first real test of finding their way home," announced Eddy as she entered the breakfast room on the morning of the next lesson day for the Weasels. "I was thinking that perhaps I could take them to Hyde Park later today. It's just the right distance for their next big challenge."

"That's very exciting." Wrexford looked up from his newspaper. "I am meeting with Herr von Münch later today, and we have several meetings to attend. However, I shall arrange to meet him at the Stanhope Gate, so that I can accompany you for the testing before we head off."

"I can manage on my own if you are too busy," said Eddy.

"I'm never too busy to help you with your projects," he answered. "Besides, for the time being, I don't want you to go anywhere unaccompanied."

She looked about to argue, but then merely nodded. "I—I understand."

"We would be happy to help transport the carrying boxes," offered Hawk, and then darted a quick look at Charlotte before hastily adding, "assuming, of course, that the training trip can be made after our lessons with Mr. Lynsley are done."

Charlotte regarded the earl and raised her brows in question.

"Yes, that will be fine," he responded.

"Speaking of Mr. Lynsley . . ." Eddy crumbled a bit of toast between her fingers. "I was wondering . . . that is, might it be possible for me to join the lessons? Moreen was very good about tutoring me, but when I listen to the Weasels talk about geography and history and . . ."

She hesitated for a fraction. "And mathematics, it all sounds so interesting, and I would . . . I would like to learn more about the subjects."

"Why, I think that's a splendid idea," exclaimed Charlotte. "I have always been of the opinion that a female ought to have the chance to be as well educated as a male."

"But I would only wish to do so if the Weasels don't object to my presence," Eddy added.

Hawk bit his lip and shot a surreptitious glance at his brother.

Raven, who was studying a series of scribbled equations in his notebook as he ate his porridge, looked up after Peregrine gave him a discreet nudge.

"What?"

Peregrine quickly whispered something in his ear.

"Of course you are welcome to join us." Raven made a face. "Why wouldn't you be? But just so you know, Mr. Lynsley gives us a *lot* of extra work to do between our lessons, and he doesn't tolerate any excuses."

"I don't mind schoolwork," answered Eddy.

"Ha! Be careful what you wish for," mumbled Raven, who had already turned his attention back to his equations.

"I will speak to Mr. Lynsley this morning about beginning the new arrangement," said Charlotte. "I will also ask if he would be available for some private lessons. That way he can understand where you are in your studies, and perhaps provide some extra tutoring."

Eddy flashed a grateful smile. "Thank you, m'lady. I look forward to that!"

Hawk and Peregrine looked at each other and made gagging sounds, which earned them a stern rebuke from McClellan as she brought in a basket of freshly baked rolls.

Eddy hurried through the rest of her meal and rose to excuse herself. "I wish to do a last check that all is well in the dovecote before we set out for the park."

She was halfway up the stairs to the rooftop when the sound of steps behind her caused her to turn.

"I—I was just wondering . . ." said Raven. "Would you mind if I come along with Hawk and Peregrine to help with transporting the boxes?"

"I thought you didn't like my smelly birds."

"They're not quite as smelly anymore," he replied. "I would like to see them in flight." A pause. "Will they really find their way home from the park?"

"Absolutely," answered Eddy.

"*How?*"

She smiled. "We don't really know. They seem to have great visual memory and learn to recognize their surroundings quickly. However, that doesn't explain their ability to find their way home from distant locations. There is clearly some unknown guiding force in the cosmos—perhaps some strange compass-like power that we humans can't sense. But I haven't a clue as to what it is."

A pause. "You probably think that sounds like silly hocus-pocus."

"On the contrary, I think it sounds incredibly intriguing," replied Raven. He, too, hesitated for a moment. "Did you really mean what you said at breakfast about finding mathematics interesting?"

"I've always thought of mathematics as a rather boring set of rules—you know, addition, subtraction, division, multiplication—designed simply to count things. But I heard you telling Hawk and Peregrine that mathematics is key to navigation, and I found that fascinating."

"Mathematics is actually very creative and has a wide range of really interesting applications," replied Raven. "If you like, I can show you a book on navigation and explain the basics."

"I—I would like that very much."

"Excellent." Raven shuffled his feet, appearing a little uncertain of what to say next. "Well, umm . . . I had better get to the schoolroom and arrange my books and papers," he quickly added. "Mr. Lynsley expects for us to be prepared to begin our lessons the moment he walks in the door."

He hurried down several stairs before turning to look back over his shoulder. "I will, umm, see you later."

"Careful, careful—not so fast!" called Eddy to the Weasels, who had quickened their pace, eager to reach the swath of meadowland where the release of the pigeons was to take place. "Jostling the boxes may make them disoriented!"

Wrexford and von Münch followed at a more leisurely pace, though the earl remained alert to the surroundings.

"You need not have felt compelled to rendezvous with me this early," said Wrexford. "I don't expect trouble, but I prefer to be cautious when it comes to my family."

"While I'm happy to assist at any time if things threaten to turn ugly, I came here because I'm curious to observe Eddy with her pigeons. I've seen messenger pigeons in action while on a mission in eastern Prussia several years ago but have never had the opportunity to watch a training session."

"I hadn't realized that the use of messenger pigeons dates back to ancient times," mused the earl. "Eddy has informed me there is evidence that they were used by the Pharaohs of Egypt several centuries before the birth of Christ, and that during the 1300s, Genghis Khan established a postal system using messenger pigeons across his conquered territories in Asia."

He shaded his eyes and took a moment to study the copse of trees that butted up to the meadow where they planned to release the pigeons.

"Have you any idea how she trains them?" asked von Münch.

"I confess, I have not inquired as deeply into the art of pigeoning as I should have," admitted Wrexford.

"You have had a few other things on your mind."

"Be that as it may . . ." He saw that the Weasels were carefully undoing the top fastenings of the three wooden boxes, which had wire screens at both ends to let in air and light, in order to allow Eddy access to the four birds in each one. "Let us go ask."

In response to the earl's question, Eddy looked up from checking that her pigeons were settling down after the journey. "It's actually quite simple, Wrex. One begins by taking the birds a very short distance away on the rooftop from the dovecote when it's time for their feeding. They are hungry—and they know that they get fed in their nests. So they quickly return. Then one gradually increases the distance—I went first to the back terrace just below the roof, and then out to various points of the garden and mews."

She reached into one of the boxes and gently lifted out a single pigeon. "This is the first real test of finding their way home. But I don't doubt that all twelve of my birds will succeed." After whispering something to the pigeon, she opened her hands and gave a soft toss upward.

It rose with a whispery whirring of its flapping wings, and after circling high above them, it turned and, without hesitation, headed back toward Berkeley Square.

Wrexford watched as the process repeated itself until all dozen birds had flown off.

"Come, let's hurry and see if they all make it back," exclaimed Hawk, his excitement tinged with a touch of doubt.

Eddy merely smiled while the Weasels quickly gathered the three empty boxes.

"I have complete faith that I will find all your fledglings back in their nests when I return," said the earl.

"I, too," chimed von Münch, still looking up to watch the last tiny speck disappear from sight. "Remarkable! The wonders of Nature never cease to amaze and delight me."

"You seem to like birds, Herr von Münch," observed Eddy as she eyed him thoughtfully.

"In my youth, I trained a hunting hawk—a very handsome merlin—and we spent many a happy hour in the meadows and woods around my home. So yes, I have a particular fondness for feathered creatures."

Her eyes lit up in interest. "You trained a hawk? I've heard that is quite a bit more complicated than training a pigeon."

He offered her his arm. "Shall we chat about it as we walk back to the Stanhope Gate? Then alas, His Lordship and I must head off to deal with less pleasant demands."

CHAPTER 28

"Damnation." Given that he was alone in his workroom, Wrexford allowed himself to give verbal vent to his growing frustration.

The rest of the household seemed to be making progress with their endeavors. Over the last week, Eddy had continued to design more challenges for her pigeons within Hyde Park's sprawling acreage, ending with a jaunt into the adjoining Kensington Gardens, which confirmed that the birds were now full-fledged travelers . . . Raven slipped away each day to work as a messenger boy at the Stock Exchange, delivering sale slips to Ricardo, along with a variety of other information that he gleaned from carefully observing what was happening on the floor . . . And Charlotte's drawings were helping to keep London calm, as she designed her commentaries to quash rumors that might set off panic.

"While I seem to be doing naught but spinning in circles," the earl added under his breath. Le Loup was made of flesh and blood, not some sulphurous vapor from Hell. And yet he had made no headway in locating him.

A brusque cough interrupted his brooding.

"Where is everybody?" growled Henning as he entered the room.

"Charlotte has taken Eddy—my sister prefers to be called Eddy, rather than Eddylina—to take tea with Alison—"

"So the existence of a sister wasn't a puerile prank created by the Weasels?" said the surgeon.

"No, she's quite real." Despite his anxieties, Wrexford found himself smiling. "And quite wonderful." The smile stretched wider. "You'll like her. She's full of piss and vinegar."

"She had better be to have any hope of keeping up with the three Weasels."

"Ha! In truth, I think they are all a bit in awe of her. She has already coaxed Lucifer into letting her ride him."

"Good Lord, you must be mad as a hatter to let her anywhere near that big black devil," muttered the surgeon.

"Trust me, Eddy could outride a Death's Head Hussar."

Henning let out a rusty laugh. "Is there anyone normal in this family?"

"Heaven forfend," drawled the earl. "They wouldn't last long."

"Well, I look forward to meeting the lassie." The surgeon ran a hand along his unshaven jaw. "But my visit today is not a social call. I received your note asking me to keep my ears open for any whispers concerning a top operative of Napoleon sent here to foment chaos."

Wrexford held his breath, waiting for Henning to continue.

"A number of our veteran soldiers—poor fellows dressed in rags and weak with hunger who can't find work here at home— were among the sick I've been helping to tend this past fortnight. But despite their shameful treatment from our government, they are still loyal to the bone."

Henning's radical views on the need for social change were

no secret to Wrexford. In fact, he agreed with them. "You know my sentiments on pensions for our veterans. But right now, a more pressing concern is—

"Yes, yes—French operatives fomenting trouble here in London." Henning turned slightly, the slanting rays of sunlight accentuating the dark hollows beneath his bloodshot eyes. His crusty exterior fooled most people, but in truth, the surgeon cared deeply about the plight of the poor, and seeing their suffering took its toll.

"I was able to treat a veteran I've helped in the past during this recent outbreak, and thankfully he survived. He knows that I'm always interested in hearing about any trouble brewing, and he returned to the clinic this morning and told me about overhearing a conversation between two Frenchmen in a ramshackle tavern last night."

Henning made a face. "By a stroke of luck, the fellow speaks passable French, as he was assigned to guarding prisoners during Wellington's march through the Peninsula. The gist of the conversation was that a varlet named Le Loup is meeting with an important government informant tonight to pass over a down payment for some sort of service." He blew out a sigh. "And before you ask what that service is, it wasn't mentioned."

"Where is the rendezvous?" asked Wrexford quickly. "And when?"

"At the Chapel of King Edward the Confessor within Westminster Abbey. And the rendezvous is for an hour before midnight."

"Westminster Abbey," repeated the earl. "Good Lord—why there?"

Henning lifted his shoulders in an eloquent shrug. "Dunno, laddie. You're the sleuth." A sigh. "Just do me a favor. Don't send me any dead bodies. I've seen quite enough of them over the last month."

*   *   *

"Absolutely not." Charlotte set her jaw and squared her shoulders, defying him to argue.

"It may be the only chance we have to catch him—" he began.

"So be it," she cut in. "I won't allow you to go after a ruthless killer *and* his accomplice on your own. It's too reckless, and you know it."

"I can't ask Kit," he explained. "He's not experienced in this sort of lethal confrontation."

"Ha! You are digging yourself into an even deeper hole," she pointed out.

"What I meant was—"

"I know damn well what you meant," retorted Charlotte.

"We can't pass up the opportunity to catch him," said Wrexford, appealing to her sense of Right and Wrong. "He's too dire a threat to our country. And we can't reach out to Grentham's operatives. It's possible the traitor is one of them."

Charlotte pressed her lips together.

Was it egregiously selfish of her to think of her family first?

Choices, choices . . .

"What about von Münch?" she ventured. "He's experienced in clandestine missions, and we know that he's a damnably good shot."

"I'm not reckless, my love. I actually thought of that," he admitted. "But I don't know how to reach him."

"Well then, it's a good thing he entrusted that information to me." Charlotte glanced at the clock. "There's still time for Hawk and Peregrine to summon him and then to make a quick surveillance of the Abbey and note whether there are any guards stationed on the grounds."

The tide was nearly at its lowest ebb, the sickly sweet scents of decay wafting up from the mudflats exposed by the receding waters.

Wrexford cocked an ear. On hearing no sounds of movement close by, he signaled von Münch to follow him into the Abbey garden. Hunched low, they crept past the ancient stone fountain and hurried into the shadows flitting along the base of the outer walls.

"This way," whispered the earl, gesturing to the left. "Hawk and Peregrine have reported that no guards are in place. Still, I think it unwise to attempt going in by the main entrance at the North Transept. There's another side door at the west end of the nave. However, that, too, is awfully exposed. It's best for us to go in through a small side door leading into the St. Nicholas Chapel. That will have us right next to the Chapel of King Edward the Confessor."

"I'm impressed that you know the Abbey by heart," said his companion with a hint of amusement as they rounded a turn and edged into a recess in the wall. "I wouldn't have guessed you to be a religious fellow."

"Let's just say I'm more interested in reading architectural plans than scriptures."

Biting back a chuckle, von Münch gave a glance at the age-dark oak door. "Dare I hope you have the key?"

"Not necessary," replied Wrexford. He had already pulled several lock picks out of his boot and was surveying the keyhole. "This lock is child's play," he murmured. "It hasn't been changed in centuries. This won't . . ."—a jiggle, and then a *snick*—"take more than a moment."

Taking hold of the latch, the earl nudged the door open, wincing slightly at the rusty groan of the hinges, and then beckoned for von Münch to dart inside.

Moonlight trickled through the tall leaded-glass windows, casting a faint glow over the carved stone and wood.

"There's a massive stone screen separating the shrine and the chapel from the main altar and sanctuary. We can take cover there." He drew the two pistols hidden in his coat pockets. "And wait."

A sepulchral silence settled over the Abbey, the centuries-old woodwork and decorative carvings standing as solemn sentinels for the tombs of Britain's monarchs.

"I understand that Queen Elizabeth's resting place is quite impressive," mused von Münch in a low whisper after a number of minutes had passed. "As a historian, I would enjoy doing a bit of exploring—"

"Shhh," warned.Wrexford. He might have missed the sound if he hadn't been on full alert. Someone was moving with a predator's light-footed stealth down the north side of the nave.

Closer and closer . . .

A dark-on-dark figure entered the chapel and took up a position by the shrine in the center of the space. Several minutes passed, and then another figure approached.

"You're late," announced the man who had been waiting. The earl immediately recognized Le Loup's distinctive drawl.

"I took a roundabout route through St. James's Park to make sure I wasn't followed." The answering voice was muffled, as if by some sort of face covering. Wrexford gritted his teeth in frustration. It sounded vaguely familiar, but he couldn't identify it.

"Given my position, I need to be even more careful than you do."

Le Loup ignored the comment and got right down to business. "Has it arrived?"

"It has," answered Muffled Voice. "No need to worry. All is going exactly according to plan." He countered with his own question. "Have you brought the first payment?"

Wrexford nudged von Münch and signaled that the moment had come to apprehend the conspirators while their attention was elsewhere. Rising from his crouch, he edged over to the opening in the stone screen and cut to the left as he stepped into the chapel while von Münch slid to the right.

"Drop the packet," ordered the earl, taking a bead on both men with his weapons. "And put your hands up."

The weak light fluttered, and then for an instant the chapel went black as a cloud passed over the moon . . .

Just long enough for all hell to break loose.

Le Loup and his companion darted into the arched openings of the massive shrine to King Edward that sat in the center of the chapel. A shot rang out from their hiding place, forcing Wrexford to dive for cover behind one of the freestanding tombs set along the outer wall.

Rising to a crouch, he ventured a look—only to see a figure slip out from the back openings of the shrine and race through the archway into the Ambulatory.

"Go after him!" he shouted to von Münch, who had taken cover behind a tomb by the far wall. Though he had only caught a fleeting look at the silhouette, he knew it wasn't Le Loup.

"Get ready to answer for your sins," he called to the Frenchman as von Münch shot off in pursuit of Muffled Voice. "One of which includes desecrating a priceless piece of British history." Le Loup's bullet had clipped off the bronze nose of Edward III's tomb effigy.

A mocking laugh. "You value all the wrong things, Wrexford. It makes you weak. And vulnerable."

"We'll see." The earl gauged the distance to the next freestanding tomb, which would give him an angle to see into the shrine. He put one of his pistols back in his coat pocket and drew the lock picks out of his boot. Setting his stance, he hurled them across the room and sprinted for cover. The clang of metal was just enough of a distraction that Le Loup's second shot missed by a hair.

"I wonder, why did you bother to bring powder and shot when this wasn't supposed to turn into a battle?" called Wrexford.

"Surrender now, and I promise that I won't put a bullet through your brain."

No answer.

Wrexford looked around to judge his options. He discerned a shadowy movement within the shrine, so a shot would likely wound the Frenchman. Or he could keep Le Loup trapped in his hidey-hole until von Münch returned—

Snick, snick.

Before Wrexford could react to the sound of flint striking steel, a barrage of lighted candles came flying out of the shrine's interior. Ducking low, he rolled away from the flames—his coat lapel had caught fire, costing him precious seconds before he was able to scramble to his feet.

Le Loup was off and running.

For a heartbeat, the Frenchman was silhouetted against the arched windows of ancient leaded glass . . .

Without hesitation, he pulled the trigger.

Through the smoke and shadows he saw a section of the leaded window explode.

Damn. The Wolf appeared to have a catlike nine lives.

Wrexford set off in pursuit, but his quarry had too much of a lead. The nave was dark, and the columns cast too many confusing shadows . . .

The sound of Le Loup's steps was fast receding and in the next moment was gone.

"Bloody, bloody hell." Wrexford slapped out the last sparks on the singed wool of his lapel. The rest of the flames had fizzled out, unable to gain purchase on the stone floor.

"Wrexford!"

He turned as von Münch skidded to a halt on the smooth stone tiles. "Sorry, the fellow darted though one of side chapels and disappeared as if into thin air."

"I imagine there are a number of hidden passageways leading out of here," he replied. "Le Loup escaped as well." He clenched his spent pistol and cursed himself again for missing the poxy bastard. "So we've nothing to show for our efforts."

"Not true, we gained two clues. The traitor is someone in a high position. And he's selling something of vital importance to the French," said von Münch. "We're getting closer—"

"Perhaps," snapped Wrexford, turning back to stare into the gloom. "But the clock is ticking, and time is not on our side."

CHAPTER 29

"How are things going?" inquired Charlotte, looking up from the note she was reading as Raven came into the earl's workroom on returning from the Sheffield residence.

"Mrs. Sheffield and I are making some headway on the mathematical calculations. And Mr. Ricardo seems pleased with what I've been able to learn," came the reply. "I know from my urchin days how to blend into the woodwork. To the traders and investors, boys like me are like the rats and feral dogs that roam the city streets. And so they assume we're dumb beasts incapable of comprehending what they are saying or doing."

"Still, you must be careful. They are canny and make a living reading people," she counseled.

"Oiy," agreed Raven. A frown flitted over his face. "Over the last few days, Mr. Ricardo has noted some increased downward pressure on the price of consols. However, he's managed to stabilize the trend by buying them at elevated prices. He's explained to me that because of his reputation for anticipating market trends, a number of fellow stockjobbers and investors simply follow his lead in bidding for the securities without doing research on their own."

"A clever strategy." Charlotte held out the note. "But it sounds as if there may be trouble brewing. Kit just sent this urgent request for you to meet him first thing in the morning. Mr. Ricardo needs to talk with you before the Exchange opens for trading."

Seeing him pat back a yawn, she added, "So you had better get some sleep."

"I would rather stay up with you and wait for Wrex to return."

"We all have our responsibilities, sweeting, and you must be sharp for tomorrow," countered Charlotte. "Wrex will be fine," she assured him, forcing a confidence that hid her own worries.

Raven hesitated.

"Go."

He did so, but not before giving her a quick hug.

She leaned back in Wrexford's chair, drawing comfort from the faint bay rum scent of his shaving soap that pervaded the room. "Wrex will be fine," she repeated, refusing to believe otherwise. "Wrex will be fine."

Her faith—and her incantations—were rewarded a short while later when she heard the familiar tread of his steps in the corridor.

Charlotte shot up and flung the door open. "Holy hell!" After pulling back from a quick embrace, she eyed his singed coat. "What happened?"

"I ought to attend church more often," muttered Wrexford. "Had I been more familiar with Edward the Confessor's chapel, I wouldn't have bolloxed things."

"Don't be so hard on yourself, milord," said von Münch, who had followed him into the room. "Le Loup is considered a very dangerous man."

"Even more reason that we shouldn't have let him slip through our fingers."

"We did get two clues," said von Münch to Charlotte. He told her what they had overheard.

"Le Loup's informant is a high government official who is selling some vital information to the French?" Charlotte frowned. "What could it be?"

"Clearly something of momentous significance," replied Wrexford. "Though I can't even hazard a guess."

"We both need to press our various contacts within the government—discreetly, of course—and try to learn what sort of delicate negotiations, either at home or abroad, might give Napoleon a weapon for blackmail," mused von Münch.

"Blackmail." The earl thought it over. "That makes great sense. Napoleon is a genius at strategy. We know he's attacking our financial markets. But our other weakness is the Allied Coalition, which is rife with rivalries and mistrust. If he can somehow foment trouble there, it gives him another important bargaining chip, even if he loses the battle."

As von Münch looked away, Charlotte saw a sudden spark come to light in his eyes. "I'll take my leave of you now," he said abruptly. To Wrexford he added, "You'll hear from me soon."

The earl shook his head in consternation once they were alone. "I confess, I'm never quite sure what he is thinking."

"Never mind that now," she counseled. "Have you any idea who the traitor could be?"

"I know his voice—I'm sure of it—but it was too muffled to identify who it was." A pause. "The man was the right height and build to be Elias Fogg. And Fogg *is* a high official at the Foreign Office." Wrexford let out a sigh. "I shall pay him another visit tomorrow. And this time I won't be so polite with my questions."

Raven jumped down from the carriage as it paused in one of the side streets near the Stock Exchange.

"I will see you later," said Sheffield, who was heading on to a meeting with a banker friend.

"Oiy," Turning away, he darted through several narrow lanes, quickening his pace as he entered an alleyway next to Capel Court.

"What do you need me to do?" he blurted out before Ricardo could finish his greeting.

"Steady, lad. A key in dealing with any crisis is to keep a cool head," counseled Ricardo with his usual unflappable calm.

Raven bobbed his head. "Right, sir. You can depend on me."

A smile. "I consider myself a good judge of character, so I am quite sure of that." He fingered the tip of his chin. "As you know, there have been a lot of willing sellers of consols these last few days, which is driving prices down. But I haven't been able to detect any specific market rumors that would cause such a movement."

Ricardo frowned. "And that bothers me. My sources of information are usually quite good in picking up any such talk. It's possible that the selling activity is simply a reaction to these very uncertain times, but it doesn't feel quite right."

After another moment of thought, he added, "I'm going to have you and a few of my other messengers circulate throughout the floor and try to discern with whom the selling originates and what the price trends are." A sigh. "Your messenger sales slips are in fact the best real-time information we have on that."

"I understand, sir."

"Good." Ricardo checked his pocket watch. "Come along, the building is about to open and I wish to take up my position."

Once they were settled in place, Ricardo studied his surroundings. "Pay close attention, as I have a specific request," he said. "It's important."

Raven swallowed hard and nodded.

"Once the floor opens for business, head in the direction of Column Three, counting down from the left side of the clock wall. You're familiar with the firm that does its activity there, correct?"

Another nod.

"I want you to pass by there frequently on your rounds of collecting slips and see if you can get a sense of what trading is going on and with whom. If you can manage to hear what they are saying, especially any mention of prices, that would be an added plus."

"I won't let you down, sir," promised Raven.

"I'm quite confident of that." Ricardo patted him on the shoulder and then strolled away.

Raven remained hovering in the shadows near Ricardo's spot until the opening flurry of trading had settled down. He was now familiar enough with the layout of the Stock Exchange interior to know all the little byways and shortcuts for maneuvering around the perimeter of the cavernous hall. It was on his third circuit that he spotted a quartet of gentlemen—their attire seemed to indicate that they weren't from London—approaching Column Three.

After pausing for a moment, Raven sidled closer to the neighboring columns and pretended to be engrossed in sorting his sale slips into order.

"Welcome, welcome, gentlemen!"

Raven waited for the stockjobbers and their visitors to finish with their effusive greetings before looking up from under the bill of his cap.

Damnation.

The quartet of gentlemen all had their backs to him, and he couldn't hear a word of what was being said.

He looked around, then moved off to disappear into one of

the recessed areas, only to re-emerge a few moments later at a different column, allowing him a different angle of view. The four faces were now all clearly visible. One by one, he glanced at the first three, straining to catch a snatch of their conversation.

No luck.

After another silent oath, he focused on the fourth man . . .

Holy hell. His heart pounding loud as gunfire in his ears, Raven shoved the sales slips into his pocket and hurried off to find Ricardo.

"It's him! It's the fellow from the warehouse—the one who kept saying 'goddamn,'" he explained in a rush. "I called him Florid Face. He and three other fellows are dealing with the stockjobbers at Column Three, but I couldn't make out what they were saying. Their English sounded very garbled. Perhaps they're from Yorkshire."

"Well done," murmured Ricardo. "You stay here. I'm going to take a stroll, and genial fellow that I am, I will, of course, stop to give my regards to my fellow stockjobbers."

Sheffield found Raven a few minutes later. "Any new developments?"

A nod. "So far, Mr. Ricardo has spotted increased selling and thus pressure on the market for government bonds. The fluctuations seem a little more than he's expecting." He then explained about having discovered Florid Face.

Sheffield frowned. "Florid Face? That's damnably odd. But let's see what Mr. Ricardo thinks when he returns."

They didn't have to wait long. And when their mentor returned, his demeanor was quite grave.

"The quartet you identified are not Yorkshiremen, Master Sloane. They're Dutch. That's why you were having trouble understanding their English. And your man from the warehouse now has a name, as I recognize him."

A small cheek muscle twitched as Ricardo tightened his jaw. "He is Johannes-Peter De Groot, an Amsterdam banker from a firm with whom I prefer not to do business. I strongly suspect the other three gentlemen are Dutch bankers, too."

Ricardo tapped his fingertips together, looking lost in thought for several long moments. "I'm afraid that I may have significantly underestimated the nature of the threat we face."

A look of alarm rippled through Sheffield's eyes. "W-What do you mean?"

"I no longer think the threat is simply a French misinformation campaign to cause consols prices to drop. Misinformation alone would have been relatively easy for us to monitor and combat."

His expression turned even more serious. "I fear what we have is something infinitely more dangerous—a full-scale French-coordinated 'bear raid' on the market for English government debt."

"B-Bear raid?" repeated Raven. Like Sheffield, he appeared utterly confused.

"It's the name of a tactic used in the financial world," explained Ricardo. "The term *bear* derives from the old adage *to sell the bear skin before one has caught the bear.* That was shortened to *bearskin jobber* and then simply *bear* around a hundred years ago. It refers to someone who attacks a company by selling stock they do not own, betting that the price will drop. In other words, a raiding short seller. But Bears, when they start attacking a target, can absolutely destroy it. Others jump in, increasing the short selling in anticipation that the raid will continue and force the price to keep dropping, thus reaping a quick profit."

His jaw clenched for an instant. "Companies rarely survive a full-scale, well-executed bear raid."

"And in this case?" Sheffield inquired.

"It has the potential to be . . . absolutely catastrophic," replied Ricardo. The note of icy calm in his voice belied the flicker of shadows beneath his lashes. "The value of British consols could be caught in a downward price spiral and fall into complete collapse due to the short selling."

He closed his eyes for an instant. "A collapse of the consol would render a number of the weaker banking institutions insolvent, because a large amount of their assets is in the form of consols. Because these banks are indebted to the larger, healthier banks, their failure would threaten even these solid banking institutions, thus beginning a sort of domino effect of failing financial institutions."

Sheffield's breath leaked out in a shaky exhale. "The banking firms in turn are all private partnerships, and their partners— the leading financial families in England—would be on the hook for the debts of these now ruined banks, not to mention that these individuals would themselves be devastated financially as huge holders of government debt."

"Correct," uttered Ricardo. "And given current events, this would all be occurring exactly when the British government needs to go to the market to raise to raise a loan of unprecedented size in order to be able to field an army against Napoleon. So you see, I can't overstate the potential consequences here."

Ricardo paused and looked at Raven. "When you thought that you overheard De Groot repeatedly saying 'goddamn' that night at the warehouse, I'll wager that what you really heard was him saying 'Gaudin' in his heavily accented English. For as I've mentioned before, I suspect that all of this is being orchestrated by Gaudin, Napoleon's brilliant finance minister."

"B-But aren't the Dutch on our side?" protested Raven.

"Yes, in theory," responded Ricardo. "But where there are business opportunities—a chance of huge profits—there are always some bankers who will seize the chance, no matter the consequences of their actions."

"Shouldn't we immediately inform the British government and have them put a stop to all of this?" pressed Raven.

"On the contrary—that's the last thing we should do," answered Ricardo. "This bear attack has been elaborately orchestrated. Gaudin is no doubt using a network of agents through which to conduct his short selling, and many of them are likely perfectly reputable firms and individuals who may not even know the identity of the client on whose behalf they are doing the short selling."

"Mind you, short selling is legal," injected Sheffield.

"The presence of De Groot and his colleagues tells me that Gaudin has been very careful to have his agents comply carefully with the law and best practices," continued Ricardo. "The Dutch bankers are known to hold a large quantity of British consols, so my guess is he has gone to the trouble of borrowing the actual securities he is selling short from them."

He shook his head. "It would take weeks or months to try to prove that Gaudin was behind all of this. Moreover, just the smallest hint that this is all happening would plunge the market into total chaos and collapse. We would only be doing Gaudin's work for him by publicizing what's going on."

"S-So, he's already won?" stammered Raven.

"Not by a long shot, lad." A martial gleam lit in Ricardo's eyes. "I'm simply saying that we're going to have to fix this ourselves."

He thought for a moment. "Why don't you both head off—not together, mind you—and meet me back at Nicholas Lane in three hours. By then I will have some next steps to propose."

The afternoon's light was deepening as Wrexford returned to Berkeley Square, the play of elongated shadows mirroring his own unsettled mood. Fogg had been away from his office, and his assistant had primly refused to answer any questions about where he was.

"Wrexford!"

The earl turned to see his friend Norwood hurry across the pavement and join him on the central garden's walkway leading to the other side of the Square.

"How are things going across the Channel?" he asked before the fellow could add a greeting.

His friend's expression tightened. "Not well. Word is, Napoleon's reassembled military might now number close to 200,000 men, many of them experienced veterans from previous campaigns. And it's just been given a name—L'Armée du Nord." A grimace. "There seems little doubt that it will soon be on the move to confront the overmatched forces of Wellington."

Wrexford muttered an oath.

"Actually, I was just coming to see if you were at home. I, too, have a question." Norwood glanced around. "A highly confidential one."

"I think you know that you can trust my discretion."

"Indeed, that's why I'm here." Norwood hesitated for an instant. "I know that you're occasionally consulted on government matters. Would you perchance be able to tell me if Elias Fogg has reason to request copies of the latest high-level dispatches from our military allies?"

Wrexford took a moment before answering. "Not that I know of," he said. "But the Foreign Office does have an interest in knowing if there are any overt tensions within our Coalition members."

"True." Norwood looked thoughtful. "It just seems a sudden change in policy."

"As it happens, I have reason to meet with Fogg in the next day or two," replied Wrexford. "Let me see what I can learn for you."

"Much obliged." Norwood touched the brim of his hat in salute. "It is likely just the way the wheels of bureaucracy turn these days. But I suppose we're all feeling a little jumpy at the moment."

"One can't be too careful," said the earl.

A nod, and then his friend turned and headed back toward Green Park.

Feeling even more unsettled—the news from Europe was disheartening—he slipped in through one of the side entrances and quietly made his way to his workroom. Perhaps a wee dram of Scottish malt would loosen the knot of dread that was forming in his chest.

Death and destruction. Damn the hubris of a single man whose unyielding ambition and lust for glory was about to plunge Europe back into war.

The splash of spirits seemed a terrible harbinger of all the blood that was soon to be shed.

"You're back." Charlotte looked into the room.

"Yes." A heavy sigh. "But I give you fair warning that I'm not going to be good company at the moment."

She came and took a seat on the arm of his chair. Threading her fingers through his hair, she brushed a wind-ruffled tangle back from his brow and bestowed a quick kiss.

Wrexford caught her hand and gave it a squeeze, savoring the warmth and the strength that her presence always brought to him.

Charlotte allowed a few more moments of silence before leaning back. "I take it your meeting with Fogg didn't go well?"

"I was told he was out. But given what I have just learned, I shall try again tomorrow." He told her about his encounter with Norwood. "I fear that when the news about L'Armée du Nord reaches the Fleet Street scribblers, they will do their best to whip up fear and frenzy simply to sell their cursed newspapers. It will cause panic and instability just when the government can least afford it."

His jaw clenched for an instant. "Official denials won't help.

The public will assume the government is lying to cover up the truth."

"Yes . . ." Charlotte's eyes look on a martial gleam. "But coming from A. J. Quill, who can remind the public that his pen has always been exceedingly good at digging out the truth, a satirical commentary downplaying the threat may go a long way to calming the country."

Wrexford pulled her into a hug. "That's a stroke of genius."

"Let us hope so." Charlotte wiggled free. "I had better get to work."

Raven and Sheffield entered Ricardo's place of business at the appointed hour and found their mentor seated at the table in the main room, his expression carefully schooled to give nothing away.

After inviting them to sit, he was quick to begin. "Our next steps are clear, but not easily accomplished. The French will no doubt increase their short-selling efforts as war nears. So my efforts to stabilize consol prices have to increase accordingly. I will need to enlist other stockjobbers and investors in the effort."

He pursed his lips in thought. "But, as I said this morning, we can't let word of the situation get out, so I will need to think of how we might accomplish our objectives without also tipping off the market—or French—as to what we're doing. And that will be challenging."

Their mentor leaned back in his chair. "I also need to consider whether any syndicate can be formed to float the massive loan for the government, given the fraught political and military situation. For that I will need some mathematical assistance from Mrs. Sheffield and you, Master Sloane."

"We are at your service, sir," said Raven.

"Finally, I must stress that everything I've suggested about detecting a bear raid by the French is based on conjecture. The visiting Dutch bankers . . . my sense of a slowly increasing 'sell' pressure on the consol . . . our young friend hearing 'goddamn' or 'Gaudin' at the time of the shooting—it's all merely a surmise of how they all tie together."

Ricardo allowed a long pause. "Which brings me to you, Master Sloane."

Raven's eyes widened in anticipation.

"Here's my dilemma, lad," said their mentor. "I need to know whether De Groot is in possession of a large number of British consols, and whether they are being used for transactional purposes. That information is likely locked in his temporary office on the top floor of the Stock Exchange."

Ricardo looked a little uncomfortable. "On principle, I don't endorse burglary. But this is war." He cleared his throat. "Just so you know, there is a watchman's station at the front of the building where a guard stands sentry. However, the Dutchman's office is at the back of the building, which overlooks an alleyway. As you've no doubt noticed, there is decorative stonework running up the four corners of the building, and a narrow ornamental ledge beneath each row of windows—"

"If you're asking whether I can get in and out without being caught, the answer is yes." Raven grinned. "Trust me, it's child's play compared to a number of other places I've had to crack."

Ricardo released a pent-up breath. "I was hoping you would say that."

"What will I be looking for?" asked Raven.

"A ledger book, which will contain the names of various trusts and partnerships which you will not recognize. Don't worry about that—all I need to know is whether the ledger indicates any transactions with these entities involving consol bonds. You may also find a portfolio of the bonds themselves. I can show you some examples."

"That sounds simple enough, sir."

"I don't want you to take anything—indeed, it's imperative that De Groot doesn't suspect the items have been touched. I simply need to confirm their existence. That will dispel any doubts that my analysis is correct and that the countermeasures I am proposing are the correct ones."

"Understood," said Raven.

Ricardo hesitated. "Now, the next obstacle is gaining Lord and Lady Wrexford's consent—"

"Leave that to me," said Sheffield.

CHAPTER 30

W rexford and Charlotte listened without interruption to Shef-field's explanation of what Ricardo needed.

"It's actually a simple task, Wrex," interjected Raven. "With Hawk and Peregrine as lookouts, I'll have plenty of warning of when it is safe to head up and come down. And the building is only three stories high, with decorative stone work for an easy climb and a ledge that gives access to the window."

"I'm well aware of your skills, lad," said Wrexford. And yet he hesitated. His own encounters with Le Loup had, he admit-ted, left him feeling all too aware of how dangerously cunning the French operative was.

What if . . .

"We're not doubting your skills, sweeting." Charlotte looked to Sheffield. "And we, of course, realize how important this is for our country."

She hesitated, and then, as if reading the earl's thoughts, a shadow of fear darkened her gaze. "My worry is that if the French plan to destabilize the Stock Exchange and ruin Britain's ability to raise money to fund a war is key to Napoleon's hope of regaining his empire, then it stands to reason that Le Loup may have the building under surveillance."

Sheffield said nothing, a tacit admission that none of them could say for sure that the danger didn't exist.

"Sometimes, when Good and Evil hang in the balance, you simply have to take a chance, m'lady," said Raven softly. "You and Wrex have set that example for us Weasels countless times."

Tears pearled on Charlotte's lashes, but in light of those words, how could she say no? In answer to Wexford's searching stare, she gave a tiny nod.

"Le Loup is big and heavy, and we know he has a hitch in his gait," pointed out Raven. "He can't match my speed and agility. He'll never catch me."

Wrexford saw Charlotte flinch. *Thinking, no doubt, about the bullet hole in Raven's rucksack.* However, she maintained a stoic silence.

"So," said Sheffield. "Are we all agreed?"

The earl gave her one last chance to voice an objection and then drew in a measured breath. "Yes."

Raven moved to the doorway. "I'll go inform Hawk and Peregrine. When the time comes—arriving a little after midnight would be a good choice—I think it best for the three of us to leave the house through our bedchamber window, so that Eddy doesn't notice any nocturnal activity."

"I'll have my carriage waiting for the boys on Davies Street," said Sheffield.

"Needless to say, I'll be coming with you," announced Wrexford.

Taking the ensuing silence as a signal that the plan was finalized, Raven slipped out and headed for the stairs.

The moon was playing hide-and-seek within the thickening scrim of clouds that had blown in from the east, its pale flutters of silvery light growing fainter and fainter. A breeze wafted through the buildings adjoining Capel Court, stirring a muted rustling of the shutters that were closed for the night.

Crouched just below the peaked roofline, Raven clung to the decorative coping stones, his blackened face and dark clothing blending into the shadows as he waited for a signal from Hawk that all was clear to make his way along the window ledge.

A moment later, the twitter of a nightingale told him to proceed. With catlike stealth, he crept across the narrow jut of stone to the rectangle double-paned window of the office assigned to the Dutch bankers and slipped the blade of his knife between the brass casements.

Jiggle, jiggle. The latch of the lock slipped free of the locking mechanism, allowing Raven to slip inside . . .

An hour passed with excruciating slowness. And when another seemed on the cusp of slipping away, Wrexford swore under his breath—only to glance at his pocket watch and discover that a mere ten minutes had passed.

"Stop pacing. You look like a cat trying to cross a red-hot griddle," grumbled Sheffield. "It's making me jumpy."

Ricardo didn't look up from the papers and ledgers spread out on his desk. "Patience, gentlemen, patience," he counseled.

The three of them were waiting in the stockjobber's Nicholas Lane office for Raven to arrive with the results of his mission.

"You've both assured me that Master Sloane has a great deal of experience in clandestine activities," he added.

Although he liked and trusted Ricardo, Wrexford had seen no point in mentioning the fact that his other two wards were equally involved in the mission. The more people who knew his family's secret, the greater the possibility of trouble.

Refraining from comment, Wrexford turned to watch the swirling currents of the dark water through the night-misted windowpanes. Even at this late hour, there were ghostly sails catching the tide in order to make the journey down to the sea.

Ebb and flow. One had no choice but to move with the rhythms of the cosmos.

If only the flow would start to turn in their favor.

"Sorry," Sheffield came over to join him. "I haven't yet had a chance to tell you, but my inquiries into Fogg's gambling did turn up the fact that he frequents a very opulent and exclusive gaming hall in St. Giles. He's had a string of losses lately—rather steep ones—but has covered his vowels."

"Which begs the question of how," muttered Wrexford. "Can you ask around among your banker friends and discern what his finances look like?"

"I'll see what I can dig up," said Sheffield. "By the by, your friend Norwood also frequents the place."

"He's related to the Grenville family. I daresay he can afford it."

"I doubt that our old university friend, Giles Arlington, can." Sheffield made a face. "Apparently he's sunk himself deep in the River Tick."

"Count your blessings that you met Cordelia when you did," said Wrexford.

"Amen to that."

They stood together in silence until the sound of steps drew them back from their thoughts.

Raven burst through the door a moment later, and seeing the expectant faces turn his way, he skidded to a halt. "You were right, Mr. Ricardo! Just as you suspected, I found a large ledger in one of the desk drawers filled with the types of names you mentioned, each followed by a notation on a transaction. And in one of the locked cabinets were several portfolio cases filled with official consol documents."

He pulled a small notebook from his coat pocket and handed it over. "I copied the first page of the ledger—it went on for quite a few more—just so you could confirm what I saw."

"It seems you may have a future in the government's Ministry of State Security, lad," announced Ricardo, after reading over Raven's list and giving a satisfied smile.

"I think there are other more attractive opportunities lying ahead for Raven," replied Wrexford. "But yes, well done."

"Any trouble?" asked Sheffield.

A grin. "None whatsoever."

"Then let us return to Berkeley Square," said the earl. To Ricardo, he added, "We'll await word from you on what your next step will be to counter the French threat to Britain's finances—"

"And how we can help," finished Sheffield.

"Yes, yes." His attention locked on the notebook Raven had given to him, Ricardo responded with a vague wave.

Taking Raven by the arm, Wrexford left the room, his mounting worries over the military situation across the Channel suddenly making him feel helpless—especially as the Weasels were doing the dangerous work here at home.

Sensing the earl's mood, Sheffield maintained a tactful silence as he followed along at a discreet distance.

Few words were exchanged during the carriage ride home, save for a flurry of whispers between the Weasels once they approached Mayfair.

"We'll get out at the next corner," said Raven, "and climb up to our rooms from the back garden terrace, just to ensure that Eddy doesn't hear us come up the stairs."

Wrexford gave an absent nod.

"Don't look so blue-deviled," chided Sheffield after the boys had slipped away. "We know what the French are up to, and Ricardo will design a strategy to strike back."

His eyes narrowed. "And knock their plan to flinders."

Leaving nothing to chance, Raven shifted his handhold on the thick vines of ivy and inched open the window casement to peer into the darkened bedchamber.

The shadows lay still, as if deep in slumber.

Satisfied, he looked over his shoulder and waved for his fellow Weasels to continue their climb before wriggling through the gap and dropping noiselessly to the floor.

"I'm famished," whispered Hawk. He crawled over to his chest of drawers and slid the bottom one open. "I've got half a bag of licorice—"

A grunt.

Sitting back in surprise, he raised his brows at Peregrine.

"Don't look at me! I didn't take it."

"No, *I* did." Eddy stepped out from behind the half-open door of the adjoining room.

"Spying on other members of our household is an underhanded trick," muttered Raven.

Harper, who was right behind her, dropped his shaggy head and let out an apologetic *whuffle*.

"So is keeping secrets," she retorted.

All three Weasels remained stoically silent.

"Do Wrex and m'lady know of your nocturnal forays?" she demanded. "And don't bother to deny that you're up to something havey-cavey."

Still no response.

"Fine." Fisting her hands in her night-rail, Eddy turned to leave. "Clearly you don't trust me—"

"Wait," hissed Raven. "It's . . . it's not that simple."

"Oiy, it is." Eddy lifted her chin. "Either you believe that I can be trusted with secrets or you don't."

"Actually, there's a third alternative," replied Raven. "The decision isn't ours to make."

"W-What do you mean?"

"I can't explain—" began Raven.

"Because the secrets involved are dangerous," interrupted Hawk. "It's not just us and our family who would be at risk."

Eddy released a shaky breath. "Thank you for at least trusting me with that." She thought for a long moment, her expression betraying a hint of vulnerability despite the challenging tilt of her chin. "Granted, you don't know me very well, but I have more experience than you might think in keeping dangerous secrets."

She looked away. "My mother was . . . a free spirit and did not always conform to the rules of society. Indeed, some of her activities would have caused a great deal of trouble had they become known. I learned quickly how to . . . keep things to myself."

Hawk stepped back and motioned Raven and Peregrine to join him.

A flurry of whispering ensued, interrupted once or twice by a low *woof* from Harper.

When finally they broke apart, it was Raven who stepped forward to speak. "Hawk and Peregrine think you deserve to know what's going on."

"And what do *you* think?" challenged Eddy.

"Actually, I agree." Seeing a smile start to form on her lips, he held up his hand. "But wait! First you have to agree to a very solemn covenant."

Her eyes widened in question.

"A blood oath," explained Peregrine. "Just as I was asked to make. The three of us swore to be brothers-in-spirit—loyal to the bone, no matter what."

"In other words, you officially become a Weasel," piped up Hawk.

"It's not something to take on lightly," said Raven. He drew out a stag-handled pocket knife from his boot and clicked the blade open. "You have to be sure your heart is entirely committed to it."

"I . . . feel at home here . . ."

Squaring her shoulders, Eddy held out her hand. "I'm sure."

Hawk and Peregrine did the same.

Raven carefully pricked each of their forefingers and then his own.

"One for all and all for one," he intoned, then signaled for their four fingers to come together, mingling the drops of blood.

Harper let out a gusty sigh and wagged his tail.

"Now the last part of the ritual is you need to choose an avian moniker," said Raven.

"Pigeon is the obvious one," mused Hawk. He furrowed his brow. "But it's . . . it's a byword for being soft and unwitting. It doesn't suit you."

"Merlin," announced Raven after a long moment of thought. "It's a ladylike hawk but a fierce one. And after all, you have a magical touch with animals."

Hawk and Peregrine nodded enthusiastically.

"Merlin," repeated Eddy, testing the name out on her tongue. "Oiy, I like that." She gave a shy smile. "I'm honored to join the flock."

"In the morning, we'll convene our inner circle for a council of war and inform the others that you're now a member." Repressing a yawn, Raven picked up a rag from the side table by his bed and began wiping off the greasy dirt from his face. "In the meantime, I'm going to get some sleep."

A sigh followed. "I don't suppose you have any licorice left?"

Eddy laughed. "Merlin might just be able to conjure up a piece or two for all of us."

Despite the added complications, Charlotte was, at heart, relieved when Raven had demanded an audience at first light to inform her and Wrexford that he and Hawk—seconded by Peregrine—had made the decision to deem Eddy a full-fledged member of their tight-knit inner circle.

Wrexford had been far less pleased as he turned to confront an unrepentant Raven. However, she had whispered, "Father and sons," to remind him that disagreements and butting heads were part of the age-old cycle.

And to his credit, the earl had tempered his fears and concerns, listening with admirable patience as Raven explained his reasoning. Indeed, after the presentation ended, he blew out a harried breath and conceded that the Weasels had made the right decision.

"Thank heavens we don't have to shilly-shally around Eddy any longer," said McClellan after Charlotte had hurried to the breakfast room and informed her of the new turn of events.

"Amen to that," replied Charlotte. "Though I must say, the more I see how well she keeps her composure in dealing with all the new demands in her life, the more impressive it is. Unlike me at her age, she's mature beyond her years."

"I have a feeling that her unconventional life and worldly experiences traveling with her mother demanded that she grow up fast," mused the maid. "That augers well for her fitting in here." A wry smile. "Our family is hardly a pattern card for propriety."

The observation stirred yet another jolt of worry for what lay ahead in the future for Eddy. Much as Charlotte embraced the spirit of individuality, she knew all too well that a young lady who chose to follow her own path was treading on perilous ground. A myriad of little dangers lay in wait, especially for one whose legitimacy could be questioned—

Laughter echoed in the corridor, and a moment later the boys and Eddy filed in for the morning meal, with the earl right behind them. Shaking off her brooding, she turned her attention back to the present moment.

Wrexford waited for everyone to be seated before settling into his own chair and regarding each of them in turn. "Everyone here now knows that we are involved in a dangerous investigation that has great ramifications for our country."

Hands folded in her lap, Eddy was watching him intently.

Charlotte felt her heart swell as she suddenly saw so much of Wrexford—the slant of his cheekbone, the arch of his brow, the sea-green intensity of his gaze—in her profile. The future held countless little things to discover about Eddy.

Joys and no doubt challenges . . .

The earl poured himself a cup of coffee. "Some of you know more about the actual specifics than others. And for now, that is how it should stay."

Eddy's response was immediate. "I understand, Wrex. Be assured I won't pester any of you with questions."

"I very much appreciate that—" he began.

"But," interrupted Eddy.

Wrexford's expression turned wary.

"But if there is anything I can do to help, I hope you will ask me." A grin twitched on her lips. "You all know how strong a kinship I feel with animals, so I am thrilled to have become an honorary Weasel and hope to contribute to our efforts."

Raven glanced at Hawk and Peregrine, which triggered a chorus of chortles. But the hilarity quickly died away as Sheffield appeared in the doorway.

Wrexford started to rise.

"No need to get up," assured Sheffield. "I just thought I would come around early to fetch Raven—"

He fell silent on spotting Eddy.

"You may speak freely, Kit," said Charlotte. "Eddy is now a full-fledged member of our inner circle."

"Ah!" Sheffield snapped a jaunty salute. "Welcome to the flock."

"Who else is a member—" began Eddy.

"Pssst—no questions, remember?" chided Raven, though a glint of teasing flickered in his eyes.

"In this case, it's a good query," said Charlotte. "She should know who has our complete trust." She waited for Wrexford's nod of agreement before continuing. "Mrs. Sheffield and Aunt

Alison, as well as McClellan and Tyler. And then there is Basil Henning, our dear surgeon friend whom you have not yet met. He has been working night and day to help a medical friend battle an outbreak of influenza in the slums of St. Giles."

"Be careful not to shake Mr. Henning's hand if he offers it," counseled Hawk. "His fingers are usually smeared with far more disgusting substances than ours are."

Peregrine nodded and added a retching sound.

A stern look from Charlotte warned them to stubble their theatrics.

Sheffield helped himself to one of McClellan's fresh-baked sultana muffins. "Shake a leg, Raven. Finish your eggs and gammon, then hurry and change into your uniform. Mr. Ricardo sent word that he would like you to be at the Stock Exchange when the doors open and continue keeping an eye on who is buying and selling as you make your rounds."

Eddy was clearly bursting with curiosity but managed to hold back another question.

Charlotte sympathized. "Why don't the two of us pay a call on Alison later this morning? She will want to be updated on the latest developments."

Hawk flashed a hopeful smile. "I'm sure she will also want to visit Gunter's and purchase a bag of Pontefract cakes."

"Is that so?" Charlotte raised her brows. "What happened to that rather large bag of licorice you brought home the other day?"

"That's a sticky question. It seems to have disappeared." A mournful sigh. "Ummm, perhaps Harper ate it all."

CHAPTER 31

Wrexford sat back in dismay after he finished poring over the latest report from Horse Guards concerning the military situation in Europe. Things, he conceded, were not looking good.

A week had passed, May had given way to June . . . and still no reinforcements had arrived in Brussels.

"Where the devil is von Blücher?" he added under his breath. Nobody seemed to know, and without the Prussian general and his army as allies, Wellington would have little chance of defeating Napoleon's seasoned veterans with the motley assortment of troops currently under his command.

Fisting his hands in frustration—a part of him was sorely tempted to head for Brussels and join forces with his former commander—the earl marched into the adjoining library to consult a portfolio of oversized maps that included one of France and the United Kingdom of the Netherlands.

Paris . . . Wrexford traced a finger northward. *Valenciennes, Mons, Brussels . . .*

His blood began to pound in his ears, as loud as the cadence of military drums. Napoleon's forces were only a three-day march from Wellington's headquarters. And God only knew whether they were already on the move.

"Geography does not seem to favor the duke," he muttered. *Nor does the devil-cursed bickering among Britain's so-called Allies,* Wrexford added to himself as he glanced up at the clock.

Be that as it may, it was time to head off to the Foreign Office and confront Fogg.

He paused at his workroom desk before heading to the corridor to gather the page of questions he had composed—

"What the devil . . ." Paper crackled as he unfolded the note that had been left atop it and read over the contents.

An oath slipped from his lips. And then another. "Charlotte may have unshakeable faith in you," he muttered, scowling at von Münch's elegant copperplate script. "But as far as I can see, you always seem to hare off on your own escapades just when your help is most needed." A sigh. "If I am going to catch the culprits, it appears I will have to do so on my own."

Raven found Ricardo in one of the secluded nooks of the Stock Exchange and passed over his last batch of slips from the day's trading. Seeing his mentor's pensive look, he looked around and then whispered, "May I ask how we're doing against the bear raid, sir?"

"The tide may be showing signs of turning," answered Ricardo. "I, and the jobbers who follow me, have been offering to buy consols at slowly ascending prices. And this has begun to really squeeze the short sellers—keep in mind that they eventually have to buy consols themselves to cover what they have previously sold short."

Before Raven could react, he forged on. "*But* it has required significant funds from me and the others to make these stabilizing purchases. Some of the other jobbers are stretched. A number of them likely borrowed significantly to fund their purchases. If the consol prices begin to fall, these loans will be called in and all will be lost."

Ricardo paused, as if to catch his breath. "I am going to have to find some new investors who might be willing to commit to this . . . stabilization effort. It's the only way to keep the necessary pressure on the short sellers. Any such investor must not only have resources but also be exceedingly discreet. I've explained why disclosure here could do us in. And given the amounts of capital potentially involved, multiple investors will certainly be required, which compounds the problem considerably."

He paused again. "Also, my sense is that the short sellers are straining hard to find more consols to borrow in order to keep up the raid. And that's a very good sign for us. However, I'm a bit worried that a few of my fellow jobbers, concerned about their own positions, are lending out consols to the short sellers that they originally purchased from the short sellers in the first place."

"Doing *what*?"

Seeing Raven's bewildered look, Ricardo gave a mirthless chuckle. "Yes, the Stock Exchange and its byzantine practices can be terribly confusing. But don't worry about those complexities. The point is that we're tightening the vise on the short sellers and Gaudin is beginning to realize that he underestimated our ability to see him coming."

A grim smile. "The next few days will decide which of us will triumph."

"Ah, you're back!" called Charlotte from the parlor, as she heard Wrexford cross the entrance hall and enter the corridor. "Alison has something to share with you."

"Perhaps it can wait," he called. "Griffin is with me, and we have some urgent matters to discuss."

"All the more reason to hear what she has to say," she replied. "This may have some bearing on what you're investigating." A pause. "And I'm sure Griffin would welcome some tea and a platter of Mac's fresh-baked muffins."

"Very well." The earl appeared in the doorway and heaved an exaggerated sigh. "He would never forgive me if I refused him the chance to fill his breadbox at my expense."

Charlotte smiled at the Runner. "I'll have Mac bring you a slice of steak and kidney pie as well."

"Thank you, milady. That would be most welcome."

"Enough about food!" The dowager rapped her cane on the carpet. "I have some interesting information to feed you."

"We're listening," said the earl.

"Charlotte mentioned the incident in Westminster Abbey and your suspicions about Elias Fogg. So I did a careful check of his family tree." Alison flashed a cat-in-the-creampot smile. "And his second cousin, who was raised by Fogg's family after the death of his parents during a local influenza epidemic, is the Archdeacon of the Abbey."

"Well, I'll be damned," said Wrexford.

"I think," murmured Griffin, "that I should make you an honorary Bow Street Runner, Lady Peake."

The dowager edged forward in her chair. "Are you going to rush off and apprehend the scoundrel now?"

"According to the Foreign Office, Fogg took an extended leave yesterday in order to visit a very sick relative in the north," said Wrexford. "Griffin and I were just about to discuss whether we have grounds to bring him in for questioning."

"But based on your information, milady, I and several of my men will immediately head north in pursuit."

"Fogg may not have gone north," pointed out Charlotte.

"True," responded Wrexford. "Which is why I will turn my attention back to tracking down Le Loup. My guess is he and his co-conspirator are still here in London—and are more dangerous than ever as we don't know what they are after."

In answer to Ricardo's urgent summons several days later—he had finally received word that the government was about ready to request bids and see if any of the financier groups would float the massive loan needed for the campaign against Napoleon—Cordelia and Raven hurried up the stairs to the Nicholas Lane office, where they found him pacing up and down in front of the windows overlooking the river.

"I have just heard that the loan needed will be unprecedented—around £35 million," he announced, after gesturing for them to be seated at the table.

"Good Lord, that's an astronomical sum," exclaimed Cordelia, as she opened her portfolio and took out a sheaf of papers and some pencils.

"Indeed." He, too, took a chair. "As you know, when the government requires annual loans of this magnitude, instead of selling bonds directly to the public it sets up a competitive bidding process among a few—hopefully at least four or five—syndicates of prominent financiers and institutions. Every syndicate forms its own list of subscribers, often hundreds of people or companies who want to buy a share of the loan. Now, this usually works well—the government gets its money right away and the winning syndicate makes a profit over time. However, in 1812, due to the perilous times, no syndicate was prepared to bid."

Ricardo made a face. "The situation now is even more fraught. I already know several of my peers who have decided not to participate."

"Assuming there are some willing syndicates, how does the bidding actually work?" asked Cordelia.

"The syndicates all bid on a security called the Omnium, which is just a name for a basket of three or four types of consols," replied their mentor. "In effect, whichever consortium is prepared to offer the highest price for the amount of the Omnium offered by the government wins the bid."

He took a document from his coat pocket and slid it across the table. "The exact nature of the bidding process and the way a bid must be formulated is actually a good bit more sophisticated than that, but I've set out the details here for you to study carefully."

Ricardo drummed his fingertips on the table for a moment. "Now, in order for me to contemplate making a bid, I need your help in assessing the current trading patterns of the consols to be included in this year's Omnium as well as their likely trading price after the newly issued consols are added to the market." A pause. "There are also various other timing, tax, and possible discount matters, which I have outlined for you."

He then slid another piece of paper—it was filled with detailed script and numbers—toward Cordelia.

She skimmed over the contents and turned pale as a ghost.

"If this was a purely straightforward matter," said Ricardo with a wry twitch of his lips, "then everyone would bid."

She forced an answering smile. "Quite right, sir." To Raven she added, "Well, we had better sharpen our pencils and get to work."

The mood in the city had grown more and more fraught as another week slipped by. News from across the Channel was confusing. Nobody seemed to know where Napoleon and his Armée du Nord were. Rumors and speculations swirled, twisting and twining with the truth until it was impossible to separate one from the other.

The morning dawned grey and gloomy. A light rain was falling as Wrexford left the house early to meet with Henning at his clinic and question some of the former soldiers who lived on the streets. Charlotte, too, was up early and drafting a new drawing to calm the jittery public, while Raven headed out the door to the Sheffield residence to continue working with Cordelia on the mathematics for Ricardo to consider as he thought about whether he should form a syndicate to bid on the government loan.

It was some hours later before Cordelia looked up and put down her pencil.

"Hell's bells. Please tell me you see something that I am missing," she said. "For no matter how many creative ways I try to factor in all the variables Mr. Ricardo gave us and come up with a report that says it's a wise strategy to fund the government debt, I simply can't make the numbers work."

Raven, who had been scribbling away on yet another sheet of paper, crumpled it up and threw it onto the growing pile littering the carpet.

"Sorry," he intoned. "I'm having no better luck."

"What's the problem?" asked Sheffield, entering the room with a tray of tea.

"Bless you," said Cordelia, closing her eyes and savoring a whiff of the jasmine-scented plume of steam rising from the pot. "As for our dilemma, Ricardo is deciding whether he should put together a syndicate to bid on the government loan. However, our mathematics say the answer is a resounding no."

She sighed. "I've sent him a preliminary report, which says just that. Though I did add that Raven and I would keep trying to see if we can make it work."

"But numbers are numbers," intoned Raven. "In the end, they don't lie."

A pinch of worry compressed Sheffield's lips, but he poured the tea and passed it around before reacting. "That's very troubling news."

The three of them sipped their tea in silence, at a loss for anything halfway encouraging to say.

With each passing moment, their brooding seemed to be adding a leaden weight to the air.

"Halloo!" hailed a voice from the corridor. "It's now official," announced Ricardo as he entered the room. "Chancellor of the Exchequer Vansittart has announced that bids for the government's £36 million loan must be submitted tomorrow."

"I—I sent you our first draft early this morning," stammered Cordelia.

"Yes, yes, and I see that your work—by the by, it's excellent mathematics—leads to the conclusion that I should *not* form a syndicate to bid on the loan because it's too risky."

Cordelia nodded. "I'm sorry, sir, but that's correct. There's simply no way to predict what the future will bring. For example, even if we were military analysts, there is no basis to compute the odds of a victory by or defeat of Napoleon—or, for that matter, an infinity of possible other nondefinitive outcomes."

She expelled a sigh. "That feeds back into the uncertainty of how the outcomes would affect trading values of government securities, which adds even more risk into the situation."

Another sigh. "And for what it's worth, our intelligence gathering suggests that three of the syndicates who regularly bid on government loans have dropped out. A fourth sounds very doubtful. That would leave only the syndicate led by Baring and Angerstein and your own group. And our sense is that Baring and Angerstein may also much prefer not to bid."

"What we are saying, sir," said Raven, "is that the mathematics show without a doubt that it's too uncertain to warrant proceeding on *any* basis—other than perhaps pure patriotism."

Ricardo smiled. "As I said, your mathematics are excellent and exceedingly elegant, and I don't dispute your calculations. But what you are identifying as an irreconcilable problem is actually a grand opportunity."

Cordelia and Raven exchanged confused looks.

"Precisely as you note, there are so many uncertainties that it is impossible for you or me to make any sensible calculation of the odds of a bet on the outcome of a battle with Napoleon. But for that very reason, I do know that I likely have no competitors for the loan, as they all analyze the situation exactly as you do."

His smile grew more pronounced. "Moreover, the government, as the borrower, is, to say the least, eager to do the deal, as reflected in the price they will pay. And even though we have foiled the French plot to collapse the consol price, the market is trading at a considerable discount in reaction—one might even say *overreaction*—to the fact that a great battle seems inevitable."

"So why—" began Sheffield, only to fall silent as Ricardo signaled that he hadn't yet finished.

"Your mathematics show me that if Napoleon wins, I would lose a great deal of money if I make the loan. I sincerely hope that doesn't happen. But the numbers also show me that I wouldn't be ruined," continued their mentor. "And should we defeat Napoleon, the windfall I will earn, given the market's certain euphoria should we prevail, would far exceed any possible losses I am risking."

Raven's puzzled frown slowly gave way to a grin. "So what you're saying is that you know a good bet when you see it?"

"This is the bet of a lifetime, Master Sloane," answered Ricardo. "I intend to proceed."

"Bravo!" Sheffield inclined an admiring bow, first to Ricardo and then to Cordelia and Raven. "By ensuring the loan, you three have done everything in your power to give our country the chance of winning a momentous victory."

He blew out his breath. "Now it's all up to Wellington."

CHAPTER 32

Charlotte shifted the parcel of books from Hatchards in her arms, smiling as she watched the four Weasels race each other over a swath of Hyde Park's meadow grass to a nearby plane tree.

"You have an unfair advantage!" huffed Eddy as she finished last. "I'd like to see you three try to run in skirts!"

"Ugh!" Hawk gave her a sympathetic grimace. "They look awfully awkward."

"Next time we'll give you a head start," offered Peregrine.

It did Charlotte's heart good to see them so carefree, especially Raven, whose work with Cordelia and Ricardo was, as of twelve days ago, mostly ended, save for the waiting. The whole family had been bearing a frightful weight of responsibility over the last few months. Charlotte found herself wishing . . .

"Let's not dally," called Raven. "It's past teatime and I've worked up an appetite for ginger biscuits!"

"Good times will come," she assured herself as they scampered off in an impromptu game of tag.

Wrexford was sitting at the escritoire in the drawing room,

sorting through the afternoon post, as the Weasels made their noisy entrance.

"Did you find some interesting books?" he asked Eddy.

"Oh, yes!" she exclaimed.

"On the Montgolfier brothers and their aeronautical balloons!" added Hawk.

Charlotte smiled. "That you're interested in flight is no surprise."

"Would you like to soar through the sky?" asked McClellan as she carried in a heavily laden tray and set it on the tea table.

"Very much so," answered Eddy. "Imagine how the world would look from such glorious heights!"

"A very thrilling point of view," agreed Wrexford. "But even from ground level, the news of the last few days certainly appears encouraging."

He turned in his chair to face the room. "Ricardo somehow managed to have his group continue to maintain consol prices, ruining the short sellers and allowing Chancellor of the Exchequer Vansittart to ask for bids six days ago in an attempt to float the loan. Only Ricardo's group—Baring and Angerstein came in as his partner—made a bid."

A smile twitched on the earl's lips. "Ricardo told me Baring and Angerstein only came in because he had made them a fortune in the past—and that, according to Ricardo, substitutes for loyalty in the world of business."

"Mr. Sheffield told me that the Omnium has apparently been trading at a strong premium since the loan closed on June 14," piped up Raven.

"Yes. And according to what Kit told me, that premium, plus the discounts the syndicate got from the government for floating the loan, means that Ricardo and his friends likely made a huge profit. How much is known only to him, but if the war news turns out to be good on top of all this, Ricardo and a few other brave souls who floated the loan will end up owning—"

A sudden, agitated rapping on one of the leaded window-panes startled the earl into silence.

"Zephyrus!" Eddy shot up from the sofa. "It's Zephyrus!"

"Why is your pigeon acting so oddly?" asked Wrexford, as the bird continued beating its beak against the glass.

"Because . . ." Eddy wrenched open the casement, allowing Zephyrus to fly in and circle around her head before taking a perch on her shoulder. "Because he has just returned from a long journey, and I think . . ."

She coaxed the bird onto her finger and examined its legs. "Yes, yes! He's brought you an urgent message! It's from Herr von Münch!"

The earl stared at her in mute disbelief.

Seeing his expression, Eddy's smile turned tentative. "H-He said you would be expecting it."

"Did he?" said Wrexford in a carefully controlled voice. Had von Münch been present, he would have been tempted to bloody the rascal's beak.

"Y-Yes." Eddy swallowed hard. "The last time he was here, he said he was going on an urgent mission and asked to take two of my pigeons with him so that he could send you vital updates on matters concerning our country."

She looked around uncertainly. "But he told me that because it was such a sensitive matter, you instructed him to tell me not to discuss it with any other members of our inner circle."

Hearing a growl rumble in the earl's throat, Eddy blinked in confusion. "D-Did I do something wrong?"

"Not at all," Charlotte assured her.

"Herr von Münch wasn't on the list of trusted inner circle members," whispered Raven.

"Let us deal with all those particulars later," counseled Charlotte. To Wrexford, she added, "If there is indeed a message, you need to read it without delay."

Eddy had already unfastened the tiny metal capsule from the pigeon's leg and passed it to the earl.

Grabbing a penknife, he scraped off the wax seal and carefully extracted the roll of paper inside it. The room was silent as a crypt as he unfurled it and read over the contents.

"Holy hell, don't keep us in suspense," whispered McClellan.

"We now know what nefarious plan Le Loup had created, and it wasn't an assassination after all," intoned Wrexford, looking grim. "A long-winded message is impossible for a pigeon to carry, so the note is exceedingly brief. It appears the traitor within our government has stolen a highly confidential—and incriminating—letter to the prime minister that will give Napoleon a potent bargaining chip with Britain even if he loses the upcoming battle against Wellington's army."

"What sort of letter could give him that power?" asked Charlotte.

He shook his head. "It doesn't say. Le Loup is meeting his co-conspirator tonight—exactly two hours before midnight—at the ruins of an ancient Cistercian monastery just past the town of Swanley, in order to make the exchange."

He paused. "I know the place. It's a little over an hour's ride south of here on the road to Dover. The note says that from there, Le Loup will head to the port and board a fast smuggling cutter that is waiting to whisk him to France."

"What—" began Charlotte, only to be cut off by Eddy.

"Look, Wrex!" His sister suddenly crouched down on the carpet. "Another bit of paper fell out of the capsule while you were unrolling the note." She held up the tiny scrap.

"Good heavens, is that a bloodstain?" said Charlotte, seeing a smudge of rusty red on one edge.

Wreford held it up to the light, trying to decipher the pencil scrawl. Frowning, he swore under his breath—and then began to laugh.

"Stop shilly-shallying and tell us what it says!" demanded Raven.

"It's dated June 18, seven in the evening," announced the earl. "The message says—*A momentous battle has just ended . . .*" He looked up. "*And by the by, we won.*"

"W-We won?" stammered Charlotte.

"We won," confirmed the earl.

"So that means this hellish nightmare is over?" ventured Mc-Clellan.

"No," responded Wrexford. "what it means is that it's absolutely imperative to keep Le Loup from getting hold of that letter. For all we know, Napoleon is still at large, and his only hope of retaining his throne is having something powerful with which to bargain."

"Wrex—"

"I know what you are going to say," said Wrexford. "Have no fear—I'm taking no chances of letting the varlets slip through my fingers again. I know just the man to ride out with me. He's battle-hardened and steady as steel in a fight."

Charlotte bit her lip, looking as if she was trying to muster an argument.

"It's too dangerous to take the chance of letting him escape, for any number of reasons," pressed the earl. "If the letter allows Napoleon to cling to his throne, God only knows what terrible assignment Le Loup will be given next and what disaster will follow for all of Europe."

When she didn't respond, he turned to Hawk. "I need you to take a message to the Home Office." He paused to write a note and seal it with his signet ring. "Tell them that the Earl of Wrexford insists that you hand it personally to Simon Norwood."

To Peregrine he said, "Tell Jem to have Sombra saddled in an hour." Catching Eddy's questioning look, he added, "I was in need of a hard gallop, so I took Lucifer out earlier this afternoon while you were at your lessons. What I require now is Sombra's speed. I need to make several stops before meeting with Norwood. The prime minister and his privy council need to know about the battle."

He turned to Raven. "Run and give Kit and Cordelia the momentous news. Then Ricardo must be told."

"Eddy, come help me take the tea things back to the kitchen," said McClellan, earning a grateful look from the earl for giving the girl a tangible task.

"Be careful," said Charlotte softly, reaching out and pulling him into her arms once everyone had rushed off.

"Always," he murmured.

They stood entwined for a long moment. Further words were unnecessary. The steady thrum of their hearts beating together as one said all that needed to be said.

Drawing back, Wrexford brushed a kiss to her brow. And then, in the space of a heartbeat, he was gone.

Raven paused in the doorway of the schoolroom, where his three fellow Weasels were trying to keep themselves occupied with a game of cards.

"Where's m'lady?" he demanded. "Don't tell me that Wrex allowed her to—"

"No, no, she went to inform Aunt Alison of Wellington's victory," answered Hawk. "Though I heard her muttering something about taking shooting lessons from Joe Manton, so that Wrex can't keep using the excuse that she's a mediocre marksman to keep her from accompanying him."

"We ought to speak with him about that, too," said Raven. "I think it's high time that we get some training with firearms."

"It goes without saying that *we* includes *me*," piped up Eddy.

"Of course," replied Raven. "You're a Weasel."

"One for all and all for one," chorused Hawk and Peregrine.

Harper punctuated their words with a *woof*.

"Would you like to join us in playing cards?" asked Eddy.

Raven shook his head. He moved to the bookshelves and chose a volume on Euclid's geometry.

The soft shuffle and slap of the pasteboard cards were soon the only sounds resonating through the room. And then . . .

Rap-rap. Another pigeon was suddenly beating a furious tattoo on the windowpane.

"It's Boreas!" said Eddy, flinging open the window and letting the bird inside. "He, too, was with von Münch," she explained, cradling the clearly exhausted bird in her palms.

"He has a metal capsule attached to his foot!" exclaimed Peregrine.

Hawk gently worked it free and pried it open. After extracting the note, he offered it to Eddy.

She handed the pigeon to Peregrine, and as she read the message, her face turned white as a ghost. Raven was up in a flash. "What does it say?"

Eddy swallowed hard and passed the note to him.

"Hell and damnation," whispered Raven, letting the paper slip through his fingers and fall to the table. "We need to get word to Wrex."

"B-But how?" Hawk looked up after reading what von Münch had written, his eyes glassy with fear. "If only it was possible to send him a pigeon."

"There's only one way," said Eddy. She shot up. "I need to change into my breeches and boots."

Raven rushed to catch up with her as she hurried into the corridor. "I'm coming with you."

"First of all, no other horse in the stables can match Lucifer's speed," she countered. "And second, you can't ride worth beans."

"I don't have to ride," he retorted." I just have to cling to your back like a cocklebur."

"Why would you do that?" she demanded.

"Because time is of the essence." Raven checked that his

pocket knife was sheathed inside his boot. "You're a neck-and-leather rider and I know all the shortcuts and hidden byways through the city down to the road to Dover. So if we want to keep Wrex out of danger, we need to work together."

"D-Do you think Mac will try to stop us?"

"Not if she doesn't hear us sneak out to the stable," replied Raven.

Eddy gave a grim nod. "Better to ask for forgiveness than ask for permission."

CHAPTER 33

Slowing his horse to a walk, Wrexford rose in his stirrups and surveyed the ruins of the abbey set on the hilltop, the tumbled stones of the cloister and the surrounding buildings just visible above the tops of the trees.

"There looks to be a cart path leading up to the site," pointed out Norwood. "My guess is the rendezvous spot is the bell-tower, as it's the most distinctive landmark."

"I agree." The last glimmer of twilight was fast fading into darkness. However, the night sky was cloudless, allowing the glimmer of starlight and the waxing moon to soften the shadows. The earl studied the surroundings a moment longer. "We're here way ahead of the appointed time. Still, I think it prudent for us to leave the horses here, hidden in the glade of trees, and make our way on foot to reconnoiter and make sure that we're the first to arrive."

Norwood, too, was assessing the surroundings. "There looks to be a shepherd's footpath winding up from the left. If we cut through the woods and approach that way, the remains of the outer building will provide cover."

Wrexford nodded in agreement.

They dismounted and led their horses deep into the leafy shadows, far from the cart path.

"This way," said Norwood after they had tethered their mounts, gesturing for the earl to follow him up past a jut of granite between a cluster of pines. They made their way with the light-footed stealth of experienced soldiers through the woods, crouching low once they reached the tall grasses to hide their silhouettes from view of the cart path.

"I brought a small spyglass," said Norwood, once they reached the first ruin of the outer buildings. "There may be enough ambient light for it to be useful."

He raised it to his eye and made a slow sweep of the grounds ahead. "It seems clear to me, but you take a look."

Wrexford took his time to search the shadows and then handed it back. "Let's find a good vantage point from which to keep watch."

They located a set of stone stairs behind the remains of a wall close to the belltower. "Excellent," said the earl as he gazed down the slope. "We have a good view of the cart path and sloping meadowland on either side. They can't take us by surprise."

Norwood checked the priming of his pistols. "How do you want to proceed? It's set as a rendezvous, so they won't be arriving together. Do we wait for them both to arrive? Or seize the first fellow and force him to lure the other one into the trap?"

Wrexford gave the options only a short consideration. "There is more of a risk in allowing them to rendezvous before we attempt to apprehend them," he said, thinking back to the mistakes of his previous attempt to capture Le Loup and his co-conspirator. "I say we take whoever arrives first and use him to our advantage."

"Agreed," responded Norwood. "Now, all we have to do is wait."

*   *   *

As the hard-packed dirt road veered closer to the marshland and the softer footing turned treacherous, Eddy slowed Lucifer from a thunderous gallop to a gentle trot.

"Oiy, are you still there?" she called, only half in jest. Given Wrexford's head start, it was imperative to pick up every possible second. And the earl's stallion could run like the devil.

"Oiy." Raven sounded awfully shaky, but added a note of bravado. "Can't he go any faster?"

Lucifer gave an aggrieved snort.

"Not in this stretch. The footing is too perilous," she replied. Raven had directed Eddy to take a shortcut. It had gained precious miles, but the going had been a little rough. "How long until we can cut over to the Kent Road?"

"Maybe a half mile," he answered, after spotting a pond to his left. "From there it's a straight gallop to the Dover Road. Once we reach it, the abbey isn't far."

"Be ready to hold on tight!" warned Eddy. "I'm not stopping to collect you if you fall on your arse."

And then, true to her word, Eddy spurred the big black stallion to a pace that threatened to rattle Raven's teeth free from his jawbone.

"Someone is coming."

Wrexford heard it, too—the thud of iron-shod hooves on the rocky cart path. Easing the hammers of both his pistols to full cock, he crept down the stairs and took up a position in one of the nooks of the crumbled belltower.

"Find cover to my right, so you can keep watch for the other varlet." He had caught a glimpse of the rider, and from the arrogant set of the silhouetted shoulders he was sure it was Le Loup. This time, he vowed, the miscreant wasn't going to escape justice.

Norwood nodded in understanding and slipped away into the shadows.

A minute passed . . . and then another. The earl heard the horse come to a halt.

Silence. Followed by slow and careful footsteps.

It appeared they were right in guessing that the rendezvous point was the belltower.

Wrexford allowed Le Loup to come to the base of the belltower before revealing himself.

The Frenchman's eyes flickered in surprise.

"Lord Wrexford," he drawled. "Like a bad penny, you keep appearing in places where you are not wanted."

"You threatened not only my country but my family. For that, I would chase you down to the ends of the Earth."

"It seems that I underestimated you."

"Arrogance has a way of clouding one's judgement." The earl held his aim steady. "Kindly toss aside the pistols I see bulging in your coat pockets. And I warn you, if you make a false move this time, I won't miss."

"Actually, it's you who will be dropping your weapons."

Wrexford suddenly felt the cold steel of a gun barrel press up against his skull and did as he was told.

"My apologies, Wrex. I sincerely wish it hadn't come to this."

"But you just couldn't drop the bone clenched between your teeth," snarled Le Loup. "Pull the trigger and be done with it, Norwood."

"Why?" asked Wrexford softly.

"*Grâce à Dieu*, kill him and be done with it!" exhorted the Frenchman, his voice sharp with impatience.

"Not quite yet," said Norwood. "As we were once comrades-in-arms, I feel that the earl deserves an answer."

"Oiy, pull up!"

In reaction to Raven's urgent order, Eddy slowed to a halt.

'It's there, on the crest of the hill." He pointed out the dark silhouettes of the abbey ruins, the ancient stones twinkling with glimmers of starlight. "There's a cart path forking off from the road—"

"Too dangerous. We'll be spotted way before we reach them." Eddy thought for a moment, then leaned forward to whisper something in Lucifer's ear.

The stallion raised his head and swung it side to side, snorting a series of inhales and exhales.

"What's he doing?" whispered Raven.

"Searching for Wrex."

Lucifer suddenly bared his teeth and tugged at the reins, his hooves kicking up clots of earth.

"Wrex is in danger," exclaimed Eddy. "Find him," she said to the agitated stallion, adding a string of lilting Celtic words. "And quickly!"

Raven quickly slipped down from the saddle. "You don't need me as baggage. Our best chance of saving Wrex lies with each of us using our skills to best advantage."

"What do you plan to do?" she asked.

"Dunno yet. But I'll find some way of raising holy hell!"

Eddy watched him disappear with wraithlike quickness into the tall grasses, then clucked her tongue and urged Lucifer onward. "Quietly," she whispered. "And then, when I give the word, run like the devil."

Aside from the ruffling of the breeze through the trees and the elemental hum and buzz of summer night sounds, the abbey grounds were quiet as a crypt.

Wrexford altered his stance as Norwood moved around to face him.

Le Loup pulled out one of his pistols. "I don't trust him," he growled.

"Patience," counseled Norwood. "There are two of us. He is going nowhere but the grave. However, I would prefer to allow him the dignity of a civilized coup de grâce once we are done with our chat."

"How noble," said the earl, not bothering to disguise his contempt.

Norwood's smile faltered, but only for an instant. "You asked me why, and I shall give you the courtesy of an answer."

Wrexford didn't give a rat's arse for his former comrade's self-serving answer, but he held his tongue. At some point he would make a move—likely a futile one, but he had no intention of going meekly to his Maker.

"It's really quite simple," continued Norwood. "I dislike being poor and dependent on patrons for my position in life." A pause. "It galls my sensibility, as I'm far more clever and talented than the overfed oafs who possess power and influence in Society simply by virtue of being born into an aristocratic family."

"Life has hardly been unfair to you. Your grandmother was a Grenville. Don't whinge for sympathy from me," said Wrexford. "If you feel so strongly about having the freedom to forge your own destiny, why didn't you go to America and make your own fortune?"

"Easy for you to say." Norwood's expression hardened. However, the smug smile was back in an instant. "I, too, have a question. How did you know about this rendezvous?"

"A little bird told me."

"Come, come, Wrexford, no need to be ungracious in defeat. I—"

"What's that?" Le Loup suddenly turned to the woods and raised his weapon. "I hear a horse."

"It's just the wind in the trees," said Norwood, but he, too, flicked a glance at the shadowed glade.

Seizing his chance, Wrexford lashed out a kick that knocked his former comrade to his knees and then dove for the cover of a nearby rock outcropping just as a spectral black shape burst free of the trees and came thundering at them.

Le Loup took dead aim at the charging stallion, but a rock came flying out from one of the nearby ruins and struck him between the shoulder blades. The Frenchman staggered and twisted away, just in time to avoid a lethal blow from the stallion's flailing hooves.

Wrexford reacted in a flash. Darting out from behind the rock outcropping, he scrambled to reach his own weapons before Le Loup could attempt another shot at Eddy and Lucifer.

Just another step—

He saw Le Loup pivot, face contorted with rage. The Frenchman's second pistol was now pointed straight at him.

BANG!

Le Loup's eyes widened in shock as a bullet hit him square in the chest and knocked him to the ground.

The earl snatched up his weapons and whirled around to confront Norwood.

"I'm unarmed," said his former comrade, tossing his spent pistol to the ground.

"I've no intention of shooting you." Wrexford waved Eddy away, hoping she would understand he didn't want her to show her face. "I prefer to let justice take its proper course." As their eyes met, he didn't so much as blink. "But I confess, I won't shed a tear when I watch you dance the hangman's jig."

"Oh, my dear fellow, I'm not going to hang." Norwood smiled. "You've totally misjudged my actions. The truth is, I'll be hailed as a hero."

With a flourish, Norwood pulled a document out of his pocket. "You see, I cleverly discovered a French plot to steal this document. At great personal danger, I took the bold initiative to reach out to the dastard and *pretend* to be a traitor, so that I could apprehend him in the act. However, I was forced to shoot him in order to save your life."

"And you expect that Banbury tale to fly?" asked Wrexford. "Here's what really happened. You sold out your country for blood money, but the appearance of reinforcements—" He gestured to the shadowy presence of Eddy and Lucifer. "—made you fear that Le Loup would be captured and give your secret away. So you shot him and now think you can avoid facing the consequences of your treason."

A laugh. "It's my word against yours, and my grandmother's family is *very* influential in the government." A shrug. "Even if there are doubters, do you think the powers-that-be will want the embarrassment of telling the public that they've been nursing a viper within the innermost sanctums of power."

Wrexford said nothing, knowing Norwood was right. He had no tangible proof. The only one capable of contradicting his former comrade's story lay conveniently dead.

"By the by," added Norwood, "who rode to your rescue? I assume it's your crony Sheffield?"

"Get out of my sight," snapped Wrexford with a warning wave of his pistol. "Before I decide to write my own tale of lies."

Norwood paused to remove a packet from inside Le Loup's coat and slide it into his own pocket before snapping a mocking salute. "Have a pleasant ride back to London."

Wrexford drew a series of shaky breaths, needing several long moments to calm the emotions roiling inside him.

"W-Wrex?"

He turned to face Eddy and Raven.

"A-Are you angry with us?"

"Angry?" He shook his head. "Angry doesn't begin to describe my feelings—"

"I don't give a devil's damn if you're angry." Raven lifted his chin, as if readying himself for a tongue-lashing. "A second pigeon arrived from Herr von Münch with the news about Mr. Norwood, so we knew that you were in mortal danger. M'lady had gone to see the Sheffields, so it was up to us. We did the right thing, and nothing will convince me otherwise."

"Oiy," said Eddy with the same unflinching tone.

Wrexford covered the space between them in two quick steps—and then dropped to his knees and pulled them into a fierce hug. "Bloody hell, you scared me half to death!" Another ragged breath. "But I'll ring a peal over your heads later. Right now I simply want to savor this moment . . ."

His cheeks were suddenly wet with tears, but he didn't give a damn. "And give profound thanks for the power of Love," he finished. "Love for my family and all the things that matter in life." *Truth. Justice. Honor* . . . the rush of thoughts tangled in his throat, too elemental to put into words.

Overwhelmed, Wrexford closed his eyes and allowed the thud of their hearts beating in harmony to flood him with gratitude.

"Lucifer is family, right?" said Eddy, looking up with a watery smile as Wrexford finally loosened his embrace. "He, too, helped save the day."

"So are your pigeons," said Raven. "Even though they are awfully smelly."

Wrexford chuckled and gave them another hug. "Speaking of pigeons, let us find our way home—and quickly. The rest of our family will be worried about us."

CHAPTER 34

"Pour me a glass of sherry, Wrex." Alison heaved a sigh as she set aside her cane and sunk into the armchair. "I know the sun is not yet over the yardarm, but given all we've been through in this investigation, I think a drink is in order." She pursed her lips. "Maybe two."

"Sherry is not a drink—it's a tipple," said Henning. "Bring the dowager—and me—a double dram of whisky."

Two days had passed since the confrontation at the abbey ruins. The news of Wellington's great victory was now public knowledge, and the heady euphoria that had taken hold of London had—judging by the drunken shouts and laughter still echoing in Berkeley Square—not quite subsided.

"You had better have Riche bring up another few bottles of malt from the cellars," said Sheffield, as he and Cordelia joined the group gathered in the drawing room. He looked around expectantly. "Are the Weasels still under a black cloud for taking matters into their own hands and rushing into danger?"

"How to respond to what happened is a daunting dilemma. I feel trapped between a rock and a stone," admitted Charlotte.

"I can't argue with their reasoning. Wrex was in terrible danger. However, how can I concede that they are free to decide on their own when to put themselves in mortal peril?"

"The rest of us do it all the time," pointed out Cordelia.

"But they are too young—"

"Age shouldn't be the only factor," interrupted Alison. "You think I'm too old to take the same risks as you. And I find it immensely irritating."

Charlotte acknowledged the reproof with an apologetic grimace.

"It seems to me that the Weasels are mature beyond their years in considering their actions," continued the dowager. "I'm not saying that they should have free rein quite yet. But perhaps the circumstances should be taken into consideration."

"Indeed, their tutor is using their actions as a teaching example," said Wrexford, "and having them analyze what other decisions could have been made, along with their likely consequences."

"We do understand the importance of thinking before acting," announced Raven, as he and his fellow Weasels entered the drawing room carrying platters of ginger biscuits and sundry sweets while McClellan followed them with the tea cart. Tyler was several steps behind her, bearing the bottles of whisky that their butler had fetched from the cellars.

"Then enough said," said Charlotte. She waited for Wrexford to finish passing out libations—to their disgust, the Weasels were given apple cider—before proposing a toast. "To family and friends!" A pause. "Though I have ceased making a distinction between the two."

She raised her glass. "To Wrex and me, you are *all* family."

"I do hope that I'm also included in that charmed circle."

Wrexford made a face as von Münch slipped into the room from the corridor.

"Don't count on it, you sneaky devil." However, the sight of the fellow's arm in a sling softened his scowl. "Welcome back."

"The duke sends his regards. He said that he would have welcomed your wise counsel and steadiness on the field of battle. But I assured him you were protecting Britain from a very dangerous enemy here in London."

"I've heard that our military victory at Waterloo came at a terrible cost," said the earl.

"The sight of so many fine men slaughtered on the battlefield . . ." Stopping to steady his voice, von Münch shook his head in sorrow. "It is a sight I shall never, ever forget."

"May it never happen again," intoned Charlotte.

"Amen to that," said Henning, and gulped down a noisy swallow.

After a respectful silence, von Münch tactfully changed the subject. "I trust your government was grateful to you for helping to save Britain from the machinations of Gaudin and Le Loup."

"As you know, the story isn't quite so simple," replied Wrexford. Aside from von Münch, only Charlotte and the Weasels were aware of Norwood's perfidy. To the others in the room, he added, "There was a very insidious traitor at work—"

"Yes, Elias Fogg!" exclaimed Alison. "But we figured it out, and surely Griffin and his men seized him before he could escape."

"Fogg was innocent of any wrongdoing. The real culprit was my former comrade Simon Norwood, who was cunning enough to drop veiled hints that made the poor fellow appear guilty."

The dowager eyes widened in horror. "But Norwood's grandmother is a *Grenville*!"

"Which along with his malicious cleverness is what allowed him to weave such a web of traitorous deceit." The earl summarized all that had happened. "It turns out that when Norwood was wounded at the battle of Badajoz, he was a French prisoner for a fortnight before being exchanged. Le Loup was one of the French captors and must have sensed that Norwood could be seduced by money, and so contacted him when he first arrived in London seeking to create havoc."

"He's even more of a scoundrel to have sold out his country when he was already wealthy," muttered Henning. "The Grenvilles are among the richest families—"

"Oh, but he wasn't wealthy," corrected the dowager. "Yes, his grandmother was a Grenville, but you all know how it works. As family connections branch out, they may retain a modicum of prestige, but the money passes down from the patriarch of the family to the eldest son in the age-old tradition of primogeniture. It rarely goes sideways."

"Yes, Norwood told me that he resented being poor while other less-clever relatives were rich," said Wrexford. "He thought that terribly unfair."

"How did you learn about Norwood's past connection to Le Loup?" asked Sheffield.

"I gave my side of the story to Grentham," answered the earl. "And apparently the minister had done his own checking of the facts after Norwood explained his so-called heroic role in saving the country."

"Assuming that his family's power would protect him, even if the authorities didn't quite swallow his lies," muttered Henning.

"Yes. However, my sense is that such hubris will prove to be a dangerous thing." Wrexford paused. "It wouldn't surprise me at all if we soon read in the newspaper about an unfortunate accident befalling Norwood."

"*Quod severis metes*," whispered Charlotte. "*As ye sow, as ye reap.*"

"Amen to that," said Henning, and drained his glass in one long swallow.

Alison helped herself to a ginger biscuit. "It may be the whisky, but I confess to being a trifle befuddled by this entire investigation." *Crunch-crunch.* "First we had the murder of an inventor and were chasing after the secret design for an electrical tele-graph, which turned out to be . . . a ruse?"

"Not precisely a ruse," explained Wrexford, "but an idea ahead of its time. Both Francis Ronalds and Michael Faraday believe the invention will revolutionize communication in the future, but they say we are still a long way from understanding exactly how electromagnetism works, which they believe will be the key to making the electrical telegraph a practical possi-bility."

"The French had concocted a frighteningly clever plan," said Charlotte. "They murdered Boyleston to make our govern-ment think that the technology existed and could be used for military purposes. But in truth, it was merely meant to distract us while they implemented their real objective—an attack on our stock market to drive down the price of government con-sols, essentially ruining our economy and making it impossible to fund a new war against Napoleon."

"However, the real genius of their plan was that there was a third option to give Napoleon a chance to retain his power," said Wrexford. "In case financial manipulations didn't work, they arranged to steal the incriminating letter, which was a highly confidential offer from the Tsar of Russia to, in effect, stab Austria and Prussia in the back by forming a coalition with Britain and forcing them to give up some of the concessions they won at the Congress of Vienna. Our government had no interest in upsetting the balance of power, but if the letter had been made public, it could have plunged Europe back into war."

"That's not merely clever, that's diabolical!" exclaimed the dowager. "But from what I have heard, the stock market wea-thered the storm with flying colors."

"Yes, thanks to the genius of David Ricardo," replied Shef-field. "With the indispensable help of Raven and Cordelia, I might add."

"Mr. Ricardo will be coming by shortly to raise a toast with us," said Cordelia, "and perhaps he will elaborate on how he managed it all."

Wrexford eyed the four Weasels. "When he arrives, please slip away and fly up to your eyrie—including you, Raven. He's a very wise man, and I would prefer that he doesn't begin to speculate as to what special skills our other wards possess."

"Mr. Ricardo has already expressed his thanks to Raven and me," said Cordelia. "Indeed, we have agreed to continue working with him on mathematical ways to spot investment opportunities." A smile. "He has a great deal of money to invest these days."

"That's putting it mildly," said Alison, after draining the last drop of whisky in her glass. "I read in *The Times* that Mr. Ricardo personally netted upward of £1 million on the government loan. That alone, disregarding the rest of his fortune, would make him one of the richest men in England."

"Now, now—this group in particular knows that you can't believe everything you read in the popular press." Ricardo entered the room from the corridor and gave a small smile as he placed several very fine bottles of French champagne on the sideboard. "That being said, all of us"—a quick wave acknowledged everyone in the room—"did quite well investing in my syndicate to fund the government's debt."

"*All* of us?" said Charlotte, looking bemused. "I thought it was only Wrex, Cordelia, Kit, and me."

"When you mentioned to me what a risk Mr. Ricardo was taking, I felt it was my duty to help," said the dowager.

"*Moi aussi,*" added von Münch, a twinkle lighting in his eye as he glanced at Wrexford.

McClelland grinned. "Tyler and I did as well."

"I still don't know exactly how you managed to support the consol market and avoid a collapse that would have made the loan impossible," said Cordelia. "Toward the end, it looked as if it was slipping away and Gaudin was going to succeed in crashing the market and thwarting the loan."

"I give great credit to my fellow stockjobbers, who did admirable work in following my lead and supporting the consol market," said Ricardo, "even borrowing great sums to do so, without demanding too much information from me about what was transpiring."

A pause. "But in the end, it was a close-run thing, and it worked only because I was able to secure the capital from an additional investor. His considerable funds allowed us to keep the consol price up until the short sellers had to run for it and cover their positions."

Ricardo allowed a fleeting smile. "And then, our victory at Waterloo caused the price of consols to rocket upward. We could have taken even more profits had we used our advance news—thanks to your pigeons—of the momentous triumph and immediately purchased even more consols. However, that would have been unethical, so I informed the Chancellor of the Exchequer at once, and we refrained from any further transactions in consols until the good news was fully disseminated."

"You deserve a medal, sir," said Wrexford. "Maybe two."

"Doing the right thing is always reward enough," said Ricardo. "Especially when it forges friendships with kindred spirits."

"*Sláinte*," called Henning with a rusty chuckle. "Someone hurry and fetch a tray of fresh glasses!"

A cork popped, and the room erupted in a chorus of cheers.

As the merriment grew louder, Charlotte leaned closer to Wrexford. "A *single* additional investor?" she murmured. "I thought Ricardo had been most clear that given the amounts involved, he would need multiple investors, which created a significant problem as to what information he could disclose and how he could count on total discretion."

"One can't help but wonder . . ." The earl maintained a sphinx-like expression. "There is, of course, one individual in the government who has the access to unlimited funds and the authority to use them."

Their eyes met.

"And above all else, he knows how to keep a secret," added Wrexford. "However, I don't think we should become too curious about that individual's affairs."

Charlotte gave a knowing nod. "Lest he—"

"Lest he become too interested in ours," finished the earl.

She raised her as-yet-untouched glass of champagne. "I'll drink to that."

"Is it always so unnervingly exciting in this family?" asked Eddy as she and her fellow Weasels lay sprawled in a circle on the schoolroom carpet, a platter of fast-disappearing ginger biscuits in its center.

The three boys looked at each other and began chortling.

Raven managed to stifle his mirth just long enough to reply. "As to that, Merlin, unless you possess a magical scrying glass, it's impossible to predict what tomorrow will bring."

Roused from his slumber, Harper added a low *woof*.

"Oiy," said Hawk, and Peregrine quickly added his agreement. "But based on the past, I would venture to guess that the future holds a great many new adventures."

AUTHOR'S NOTE

Those of you who are familiar with my Wrexford & Sloane mystery series know that I enjoy sharing some of the back stories on what has inspired my plots and the cameo appearances of real people from the Regency era. And with this particular book, which is a little different from the previous ones, I have a lot of details to share.

You may have noticed that the mystery combines elements of both a "whodunit" and a "procedural," and the story has more "moving pieces" than usual—including a major reshifting of the family. Not only is it fun for me as a writer to "shake things up," but I also don't want the books to become formulaic and begin to sound repetitive to readers.

As someone who loves the colorful arcane details that are often hidden within the grand tapestry of history, it's really exciting for me to fall down research rabbit holes and find myself tripping over fascinating facts that suddenly spark those wonderful creative "what if" moments. And that's how the two major plot threads of the story—the electrical telegraph and the London Stock Exchange—came into being, which in turn drew in the real historical figures who join with Wrexford, Charlotte, and their inner circle to help ensure that Good triumphs over Evil.

In researching a fairly simple question concerning voltaic batteries (which were used during the Regency to generate electricity) for a previous book, I followed an ancillary link that led me to Francis Ronalds—who in Britain is revered as the first electrical engineer and the "Father of the Electric Telegraph," along with a host of other amazing accomplishments. Most of us have been taught that Samuel Morse invented the electrical telegraph in 1838. So imagine my surprise when I read about Ronalds and how he constructed eight miles of electrical wiring through his mother's gardens in 1816 to test the speed with which electricity could travel . . . and that led him to experiment with sending electrical messages.

I found Francis Ronalds and his invention fascinating and decided it would be great fun to use it in a plot. Now here is where it gets very interesting! (Yes, there is science coming, but you have come to expect that from me. I shall try to keep it simple!) As I did more reading about electricity and messaging for this book, I realized that there was a fundamental reason Ronalds and his fellow inventors couldn't create a practical messaging system—the science of their times didn't have a full understanding of the phenomena of electricity and magnetism—what we today call electromagnetism.

Why is this important? Because understanding electromagnetism literally changed our world! In a nutshell, it allowed scientific innovators to create technologies that converted electrical energy into mechanical motion, or vice versa. In addition to the telegraph, it is the principle which underlies the electric motors, generators, and transformers that power our modern world.

How the electrical telegraph ultimately developed from the time of this story is fascinating and happened fairly quickly. As I show with Francis Ronalds and his fellow inventors during 1815–1816, they understood that information could be encoded in electric current—think pulses or dots and dashes—but were stymied by how to read that information at the other end of the wire. Ultimately, through a series of discoveries, inventors were able to utilize the magnetic effects which they found were created by electric current to move metal levers or pointers and thereby create a visible or audible signal.

A major step in the story of these discoveries occurred in 1820, when the Danish scientist Hans Christian Oersted discovered that an electrical current running through a wire created a magnetic force around the wire. André-Marie Ampère (who is mentioned in the story) went on to specify various aspects of the interaction of electricity and magnetism, and his development of the earliest theory of electromagnetism first demonstrated how electricity flowed through conductors, a key element for transmitting signals.

It was Michael Faraday (who also makes a cameo appearance in the story), one of the greatest scientists of all time, who first proposed the concept of electromagnetism as a "field," which was vital in developing an understanding of how the force worked.

As the Royal Institution website explains, "Faraday was the first to understand what these discoveries implied." In 1822, he created a simple apparatus consisting of a stiff wire and a magnet in a glass container filled with mercury (which is a good conductor of electricity). He then ran an electrical current through the wire, which created a circular magnetic field around the wire, causing the wire to rotate around the magnet, transforming electrical energy into mechanical motion. This critical discovery—that the magnetic field could induce continual motion and thereby create a visible or audible signal—was the "aha moment" that led to the development of a functional electrical telegraph.

In the 1830s, Joseph Henry made further discoveries regarding the principles of electromagnetism—the "Henry," a basic unit of electromagnetism, is named after him—and he created a rudimentary signaling device using pulses of electricity. Other inventors were also tinkering with messaging technology, most of them using the electrical current to move a needle on a dial showing the alphabet—a messaging system that proved unreliable.

It was Samuel Morse who came up with the idea of the simple Morse Code of dots and dashes—short and long pulses of electricity (which anticipated the binary code of today's modern electronic communications). And so the first truly functional electric telegraph came into being in 1838. (To debut the world's first commercial telegraph system, Morse sent the famous message "What hath God wrought?" in 1844.)

In reading about Michael Faraday, I went down yet another research rabbit hole to discover Jane Marcet and couldn't resist giving her a small role in the story. As you probably know by now, I love finding unsung women in the history of science, and she was a fascinating discovery. She wrote innovative books for young people—especially young women, who she believed should have the chance to understand subjects that were considered too difficult for the feminine mind to comprehend. They were hugely popular in the Regency, and in fact, Michael Faraday credits her books for inspiring him to seek a career in science. I found that a really wonderful anecdote and wanted to pay homage to her.

On reading about Ronalds, Faraday, and Marcet, it occurred to me that an electrical messaging system could be a fun red herring for a book set during the time of Napoleon's escape from Elba and the ensuing Hundred Days . . . so I took the liberty of assuming Ronalds likely had his electrical wires strung up in 1815. (However, while Francis Ronalds is a real-life person, his redoubtable mother is wholly the creation of my imagination, as are the villains in the story.)

One last note on the electrical telegraph before I move on to other inspirations for this book is why Atticus Boyleston, the curmudgeonly inventor, was murdered in the Prologue for hinting that he had discovered a theory of electromagnetism. History shows us that scientific innovation has always had huge implications for the military. In this story, Boyleston was an important red herring, because the British government would have had every reason to be terrified if the French had indeed succeeded in inventing an electrical telegraph, which could give them a daunting advantage on the battlefield.

The final plot thread in this book was inspired by the many

rumors over the years that the famous British financier Nathan Rothschild made a fortune on the stock market because he learned via messenger pigeon of Britain's victory at Waterloo before anyone else. The story has largely been debunked, though it's true that the powerful Rothschild banking family did occasionally use messenger pigeons for communicating between their various offices in Europe.

This got me to thinking. . . . The British government was indeed dependent on floating massive loans to run its far-flung empire, especially in times of war. And we all know from our own times how fluctuations in the stock market can have profound political and social implications . . . and then I remembered reading an intriguing account of a famous "bear raid" by short sellers on the New York Stock Exchange in the 1920s in which it was observed that financial battles are, in a sense, often more ruthless than war itself, because of the impossibility of distinguishing friend from foe with any certainty. . . . So that's what sparked the (purely fictional!) idea of having the French launch an economic attack on the London Stock Exchange just when Napoleon's escape created a time of maximum confusion and crisis throughout Europe.

For those of you who would like to explore a more detailed explanation of consols and other financial workings of the London Stock Exchange, I have posted additional information (yes, more mathematics!) under the diversions tab on my website (www.andreapenrose.com). I've also included a photo of Jane Austen's consol certificate!

Doing research on the London Stock Exchange led me to one of Rothschild's fellow financiers, David Ricardo, who was not only a brilliantly successful investor but also one of the most influential thinkers in the history of economics—and someone who actually was a key player in floating the British government's loan in the critical days before the Battle of Waterloo.

A legendary figure of the Regency era, Ricardo plays a major role in this story, and it's hard to do full justice to his extraordinary accomplishments in the short space of this Author's Note, though I will give you a short overview. Ricardo is perhaps best known in popular lore as "the richest economist in history." This renown stems in large measure from the writings of Paul Samuelson (himself a modern-day economics icon) about the returns realized on Ricardo's purchase of British government bonds four days before Waterloo. I incorporated the story of that bond offering, with only minor literary license, into the book. (The dowager's observation in the last chapter that she read a newspaper account saying Ricardo "netted upwards of £1 million" from that single investment is in fact a quotation—which I admit to moving earlier in time for purposes of story-telling—from Ricardo's obituary in 1823.)

A remarkable piece of recent scholarship by Wilfred Parys, *Ricardo's Finances and Waterloo*, however, argues that while the returns on the Waterloo loan were significant, Ricardo instead built his immense fortune more gradually over time working as a phenomenally successful stockjobber and investor on the London Stock Exchange and as a contractor for seven British loans—particularly the 1813 financings. Parys also wonderfully describes the process and structure of these Napoleonic loans, and I drew heavily on his analysis (while attempting to spare readers some of the technical details!). For readers also interested in a theoretical treatment of the decision-making processes and investment analysis underlying Ricardo's decision to swim against the tide and underwrite the Waterloo financing, I heartily recommend a superb piece by Richard J. Zeckhauser, *Investing in the Unknown and Unknowable*.

In addition to Ricardo's decision to underwrite the Waterloo loan, the description in the story of the nature, origins, and vital importance of the British consol, as well as the practices of short selling as existed on the London Stock Exchange during the Regency period, are also based on fact and history. That Britain relied almost solely on the public marketing of loans as a way of financing a decade and a half of war against Napoleon underscores how perilous the situation was in the few days before Waterloo as the British government struggled to put a massive loan in place.

However, as I mentioned above, my plot regarding Gaudin—the brilliant real-life finance minister of France who managed to make it economically feasible for Napoleon to keep armies in the field throughout years of continuing battle—and a short-selling bear raid on the British consol designed to thwart Britain's ability to finance this final campaign of the Napoleonic era is entirely fictional.

Possible exaggeration of Ricardo's actual profits from the Waterloo loan may have led historians to understate the extraordinary success he demonstrated throughout his relatively brief career on the Stock Exchange. As noted in the story, he began with an unusual social background, limited capital, and no familial support. And yet, within just a few years, he had become one of the wealthiest men in England. He simply astounded his contemporaries. As one noted, "his surprising quickness on figures and calculations—his capability of getting through, without any apparent exertion, the immense transactions in which he was concerned . . . enabled him to leave his contemporaries at the Stock Exchange far behind."

Ricardo's career is probably unique in that he was not only the most successful investor of his day but was also a leading economic theorist. There is generally a sharp divide between those active in business and those who theorize. Ricardo was arguably the best at both. One poll of US economists ranked Ricardo, along with Adam Smith, author of *The Wealth of Nations* and often considered the father of modern economic analysis, as the two most important economic theorists prior to the twentieth century. His contribution to economic theory is far too broad and complex for a discussion here. I'll simply note that his masterwork, *On the Principles of Political Economy and Taxation*, is considered one of the most important books ever written on economic theory.

Ricardo essentially retired from the business world shortly after Waterloo, having become one of the wealthiest people in the country. He moved to Gatcombe Park, his recently-purchased country estate, and remained quite active. Among other projects Ricardo "bought" (as was not uncommon then) a seat in Parliament. He quickly achieved the status of outright veneration among his fellow parliamentarians. Known for his insightful analysis, he was called upon by both sides of the House to speak on the major issues of the day. For those of you who are interested, I have an even more extensive profile of David Ricardo posted in the diversions tab on my website (www.andrea penrose.com) as he is one of the truly influential figures of the Regency era and modern economic thought.

And now, moving on from fact back to fiction, I should also mention that the traitor within the British government and the incriminating letter that might have upset the balance of power in Europe are also purely figments of my imagination—though given the squabbles between Britain and its allies on how to re-structure Europe once Napoleon had been removed from the chessboard, it seemed very plausible to me.

Lastly, I would be remiss if I didn't mention the new addition to the family! It occurred to me that adding a girl to the Weasels could be great fun and give a whole new twist to the relationships and possibilities for their adventures. It will also add a new range of challenges for Wrexford and Charlotte.

Given that Raven, Hawk, and Peregrine all have a special skill, it seemed only fair that Eddy have one, too. As I built her imaginary back story in my head, I had the idea of her mother possessing an uncanny ability to communicate with animals, which was passed to her daughter. That also allowed me to add my own fictional messenger pigeon twist to the Battle of Waterloo. As for the future—stay tuned! More plot ideas are percolating!

I hope you enjoyed this behind-the-scenes peek at the quirky ways an author's mind works and how a story comes to life.

—*Andrea Penrose*